"I ask recompense of you, my lady . . .

"A gift for having saved your life. Once in the woods, and now. An eye for an eye, it might be said."

Luisa stared, the warm wind whipping her brown hair. "We have little enough as you may have guessed, but I am sure that you are welcome to whatever you will take."

"Whatever I will take," he repeated. "That is well said. But I will ask that something be given as well."

He bent to her then and touched his lips to hers, probing her mouth gently until her whole being opened and moved. They locked together in a passion-filled embrace, as the world spun around them. Luisa lost all power of thought, so strong was her longing to be closer and yet more lost in this man. He drew her more fully into his arms.

Her back was against the bole of a tree and her whole being was fluid with desire. His hands were gently urging her down toward the ground. His mouth caressed hers until she had no will, only hunger.

Lady Defiant

ANNE CARSLEY

PAGEANT BOOKS

PAGEANT BOOKS
225 Park Avenue South
New York, New York 10003

Copyright © 1988 by Anne Carsley

Cover artwork by Pino Daeni

Printed in the U.S.A.

First Pageant Books printing: November, 1988

10 9 8 7 6 5 4 3 2 1

To Cadwallader–Ethelred–Taliesin: Tripartite,
who is both reality and myth,
and knew it all along

Lady Defiant

Chapter One

CHALLENGE

THE GORGEOUSLY CAPARISONED horsemen streamed down the dusty road in search of the small castle, which their charts indicated should be near. Sweat streamed from their faces, darkening the red-gold and white of the tabards. Clerks, scribes, and servants rode in the back struggling to keep up the pace set by their masters. It was to be the last evaluation of the day, then on to the next town and rest.

The group rounded one curve, then another, but saw only a wide expanse of field baking in the midsummer heat. The road stretched on into the distance with no sign of human habitation, and the leader, Sir Edward Buran, frowned in frustration. Just then the clump of brush on top of the next hill swayed and tossed as an old peasant woman emerged carrying a hoe.

"Wait!" The leader applied spurs to his horse,

1

and the big stallion flew over the ground to halt just inches from her. He snapped his fingers and the clerk hurried up with the chart. Unrolling it, he consulted the Latin for a moment, followed the lines of the map, then looked up. "Is this the land of Sir Arnauld Edwars, holder of the Marmoor estate?"

The old woman had moved further away from the men and readjusted the gray homespun hood over her head. Her hands, wrapped in the same material, clutched at her skirts while her feet shuffled in the dust. When she spoke her voice was cracked and rusty.

"Who?"

One of the knights laughed. "Make it plainer, Sir Edward. The crone is doubtless simple as well as ancient."

The clerk bent toward her, but she clutched her hood and began to mumble to herself. He pitched his voice low and soft. "The great house, mistress, the one where the lord lives. Is it close?"

"Aye. Few remain. The sick. The sick." She waved a palsied hand toward the east.

"Few are left from some sickness? Why so? Speak up, you need not fear us. This is a noble lord, Sir Edward Buran."

She looked around fearfully and made as if to scuttle deeper into the bushes. The clerk caught at her sleeve and missed. Sir Edward snorted. He had had enough; all his authority was in his voice as he demanded, "Where is your master, then? I will speak with him! We travel in the name of the king."

Her eyes went up to the leopard banners. "He

has the plague, the master does. He's getting better but one of the young lads who tended him died this morning. I had it a long time ago."

Noblemen and clerks alike jostled away from her. It was no cowardice to fear the plague—every sensible man knew it walked in weather such as this. You took what precautions you could; you prayed; often you died.

"How long has he lain ill?" Sir Edward called to her from what he hoped was a safe distance.

"Long." She hobbled back to the shelter of a small tree and fiddled again with her hood. Her hands were shaking.

"Is the plague in the village?"

"Aye, many have died there in the past month."

Sir Edward put a length of sweaty cloth up to his face and backed further away.

The clerk called out, "If your master still lives, say that the king's commissioners will return soon to see him about the estate."

She gaped and advanced, cupping her ear. "Sirs, what do you mean? I don't understand."

They backed away, discipline forgotten. The frightened clerk bawled, "Tell him the king's men are coming about taxes! He'll understand if he lives. If he does not, there will be other business."

The troop wheeled around as one and fled down the road in a cloud of dust. The old woman stood and watched until there was no sign of them. Then she hobbled carefully into the thicket, paused to peer about for another few minutes, then jerked up her skirts and ran gracefully into the deep woods.

Luisa Marmoor threw herself down on the mossy bank of the little stream, whipped the hood from her head, and drank deeply of the cool water. She began to laugh as though she would never stop. Her chestnut hair came unbound and tumbled down her back. She pushed it back with one hand and put the other to her side where a knifing stitch had formed. Then a sobering thought came, silencing her amusement. Marmoor seemed safe but for how much longer? The will of the king could not be held at bay forever.

Luisa shook her head defiantly. She would not allow herself to think of such possibilities. Quickly she rose, stripped off the remainder of the disguise that had served so well, and plunged into the bracing waters of the stream. She swam back and forth, floated on her back, and finally lay in the shallows to luxuriate in the combination of warm air and water on her naked body. Her skin was touched lightly by the sun and had a burnished sheen to it. When Luisa sat up to stare at her face in the stream, she studied the combination of features and wondered if anyone would ever find her fair. In her early youth she had often wept over her squared-off chin, full mouth, high cheekbones, and strange, slanting, green eyes below emphatic dark brows; all the heroines of minstrels' songs were blond and blue eyed like the Queen of Heaven. Why wasn't she? At twenty, she knew her looks were unusual, but the old, pointless doubts returned at times.

She shrugged impatiently. There was little time to plan her next strategy; she should not waste it sitting here contemplating herself. Yet she lingered to run her fingers over her flat stomach and down her long, slim legs, enjoying the prickle of excitement. Her breasts were round and full, the nipples slightly erect. What might a man's hand feel like on them? She thought of the dreams she often had and a flush of color stained her cheeks. Once, and only once, she had confessed them to the priest and he had been horrified. Devil sent, he called them. Luisa was glad she had not told him she enjoyed the dreams. She grinned. It was better to keep some things to herself.

She rose, quickly drying her skin and hair, and dressed again in the baggy homespun. Leaving the wrappings where they were she headed for Marmoor Castle, which was a mile distant. The road was overgrown with bushes for few travelers came this way anymore. The sun was low and lush scents drifted to her as she walked. Soon the walls of her home came into view, their weathered gray seeming to merge with the surrounding forest. The moat had long since dried up, and there were no guards at the castle's entrance. Her ancestors lay in the nearby churchyard. Her cousin, a very distant one, Sir Arnauld, had been dead these seven months and rested among them in the peace that had not been his in life. Luisa reminded herself to pray for his soul, then went through the tiltyard and keep, past the one guard who was simple and kept only for his great size, up the narrow stairs, and into Dame Matilda's rooms.

To Luisa's way of thinking Dame Matilda was immeasurably old. She had tended Luisa's father in his infancy and early years, remaining to care for the only child of his brief marriage after the young parents died together of the plague. Now Matilda sat in the deepening gloom for candles were precious. Her chair had been taken from the great hall below, and many soft coverings were placed in it to soothe her aching bones.

Luisa came up beside her nurse and spoke excitedly. "I knew they would come soon. That's the third time and always I have a different look and excuse. My schemes work, Matilda! Eventually Marmoor will be forgotten! I know it. The same person never comes back, you know. This time they really ran. Everyone's terrified of the plague."

Dame Matilda had been nodding, but at Luisa's words she jerked upright. "They'll keep coming, Luisa. We can't hold out against them. It is impossible. The writ is plain. The property descends through the male heirs. Your cousin Arnauld was the last and so Marmoor reverts to the king. Dear child, what can any of us do?" The easy tears of old age stood in her faded brown eyes as she twisted her hands together. "It might be best to let Marmoor go. The king could find a husband for you; there would be a home, children, a quiet life of security." She sighed heavily and looked at Luisa in entreaty.

The silence was palpable, heavy in the dark room. Dame Matilda was suddenly a harbinger of doom, like an ancient prophetess out of a legend.

Luisa's strong voice rose as though Matilda had not spoken. "I'll tell you what we can do! When they come again I can be a nun about to enter an enclosed order, a madwoman whom

you tend, or even a widow gone into seclusion
on a vow. Anything. Lie! Dissemble! Cheat! The
Lion-Heart gave this land to my ancestor and
now it is mine! Mine! I intend to hold it!"

Dame Matilda's attention was already wandering. "Yes, of course. Yes."

Luisa's eyes filled with tears as she turned
away. Bravado was all very well, but what could
she do for the one person left in the world who
loved her? Months ago a passing leech, given
bread and ale, had said, "Anytime." Her lack of
tears must have puzzled him. He had not known
of her inside anguish.

Dame Matilda was drifting in the past now.
"Sir Rafe came that spring before your father
was wed. Or maybe it was the one before that.
So handsome . . ."

She loved to talk this way and usually Luisa
was fascinated, even though the times often
merged or the threads of one story became com-
plex skeins of many others. Today she left Matilda to dream and took her customary route
through the area of the castle they used daily.
Much of the rooms remained shut off for lack of
servants and coin.

She and Dame Matilda lived in a few of the
rooms upstairs. The great hall below remained
unused. Even the kitchens were only partially
utilized now, and several maids and guards lived
beyond them. Luisa oversaw the castle, check-
ing that the rushes were reasonably fresh, the
products of the gardens were being prepared
against the winter, deploring the condition of
everyone's garments.

The unused great hall was still hung with old banners, trestle tables were stacked against the walls, and the throne chair of the lord stood empty. Luisa stood for a moment remembering a Christmas long past; a fair face bent to hers and a soft laugh rung out as the assembled company saluted them all. The sounds faded before the chill, which persisted here even in high summer.

She climbed next to the battlements overlooking the woods and the few remaining fields, which were worked by fewer tenants each year. The castle was given a share of the crops and they, in turn, were given work and protection. For much of Luisa's life the returns on both sides had been meager. She had worked alongside them at times in her own gardens and kitchens. Her back had felt the strain of hard work, and her hands showed it.

As she looked out over the battlement twilight was turning into darkness, and elongated shadows grew in the fragrant summer night. A night bird called and was answered by another. A slight breeze ruffled her hair and sent strange longings over her, a deep yearning for something beyond her present knowledge.

Was it fear of the future? She had always known she would not inherit Marmoor, although she thought little of it while Cousin Arnauld lived. After he died life had gone on as before, although there was far less money. The castle was remote, the nearest town miles away, and the nearby village was tiny. There were her books, her friends among the servants and tenants, Dame Matilda, the woods, and the estate itself. Life was peaceful if not exciting, never easy but generally predictable.

Then, last month, news of the death of King Henry IV had come. Dead of leprosy, it was said, and his son crowned in his place. Bad luck for certain. One king was much like another, but a new one meant a rise in taxes. From the time she heard the news, Luisa had either kept watch herself or set one of the tenants' young boys to do so. It had been part caution and part fear for the future, but this afternoon had proved the worth of her caution. She knew the king's men were bound to return with more orders. Luisa had always loved mumming and posturing; they would stand her in good stead when the next challenge came. Still, Marmoor was small, isolated. Surely it was of little strategic value to anyone and not well known except on obscure rolls.

She shifted uneasily. What was this odd hunger that pulled at her senses and stirred her blood? This might be another night of restless dreams, a time when her body seemed to turn toward an unknown lover and she waited for caresses tantalizingly out of reach. At the thought she felt her breasts swell and her mouth go dry. Sometime soon the dream would have to be reality; the Marmoors were not among those who curbed their passions. Although it was not marriage she sought.

She remembered Lady Isobel Dorout, a friend from her convent days, who had written to her over two years ago telling Luisa how pleased she was in her marriage. Luisa had not answered. Did Isobel think she had forgotten the tears and entreaties, the attempt at flight, and finally the force brought against an unwilling girl before she yielded? Luisa hoped Isobel was content now, but she doubted it; she was only thankful that there was no one to force her into matrimony.

"I'll not be ruled!" She spoke emphatically into the soft evening and then tried to laugh at her own intensity. Suddenly she felt the shadow of an old dread; she was caught in a pool of hushed voices, sparkling jewels, spreading blood, and the silence before horror, and then there was a giddiness and sense of falling. All this had been one of the specters of her childhood and early girlhood, but it had faded as she grew. Dame Matilda had explained away her dreams in her blunt way. "Too many fanciful stories! No need for a woman to have learning, anyway. God never meant it." Despite Matilda's disbelief, Luisa had come to believe that in her dreams she was living something out of Marmoor's past.

Now fear touched her and she fought it back with anger. Why was she standing here brooding, thinking of the past? There were plans to make, the future to consider. It would take ingenuity to hold her beloved Marmoor, but she was capable of it and more as well. She turned slightly and saw the flicker of movement through the trees as they bent before the wind. Riders! Quite a number of them and moving closer rapidly!

"Damnation!" The oath burned her lips and she squared her shoulders as she readied herself for the challenge.

Then there was a clatter of hooves below. Male

voices called out and one rose above the others. "Who is in authority here? This is the business of the king and cannot wait!" The clear moonlight showed Luisa the sight she had long dreaded. They had come to take Marmoor; this was the troop of the afternoon, and their leader was even now preparing to mount the stairs in search of her. She heard one of the maids cry out and knew it was time to assume the role that was rightfully hers.

The tramp of booted feet rang against stone, and she heard harsh words. "By God, this place is falling to pieces! The records do have the woman down as living here, don't they? Find her! That's an order!" He was answered at once. "Yes, Sir Edward. Certainly, Sir Edward."

Luisa's chin went high and she tossed her hair back. How dare they take over in such a way? She went out to meet the intruders, standing halfway down the flight of stairs so that they had to look up at her. "I am Luisa Marmoor. What is your business here and why have you entered without leave?" Best to affect a haughty note at once. They must not treat a daughter of Marmoor as if she were a peasant.

Sir Edward, dark bearded and ascetic in appearance, had the look of boredom Luisa knew she herself wore when Dame Matilda gave endless lectures on worthiness. She would dispel his boredom! He did not deign to speak but lifted one hand to the clerk, who scurried forward and spoke from memory.

"This castle and lands belong to King Henry by virtue of the death of the male heir. Always

previously there was an heir to take over, no
matter how remote might have been his relation.
When your father, Philip Marmoor, died un-
timely, it went to his oldest living brother, who
quarreled with the then king, Richard II, and was
exiled for it. When he died, Sir Arnauld Edward
was informed of his inheritance and came from
the Holy Land to claim it. He was in the process
of dying then and sequestered himself for years.
You, daughter of the Marmoors, and your nurse
remained here as part of the household. You are
convent educated and well over an age to marry.
Sir Arnauld has been dead for months and the
matter unreported to the king."

He paused for breath and Sir Edward spoke in
the sudden silence. "A consideration which
might be viewed as treason. Our sovereign lord
is most swift to punish, as well he must be." His
thin mouth lifted unpleasantly.

"I am the heir of blood and right. Marmoor is
mine. My family has always served the ruler of
England." Luisa tried to speak quietly, but the
flashing, fatal fury that belonged to all the Marmoors was about to blaze out. "Always."

The clerk was now fumbling with his papers
and preparing to continue the recitation. Sir Edward gave him a savage look and he faded into
the background. "Believe what you wish. It
counts for little. This castle is to be manned immediately and steps taken to begin making the
area a profitable one for the Crown. The records
of these remote castles and properties have been
studied for months. Marmoor is one of many on
our lists." He grinned. "They told us in the vil-

lage that the plague had not been there for over a year. It was fortunate that I stopped to ask and hinted that we carried good news for the lady of the castle."

"And if you take my home what do you propose to do with me? And with Dame Matilda who is too old and ill to be moved?" Luisa gritted her teeth, trying to maintain her control. Did they think her a hart brought to bay? A meek and obedient maiden?

Sir Edward shrugged and ran a finger over his mustache. "All will be done properly. You may return to the convent. They will take you willingly for a small dowry. Or a suitable husband will be found from around here and money will be settled on him. You have a choice, you see, and should be grateful for it. Few women do, but our king is just."

Luisa came down the stairs, her fists clenched and her face white. Sir Edward backed away. "Justice! Is this the king's justice? I'll not be dispossessed of my home and my future determined for me!"

"Take care, lady." The clerk barely breathed the words. His eyes were round with amazement and barely concealed admiration.

"Care, indeed! Why should I fear? No wonder your king seeks money so hungrily! Even in the depths of the country we have heard of his eagerness for his father's stolen throne! Now he takes from his subjects with greedy hands and calls it right!"

They stood transfixed as she uttered words no man could say and live. The maids had brought in smoky torches which illuminated the great walls and picked out the beads of moisture on them. Luisa was beyond thought now. The brown skirts swirled around her bare ankles as her hair tumbled in masses over her shoulders with the force of her anger. Even the proud Sir Edward was speechless.

"I am a free citizen of this land and my ancestors have been likewise. I will ride to London to demand true justice of King Henry. Not justice by the whim of a long-dead ruler, but that justice which comes by living and working with the land, the right of love. Marmoor is mine!"

The challenge had been issued.

Chapter Two
PERILOUS ENCOUNTER

Luisa pushed her hair under the dark green hood and cloak that had once been her best. The matching gown was patched and worn, but it would do for travel. The only decent one she had was of black wool and she must wear that to court. Her smooth brow was creased as she thrust a few belongings into a bag and stepped quickly to her one pair of slippers.

Sir Edward's reaction to her defiance the previous night had greatly surprised her. Instead of the expected whiplash of rage, he had said,

"Since you feel so strongly about it, you shall go to London on the morrow with some of the men who are sent to report. I will give you the name of the person to whom you may address yourself. I trust you can be ready early? And that you will not mind traveling with men?"

He thought she would refuse his offer, but she had given him look for look. "I will be ready at whatever hour you choose. There is a small convent some twenty miles from here. We will stop and ask if any of the holy sisters can be spared to go with us to London. Once in the city I intend to ask shelter at their convent until such time as I may have audience of the king. No minor official, but the king!"

Sir Edward had snorted, nodded, given her a strangely veiled look, and left his men in search of accommodations. She had won the first skirmish but was still uneasy.

Now there was nothing to do but go. Dame Matilda had retreated inward, as she often did, to a happier time when she and her husband had served other Marmoors at the court of King Richard II, that elaborate, dangerous, and fascinating place. Luisa smiled indulgently at the older woman. Dame Matilda and her dreams would be tended by one of the stout girls from the village while Luisa was gone. But she herself was preparing for battle. She had to try to save Marmoor.

She did not look back as they rode away from her home. She would hold it in her memory and cherish this land of hers; it was a part of Luisa herself. Her spine was straight and her chin was set as she controlled the black mare she had been given. The five men-at-arms, one young clerk, and two servants all stared covertly at the woman who had jousted with Sir Edward and lived. She felt their awe and was pleased; it gave her courage to leave Marmoor and Dame Matilda, who she feared might not live to see her charge return.

They reached Burney Convent at twilight after a long exhausting ride and settled in. The abbess was austere but agreeable to sparing two sisters, Agatha and Martha, for the rest of the journey although she expressed doubts as to Luisa's mission.

"It may be that you attempt to flout God's will for you, Lady Marmoor. You should pray long and earnestly."

Luisa smiled and nodded. She had long since learned not to argue with nuns and priests. One always lost. Father Peter, who served Marmoor and the village near it, had begged her to become a nun. "I feel it to be God's will, my dear," he had said. Certainly it was the way of safety for a woman alone, but it was not Luisa's way. She said mildly, "I must do this, Mother, but I will pray as you say."

The journey was slower after the nuns joined the party and Luisa found herself wild with impatience. Both were calm and reflective; although she was very glad of their presence, she had nothing in common with them. She was ready to reach London and embark on her mission. It was hard to move sedately, pause at appropriate shrines, or stop frequently for prayer. Yet the church was her bastion, for with its support even the king of England must give way. She could claim its protection to ward off any forced marriage while seeking an alternative.

On the afternoon of the fourth day, they entered a large wood which was thickly covered with underbrush. The path was narrow and they were forced to go single file. Luisa was riding behind the nuns and, for once, her urgency was stilled. They were a silent party for the most part and each dwelt on his own thoughts. She breathed in the soft air, which was redolent of flowering shrubs. Light lay in warm pools, birds cheeped softly, and insects droned. Peace was everywhere. Already Luisa had planned what she would say for defense of her claim and the manner in which she would present it.

Suddenly there was a cry and the lead horse rose up on its hind legs with a whinny as the bridle was jerked down. The party was surrounded by men in hoods and ragged shirts, who held staves and knives, their faces set and savage.

The rein of Luisa's horse was caught by a gap-toothed man who shouted, "Jewels, coins, pouches, cloaks, horses! Yield everything quietly or you'll lie dead and we'll have it anyway!" He laughed as Luisa recoiled from him.

Sister Agatha lifted her crucifix and closed her eyes in prayer. Sister Martha started to remonstrate with them, but one of the robbers pushed her aside roughly. The man-at-arms nearest Luisa took advantage of the distraction and lashed out with his own stave. He was instantly slammed from his horse to lie prone in the path with his head broken.

The gap-toothed man went mad with rage. "I warned you! Now you'll pay!" He reached for Luisa to pull her down, and she saw the lust in his eyes.

She twisted backward as the horse reared. She tumbled from it and into a prickly bush. The robbers hurled themselves on the guards and began to beat them cruelly. Several came at her but she caught her breath and screamed until the air rang with it. Then she snatched the dagger out of her belt and prepared to sell her life as dearly as possible. Rage blotted out fear as she faced them.

Her wrist was seized from behind, and she felt a paralyzing pain in her arm. Her captor swung her around and shook her. "Peasant wench! I'll teach you a thing or two after these holy ones give up their riches!"

"Leave them alone!" Luisa momentarily forgot her own danger when the others began to pull at the praying nuns. "Leave them alone, I say!"

The gap-toothed man laughed harshly and advanced toward her. His muddy brown eyes flamed and she saw death there. His face was frenzied in the dappling of light and shadow. "The church is rich! We'll get our share!"

His men cried out in agreement. Luisa spat at one of the men and his fist slammed against her head.

"Stop or you die this instant!" The command

was hard and authoritative as it cracked like a whip across the melee.

Two archers stood with crossbows at the ready. She could not see their faces in the gloom, but they wore sturdy brown garments and swords hung at close reach. The surprised robbers slunk back. The supplicating voices of the nuns rose in continuing prayer.

A tall man stood behind the archers. He wore homespun and his black hood was pulled well over his face, but the span of his wide shoulders and stance of his booted legs proclaimed his authority. As he moved his head, Luisa saw that his nose had an arrogant thrust. He held a heavy sword in one gloved hand and was immediately joined by other archers.

"Ladies, are you all right? This scum will bother you no more. I think they plan to run for their lives." The man spoke in heavily accented French, laughing as the frightened robbers dashed into the undergrowth, a hail of arrows following after them.

One, braver than the rest, called, "Our time will come, you spawn of France! Wait and see!" The rattle of breaking branches accompanied his howl as an arrow found its mark.

Luisa leaned against a tree trunk, her knees shaking under her. "Why didn't you kill them?" she demanded in French. "They would have done as much to us!"

"Bloodthirsty, aren't you?" The leader turned to her and she caught the undertone of anger in his voice.

She continued in French. "They will only rob

again and next time their victims may be killed. If that is a bloodthirsty viewpoint, so be it." The narrowness of the margin between death and life shook her and her words came from the heart. "I thank you for us all. You have saved our lives and virtue. We are grateful."

He nodded absently, sheathed his sword, and looked about for his horse. She moved closer and he gazed directly into her face. The light fell on him in one long, last ray. His hood was now swept back to reveal wavy, black hair, a tanned face, and a mobile mouth with a slight downward curve at one side. Heavy lashes framed eyes of a deep and brilliant blue. She could not look away. He exuded a magnetism so powerful that it pulled her toward him. It was as if all her blood lifted and sang in her veins. Her mouth ached to know the shape and texture of his lips. Over the roaring in her ears she heard him speak in English. His accent was faintly lilting.

"Go and gather those you serve. These woods are not safe. Hurry."

Luisa stared at him, wondering if he thought her a simple girl bemused by a handsome man. Had her feelings been bare on her face? She matched his brusque manner.

"We are headed for London on urgent business. I know it is less than one full day's journey. Could you see us at least to the high road?"

"I cannot. Come, we must go before it is full dark."

Something opened between them as they took each other's measure. It was an awareness so keen as to be searing. Luisa moved away, shaken to her very core. Was he also? She wondered.

One of the men-at-arms was dead and the other severely wounded. The clerk was found in the bushes, where he gibbered with terror. Their rescuers took them all to a small village less than two miles from the place where they had been attacked, and there arrangements were made to tend those hurt in the struggle. They learned that it was not far to the convent where they had originally planned to spend the night. In a moment of brief respite, the parties paused to drink a cup of sorely needed ale and rested on benches outside the tiny inn.

By now the nuns had recovered sufficiently to call down blessings on the tall man and his men. Sister Martha tangled Latin, English, and French together as she ended, "You came in answer to our most fervent prayers. You were sent. God heard us and gave us his instruments."

He bowed politely over their upraised hands as they began benedictions again. Luisa felt only irritation when Sister Agatha made a beckoning gesture toward her. The night wind blew her hair back from her face and her torn clothes felt sticky on her skin. Luisa's words rose unbidden.

"I fail to see that your prayers, sisters, accomplished very much. Your pardon, but it seems to me that if we had not first fought for our lives we would have been dead before anyone came."

Sister Agatha regarded the heathen in their midst and sniffed. "Prayer and submission to His will are all the answers we need."

"But we are given mind and thought to use."
Luisa felt herself growing angry and knew it was
pointless to continue. She turned slightly and
met the blazing blue gaze of the dark man.

"You are a pagan, mistress." The words themselves were casual but some question lurked behind them. "Greek, Roman, or beyond either?"
He smiled slightly, appearing younger than his
thirty-odd years.

"Perhaps any or all." She meant to be casual
but the nuns looked horrified. The matter was
best dropped, she knew. Religious discussions
of any sort were often the source of great anger.
"But certainly a good Christian, sir, as we all
are." Even in the small village near Marmoor she
had seen men come to blows over the interpre-
tation of a verse by Father Peter or another priest
if the opinion differed. She shook her head in
annoyance at the ways of such. The dark man
rose abruptly to go to his men.

They had planned to resume the journey
within the next few minutes, but the two nuns
were still upset and needed more time to compose themselves. The archers were to ride with
them to the convent but it seemed that their
leader had business elsewhere. He was speaking
urgently to them now.

Luisa sighed and expelled a long breath. She
was ready for action and hers was not a nature to
sit idly by.

"You are impatient even as I." The French
accent was heavy on his words as he bent toward her. His mouth was unsmiling.

Luisa saw that the archers were bent over their

weapons and ignoring them. Whatever he had said had been effective; he was not a man with whom one trifled. She longed to prick him; no one should be that sure of himself. Yet she was very conscious of the debt they owed him. She rose and held out her hand. He bent gravely over it but amusement flickered in the blue eyes and she knew that he considered her a servant who was putting on superior airs.

"I would know your name, good sir. I am the Lady Luisa Marmoor."

He looked boldly at her. "Lady Marmoor? And you travel so? With no attendants? Is your father or husband quite mad?"

Luisa was nettled and rage skimmed her words as she said, "I have neither but you need not doubt the validity of my name, which is old in the annals of this land. Can you say as much?"

His face went dark and cold but he said nothing. Luisa was instantly ashamed. But for this man and his followers all their lives would be forfeit. The warm wind lifted her hair, blowing it against her hot cheeks. Luisa raised both hands to them.

"I have been unpardonably rude, sir. Forgive me."

He smiled quickly. "It is forgotten. You have asked my name. Call me 'John.' Yes, do call me that."

"And your family name?" She could not hold back her curiosity. There was an air of mystery about him that lured and fascinated her.

"I have made a vow not to divulge it until certain matters have been accomplished." His voice was suddenly flat as he looked beyond her.

Luisa said half-musing. "John, the one who goes before—"

He swung her around so hard that the bones in her wrist crunched together and his blue eyes filled with the bleakness of death. "What did you say? Who are you?"

Chapter Three
LIFE'S LOTTERY

JOHN'S TOUCH BURNED her skin and she fought back her fear. "The sun has addled you. It was but an idle remark. John the Baptist, who went before the Lord." Her laughter was forced but some of the tension left his face. "Silly, I know. I am Luisa Marmoor, as I told you."

"A coincidence only. Perhaps. We will not speak of it." He drew her into the shade of the tall tree a few steps away and she followed willingly, all her senses alive with excitement. His face was grave but he was half-smiling as he loomed over her. "I ask recompense of you, my lady. A gift for the gift of your life. Once in the woods and just now. An eye for an eye, it might be said."

Luisa stared, surprised at this apparent crudity, suspecting him of base motives. "We have little enough as you may have guessed, but I am

sure that you are welcome to whatever you will
take."

"Whatever I will take," he repeated. "That is
well put. But I will ask that something be given
as well." There was a hint of laughter in his
voice and something else that made Luisa involuntarily step away from him.

He bent to her then and touched his lips to
hers, probing her mouth gently until her whole
being opened and moved. They locked together
in a passion-filled embrace as the world spun
around them. Luisa lost all power of thought, so
strong was her longing to be closer and yet more
lost in this man. He drew her more fully into his
arms, and she felt the hardness of his manhood
against her suddenly shaking legs. She felt herself grow warm inside and she ached for him to
hold her tighter. Her arms slid around his wide
back and her breasts throbbed as he dropped
one hand to them under her thin gown.

Her back was against the bole of the great tree
and her whole being was fluid with desire. His
hands were gently urging her down toward the
ground and she did not have the will to resist.
Luisa heard herself moan as if from a distance as
his warm fingers caught an engorged nipple and
began to massage it very slowly. His mouth caressed hers until she had no will, only hunger.

Suddenly she was set back from him, her desire naked on her face in the light of the rising
moon which now shone brilliantly through the
leaves. She shook with the force of her feelings
and her mouth trembled. The mad thought
chased through her head that she must resemble

one of the wood carvings in the church, crafted to represent lust.

John was laughing softly, the moonlight glinting off his bold face which now showed no trace of desire. "I see now why the cloister does not appeal to you. It is ever thus with you bold ones. I would suggest that you get yourself wed swiftly, mistress or lady, as you be."

Luisa went from sweet immolation to red rage as she raised her hand to slam it across his face. He caught her arm and forced it back down, laughing as he did so.

"How dare you treat a gentlewoman as if she were one of the trulls with whom I do not doubt you bed constantly?" Luisa cried. "What do you know of respect? You should be whipped for insolence!"

"And you for lusting, sweet mistress." He stepped back from her and gave a low whistle.

Luisa wiped the sweat from her forehead and tried to speak but fury choked her. There was a crackling sound beside them then as one of the archers appeared with John's great black horse. He mounted with quick grace and instantly seemed as one with the beast. Involuntarily, Luisa thought of the centaurs. The archer spoke softly to his leader in that strange language that teased the ears. John answered as he waved one hand toward her and the inn.

"Demons go with you and attend you!" It was a childish response, Luisa knew, but it gave her some satisfaction. She longed for words yet more savage and cutting, as she stood boldly before him, both hands on her hips.

The beautiful horse snorted, its nostrils spread wide, and the archer edged away as if unwilling to be a witness to whatever was going on between Luisa and his master.

John spoke softly but she could hear the edge in his words. "You need not fear, they already do." He moved the horse closer to her until she felt the warm breath of the animal almost directly in her face, but she did not deign to move back.

"Then my wish is fulfilled." Her legs were shaking again but she kept her haughty demeanor.

"Think of me when you are wed to your fat merchant or aging knight!"

The black horse was merged with the night and the hoofbeats were fading on the coast road before Luisa realized that the French accent had vanished from his voice, and he had spoken those last taunting words in perfect, unaccented English.

Luisa moistened her dry lips, straightened her rumpled gown, and fought for composure. Then she stepped out into the torch-lit area and called for all to hear, "Can we not go on to the convent this night while it is yet early? Are the sisters restored?"

Luisa smiled a little to herself. Of a truth, the convent was not far, and with the protection of the archers it should be simple for them to reach within an hour or two. The good sisters would flinch at the thought of a night spent at so worldly a place as an inn. And Luisa wanted to remove herself as quickly as possible from the place of her humiliation.

"I am still Luisa Marmoor. I am still myself," Luisa repeated under her breath. Since earliest childhood she had said these words to herself in times of stress and when she was in need of comfort. They helped her now even though the odd feeling of loss remained with her.

The nuns soon appeared and declared themselves ready for the journey. She could see they were still shaken, though not by the assault on their persons but by what appeared to be a slight to the church. Always self-sufficient, Luisa might not have understood even a day ago, but her attitude had softened since her own being had been defiled.

From then on the journey was uneventful, and at the convent the archers bade them farewell and departed to join John. Luisa wondered again at his guise, the strangeness of his language, and the way he had toyed with her. She heard his laughter over and over as she recalled the shameless passion she had displayed. Never less than honest with herself, she knew she had experienced the kind of passion that altered human lives, not the delicate weaving of the ballads or the pretty puzzles of the courts of love, but rather a force by which men and women lived. She must accept her weakness and go on.

During the time of rest at the wayside convent and the slow journey to London in a driving rain, Luisa tried to think little of John. Some odd fatalism told her that they were fated to meet again, but Marmoor was her chief concern now. She practiced the words she would say in its defense many times over as they made their way toward the city.

Several days later they approached London in the dim light of early morning. Already peddlers, rich merchants, pie sellers, soldiers, members of the clergy, guild representatives, and many others swirled through the narrow streets where the roofs of houses nearly met. Passersby walked in real danger of pots being emptied on their heads, and the varied smells were enough to stagger the senses. Everywhere there was movement and excitement; people rushed frantically, some intent on business and some on mischief.

The small company went along wider streets and smaller lanes while Luisa stared as much as any bumpkin. She saw London Bridge with its lines of shops and dwellings. There were the houses of government, the great palaces on the river which ran to the sea, the well-known churches, and the gray sprawl of the convent to which they were bound. Luisa knew a wiser person ought to be afraid of this teeming city and of confronting the king, but she entered into battle for herself and Marmoor; all her will readied itself for that challenge.

She spoke silently to the city, I am ready.

When they reached the religious house, Luisa was given God's welcome as had been the custom since the earliest days of the church. The community closed over her without a ripple; she was given a tiny cell to herself, instructed to attend services, issued sewing materials so that she might repair the few clothes she had brought, and was otherwise ignored. No official notice was taken of her presence, but the nun who dealt with petitioners grew weary of her determined questions.

"You are one of many, Lady Marmoor. These matters cannot be hurried. Channels must be utilized, everything done properly. Requests must be very carefully checked. Patience, patience. It is a virtue favored by our Lord."

Luisa was heartily sick of maidenly obedience, but she bent her head and murmured her gratitude. All her efforts must be directed toward the coming battle. In spite of all her efforts to be calm baffled frustration shook her. What law decreed that a woman should hold no property in her own right or that she should be married or a nun? It was unjust!

The next afternoon a message was brought to Luisa as she paced the narrow confines of her cell. She whirled about as the door swung open. Did none of these holy women knock? Sister Helena, mistress of novices, entered. Previously she had only nodded casually to Luisa and passed on. Now she watched her assessingly.

"A litter will call for you early in the morning. Charles Arban, the chief clerk of taxes and accounts, a most important man, has declared his readiness to speak with you. His decision will be final."

The nun's austere habit loomed large in Luisa's gaze. "I asked audience with the king! It is my right as a citizen!"

"Anger is unseemly, my child. The king cannot be everywhere and surely there are important matters of state with which he must deal. Be calm and obedient. God commands it." Her black eyes burned into Luisa's.

"Has He not given us our minds to use?" Luisa asked, impatiently. It was the sort of comment that had once made her old tutor set her to construing endless lines of Greek.

Sister Helena only replied, "Remember what I have said." She waited until Luisa bent her head in apparent agreement before leaving.

Luisa sent both shoes slamming into the wall. "Obedient, indeed! I'll spin that clerk such a tale of woe as will make him have me before the king instantly." She had to be optimistic; was she not about to be at the mercy of a strange man in the corner of the palace? A man used to papers and laws and accounts! She thought of the delicate towers and green fields of her home, and her eyes misted with the tears that were no part of Luisa Marmoor. Her chin went up as she began to plan.

The next morning she peered critically at herself in the mirror of polished steel. Her black gown was of aged velvet and worn from much use, but it lay softly against her slim body. Her face was still touched by the sun. It shone a pure oval against the severe gray headdress, which was softened by a drifting white veil. She stared at her high forehead, arched brows, and determined lips; the brilliance of her hair was the only color. Too subdued? Too vivid? She did not want to look the humble supplicant. Daughter of a proud line, proud in her own right, secure in the justice of her cause, Luisa spun before the mirror and saw the slender, floating figure there. Her ancestors had gone forth to battle; so now did she.

The journey in the litter to see Charles Arban seemed to take an eternity. The bearers paid no attention to her as they rushed swiftly along the busy streets. Her head buzzed and spun while the city noises came faintly to her ears. She tried to think objectively but concentration was not possible. She must not lose her temper; that was the most important thing. Even if this clerk handed down a ruling, she would demand audience as was her right. Her family had helped make the history of England; they had been peers, honored and respected. King Henry V could not refuse a simple request from one of her rank. He had once been gay Prince Hal who laughed and sported in London with his friends—now he was considered by many to be pious and rigid, determined to set England right. *Dissemble!* Luisa told herself. But while she knew she had to heed her own warnings, foreboding was deep in her.

The litter dropped to the ground abruptly and the curtains were roughly pulled aside. A brown-haired, nondescript man looked in. "Come. There's no time to waste." He left her to scramble out unassisted as he led the pace across a small courtyard, gray and cold at this hour, and then through a network of passages. Water dripped down the walls and the chill was palpable. As Luisa had no cloak, she was grateful when they came to a level where torches set in sconces gave both light and warmth. She was ushered into a little room furnished only with a high stool and a rickety table laden with papers. An open door led to another room filled with ironbound chests.

"You will wait." The servant shut the door with a bang and was gone.

Luisa stood uncertainly for a few minutes, then began to pace back and forth. Her throat was parched, her legs weak. When she went closer to the table she saw a flagon which must have been filled with ale or wine and several cups half hidden in the morass of papers. How she would love a single swallow! She had to be ready to speak. So much depended on the impression made here in the first few moments. Why had she been rushed here and then made to wait? Who was a mere clerk to treat Lady Luisa Marmoor this way? And Lady Marmoor I will stay only if I handle this properly, she told herself. Remember Dame Matilda! Remember Marmoor. Almost wildly she thought of her ancestor, who had gone on Crusade in the long years after the Lion-Heart's death and whose battle cry had been not "Deus Veult!" but "Remember Marmoor!" "I, too. I, too!" she said aloud, and felt somehow reassured.

Instinct made Luisa pause in her pacing. She felt watched. She lifted a hand to her head and allowed a sigh to escape, then rubbed her forehead as if it ached. When she looked around between her fingers, she saw nothing. She swiftly walked to the wall where she leaned as if drooping with fatigue or worry. Another glance showed nothing. An uneasy feeling still pierced her and she felt as if the watcher, unseen as he was, was gloating, enjoying her discomfort.

She started to swing around, but then a panel on the far wall moved smoothly back and a cold voice encircled her.

"Luisa Marmoor, who disputes the law, come for reckoning? That you shall have and promptly!"

Chapter Four
THE STALKING GAME

CHARLES ARBAN SEEMED to have grown old among ancient records. His face and hair were the same shade of yellow-white, his skin papery, and his eyes pale gray. The black robe he wore, with its fraying edges, was the most colorful thing about him. His thin lips lifted away from yellow teeth, reminding Luisa of a weasel or a ferret. She did not make the mistake of considering him ineffectual for, though short and very thin, his body exuded power and confidence. She knew he had watched her since the door first opened.

"Well?" He did not move but his gaze bore into her. "Speak up!"

She would show him that she understood his power. Surely maidenly submission was the key here; his sharp words were meant to make her fearful. Luisa clenched her hands together in front of her and saw his quick glance go from her twisting fingers to her trembling lips. Good.

"Marmoor has been long in my family, sir." She let her voice go soft with appeal as she spoke of her life—from orphaned daughter to nurse to Sir Arnauld to companion of Dame Matilda and finally to her own wish to live quietly, modestly, at Marmoor. "Of course, it is a small estate, but it can be self-supporting and who can care for it more than the bloodline? The king's purse will suffer no loss. Leave us in peace. This is my home; my only refuge."

Luisa had kept her head partially bent during this speech and now she drew her veil closer over her face as if to hide tears. Would this be a good time to launch into the speech about her ancestors and the probable intention of the Lion-Heart when he bestowed Marmoor, as well as the long tradition of service to the Crown that her family had? It seemed not. Master Arban's eyes were looking past her with an expression of utmost boredom.

"You waste your time and mine, Mistress Marmoor. You know that the castle and land belong to King Henry by law. I do not propose to stand here and argue about it."

"Sir, I beseech you . . ."

He folded his arms and stared her down. "My time is far too valuable to be wasted in this way."

He made no move to go and Luisa took heart even as the blood hammered in her temples. Fighting back her shame, she held her submissive pose and spoke softly. "Yours is the power, sir. All know of it and I am grateful that you chose to see me this day. I ask a thing that is little to you and much to me. Can you not, will you not, of your charity, leave me this one thing? Charity is most pleasing in the sight of our blessed Lord and I will pray for you all my days." Luisa lowered herself slowly until her knees touched the floor and she knelt before him in supplication. What more could the man want from her?

The silence stretched out for an eternity before she heard a rustle of movement and his padding steps as he came close to her. When she dared look up, she saw that she had made a fatal error. She had thought him old but he had yet to reach his mid-forties; only the pallor of his skin made him appear aged. Now there was a flush on his cheekbones and amusement in his eyes. Her performance had made her a prey for him. How could she have been so foolish?

"You can take the veil or have a marriage arranged as was mentioned to you. You are fortunate you have a choice. I shall direct that the matter be settled within a week. Go now; you are dismissed."

Arban turned to the table and reached for a small bell which stood close at hand. He paused to riffle in some of the papers, his interest apparently caught and Luisa was forgotten. She rose to her feet, dug her nails into the palms of both hands, and summoned all her strength.

"Master Arban, I can understand legalities but they may surely be tempered with mercy. What use is my heritage to the realm? What can it offer? To me it is everything. What harm can be done by allowing me to keep my home?" She tried to speak reasonably and with a faint undertone of supplication, but her voice shook with rising fury.

He did not turn around. "Why are you still here? You shall be removed immediately." The bell was in his upraised fingers.

Luisa was beside him in a few short strides, eyes blazing with fury. She stared at the object of her fury. "Pig of a clerk! You never meant to help me or even listen, did you? You took gloating pleasure in my pleas, in my humility before you! That's what happens when such as your ilk is given power to use without check! Well, I intend to take this higher!" She thumped her fist on the table, sending the papers flying.

Arban's face did not alter. His mouth barely moved as he said, "There is none higher. Full power is mine."

"So it pleases you to think! I doubt clerks yet rule England!" She could not check herself now; it was intoxicating to speak her mind. "Lowborn louts must often think so!"

"Dangerous words. You need ruling." His manner was deceptively mild in contrast to the earlier peremptory one. "I must make a note of that. Your husband, when he is selected, will find it of interest." He made as if to reach for a fresh quill.

Luisa was now so furious she could not speak. Her throat was totally dry. She spat a single Latin epithet, stamped her foot, reached for the wine and a cup, then poured out a generous dollop and drank it down.

"Even your wine is thin and sour." She threw it, cup and all, on the floor at his feet and had the inestimable pleasure of seeing the thin lips tighten as his fingers curled convulsively.

"I see, my lady—you see I no longer omit the title that you give yourself—that you have unexpected facets to your character. Such spirit is wasted in the cloister. I quite agree. But, look you, I know just the thing for your future." He smiled, showing the tips of his yellowed teeth.

Luisa's rage evaporated as the quiet words froze her. Her hellish temper had led her into deadly peril.

He continued. "There is a certain lord I have in mind, he has had ill luck in his marriages. Three of them and no son. Is that not sad? I have grieved for him. There was been difficulty, we have often remarked on it, in finding just the right lady for him. He is very particular and I think you may be a suitable candidate. A man of sixty-odd years must have sons."

He paused and Luisa felt the sweat run down her back. She could not regret the anger she had let free for she knew that this man took pleasure in those who crawled.

Arban was smiling malevolently as he said, "Now I rejoice that you have come this day."

Her voice was rock steady. "You cannot force me into a marriage for the spite of a moment."

"No?" He paused. "Where are those who will protect you? I see no one. I rather think that the solicitude of the king's servant does our master credit. A penniless female must be cared for."

"I will not marry and you cannot force me. I will appeal to the king himself."

Arban allowed a grimace to cross his face. "The king has personally thanked me for lifting many mundane matters from his shoulders. You do understand me, I suppose?"

Luisa understood that she was virtually powerless. She knew she had probably made the situation much worse with her temper, but how could she have submitted tamely?

Arban continued, "I have the power and will use it. Make no mistake. You were safer when you were unknown to me—anyone who knows me will tell you that. Begin to prepare yourself for the happy day of your marriage. The convent will be notified of the king's will in this."

Luisa spoke in a hard tone. "Your friend had best look to his manhood, lest he lose it before he can find it."

Arban lifted the bell and rang it twice. The servant opened the door and stepped inside. "Take two of the guards and see the lady here safely to the convent. Tend her well for her own sake. A message will follow." He turned to Luisa, his manner that of the polished courtier. "May I wish you happiness on your coming nuptials?"

"To the devil with you! May the evil that you have sought for others come upon you!" She marched proudly from the room, the servant behind her. In the long stillness of the hall she heard his chortling echo. There was a self-satisfied sound about it which made Luisa suddenly aware that she might have played directly into the manipulator's hands.

For the rest of that day and all night Luisa tossed on her hard bed at the convent and paced in her cell. No one came near and she was thankful for this mercy. Her pain was so intense she felt she would shatter if forced to speak. Marmoor was truly lost; she berated herself for her folly, her playacting, her temper.

What could I have done to alter things? she asked herself. The despairing question beat at Luisa until her tears and anger were gone. Finally she lay down because she could no longer stand and sleep came as a bludgeon.

When she woke, Luisa realized that she stood in mortal peril for Arban meant every word he had said. If only she had been meek and mild! But then Arban might have devised another torture. Who could know? She must not think of Marmoor now, but of herself. Flight was the only answer and too much time had already been wasted.

A few minutes later, Luisa slipped down the long stone corridor toward the chapel. The black woolen gown she wore was covered with a long, coarse cloak and her hair was bound back. Her face was scrubbed and pale, her swollen eyes puffy. Her hands were clasped before her and her proud head was bent. She heard a flurry of movement behind her but did not pause until a firm hand took her arm. It was Sister Helena.

The nun was composed and cool but her voice was warm. "We were beginning to worry, Lady Marmoor. You kept to your room so long." She drew Luisa into a small alcove where they might have privacy from those passing. "My dear, instructions concerning you have arrived."

Luisa looked at her and then away. "I know. Tell me what they are."

"You will be given in marriage to Sir Adam of Wenlock six days from now. This is the will of the king whose ward you are. It is final. You will remain here until your bridegroom arrives from the north to claim you." Her fingers raised Luisa's chin and held it. Her assessing gaze could not be avoided. "Pray for strength; it comes when least expected."

In spite of all her efforts, Luisa heard her voice shake. "He is an old man, experienced and dissolute. Master Arban said as much. I am but twenty." The warnings rang in her brain. She must not say too much. Careful!

"It is time you were wed. Obviously you have no calling to the cloister." Sister Helena was brisk and practical. "Many would be pleased to wed a noble lord. Sir Adam is older and has had varying difficulties. No sons, battle injuries, even rebellion amongst his followers. But he is a devout Christian gentleman and favored of the king and church. Your future is settled."

Luisa forced her words through stiff lips. "I will pray for acceptance in the chapel and rest alone in my room later if I may. This is not easy for me." She thought bitterly that this must be the greatest of all understatements.

"I can tell the abbess that you will obey? You know all our prayers go with you." The nun was insistent.

Luisa repressed a very strong urge to tell her

just what could be done with the abbess, convent, prayers, the king, and his servants. "I will obey, Sister, but it is bitter for me." Now the tears misted her eyes and ran down her cheeks. They were of rage but the nun could not know that. "Please escort me to the chapel now."

She was left alone in the chapel, a glory of stained glass, velvet, and incense. When she knelt the rough stone bruised her knees but at this stage she wanted no comfort. Somewhere in the depths of the building a lone voice lifted in a limpid chant about the peace of green valleys. Eyes seemed to pierce her back. There was no doubt she was being watched, possibly by guards. Had she waited too long? Why so much bother over one girl with a small castle of no real importance who had angered a clerk? Luisa heard the rustle of robes and adjusted her face in suitable lines of piety. She fixed her gaze on the nearest window, which depicted Abraham about to sacrifice Isaac. The detail was far too graphic. With a gasp that was nearly a nervous giggle, she looked away. She pictured brilliant blue eyes, and in her inner vision she stood again with John in shared laughter and excitement. It was little comfort in the long hours she spent in the chapel as the day wore on.

Luisa grew cramped and tired but she dared not leave. In a just society she would be helped to regain Marmoor or would never be in danger of losing it. Now even the church was unwilling to help her. She was alone and must fight her own battles. This time it was a struggle for her very life.

She shifted uneasily and counted the passing seconds, reviewing her plan again and yet again. "I won't fail. I can't." She spoke the words as though they were prayers and in a sense they were.

Chapter Five
PILGRIM PATH

"WHAT ARE YOU doing here, boy? Don't you know these places are forbidden? You cannot just wander around in here!" The fat guard scratched under his helmet and peered at the scruffy youth who had just emerged from the narrow passageway that led into the kitchen courtyard. The guard's mouth hung slightly open and his vague eyes did not focus. "Where did you come from?"

Luisa tapped her ears and lips, rubbed her stomach, and made pushing motions. She did not have to pretend desperation; it was welling up within her. The dawn would soon give way to full morning and the nuns, now at the second service of the new day, would turn their minds to practicalities—one of which was Luisa Marmoor.

The guard bawled, "What is it? Are you deaf? Daft?" He leaned forward, fully prepared to howl in her ears once more.

Luisa doubted she could bear that burst of

sound again without flinching. How could this
work? He must smell her fear. She made pointing motions toward the gate and let her mouth
drop even more open as she grunted.

This particular tableau had not yet been noticed for the courtyard was alive with activity.
Carts filled with the produce of the countryside,
eager tradespeople, beggars, petitioners, farm-
ers, lay servants of the convent, and a few
townspeople swirled back and forth. The iron
gate with the great cross above it would soon be
closed for the day; this hubbub was only permitted early so that food, trading, begging, and true
petitioners might all be separated into their
proper categories.

"Let this one out!" Even in the moment of her
relief, Luisa wondered if the guard thought she
was about to have a fit, defile the convent in
some way, or simply take up his time which
might be better spent sampling the wares
brought in. Perhaps he was bored with the business. At any rate, she was being given leave to
go.

"Out! Go! Go!" He made flapping motions at
her just as a sturdy woman turned too quickly at
the gate and several chickens flew from her cart,
scattering in different directions. Her children
sped after them while the people laughed, joined
in the scramble, or spoke significantly of the
need for quiet in this holy place. The tower bells
began to peal and the sun shone warmly through
the cloud banks.

Luisa mumbled to herself, rubbed her stomach harder and walked toward the gate as rap-

idly as she dared. She was nearly out when she saw four men standing near. They seemed to be chatting but their eyes missed nothing. Their livery was yellow and they wore badges of a wheel surmounted by a boar in full charge. Wenlock's men? Maybe. Arban's? Likely. No, she told herself, she was probably seeing pursuit where it did not exist.

"Slow there, boy. Don't be pushing your elders about." The big, heavy-handed farmer stood in her way, grinning, ready for a bit of sport.

Luisa started to go around him but he stepped in front of her. She gave him a slack look of incomprehension and prepared to step heavily on his foot. She had to get out. She had to! Any minute now the nuns would be coming to take charge.

"Henry, you get over here and help unload this cart. You hear me?" The man started and whirled in the direction of the voice. His fellows roared with laughter. Luisa darted between them and went around a carter, two children, and a fat woman who stood berating the world in general. She moved through the gate and into the narrow street, imagining that every eye was upon her but forcing herself to walk normally until the next corner was rounded.

Now caution left Luisa and she began to run as hard as she could, as fast as she had ever run in the fields and forests of Marmoor. She was not challenged as she sped through streets that narrowed, widened, and grew small again. What, after all, was one more cutpurse or fleeing apprentice in this city where anything might happen?

Luisa ran. Her breath came raggedly and the sweat poured from her body. Drums beat in her head as her teeth chattered. Finally she had to stop, no matter if all the hordes of Attila were upon her. A deserted shack stood on the corner nearest her and she collapsed thankfully on the one stone stair before it.

In the aftermath of her escape she recalled how easy it had been. Too easy? She looked up in sudden horror, but the dark little street was empty. People drank deep here and slept late. She edged to one side of the tumbling dwelling and into even deeper shadow. There she unwrapped the cloth from around her stomach and pushed it under the old boards. She had taken it from her bed in order to make herself seem larger. How fortunate it was that she had brought her boy's clothes from Marmoor. Now she looked like a slender youth with a rather dirty face and a hungry look, a youth seeking a quick way out of London.

How long would it be before her absence was noticed? She had eaten every scrap of the food left for her, had been seen wrestling long with her emotions in the chapel, and the covers on the bed were adjusted to show a sleeping body. It was possible discovery could come as late as tonight, or as early as noon today. She must get out of the city. A watch would certainly soon be set at the gates.

The sun grew hotter and Luisa became conscious of the smells abounding here. It would be

best to keep moving. She began to walk purposefully as if on an errand. Dame Matilda had
told her much about the city, but that knowledge
had been based on court life here. Luisa did well
just to recall directions as she headed for one of
the gates. She soon encountered inns, taverns,
alehouses, stalls of all sorts, and plenty of customers for them all. There were odors from rot-
ting vegetables and fruits, unwashed bodies,
pungent ointments, incense, and sour drinks.
Cries to buy, eat, and drink rose on the air. A
golden-haired woman well past her first youth
strode by with several men in her wake. Luisa
stared; she had never seen so much exposed
bosom in her life.

"Watch where you're going, boy!" A young
man brushed past her in his attempt to catch up
with the woman. "Wait there, Eliza! I'm
coming!"

Luisa looked at his rich clothes and then at his
hat. A pilgrim's cockleshell shone against the
red velvet and a golden cross hung on his chest.
Of course! He had been on a pilgrimage and
wore these emblems proudly. It was perfect! She
would join one of the local ones. Fortune's
wheel, so long down, was beginning to turn for
her. She intended to help it along.

It was well past noon when Luisa strode into
the side yard at the Red Wolf Inn. Business was
roaring: people were shouting at each other; children howled; bags were dropped, trampled, and
rescued; several fights were in progress; a band
of priests held an animated discussion, and no
less than three separate trains of riders, pack

animals, and escorts were tangled together and shouting. The despairing landlord, recognized by apron and shrieks for order, was waving his arms at the servants who ran back and forth.

In spite of all her worry, Luisa grinned to herself. This was the place. Only two streets away from the main gate at the near section of the wall, wild with people setting out late, the Red Wolf was the seventh inn she had investigated. It appeared to be the sort of place that would not notice the king himself in full regalia if he chose to come now.

The din grew louder. Luisa saw a fat woman who might be fifty or more standing with a younger version of herself who looked about to weep. Bags were scattered around them and the older woman was talking so rapidly that her face grew redder by the instant. A child of perhaps a year sat at their feet busily cramming dirt into its mouth.

She would have no better chance. A moment later she was before the ladies, making a crude bow and saying in a faintly whining voice that she had practiced all morning, "Begging your pardons and all, but would you be needing some bit of help here? It looks it, I said to myself." She waved at the child and the litter.

The mother shrieked and gathered up the baby, which began to scream. The other woman snapped, "I don't know what beggars like you hang about for. Go find an honest day's work and leave us alone."

Luisa jerked at her hood and let her voice rise over the added noise. It was difficult. "I'm not a

beggar, God's truth, I'm not. I live over Berkeley
way and want to travel in company. My pocket
was picked, you see. The neighbor I came with
went on up to York on business. I just want to
get home!"

Luisa had listened to the talk long enough to
know that these travelers were banded together
for personal business or a pilgrimage to the
shrines of various saints. Robberies and murders
often happened to those who were foolish
enough to go unprepared. Had it not been for
John and his men, her own party would have
been dead.

"We go to Bristol." The daughter gave Luisa a
faint smile as she jiggled the child, which yelled
even more loudly. "To visit the Shrine of Saint
Eustace."

The mother glared. "Gwendolyn, stop that!
He may be a robber hoping to ingratiate himself
and slit our throats later."

Luisa wanted to scream. Why had she settled
on these people? They had looked inept. Suddenly inspired, she leaned forward and snapped
her fingers under the child's chin, pulling a truly
terrible face as she did so. Surprised, it ceased
howling and reached out a tentative finger,
which she took. She could admire the child if
only she knew the sex, but the hot woolen robe
offered no clue.

"How brave to do that to a stranger!" She
smiled at Gwendolyn who regarded her with
awe.

"No one can manage Roger except me. How
very odd."

Luisa thought so, too, but she smiled modestly. Roger stared unblinkingly but did not resume his wails.

"We're leaving now. Ladies, are you ready?" A portly merchant, mounted and secure, beamed down at their confusion. "Better mount up. Get that to working!" He went on behind two nuns and a young couple who clutched hands as they rode. One of the priests, a tall man with a bleak face, climbed up on his mule and moved slowly by, staring as he went.

"Where are your animals?" The voice was that of Luisa Marmoor and her authority, but in the fear of being left neither of the women noted the lapse. Gwendolyn pointed them out and began to argue with her mother. Roger began to scream again. Three mules, partially loaded with baggage, and their two horses made up the personal train. Luisa tossed bags about with abandon, grateful the work at Marmoor had taught her what to do, mounted the calmest looking mule, and looked at the mother who sniffed.

"All very well for now, young man, but I'll be watching you, I can tell you that." Her cheeks puffed red and the tiny brown eyes drilled Luisa. "What's your name?"

"Willie Cobbler, ma'am." As good a name as any and easy to remember.

They were riding now. She had done it! Soon. Soon, they would be out of London and she could go to ground, bide her time, and win back Marmoor. In the meantime she might look for work in boy's guise; a woman had little chance of safety. Freedom was intoxicating!

"I am Lady Martha Terence. This is my daughter, Gwendolyn Regis. She is lately widowed. He was a merchant in Colchester who had lived in Bristol and demanded she make yearly journeys to his birthplace there. It was said on his deathbed so she agreed, in presence of witnesses. Gwendolyn came down in the world when she married a common merchant." The last pronouncement she made haughtily.

Gwendolyn, doubtless from long practice, said nothing. Luisa struggled not to laugh. The lady spoke in exclamation points and seemed perpetually affronted. A difficult life for the girl and her child. Luisa did not care what the women were like, though—she would have ridden with Grendel and his mother to escape the fate Arban had set out for her.

It appeared impossible that such a collection of people could ever evolve into anything orderly, but as the group approached the gate, it was surveyed and waved through in a matter of seconds. Luisa was thankful; she was merely another indistinct face under a hood and glad to be so. Lady Martha kept up a rapid scolding that did not alter as their pace increased. She was furious because the two maids who were to have traveled with them on the journey had taken a fever at the same time and had remained in London. This was yet one more reason why Luisa had been accepted as she had.

She wanted to turn and look back at the great city but dared not; it was sufficient to gaze at the western road and think that Marmoor lay far off in that direction. She planned to leave the pilgrims well before Bristol, and devise a new story for her next stop. The warm wind blew over her face and the sun beat down. She could smell the distant woods and flowers mixed with the London odors pursuing them. Clouds built battlements in the brilliant sky. Luisa reveled in her new freedom, won by her own wits and courage. The future might hold defeat but she would always know that she had gone out to meet it, had not yielded tamely to Arban or the expectations of her world.

"My daughter, cease this quarreling. Some are going to the holy shrines and it is not proper that you continue in such a manner."

Luisa's head jerked up. Lady Martha was quiet for the moment, but her face was mottled and her cheeks swelled out. The tall priest had ridden near to keep pace with them. The others pulled back to give room. It was he who had spoken in a flat voice that left no room for disagreement. His thin mouth folded down and his chin was set. The black eyes burned with a zeal that was almost frightening.

"Have done, I say." He was like a darkness over them all.

Martha clutched the bridle. She had been amusing before but was now suddenly pathetic. "Yes. Yes."

Luisa felt the power of this priest who was surely no ordinary man. She found herself unable to take her gaze away.

He looked around at her and their eyes locked. She knew then that his was the power of evil.

Chapter Six
NONE BUT THE BRAVE

By a single concentrated effort of will Luisa was able to look down, away from those compelling eyes that sapped her ability to think. Her hands fumbled with the mule's bridle. Quiet surrounded them; even Roger was silent. She longed for him to howl.

"Very well. Let us continue." The priest's voice did not change inflection and he began to move away.

Luisa felt a shudder of foreboding which she could not suppress even as the group rode on into the bright afternoon. Everyone had been touched by the encounter. The priest now was far in back, but his head was upright as he watched and listened. Martha and her daughter kept close together, eyes fastened on each other.

Luisa surveyed the company curiously and tried to keep her mind off the danger. What was one purse-lipped priest more or less? She saw several nuns, pale and timid as they clustered about the older one who seemed to have them firmly in hand. Four buxom ladies in their late fifties rode with a younger man who kept pointing out scenes to them. All five faces were alike. A slender young girl on a white horse was obviously with her parents. The earnest young man just behind her must be her suitor Luisa thought, for his eyes never left her. There were a few men-at-arms hired for this journey, two very young priests of a different order than that of the demanding one who had chastised them all by his look, some merchants who talked of business, two brilliantly clad young men exchanging languishing gazes, and a very old dame who spoke of her infirmities to the long-suffering servants with her. There were others of the party but these were closest to Luisa. She passed the time making up stories about them and plotted when she might leave without incurring suspicion.

They spent the night at a wayside inn. Luisa was kept busy running errands, tending the animals, watching Roger, bringing food to Lady Martha's room, and listening to her complaints which were now far less voluble. By the time she was allowed to return to the barn and rest, she would not have cared if an army of black-eyed priests had walked around her chanting imprecations.

The next day was different. The flowering hedges beside the road gave out haunting scents and birds called high overhead. The air was fresh and sweet, the sky cloudless. One of the young men took out a small pipe and began to play. His companion started a well-known ballad and one of the buxom ladies took it up in a high, cackling voice. The nuns looked shocked but one of the young priests smiled and beat time with one hand. The older priest was far in back, bent over as if in contemplation and his head was concealed in his cowl. The company rode briskly, chattering of purchases to make, boons to be requested of various saints, the bandits of the neighborhoods, past wars, and gossip as to whom the king might or might not marry. Martha and Gwendolyn talked nonsense to Roger, who wailed now and then, clearly unimpressed. Luisa's mind drifted, glad to relax and think of nothing in particular.

They paused in midmorning to rest and refresh themselves. Many of the party went to a respectable-looking tavern just across the road. Luisa was left to mind the horses but decided to go toward a well close at hand and draw up a drink for herself. That at least was free. The bucket was nearly at the top when a voice spoke behind her.

"Give me some, lad." The harsh voice was muted but still grating. "My fast has been long."

Startled, she dropped the bucket back and swung around to see the priest staring at her. He looked even more skeletal in the brilliant light of the summer day. Exhaustion was stamped on his features and his skin seemed parched. His mouth tightened as he gestured toward the well, not bothering to repeat himself. Luisa wanted to escape but dared not show haste in drawing up the water once more. What if he looked at her hands and saw they were not those of a stable boy? Or happened to notice her face as she had his?

"Drink." She forced out the one word and shoved the dripping bucket at him. He took it and she turned away, moving as rapidly as she dared.

A young girl of perhaps twelve or less had paused a few feet away and was regarding the priest with an instantly recognizable revulsion.

She was gaunt and pallid but fury burned red
spots high on her cheeks.

"Sir Priest, you and all who ride with you
ought to be praying in the churches and showing Christ's way by works and faith! Humble
yourselves with the poor! Each man before his
God! Examples! We must all be that, not out in
gay clothes and for sport!" Her voice was high
and piercing, painful to the ears. There were
flecks of foam at the corners of her mouth as she
shook with the fervor of her words.

Luisa thought no one could say she and the
priest were richly dressed, but some of the company across the way had turned to stare and
murmur. They were gay in purple, reds, greens,
and other colors. The girl's venom was primarily
for the priest, however. Now she advanced toward him, shouting all the louder.

The priest moved to meet her, his motion so
swift it was barely a flicker. His black eyes
seemed to engulf his cadaverous face as one
hand went up to strike the child. Luisa had time
for only one sharp thought: Fanatics, both of
them! Then she was darting in front of the girl
and twisting her away. The child struggled; the
priest's upraised fist hit Luisa's shoulder in a
heavy blow that appeared beyond his capability.
They tumbled to the ground and he stood over
them, his face a devil's mask. The child's fingers
went up in the sign meant to ward off evil. Luisa
scrambled up.

"How dare you interfere, boy? Get away at
once!" The priest fairly hissed the command.

"She is simple, Father. Just look at her face.

She cannot know the meaning of disrespect." Luisa pulled her hood more closely over her head while blocking the priest from the girl, who had scrambled to her feet and moved a few feet away. "Let her be." She met the man's astonished gaze and realized that she had again spoken with the authority of Luisa Marmoor, not a subservient boy.

He spoke slowly, taking pleasure in the roll of the words. "Perhaps you agree with what she said? Do you approve of taunts made to priests and the Holy Mother Church and her faithful? There is heresy everywhere and I, Father Sebastian, am committed to finding it and destroying it! This is my holy mission! This kingdom is filled with disputers, rebels against the pure faith! All shall pay. All." The harsh voice was like a hammer as it rose and fell.

Luisa could not help backing away. Ashamedly she said, "I, Father? I have been taught to honor the church and those who serve her. I know nothing of heresy. This child babbles anything she hears. . . . You can hear anything on the high road or around inns. Surely you can't think . . ." Her voice trailed away before his upraised hand.

"Here come more of her ilk. I shall deal with them!" His interest was diverted from Luisa by some shabbily dressed people rushing toward them from the nearby woods. The group of travelers were watching avidly but made no move to come near. As soon as the priest turned fully away, the child ran wildly in the other direction. Luisa longed to follow suit but did not dare. She slipped a few paces backward and was thankful to see that some of Lady Martha's pack animals, along with several other mules, had taken the opportunity to wander close to some succulent bushes near the well. She started for them.

"Stay, boy. You need teaching about the evils of heresy." Father Sebastian was not at all perturbed by the fact that he stood alone. "Or perhaps you are one of them, despite what you say?"

Luisa pulled at her hood. "No. No. The animals might get away and I have charge of some of them."

"Better to lose the beasts than endanger your immortal soul."

She gave up. Any minute her voice might slip down into her normal one and lose the boy's gruffness. "Yes, Father. You are right."

The priest stepped out briskly and was immediately engulfed by a group of ten or so peasants in heavy work clothes, all endeavoring to speak at once. Their accents were so thick Luisa could understand only a few words of apologetic explanation and supplication. Their dirty, earnest, near ignorant faces and clenching hands made her shake with pity.

The clamor rose and swelled. Father Sebastian raised both hands and held them out while he listened. Luisa thought of the cruelty of his voice and eyes. He would take pleasure in the flames that were known to be the only true cure for heresy. She remembered a girl at the convent who had been taken to a public burning while at home on a visit. On her return she had been

encouraged to tell of it. Luisa could not approach
a hearth fire for days without wondering how
her own flesh would crinkle, sear, and agonize.
Only a fool courted the anger of the church.
What had come over her?

"You are heretics. You harbor that girl in your
fellowship. Who are you? Where do you come
from? Who else among you speaks and thinks as
she does?" There was no mistaking the fact that
he was enjoying himself. In another minute they
would be kneeling and cringing before him. He
turned toward Luisa. "Boy! Confess your error.
Repeat what that heretic said. I am God's scourge,
his lash on the earth. I cannot defile my mouth
with it. Repeat the wicked girl's blasphemy!"

"No!" Luisa did not have to pretend terror.
The priest's eyes brightened. He delighted in the
fear of others. "No. I can't!" she yelled. "I'm
afraid of 'em! Scared! No, no, no!" The syllables
ran together in her mouth and she turned from
right to left as though deranged.

Father Sebastian was caught off guard and his
exhortations stopped. A woman took his hand
and began to gabble loudly. He tried to free himself but could not. Another threw herself at his
feet.

"I'll have all of you arrested! Men! You men-
at-arms! Get over here and round these people
up!" He was utterly without fear, confident in
the boundless power of his church.

Luisa thought she was going mad. The peasant men seemed to stand more erect and their
eyes, which had been dull, began to blaze with
quite a different light. One of them had begun to

fumble purposefully in his ragged clothing while another shoved the children back. But it was not this that made her brain tilt. A figure had stepped from the trees and was coming toward them, leaning on a staff. She knew him, would know him anywhere. Had he not haunted her night dreams and daily thoughts? It was John.

He was not a John any of the old party would have recognized. He was clad in a flapping brown robe, old sandals, and a cap of ancient vintage covered his head. Folds of it sagged over his forehead and neck, but when he looked up Luisa again saw the brilliant blue eyes and the arrogant nose that no disguise could hide. His shoulders were hunched up and his back bent; their strength was evident to her alone.

She feared to trust her eyes. Had she conjured him up out of some wild dream or an impossible longing? That must be it for now she saw other men half-concealed in the sheltering trees, the green and brown of their garments mingling together. She squeezed her lids together, trying in vain to plan her next move.

Two separate cries cut across her consciousness as a familiar roar began. Roger was unhappy and intended to let the world know it. Another was a bitter lamentation. "My humors are rising up! I must get to my saint's shrine before I die! We have to go!" Lady Martha was joined by Gwendolyn. "We have to go!" Then one of the merchants barked, "Let's get rid of that rabble and be on our way!"

Luisa opened her eyes. It was no dream; there stood John, about to confront Father Sebastian, who had both hands planted firmly on his hips as if geared for struggle.

"Do you command the king's road, priest?" It was an old man's voice, sharp and irritated, the accents broad, with nothing of John's previous cadences.

Father Sebastian started to say something but his voice was lost in the surge of other voices as the pilgrims protested and the men-at-arms reached for their weapons. Several of the women cried out and were silenced. It would take very little for all-out war to begin.

Luisa suddenly let out a long, low wail that she had perfected long ago at the convent. Many a dull winter's night had been enlivened by it. One of the Irish girls swore the family banshee had arrived. The nuns were of the opinion the devil was not far behind. Luisa had reason to be proud of this particular wail for it was chilling even on a bright summer afternoon. As she wailed, she ran straight for the pack animals which sensibly scattered before her.

She seized one laggard and drove her sharp nails into its soft, hairy ear. The mule gave a startled bray, then a louder one. She hung on as it started to move, still braying. In one quick motion she was on its back, guiding it into the group of peasants without appearing to do so and toward Father Sebastian, who had to move rapidly in order not to be trampled.

Other mules joined in the braying and the cacophony drowned out Roger. Out of the corner of her eye she saw the loud-voiced merchant rallying the company toward their beasts. Men were putting aside their weapons and some were frantically trying to conceal their laughter. A few of the peasants retreated, shoulders shaking.

Her mount swung around and Luisa found herself facing John. Their eyes met, and underneath his startled look of recognition she saw his utter gladness. Her mouth curved upward and without words or gestures they saluted each other.

Chapter Seven
THE FAIR HOUR

THEY WERE FOLLOWED down the high road for the rest of the afternoon. The watcher saw them take two side turnings, skirt the little village, and come to the Inn of the Proud Pilgrim where the travelers broke their journey. He was waiting for darkness to come. Little gusts of rain had started earlier and the breeze was chilly. It would not be long now.

Luisa sat on her spread cloak just inside the side door of the far barn. All her senses told her the watcher was John, and that he was coming for her, but logic denied it. Would he follow a girl met only once and with whom he had exchanged sharp words? It was foolish to expect it, yet she felt he was not far away from her now.

Rain drummed on the ground and the scent of fresh grass drifted to her. Horses, mules, donkeys, and cows munched hay, the sound peaceful and contented. There was a roar of song from the inn. The men-at-arms would drink long tonight and the travelers would relive their harrowing day. Some would pray and give thanks.

Luisa smiled to herself. She was alternately in disgrace and honor, according to the various speakers. Her fear was natural, they all agreed on that, but was she prone to such fits or simple in nature? Her behavior *had* stopped a near fight and Father Sebastian had been so eager to investigate possible heretics that he stayed overnight to do so. He would rejoin them later and Luisa meant to be gone by the time he did. Lady Martha defended her servant loudly, pretending at this time that she had chosen him carefully. Luisa bobbed her head, sniffed, and said, "Just real scared, that's all," to any questions. Now she thought she had been lucky but she admitted to herself, however modestly, that her wits had been at the ready.

A hand grasped her arm and another slid across her mouth. The motions were so sudden that she resisted in spite of her expectations. She was jerked to the ground and a familiar voice hissed in her ear.

"Stop that. You're perfectly safe."

It was John. There was no other place she wanted to be at that instant. Excitement made her shiver. This night would change her life. She knew it and gloried. She lay still in his arms as he lifted her up and carried her out into the diminishing rain. He halted in the shelter of the tall oak just behind the stable.

"There is unfinished business between us, Luisa Marmoor." His hood was pushed back to reveal the strong jaw, clustering curls, and proud face. "Do you agree?"

The decision was hers to make. He would not push her if she suddenly became a frightened maid, fearful of what might be unleashed. She looked up at him. "I do."

"You are a brave woman. That priest is a hunter of heretics and carries a commission from Bolingbroke's spawn to destroy them. I watch him. Your action today prevented burnings." His voice was husky and laced with bitterness. He leaned close to Luisa. "I thank you for us all. Don't question me. There are things too dangerous for you to know and I did not come to you for that."

"I know." She spoke softly, conscious of the wind in his hair, the clean odor of his body, and the sharp modeling of his lips. It was not the time for questions or answers, but one slipped out unbidden. "Is John really your name?"

He gave a short laugh. "One of them. The last you should not know, for your own safety. I am John Marcus, called by both, but Marcus to those close to me." He took her hand and tugged gently.

"Then I shall call you Marcus." Her heart was hammering and her awareness of him was so keen she knew his blood raced as did hers.

He said, "Come." She followed him willingly, but he did not relinquish her hand as they went through wet leaves and grass, several thickets, and into a forest where the trees grew so thickly that the rain barely penetrated. They moved past a small stream, wandered in total darkness for a few minutes, and then forded another stream. "Now, bend down and do just as I do." He went to all fours, slipped down, and vanished.

Luisa spared a brief instant to wonder what she was getting into, but then did as she had been told. She scraped her shoulders against rock, heard the sound of moving water, and felt its spray on her face. A thorny branch pulled at her sleeve. Fear again snaked through her. What did she know of this man, after all? She might be entombed in this strange, dark place.

Then strong arms pulled her up into the light and Marcus was smiling down at her, his face curiously young and smooth. "I think people must have hidden here for centuries." He watched her as she took in their surroundings.

They stood in a small, natural cave lit by a flickering candle Marcus had set in a crevice. Water ran through one side of it and some hardy bushes grew at the edge. A portion of the area above their heads was open to the sky and covered over with vines. A summer freshness pervaded the area and mingled with the scent of sandalwood. In one corner, Luisa saw a pile of cloaks, two wooden chests, and several gleaming swords, battle-axes, and knives.

She cried out, "You and your men are dissidents? Rebels!" She tried to think clearly but his nearness was intoxicating. "I thought they were *religious* dissenters."

The blue gaze darkened. "Think what you wish. There are many ways to shake a throne."

He tilted her chin up with one hand and pushed the hood from her head with the other. "Ask no questions. I ask none of you." He loosened her braids and her chestnut hair tumbled free. Then he pulled her into his arms.

Luisa clasped her arms around Marcus as he held her tightly. His mouth came down on hers and his tongue began to explore the softness of her lower lip. She felt the powerful thrust of his manhood against her body. Her lips parted under his; their tongues met and melted together.

"Luisa?" He whispered her name as his tongue tip flicked in her ear. His warm breath on her neck made her shiver with delight. "Luisa? Now?"

All of her being strained toward him. This was the only reality. "Yes," she answered. She put both hands on the sides of his face and drew his mouth down to hers. Their kiss was deep. She sought to drink of him, prolonging the sweet, terrible moment.

Marcus pulled her shirt loose, ran his hands up and down her back before loosening the binding that held her breasts. He cupped their white firmness in his fingers before bending to touch them with his warm mouth. Luisa shivered with pleasure and arched her back. His dark curls tickled her chin. She put one hand on them to feel their crispness. Tenderness welled inside her and once more she gathered him in her arms.

He stripped the remainder of her clothes away and carried her to the improvised pallet. When he sank down beside her and began to remove his own clothes, Luisa thrust his hands away and slowly undressed him. She both wanted and did not want to wait. His body was long and muscular, darkly tanned to his waist and then more lightly below. His skin was taut, marked with several old scars. It was the body of a warrior. His shaft was hard and jutting, the passion barely controlled. She stared at the rippling smoothness of him, the powerful shoulders and tapering waist.

"You are beautiful." She might have been adoring a pagan god.

He gave her a sardonic glance, then saw that she meant it and smiled. "What words do I use for you? Nymph? Love goddess? You are these things and much more." He touched the palm of his hand to her nipples and watched them rise. Her hair swung forward over her shoulders and gleamed in the candlelight. "But you know that, don't you, my temptress? I did, the first moment I saw you on the road. That mouth, those eyes and hair, your delectable body—you're made for love and it shows." The blue eyes went dark as he brought her down to him.

Strange sensations thundered through Luisa as he touched and caressed every part of her body, causing trickles of flame to begin until she ached and shuddered. Instinctively she reached for the very spear of his passion, gently stroking it. He twisted convulsively as her hand dropped lower.

"Kiss me."

"Where?" She half teased, half asked. Her lips brushed across his flat stomach and he groaned.

Then she was beside him, fitting her body to

his lean length, moving her fingers over his muscular shoulders and back. "Marcus!" she cried out as he thrust deeply into her once, hesitated, and thrust deeper. Luisa felt as if she were being torn to pieces. Pain was all around her but she could not cry out for his mouth was on hers. Then he was very still inside her. He released her mouth and rose slightly on his elbows. The brilliant eyes shone down into hers. His nostrils flared with the effort of control.

"By all the saints, Luisa, I did not know you were virgin. If I had, I would never have touched you." His voice was soft, very gentle.

She thought of those who wanted to dispose of her body: Arban, Sir Edward, the old man chosen as her husband, even dear Dame Matilda and the nuns. How often could a woman make her own free choice? She put out one hand to the furrowed brow of the man who cared enough, even at this intense minute, to allow her that choice.

"Better a man I choose, Marcus, than one ordered upon me."

"I'll be more gentle the next time. I don't want to hurt you."

She started to speak but he kissed the edges of her mouth, her neck, and her cheeks. Returning to her mouth, he set his lips tenderly on it and cherished it while he began to move slowly inside her. She clung to him at first, then grew bolder, letting her back arch and her hips move. The pain was bittersweet now, ripening into joy. Marcus turned her carefully so that she was on her side, facing him. Their joining was undisturbed and now they swayed together in an ever quickening rhythm. Luisa let her fingers move on him, caressing him with a knowledge that came from deep within her. They fit together, belonged together in a way that was ordained.

Luisa and Marcus were kindled into one flame now. She had no thought or feeling apart from him, nor he from her. They wound savagely about each other. When he thrust into her, she rose to meet him with demands of her own. Her head was light and her blood pulsing. An aching need encompassed her. She hung on the edge of something beyond experience. Her voice called out to him and she heard him speaking but the words made no sense.

They clung, separated, and melded. He pierced her so deeply that her breath was taken away, and then he lay shuddering in her arms. In the next instant Luisa moved into the flame-colored darkness, up and out and into the endless abyss with no mortal name. She felt her very core being unlocked; she was drawn out into life and beyond it toward timelessness.

Their breathing slowed and meshed so that it was as one. They lay in a mutual embrace, elemental and replete.

Twice more that enchanted night, Luisa and Marcus explored the ways of passion. They bathed in the little stream, splashing and ducking each other's playful advances, then racing for the nearby cloaks where they shortly created their own warmth. Luisa planted kisses all over his body. They soon began again and this time it was he who caressed her with lips and tongue until she cried out. They lay together in the aftermath, wrapped in a languorous warmth, Luisa's head on his shoulder. In that moment of contentment, she found it easy to speak.

"I don't even know your last name, John Marcus." She knew she could expect nothing from him; he was engaged in treasonable activities. But it seemed reasonable to think he might help her avoid the pursuit of Arban's men. Possibly she could convince him that she would be an asset to him and be allowed to travel with him. A flush stained her cheeks as she thought of more nights like this one. "I understand these are difficult times and one shouldn't inquire too—"

Her words broke off as Marcus came upright, chin set and blue eyes distant. In one brief instant the tender lover had become committed rebel, suspicious of her questioning. No matter that the long planes of his body moved enticingly in the faint light, the powerful muscles rippling under his tanned skin. The long fingers which had stirred her flesh to glory now reached out to catch her arm in their hard grip—he was a stranger.

"Then ask nothing." He spoke the words plainly, but decisively. "I don't want to know about you. You are brave and beautiful; if circumstances were otherwise I could very easily yield to your soft trap, but I have other responsibilities. We must soon go our separate ways." He wanted to hold back from her in one moment and in the next share all things. He knew it was dangerous to trust anyone, least of all a woman as alluring as this one.

"I wasn't trying to persuade you to forsake anything!" Luisa sat back on her heels and shook her streaming hair. "Trap, indeed! We had mutual pleasure, I think." She pushed back the thought of their shared tenderness for it nearly brought tears. Why was his reaction so extreme?

"Can you deny that you were about to take advantage of the moment? About to demand knowledge or action of me? It is always so with women!" He looked about for his clothing, his mouth set firmly. "Get dressed. I'll take you back."

Luisa knew he was burdened with his own demons and the problems of others. She well understood his struggles against the powerful attraction they two had for each other. But it was not enough. Her anger rose to meet his and swept away the humiliation of his behavior. She rose to her feet and took several slow steps toward him. This was not innocent longing but deliberate invitation as she let one hand trail downward, the fingers moving softly in manipulation, her shoulders back to lift her proud globes with their pink tips. Her tongue touched her open lips.

"Not yet." She almost sighed the words as she came close.

Marcus moved back, trying to keep his face impassive, but he could not control his body. His eyes seared her skin and he crossed his arms over his chest for an instant, then remained still.

"The odds are against you and me. What are you trying to do, Luisa?" The deep voice was now only a thread of sound.

She knew they now faced each other on a field of battle. Her hand left her own flesh and went to his throbbing manhood. "Marcus?" Her lower body arched toward him in one slow, smooth movement. She guided him toward her and felt the savage response he made against his own will. Vindication was sweet. She gave a low laugh, reaching out to pull him close.

"By the saints!" He pushed her slightly and she lost her balance. A second later he swung her up in his arms, kissing her with harsh passion as they slid down together onto the piled cloaks where they had earlier known ecstasy.

Time and dimension now ceased to exist for Luisa. Before Marcus had been gentle, fearing he would hurt her. Now pain and pleasure, passion, and lust were one.

She woke once in the aftermath and shifted to a more comfortable position in his muscular, brown arms. Whatever happens, I have had this night, Luisa told herself. It was comfort to take into the long loneliness that lay ahead.

Chapter Eight
SPIRIT OF IRON

LUISA RAN THROUGH the fog-shrouded woods. Wet branches slapped her face and she slipped several times on the grass, but she was beyond caring about discomfort. It would be dawn soon and she needed to slip back into the stable without being seen. She tried to think only of the time ahead and what she would do when it came time to leave the pilgrims, but her mind returned inexorably to the parting with Marcus of a short time ago.

They had slept little for their passion was rekindled with every touch. Luisa was drained and exhausted when he kissed her for the last time and turned to dress. There was nothing they could say to each other in view of the circumstances. Luisa wanted to cling and weep but that was not her way. She knew that the matter-of-factness he showed was a shield to conceal his own feelings, but it was still hard to bear.

"I'll say farewell now, Luisa. We may meet again. If not, you shall always be in my heart." The dark brows drew together and he lifted one hand. "Be careful, my lady, and may God guard you always."

She forced herself to give him a watery smile. "You, too, Marcus. May God and His blessed Mother watch over you." Her fingers did not shake as they clasped his.

They turned simultaneously and went their separate ways. Luisa dared not allow herself the luxury of tears; she did not think she would be able to stop. "Don't think about him right now. There's no time." She spoke the words to her inner self, but already the savage longing for him shook her to the core.

She was almost across the last patch of woodland which bordered on the grounds of the inn when a tall figure moved out from the bole of a tree and caught her by the arm. The action was so unexpected that she fell back and her loosely bound hair tumbled from the hood.

"A woman! I knew there was something strange about you, but I thought you were a spy sent by those who dare oppose me, fools that they are!" Father Sebastian, eyes glinting cruelly in the gray light of morning, clutched her so hard that the bones in her arm crunched together. His tongue slipped out from his thin lips and moved into their corners as he smiled. "Hot from a night with your lovers, I take it? I can smell a slut, did you know that?" He shook her. "How many are here? Confess it, slut!"

Luisa stared in horror. There was no mistaking the pleasure he took in twisting her arm. He would enjoy burning the heretics he found. How many of them had rejected his advances? She remembered the glory of the night just passed and thought she would kill him before allowing one touch from those defiling hands.

"Confess? But the time is short and we are due to start early, Father. You have only just arrived?" She kept her voice low, acting as though they stood conversing on the high road in the noon sun. "At another time might I be allowed to ask your counsel?'' The words had a suggestive lilt that cost her great effort.

"Do not dare toy with me, woman. I can have you jailed and worse! Perhaps you are both slut and heretic." He tilted his head as the sounds of travel preparation came from the direction of the inn. "Women in men's clothes might be considered such." Lust and cunning mingled in his sharp face but his grip lessened perceptibly.

Proud Luisa Marmoor might once have cried out in anger, used nails and dagger to free herself from this false servant of the church. Luisa the fugitive had only her wits and courage. "It is not what you think, Father. My husband deserted me not long ago. I have word that he is in Bristol and I go to confront him there. I have no money and found it easier to travel as a boy. I went walking this morning because I could not sleep. It is the truth." She let her voice beseech and her gaze slide by him. If only he would take the bait and release her!

"You are lying. Is it because you are afraid of me?" He waited for her ashamed nod before continuing. "We will discuss this tonight after the others are in bed. Do not think about escaping. You cannot. I will find you. Now go and remember that I am watching." He flung her arm aside but kept his impaling gaze fastened on her face.

"Yes, Father. I understand. You are most kind." She gave him a bobbing curtsy and backed away. Her fear was not feigned and this pleased him.

He watched her all the way to the stable and

his gaze did not shift even when she paused to bind her hair tightly around her head and secure the hood. He would wait and have her that night; she knew it for a certainty. She must vanish into the crowds of the first city they entered. There was no time for planning, only speed.

Luisa thought later that luck, fortune, and the saints all combined to forsake her that day. Father Sebastian was constantly in view, Lady Martha had a dozen orders to be instantly satisfied, the mules were balky, Roger howled continually, and the pilgrims muttered about the growing heat just as they had complained about the rain the night before. The tension among them made tempers sharp and Luisa found it hard not to retort angrily when Lady Martha began to make disparaging remarks about "young louts dashing about the countryside when they ought to be at home working for their betters" and staring directly at Luisa when she did so. Luisa felt her nerves strain and retreated into thoughts of Marcus, but their passionate night together now seemed like something out of a dream. She forced herself to think only of the lecherous priest and to stay alert for any opportunity to escape. Her struggles seemed suddenly overwhelming and she fought to hold back tears of weariness.

The day turned clear and hotter as noon approached. The air was heavy and sweet with the scent of roadside flowers. Dust coated their mounts, parched their throats, and stirred up in little clouds on the road ahead. Luisa hunched deeper in her swathing hood, wondering if a chance to escape would ever present itself.

"Look, a market! Let's stop for a while!" The cry came from a young man named Gilbert, who was traveling with a friend whose name Luisa did not know. The pair had stayed close together, carrying on low-voiced conversations and mingling little with the others. Father Sebastian often glared at them but was ignored, a difficult thing to do. "We need rest, refreshment, a chance to cool off."

Father Sebastian countered, "We need to go on while the weather is good." His tone was commanding but for once another voice rode over his.

"My grandson is faint. Exhausted. This is not an endurance course. We must stop." Lady Martha pointed to Roger, who sagged before her on the saddle, his eyes heavy. "The pace is too much for him."

Some of the others tried to hide smiles but there were several disapproving looks. Luisa smothered a giggle; the child was merely worn out from all his screaming. A babble of comments arose and after a few minutes the issue was decided. They would remain here in the noon heat and set off an hour or so later.

They advanced into the little market town of Helstow, threading their way through streets lined with stalls filled with trinkets and all types of cloth, ribbons, food, and drink. People moved back and forth, chattering with each other and arguing about prices. Prices were better here than in the larger cities, and the women's eyes lit up at the bargains they saw.

"Willie! Come along, boy. You shall carry my basket while I shop." Lady Martha headed for the common ground, a wide grassy space at the edge of the outdoor market. "Gwendolyn, you mind Roger rests now."

Luisa was glad enough of the orders. Surely it would be simple enough to lose herself in the crowd and head for the other side of town where she could set off in the opposite direction. Obediently she helped Lady Martha dismount, tether the mules, and settle Roger with his mother. The other pilgrims were following their examples; some stretching out to rest, others heading for the nearest tavern.

"I must borrow your servant for a short time, madam. I have business in this town since we remain here for a few hours and he can be of help to me." Father Sebastian's firm grip took Luisa's shoulder.

"But, Father, I need . . ." Her protest trailed away as he fixed hard eyes on her face.

"It is the business of the holy church, Lady Martha." He spoke softly but all of them felt the menace just under the surface.

"Of course, I understand." The familiar heartiness of her voice had faded. "Take him."

The priest pulled Luisa along so rapidly that she could barely keep on her feet. Even if she had fallen, no one would intervene or interfere in a church matter, especially in these days of disquiet.

"I know an inn, very discreet, not far from

here. We shall have not only tonight but this afternoon as well." He hissed the words into her ear and they sent shudders over her flesh. "Do not think to resist, girl. Your danger is great."

Luisa knew that but she said, "I thought the church demanded celibacy. Are you a new breed, then?"

He jerked her around to face him. Thin as he was, his hands held such power as to render her, strong as she was, immobile. "Slut! Our association will be interesting, I vow. I am above petty rules; I work for the greater glory of God and my king! Every sinner shall be delivered to punishment and the flesh shall be as nothing!" The savage eyes grew larger and it took little imagination to see the flames of evil in them.

Luisa let herself go limp. "I should not have questioned you. Protect me, Father, I beg you."

"I promise you, girl." His grin might have come from hell's very depths.

Luisa let him pull her onto a side street, around several chattering women, and past a group of small boys engaged in a fierce fight. Her very acquiescence must have disarmed him, for when one of the boys bumped into them, his grip lessened momentarily and he snapped, "Watch where you're going, boy! You want a good hiding?"

In that instant Luisa jerked free and ran as she had never run in her life. It did not matter where she was going, only that she get away from that abomination in church garb. He was as corrupt as Arban. The thought sent her all the faster down the rough streets, past the close-set houses, dodging around people and animals as she ran.

"Stop, thief! Stop, I say! Get him! There he goes!" The cry was raised behind her and taken up by others. Now those in front of her looked to see what all the commotion was about and tried to impede her progress also.

Luisa knew all was nearly lost. Cutpurses abounded in markets and crowded streets, a menace to everyone. Once apprehended the culprit was fair game.

Her hood was smothering her. She loosened it with one hand and her braided hair tumbled out. She saw a mass of people just ahead and dodged back, but the press was too great. Several grinning apprentices moved directly into her path. She veered to the left, went between two ramshackle buildings, and came out into a wider street where a small procession was moving at a stately pace.

Her pursuers were at her back and one was pulling at her tattered shirt. It ripped and tore free just as she gave a last, desperate burst of speed which took her into the very center of the procession. She careened off a large, jeweled personage and both women fell into the dusty street.

Hands grabbed for Luisa, who tried in vain to roll away. She heard alarmed voices run together. "My lady, are you hurt?" "These louts! No one is safe on the streets!" "Find a leech!" "Oh, madam, are you all right?"

"By all the blessed saints, it's no thanks to any of you that I am!" The woman spat out a string of rich oaths and took her time about rising. "Get up, girl, and let me have a look at you."

Luisa scrambled to her feet and ignored those who shouted behind her. The woman was tall and robust, loudly and richly dressed, perhaps in her midthirties. Authority exuded from her and was apparent in the manner of those who stood around her party of servants, priests, men-at-arms, and ladies. She had black hair on which an ornamental headdress was awry, piercing brown eyes, and fat fingers—every one adorned with a jewel.

"Who are you? Speak up! Why are all these people after you?"

Luisa opened her mouth to speak but the mob drowned her out with howls of "Thief!" The woman took a step toward the nearest man, who paused in midyell and retreated. She put both hands on her hips and looked at Luisa.

"I have stolen nothing. I would speak privately with you, my lady, if you will grant it. This is a matter of great urgency." Luisa's head was high, her chin tilted, and her chestnut hair tumbled down her back as she stood proudly despite her situation. She was Luisa Marmoor, equal to the highest in the land, and so she would stand before the king himself.

The woman roared with laughter. "It's a bold gamine you are! Come, what have you done? Run away from your lover or husband? Or did you take a rich man's purse? Feel free to say. There's nothing to fear. You have amused me and taken my mind from this boring journey. That alone is worth something."

"If that is so then let me speak with you. I promise you the boredom will be less." Luisa let her voice drift lightly into the court accents Dame Matilda had taught her. Amuse, lure, never implore, make little of great matters. Would this work?

"What is going on here? Why has this criminal not been brought to me?" Father Sebastian strode up to them, black robes flying, his face contorted into a scowl. "Someone shall pay for this!" He reached for Luisa who, pretense done, struck his hand away. A mutter went up from those surrounding them. The woman stepped close to Luisa and the priest snapped, "Madam, I regret you have been disturbed by this person. She is a London thief, quite notorious. She has taken money from the holy church and will go to punishment. You may go your way."

"I will not go a step with him. He soils the church itself." Luisa's voice was as hard as his own. "He is a lecher."

The crowd drew in its collective breath, silent before the enormity of the charge. Luisa looked straight at Father Sebastian and swung her gaze to the woman who burst into laughter again.

"Very good, girl! You interest me and I have not said that in many a long day. You shall come with me." She waved to one of the watching women. "Bring a cloak to cover her and some wine for us both. Hurry up with it!"

Luisa decided to play the game to its fullest. She sank in an elaborate curtsy she had learned in her youth. "I thank you, gracious lady."

Over her bent head, she heard the priest say,

"You are in error, madam. The holy church has jurisdiction here. This is a special matter which may touch the highest in the land. I am given that power and have the commission to prove it. Now, stand aside."

Luisa rose, determined to fight with bare hands for her freedom if she had to. She would not be the first Marmoor to die in hopeless battle. In her memory she saw the brilliant blue eyes of Marcus and held them as a talisman.

Chapter Nine
LEGACY OF THE SWORD

"You do not know who I am, I take it?" The tall woman spoke mildly, but her eye caught Luisa's and she winked. Even in these desperate straits Luisa could not but smile.

"It does not matter. My orders, though secret, come directly from His Grace of Canterbury. I have supreme authority. I have explained all I intend to." Father Sebastian's anger was gathering. Red splotches stood on his cheeks and his eyes burned.

"Priest, I am Lady Cecilia Barthampton. If you truly do not recall the name, I will refresh your memory. I hold many properties in the Welsh marches, more in Kent and Suffolk and Cornwall. My husband, Barnabas, was killed fighting with King Henry in Wales when he was prince. You may know of those battles with Glendower?" She grinned at the expression of consternation on his face. "Moreover, I am a close friend to Queen Joanna, stepmother to our king and have been given the honor of addressing both of them—both, sir priest—by their first names. We dined privately only last month. Now, what have you to say?"

He stood stunned for the briefest second. Luisa had to admire the skill with which he recovered. "Forgive my zeal, Lady Barthampton. Had I the slightest idea of your identity I would not have spoken so. You now have but to command me. I must warn you as my Christian duty, that woman is dangerous and deceitful—"

She cut him off. "That is enough. I do not like sycophants. She comes with me and that is final." Turning to Luisa, she snapped her fingers at the maid, who now rushed forward with a full green cloak and a flagon of wine. "Have you lied, girl? I will know it shortly if you have."

Luisa pulled the cloak around her shoulders and all the power of the Marmoors was in her as she answered, "I have not lied. I thank you for the charity you extend, and I believe you will know the truth when you hear it." Had she gone too far? What would this noblewoman take as individualism and what as insolence? Luisa knew her rescue was no more than a whim on the lady's part. If she ceased to interest her benefactor she might well find herself in Arban's hands again or far worse. "May I now speak with you?"

Father Sebastian stared at them both, not bothering to mask his blazing hatred. "It is as you command, lady. Justice will be served." He sketched a swift bow, swirled his robes about, and strode away, scattering the onlookers with a gesture.

Lady Barthampton ordered, "Mount! We ride on immediately. This town cloys my spirit. We'll make early camp." She swung round on Luisa. "Are you able to ride?"

If Luisa had been incapable she would not have admitted it. She had the distinct feeling that few people went against what this lady desired. "I am fully able." The sip she had taken of wine was going to her head and she resisted the impulse to giggle.

She was mounted on a sturdy black horse and a watchful groom rode close by. In a few minutes the whole troop, some thirty or more persons, clattered off the high road onto a narrower one and sped rapidly away. Luisa thought of the pilgrims, wondering if Lady Martha would give a thought to her useful servant's absence and what Father Sebastian would do. Then, looking at the massive figure of Lady Barthampton on her stallion, she decided it mattered little. She would tell her story, spicing it with the proper details, and hope that help would be forthcoming. It seemed that fate had brought her to this encounter.

The sunny day dwindled toward dusk and birds were beginning to make night calls when they finally paused on a flat plain not far from a village. Luisa was so tired that she was numb but she noticed the speed of long practice in the way the tents were erected, furnishings spread about, and guards posted. Cooking facilities were arranged and soon the smell of roasting meat was on the air. Evidently Lady Barthampton traveled a good deal.

"I'm Milla, mistress. You're to be bathed and gowned, then I'll take you to my lady." The maid had flaxen hair and a hesitant manner. She was no more than fifteen.

Luisa followed obediently. She had lost count of the hours since she had last slept. She tried to smile at the girl but her lips seemed frozen; it was easier to drift.

She was taken to a curtained corner of one of the tents and sponged with cool water from the nearby brook. When she protested, Milla said she had her orders and Luisa was to do nothing for herself. Her chestnut hair was combed until it fell to her waist in a shimmering mass. Soothing lotions were applied to her face and hands. She was given a shift of thin cloth and a white homespun gown which accentuated the curves of her slender body. The low slippers were too large but felt much better than the old shoes she had worn in her boy's garb.

When she was dressed, Milla brought more wine, some bread and cheese, and roasted meat. "Hurry, please, mistress. My lady does not like to be kept waiting." The thin face was apprehensive.

Luisa imagined Lady Barthampton might be a hard person to serve. "I am ready." She was too nervous to eat, but the wine gave her courage.

This might be her best chance to save Marmoor and herself. One must use every opportunity.

Lady Barthampton's tent was brilliant inside with silks, cushions, and shielded candles in golden holders. She wore red, a long flowing garment that enhanced her height and rendered her figure even more commanding. Luisa thought of the Amazons of Greek myth; power exuded from Lady Barthampton. There was amusement and curiosity in the dark gaze she turned on Luisa.

"Now, girl, I am ready for your tale. You look quite different, no longer the waif. I can understand that court manner you have." She waved toward one of the cushions. "Sit."

Luisa sank down, pushed back her hair, and said, "I owe you my immense gratitude, Lady Barthampton. It is dangerous to have me here, is it not? Father Sebastian spoke of a special commission, particular powers?"

The woman's mouth went hard. "Fanatics such as he are everywhere. They will be dealt with in due time. Besides, we are on our way to Wales where I intend to remain for some time seeing to my lands and making sure that all is run properly. He cannot follow us. Other heretics are closer at hand." She gave a sharp laugh and waited for Luisa to speak.

She hesitated. "The tale is long. I do not wish to bore you." There could not be a better moment than this to explain everything to this woman who appeared fully capable of managing not only her own destiny but that of others and had influence at the royal court. Something moved across the surface of Luisa's mind, fading when she tried to recall it.

"I have commanded you, girl. Do not delay unless you are making up lies as I warned you not to do." Lady Barthampton's cheeks were touched with color and her eyes narrowed. "Why do you hesitate?"

Luisa did not know; she only knew that she dared not tell the whole truth. Some danger lay in Cecelia Barthampton and she must trust her instincts. She could not reveal herself completely. She lowered her gaze and began to weave the fabrication.

"My father was a very minor noble who lost favor when King Richard II abdicated. We lived very quietly, but I was trained in court ways and sent to a convent for instruction. He died long ago and I was reared by an old relative. There was a man I was ordered to marry. He was old and I couldn't bear the thought of him so I ran away." She did not want to give her full name as yet. Perhaps if she came to fully trust Lady Barthampton and to understand her own hesitance—but not now. "I thought to look for work, any sort. It would be better than being sold into bondage."

Her listener snorted. "Old men die and leave you the richer. My husband was very useful in his time. The young are foolish."

Luisa's lips quirked at this bit of realism and thought it better not to comment. Now she told of the pilgrims, the labor she had done, and of the priest who had looked at her with hungry eyes. She left out the encounter with the dissidents and gave no mention of Marcus. "He brushed against me several times, saw me adjusting my clothes, and made foul advances. There was nothing to do but run away. If I return to my home—although it is not really home anymore—in Kent, I will have to wed the old man and I will not. I will not!"

"You have a determined spirit. I might have been as you in my youth but I hope I would have been wiser." Lady Barthampton patted her hair complacently. "I have yet to know your name. Give it at once."

"Luisa Martinson." It was close enough to her own so that she would answer and still it was clearly not a noble name. How painful it was to disavow Marmoor! But she must in order to save it. She raised her head and saw, behind the faint amusement and benign manner of her protector, something else—a thing not very different from Father Sebastian's interest in her soul and body. Taken aback, she stared and wondered how an animal felt caught in the painful jaws of a trap.

Lady Barthampton saw Luisa's reaction and instantly became brisk. "Well, I have taken risk for you. You owe me for that, I think you will agree. If you had other history I should not suggest this, but you have done many things and can prove useful to me in Wales."

"How so, my lady?" Her chin went up. The words were true and Luisa Marmoor paid her debts.

"You have some experience of the rough-and-tumble world, can deal with circumstances as they come, possess a quick tongue, and have been trained in gentility. I think most people are frightened of me, but if you are you hide it well. You are a type of person of whom I know very little. Most women have little opportunity to be independent. We shall speak together often. You can read to me in the long evenings, pass my orders to my servants, alleviate my boredom. I will give you a small wage and when we return to London I will suggest your services to other ladies for by that time there will be no need of you in my service."

Luisa wondered if the noblewoman deliberately sounded insulting to test her reaction. She struggled to keep her anger back. Here was a safe harbor, a chance to earn money and plan for the future. Her intuitive feelings about Lady Barthampton might simply be the product of her exhaustion. Luisa would not luxuriate in pride but bend to this fortune and be thankful for it. If the woman spoke as though she were a toy or a pet possession, Luisa would ignore it and accept with silken words and have done.

"I am grateful for your good offer and will serve as best I may. You are most kind, Lady Barthampton. I hope I can fulfill your orders but it is only fair to explain that I have little singing voice, less skill with a needle, and no sense of the hang of a gown." Surely that was humble enough!

"But I think you can tell a good tale. Is it not so?" She looked at Luisa with a knowing smile. "We shall see. The matter is settled. Go to your tent now. We rise early to travel." She dismissed

Luisa with a wave of one beringed hand and shouted for Milla.

Luisa made her curtsy and went out into the windy dark. In time to come she would walk carefully for she knew now that Lady Barthampton did not believe her story and would make use of her for reasons of her own. She, Luisa, must be ever watchful.

In the next few days they rode hard and long, pausing to rest for a brief respite in the darkest hours of the nights and rising before dawn to continue. Lady Barthampton kept the same opulence of the first night, but she did not summon Luisa again and the others of the party stayed away from her although they were unfailingly civil. She was just as glad for it gave her time to strengthen her resolve so she might conduct herself with caution.

The character of the land changed as they traveled. It became craggier, cooler, and the vegetation grew more dense. They saw fewer people and dwellings. The occasional individual who was encountered did not acknowledge them at all. To Luisa the feeling of encroachment was palpable. Close by the border a large troop of armed men joined them, much to the excitement of the maids. Lady Barthampton consulted with their leader, waved them to the back, and angrily rode up beside Luisa.

"They are telling me —*me*—to turn back! That it is not safe! When was it ever safe in Wales? I have my lands to attend. Cadan may be a coward but I'm certainly not!" Her wide face flamed with indignation as her hands clenched hard together. "Ride on!"

"Is it so dangerous here now? I thought the Welsh wars under control." Luisa privately wished them well if they rebelled against the authority that did not even consider a citizen's rights. She remembered, as did all England, that Henry IV and the present Henry had carried out expeditions each summer in Wales against Glendower with little success.

Lady Barthampton snorted. "Wales is always afire with something. Now it seems some of our officials set to rule here have been found cheating and failing to administer justice. A commission has been sent by King Henry to look into the matter. There have been complaints of venality and oppression, murmurs of retaliation. My neighbor, Lord Cadan, has gathered his family and servants and hied himself to London. These men were dispatched to escort me back for he had heard of my incipient arrival. Nonsense! Glendower hasn't been seen in a long time; that self-styled Prince of Wales may be dead and I hope he is!"

"Perhaps the Welsh only want to be left alone to carve out their lives as best they may." Luisa felt her sympathy rising. "English arms will never conquer Wales completely or so I have been told."

"That could be treasonable talk. You are not an expert on battles, Mistress *Martinson*." She slapped her hand on the saddle horn and emphasized the last name sharply. "Discretion is a virtue, is it not?"

"Yes, my lady." Luisa cursed inwardly. How was she to know which balance to strike?

So they went deeper into the Welsh country, around narrow curves, through valleys lush with summer, far into the wild untamed land, and nearer to the mountains where it was said Glendower bided his time. Luisa often saw tumbled bridges and burned out houses, signs of a war that continued. At times she would see a vast castle now no more than a pile of stone brooding over a strategic road and would believe it to be the mark of the English hand on this remote world. At such times she had the feeling she rode toward her ultimate fate, and she made the sign of the cross against it.

Chapter Ten
SAVAGE MEETING

LUISA PEERED AT herself in the steel mirror and fancied she looked very much the court lady. "We are now on my lands and shall reach Abbewas Castle, my stronghold, tomorrow afternoon. We'll act as civilized folk should tonight. Dress elegantly, Mistress Martinson, in what is provided for you. I must see if you will be a credit to me. I plan to test your reading skills as well so make sure your voice is fit. Milla shall bring wine and honey for you." As always Lady Barthampton was lengthy and explicit.

Luisa obeyed. The full-skirted green gown brought out the brilliance of her slanting green eyes and emphasized her small waist. The flowing sleeves made her hands seem slim, the fingers tapering. Her hair was bound up in an intricate coil seeded with tiny pearls. A gauzy veil of paler green drifted over her shoulders. Her dark brows were emphatic against the pale oval of her face. The gown was cut straight across the bosom and was a bit too large, but Milla's skilful needle had taken care of that. Luisa wondered to whom the ensemble had belonged but was afraid to ask.

She examined the necklace Lady Barthampton had sent for her to wear. It was obviously one of her least ornate and still it was almost vulgar in the heavy settings of pearls and emeralds intertwined with gold leaf. She had looped it twice around her neck but it hung below her waist. The value of such a thing would buy Marmoor many times over and keep the property going for years. Luisa sighed over the inequities of life, then told herself sternly to be thankful that she had escaped the horrors of Father Sebastian's attention, not to mention the marriage to Arban's friend.

"Mistress, you are beautiful! Just as my lady commanded!"

Luisa whirled to see Milla standing in the door of the tent. Admiration shone in her eyes. "Thank you, Milla. It's the borrowed finery." She grinned at the thought that even beauty could be ordered by the formidable Lady Barthampton. If only Dame Matilda could see her now. She wondered if the Dame lived and if she had been turned out of Marmoor. Her face clouded as she turned to follow the maid out into the cool night.

Suddenly there was an unearthly scream to their left as a flaming arrow crashed into the breast of one of the guards at the main tent. A shower of them lit up the sky as they fell to claim their human targets. At the same time the clang and rattle of swordplay rose up. Curses and shouts rang out as men struggled together.

"My lady! I must go to her!" Milla dashed toward the tent which was already aflame, the thin silk crackling briskly. But before she had gone more than a few steps, an arrow found the maid's back. As soon as she fell, Luisa threw herself flat beside her. More arrows went overhead and landed in the tent. The deep voice of Cecelia Barthampton could be heard cursing from within as she interspersed oaths with shouts of "Treason!" and "Treachery!"

Milla was dead instantly. The arrow had gone completely through her body. Luisa saw that much by the light of the torches and the other flaming arrows that continued to rain down upon the camp. One of them pinned Luisa to the ground by her full skirt. The arrow's flame spat and went out as she pulled at it frantically in a desperate effort to be free before the raiders found her. She had no doubt that their intention was to kill everyone in the traveling party. Now Lady Barthampton's cries were ominously silent; her tent was one full sheet of fire.

Luisa's one thought was to escape. Her skirt

tore finally and she was free. She rolled over in a quick motion and started to rise only to be slapped back by a man who suddenly rose from nowhere. He was covered with blood and his beard was singed. The dagger in his hand lifted toward her throat as his lips drew back from uneven teeth. He hurled a stream of words at her in what she assumed was Welsh and dashed at her.

"Murdering fiends!" Luisa forgot her own danger as she twisted back and thrust out one foot to trip him. His own fury caused him to overbalance and he went down, throwing the dagger free. She caught it up and held it before her, well aware that anyone might take it away with one gesture.

The man jumped up, shouted something, and then said in English, "You hell spawn! I'll just have my fun now and kill you slowly." He began to stalk her with feinting movements.

Luisa knew she should save her breath but rage and fear fueled her words. "Not before I sink your dagger in your throat, murderer!" She circled as he moved. It seemed hopeless, but she had to fight. In the one brief glance she dared take of the camp she saw that bodies were everywhere, and now raiders dressed in dark clothes, weapons ready, were gathering to watch this battle.

"I get her after Ned!"

"Look at the jewels on her! They'd buy an army!"

"Jewels, nothing. Look at her. I'll make her want to fight!"

Luisa knew the calls were to distract her and they did. This was the climax to the bloodshed. She wondered what had happened to the maids in the party. If she were the only one left alive it would not be for long. Even at this moment she wanted intensely to live, no matter in what circumstances. The dagger was slippery with sweat as she clutched it. She feared she could not stave them off much longer.

"By God's blessed bones, stop this immediately!" The command rang out over the crackling flames and the blood lust of those gathered around Luisa. The jeering men backed away slightly but her attacker did not, so intent on her was he. She looked up enough to see a tall figure step forward almost leisurely, jerk him back, and speak to him in Welsh. The spell broken, he bent almost double in an attempt to escape a loud slap from the tall man.

Luisa stared incredulously. The world swayed dizzily before her eyes. The tall man turned in her direction and she gasped out the one word, "Marcus!"

"What are you doing here?" The incredulity in his voice matched her own. He strode forward and put both hands on her shoulders. "The waif of the road, the proud threadbare lady who needed rescuing, the elegant woman who wears a queen's ransom and faces one of my most dangerous men in battle. Who are you? Who in hell are you that you travel in such company as Lady Cecelia Barthampton, whose soul God curses?" The bitter savagery in his words was reflected in the twist of his lips and the harsh glitter of his blue eyes. His dark hair fell over his forehead; the aquiline nose and flat planes of his face might have been cut from marble. In this setting of wild mountains and flaming death, he could have represented Lucifer himself.

"I say the same for you, Marcus Whoever-you-are! Slaughterer of innocents. This was not an open war but an ambush!" She pointed to Milla's body. "The little maid ran to see about her mistress and took an arrow in her back. She was perhaps fifteen! Do you curse her soul?" Luisa felt the numbness leaving her as her fear retreated and was replaced with anger. It was as if she had never lain in loving tenderness and passionate desire with this man, had never felt his sweet caresses on her body and his distracting presence in her heart. But she had cherished his hard-muscled flesh, drunk of his kisses, and listened to his murmurs of longing. He had given her so much; she had offered all that Luisa Marmoor was in those tender few hours of the cave. Now nothing remained.

"You are to come with us. I *will* know what is going on. Perhaps you are a spy and if so I vow you will give us every detail of your plots." He waved at one of his men who came forward eagerly. "Prepare the lady for travel."

It was too much for Luisa. The madness of her anger was in her next action. She hurled herself at Marcus, fingernails curved to slash his face. Suddenly he was all enemies personified, even if he had just saved her life. He caught her around the waist and swung her toward his man in one motion.

"Make sure she goes calmly. Bind her if you must but do not touch her otherwise. Is that perfectly understood?" His voice was frigid.

His man spoke in Welsh and Marcus nodded. In another minute Luisa found herself hoisted on a large black horse, and her hands were bound in front of her. Only then did the raider, now mounted behind her, pull the necklace from her and toss it to Marcus.

"What is a bit of thievery after murder? Is that how you see it? Why quibble? What do you plan for me?" Luisa slammed the questions at him, daring to provoke the anger she knew lay just under the cold, controlled surface.

"One more word, madam, and you will make the journey well gagged." He came to the side of the horse and looked up at her. No trace of laughter or gentleness remained, only a fierce determination.

Luisa understood that he meant his every word. She subsided and looked away at the bodies of her fellow travelers, then shut her eyes. She had endured less than they and could take no more. Tears burned against her lids.

"You show sense at last. Take her, Morgan."

The raiders rode to the top of a crest and paused to look back. Luisa saw the flames dying out while the quarter moon shone cooly down on the devastation of a noblewoman's pride. A wolf howled in the distance and was answered by another at close range. Morgan turned the horse and headed toward the mountains. The others followed quietly. Their pace was slow and steady. Presently Luisa slumped back in exhausted sleep.

She woke to Morgan's voice in her ear. "Wake, lady. We are at our camp. Don't be afraid. Marcus will speak with you later. I do advise you to be civil."

His English was perfect, his manner proper. One would not have thought him to be a murderer. Luisa said, "I will remember your words." She looked about at the ring of fires which bordered cave entrances in the side of the mountain. Men and women were preparing the morning meal in the early dawn. The green forests stretched out on all sides and she heard the sounds of rushing water in the distance. The air was fresh and cool, and Luisa drew it in hungrily.

A woman came up to them and spoke in Welsh to Morgan. He answered her and lifted Luisa down. She said in accented English, "I am Talwis. I will take you to shelter."

Luisa wondered what sort of woman allied herself with outlaws and raiders. She was perhaps in her late twenties with a smooth brow and pleasant face. "I am Luisa and I would be grateful." She forced herself to smile and Talwis returned it. She must not struggle against this new development until she knew what it meant. Morgan leaned across to slice the bonds on her hands with his knife. She rubbed them together to restore the circulation and followed Talwis meekly.

In a secluded corner of the small cave, Luisa was allowed to rinse her face and body, put on a loose white gown with a warm overrobe of dark fur, and make a hurried meal of bread, cheese, and weak ale. She thought longingly of sleep and forgetfulness but Talwis had other instructions.

"Our leader will speak with you while he has the time. Come."

In spite of all that had happened Luisa felt a quick heartbeat of excitement. If only she and Marcus had met again without blood and hatred! His face swam before her as she had seen it when they made love and then as it had been only hours previously, hard and cold. How did a man come to change so?

Talwis was saying, "Do not lie to him, Luisa. He hates that above all things. Be warned."

Luisa thought of all the lies and half-truths she had been forced to tell in her own good cause. It would be a relief to tell the truth for a change. She thanked the woman and once more followed her to a changing fate.

They went around an outcropping of rock, emerging on a narrow path which led between some boulders and a sparse growth of trees, up to another and larger cave where two men waited. Talwis dropped back as one of them came forward to take Luisa inside.

Just past an entrance shielded with timbers, she saw a room that would not have been out of place in a castle. Furs of all sorts lay on the floor and hung on the walls. One section of the roof was open to the pure air and grouped candles provided more light. A faded rose and silver tapestry hung close by. Several carved chests stood about. One held at least six books in elaborate leather bindings. There was a bed of furs in a high alcove and a boulder draped with cloth held flasks as well as some wooden dishes. A lute was placed against a stone that must have served as a seat.

Her escort faded away and Luisa stood still for a moment before she saw movement from the shadows of a far corner. Marcus wore a loose blue robe that in no way concealed the litheness of his body. The brilliant eyes were a deeper blue than the robe and his dark hair clustered in curls over his head. The tanned face was hard as he waved her to a seat.

"Your full name? Your station in life? Your business with Lady Barthampton?"

"You know my name. What is yours? Your station? Your business besides that of raider and murderer?" Luisa felt her heart twist with pain. One part of her wanted to berate him, the other to be held securely in those powerful arms and again have him deeply inside her. She fought the longing she had for him and resisted the thought that her hunger would not subside until they made love once more.

He was casual. "I am John Marcus Lenley, outlaw to the English, soldier of Wales here. That is enough for you to know. Your own plight should interest you, however. I mean to hold you for ransom. If your own family or betrothed does not claim you—though they are mad to let you run about the country as you have—then Lady Barthampton and her minions will certainly pay. I'm not particular, you see. An outlaw takes his money where he can." He sank down on one of the rugs and grinned mirthlessly at her.

"I am the Lady Luisa Marmoor. My estate is forfeit to the king, who declares it his own. I went to London to ask audience but angered a clerk who swore I should be forced into marriage. I ran away and joined a group of pilgrims. A priest with them made advances toward me. I attempted to get away and ran quite literally into Lady Barthampton, who protected me for her own amusement. All that I wore belonged to her." Luisa paused for breath.

Marcus jumped up and came to loom over her. "You are lying! No woman could survive going about as you did. You shall tell me the truth."

"How dare you speak to me so!" The words were involuntary. Luisa realized how foolish they sounded in this world ruled by Marcus.

He glared at her furiously and Luisa's eyes met his defiantly. For an instant his resolve wavered and his face softened, but then his expression hardened again.

Suddenly his bitter laughter rang throughout the room. He had listened to her lies from their first meeting, believed her, even seen her fair beauty in his dreams and wondered at the mystery around her. What was she truly? Spy? Harlot? Lady? Marcus continued to laugh. It should be a rich jest, he thought as pain wrenched him. Before he had taken women for his own pleasure and theirs. Not since his youth had one haunted him as Luisa did. He knew he must not yield to the feeling for her. He was the leader of these people, this band. The cause of Wales, of Glendower, was his. No matter her beauty, he must remain true to his cause. But even as he glared at her, Marcus saw that she did not fear him and he unwillingly rejoiced in her courage.

"I have pressing business at present. Think of who is most likely to pay your ransom for the messenger leaves within the hour. We keep no prisoners!" He heard the blunt words and hoped they had the desired effect even as another part of him wanted to cradle and protect her. Long ago people had lied to him and he could not forget. Would not forget. He had learned that anger held people back from him. It was safer that way.

Chapter Eleven
EARTH'S CENTER

LUISA STRUGGLED to maintain her dignity in the face of such hostility from the only man she had ever given herself to. "Ah, yes, more killing to do. I can see that you are very busy. I suppose you will kill me when you discover there is no one to pay anything. Spare me the sight of your evil face until that day!" She almost screamed the last words at him.

"Get out! Get out! Guard!" He turned his back to her, and when the men dashed in, cried, "This woman is to be watched. Order Talwis to see to it!"

The guard motioned to Luisa who was glad to move ahead of him and go out the door. As they shut it she heard the sounds of breaking crockery and curses. Marcus was venting his fury at more than Luisa.

She was taken back to the cave where she had changed earlier. There was no sign of Talwis but it had been made more habitable with several low stools, a pile of covers for a bed, more water for washing, and even a wooden comb set out for her hair. A gown of brown homespun was lying across the bed. As in Marcus's cave, this one had a crude door affixed at the entrance, and a curtain could be pulled over that. Luisa was thankful for the privacy. She wanted to cry but did not dare give way.

She paced up and down for a few moments before washing her face, braiding back her hair, and pulling the gown over her chemise. Once dressed she felt better. What would happen when Marcus learned she was telling the truth? She did not really think he might harm her but he was capable of going away and leaving his men to deal with an inconvenient prisoner. What had Lady Barthampton done to have so evil a reputation in his eyes? She thought again of his tenderness on the road and of the passion of their lovemaking. Now he made mockery of it all. Luisa shook her head impatiently. Here she went in danger of her life and was mooning about romance! How foolish she was being! But she could not drive these thoughts from her head.

Time passed with dragging slowness. Luisa sat on the bed and remembered Marmoor in every detail until she was torn with a painful longing for it. She tried to hold thoughts of Marcus at bay. Her mind whirled until she was ready to pound on the door for release. She paced her stone dungeon.

The door opened soundlessly and Talwis entered, her manner as calm and agreeable as if she were calling on a welcome guest. She carried a beaker of wine, a piece of roasted meat on dark bread, and a wrapped package under one arm. Luisa decided no one was ever more pleasant to see.

"Time can be long here. I've brought you something to look at. The illustrations are beautiful. I don't suppose you can read?"

"Of course, I can." Luisa was faintly indignant but she knew that few women were taught to read or cipher. That was thought to be men's work. She loosened the bindings and gasped with delight. "Boccaccio's *Decameron!* How wonderful! Where does it come from?" She touched the pages reverently, noting the rich workmanship, brilliant colors, and perfection of the bindings. It was translated into French.

"Marcus has a number of books. I took the liberty of borrowing one." The color came into her face as her voice lingered over his name.

Luisa felt her blood chill. She knew now with certainty that Talwis and Marcus were lovers. Her face flamed. Luisa Marmoor refused to be just one in a string of women!

She made her voice gentle. "This will give me comfort. I thank you, Talwis."

Talwis smiled complacently. "The messenger has been gone these many hours about your ransom. It won't be long for you, I hope." She moved toward the door and silently slipped out.

Luisa wondered if Talwis might help her escape when news came of the lack of a ransom. Surely the woman would not condone murder yet would be eager to rid herself of a rival. She must think of concocting a plan. If nothing else, it would pass the time.

She dipped into the *Decameron*, recalling the first time she ever read the racy, diverting tales. The book was an old friend, and as she went through it, she was transported once more to the solar at Marmoor where she sat close to the fire on a winter day and hoped she would encounter one-tenth of the emotion found in those stories. When the light faded in her prison, Luisa found that she was sleepy. The pain of her current plight had lifted a little. At least the Black Death is not abroad! The thought amused her and gave wry comfort.

The next day and night were endless. She was allowed out only twice, both times to a separate area where she saw no one, and escorted back by a young girl who apparently spoke no English or French. The rest of the time Luisa paced, read, considered and discarded a dozen schemes, and alternated between anger and tears. It did not help that she woke several times from dreams of Marcus in which he bent over her, blue eyes passionate and his body tender on hers. "Luisa, my love, my dear, dear love." She heard the words over and over until she woke, shaking and alone. Then she recreated the ambush at the camp and his harshness toward her in the hope of counteracting her passionate dreams. It was not helpful. She remembered only that he had protected her, perhaps not totally for the sake of a ransom. There was no peace for Luisa, torn as she was. She stalked up and down impatiently. Was this to be the pattern of her days for all the time it took to discover the fact that Luisa Marmoor had nothing, was missed by no one, and her property was forfeit to the English king? Soon it would not matter to her—she would be driven mad from confinement. How did prisoners in the Tower and such places endure it?

There was a knock on the door very early on the third morning of her confinement. Part of the cave was open to the light; she was very thankful for that. The nub of candle she had been given had long since gone out and it would have been awful not to know night from day. Now she sat up, thinking it strange that anyone would knock on a captive's door.

"Mistress Marmoor? May we enter?" Before Luisa could call out, a young man and woman of perhaps eighteen or slightly less came in and stood looking at her. "I am Edra and this is my brother, Ian."

Luisa smiled tentatively and was rewarded with two large golden smiles in return. The visitors were both brown-eyed and fair, dressed in rough clothes, and appeared frankly curious. Fellow prisoners? More outlaws? She must not be discourteous. Waving at the small area of the cave, she spoke with as much lightness as she could muster. "Will you sit? And I am Luisa, not Mistress Marmoor."

"I, that is we, have to go on an errand in the hills." Ian stopped and motioned to his sister who moved closer to Luisa. "Maybe you'd want to go with us. The guards would go, of course. It was suggested . . ." He stopped, staring imploringly at Edra.

"The air will be good for you. Close captivity is wearing." She spoke the platitudes solemnly.

Luisa did not care what their motive was. Anything was better than staying there. She tried to control her emotions but laughed instead. Not wanting to offend them, she said swiftly, "I'm sorry. It's just that I have missed the outdoors so." Had Marcus remembered her kindly after all? Had they come on his orders? She asked no questions, deciding it unwise at this juncture.

"We understand." Ian was solemn in his turn as he turned to lead the way out.

Three tall brawny guards accompanied them as they threaded their way out between the trees and boulders of the lair, across a clearing, and up the hill onto a narrow trail which led up to a ridge crowned with tall flowering shrubs. The sun was just rising, the golden warmth caressing the distant peaks with light. The scent of earth rose richly. Luisa drew in hungry breaths as she pulled up a handful of pink flowers and hurried to keep pace with the others. They walked for a time without speaking, enjoying the new day.

Luisa's natural curiosity came to the fore as she asked Edra, "Are you not of this country? I thought most of the Welsh were dark."

The girl was matter-of-fact. "Our mother was English, our father French. He came to fight with Glendower in the great days when all Wales belonged to him. He sent for us but our ship foundered and sank just off the coast while in a storm. Our mother drowned and he fell in battle the next day. We were saved by a seaman who brought us to Prince Owen." She gave reverence to Glendower's name. "We were to be reared at Sycharth with his children. When the battles turned against us, everyone went deeper into the hills. Now Ian wants to fight and his right cannot be denied. I go where he goes."

Luisa was silent. She did not want to bring up vexing questions, and there was no other way she might find out about her own status. She began to talk about the vegetation and the beauty of the landscape as she tried to forget the peril in which she stood.

They went higher up the green slopes and then down into a little valley so deeply hidden that it was not discernable from the trail. Ian went off with one of the guards and the other two guards sat down a good distance away. Luisa and Edra were alone on the bank of a rushing stream.

"Let's go in!" Edra peeled off her dress and,

wearing only the thinnest of undergarments, jumped in the middle of the icy water.

Luisa stuck one finger in and recoiled, but not to be outdone she did as Edra had. The first shock of cold was fierce but after she was inured to it they played as children, chasing each other from rock to rock, diving for a probably non-existent fish, jumping high to see who made the greatest splash, and finally collapsing in the now-hot sun to dry out and dress. Bees hummed in the flowers nearby and birds resumed their chatter. When Ian came up a little later, he brought with him brown bread and cheese. It was now a banquet topped off with water from the stream. Afterward they dozed in the shadow of a hanging bush.

"Wake up! I want to show Luisa something!" Ian was grinning but his eyes were serious. "You don't want to sleep the day away."

Luisa scrambled eagerly to her feet. The early morning's heavy heart was completely gone. This was a time spent with those who might be her friends; the moment was to be taken for what it was, a pleasurable interlude. "I'm ready."

Nearly an hour later they were still climbing up through vines, spindly bushes, and outcroppings of rock. Luisa's hands were aching and her legs were sore. She considered herself reasonably agile but now she began to think again. "I hope whatever you want me to see is worth all this scrambling about," she complained at last as she mopped sweat from her forehead.

"Wait until you see." Ian and Edra spoke as one.

A great growth of bushes loomed up ahead, seeming as impenetrable as the walls of rock around the climbers. In the lead, Ian moved competently and surely through the branches, then took a sharp turn to the left and beckoned to Luisa. Edra came to stand beside her. They smiled at Luisa.

"Wales."

The panorama before Luisa's eyes was a land in miniature. Smooth green fields, a lake whipped gently by the breeze, a far fall of golden flowers, cattle grazing on a rise, a waterfall tumbling down from a crag, distant mountains touched with clouds, a dark forest, and a sweep of bracken. She looked down from the heights and, as she did so, there was a crash of wings close to her and an eagle soared high, paused to drift on the wind and rose to meet another. Both went toward the highest crag, the sun glittering on their wings.

Luisa felt tears brimming in her eyes. She wanted to speak but there were no words for this pervasive loveliness. When she turned to look at Ian and Edra she saw that they were as moved as she.

Ian began to speak in the strange cadences of Wales, the words lilting and rising one second, tearing and harsh the next. Luisa knew somehow that they spoke of love and death and beauty, a song out of time for this particular moment that bound them together. She thought of Marcus with a wrenching longing.

Edra murmured, "'It is our great poet, Dafydd ap Gwilym. He may have stood here at one time and fashioned those words." She did not offer to translate; there was no need.

Luisa felt a sudden overwhelming desire for Marcus. She wanted to stand here with him, share the beauty, let her pain for her lost home mingle with his for this country, be at one with him in love's battles.

She said, "Thank you for bringing me here. For sharing. For being here." She could say no more but she saw that they understood.

It was so silent that she fancied she heard the tumble of the waterfall far away. Insects chittered in the grass at her feet and the mountains shone purple in the distance. They sat down at the edge of the overlook and it was only natural to speak of her home and all it meant. And because Marmoor had been wrested from her, Luisa could understand all the better now the feelings of the Welsh. As she talked, her hurt was eased. Soon she was able to say lightly, "Enough of this! I'd like to read your poet someday. Will you try to teach me your language?"

They were delighted and the feelings of friendship grew all the stronger for their sharing.

For the next five days the trio was inseparable. Luisa soon ignored the omnipresent guards as she, Ian, and Edra walked the trails, talked endlessly, played at dice, bowls, and darts, sang ballads, and struggled with Welsh lessons which usually ended in spurts of laughter. Luisa was regaled with poetry and music and wild tales of Welsh valor, which she felt bound to counteract with stories of heroic Englishmen. Best of all were the times when Ian recited the words of the great Welshman Dafydd ap Gwilm, his poetic passion plain in each syllable.

It rained on the sixth day, a hard and droning downpour. Thunder cracked around the camp and a penetrating chill hung over everything. Luisa had had no contact with anyone else, not even Talwis, but she had the feeling that everyone was waiting for an unknown event to take place. The isolated bliss of the past days must soon end. The roaring wind crackled in the branches outside as the day went on. They had kindled the fire in the corner of the cave and Luisa sat on a bearskin rug before it. Ian was correcting her pronunciation of a phrase. "It's physically impossible to say that!" Luisa declared. "My tongue cannot twist so!" Edra was staring into the flames, lost in dreams of her own.

"My Lady Marmoor." The words fell like pellets into their coziness. "I see you are not at a loss for entertainment." Marcus stood by the door with his leather coat dripping, his dark face inscrutable.

"Sir." Edra and Ian came to their feet immediately, respect clear in their eyes.

His chilly gaze locked with Luisa's and pierced through her. Reluctantly she stood up. "They have been my very good companions in these last few days." Ominous phrase. All too likely it would soon refer to her in quite another way. Would she live to be with them again?

"I must speak with you alone." Marcus shed his coat, crossed his arms over his chest, and waited. "They will excuse you."

Ian and Edra withdrew so rapidly that they almost seemed to run. Luisa pulled the shawl she was wearing more closely around her shoulders, hoping Marcus could not tell she was shaking. She tilted her head and stared at him challengingly.

"I am ready," she answered, without a quiver in her voice.

The sword lay between them.

Chapter Twelve
PROTEUS

"I sent messengers to inquire about your story. You know that. We know the news very quickly here, remote as we are. I had business across the border so I waited there. Naturally I wanted to know where the ransom demands might best be placed. My people were discreet; they have to be for that spawn of Bolingbroke who calls himself king would root them out and call them traitors." His eyes were unreadable.

"Say what you came to say and leave me in peace." Luisa could not be civil and pretend. Let the war between them continue! It was better than waiting supinely for his decision.

He continued as though she had not spoken. "You have called me murderer, yet Lady Barthampton lives to plot again as she has done for

years. The women also. I gave orders they were
to be left alone. She was badly shaken and a bit
wounded. Now she is across the border. Oddly
enough she never heard of you under any name.
Nothing happened in that camp to a strange
woman. No ransom."

"I did not expect it." Luisa was thankful Lady
Barthampton and the women were all right.
Why should it be painful that she was dis-
avowed? She was just another bit of flotsam to
the bored noblewoman.

"Luisa." He said her name so softly that she
barely heard it. When she looked at him again
she saw very real warmth in the brilliant eyes.
"Your estate is fully forfeit to the Crown. An
overseer has been appointed and workers have
been sent to make the place as productive as
possible. Every possible avenue of income is to
be explored. Then Marmoor will be sold to the
highest bidder." He stopped. "Also . . ."

"There's more?" She choked the words out
fearfully.

"Yes." He was so close to her side that she
smelled the freshness of the rain on his clothes,
the rough garments of a peasant. The magnetism of him surrounded her, causing her senses
to whirl. When he put his hands squarely on her
shoulders the touch blazed over her.

"Tell me! Stop tormenting me!"

"Your Dame Matilda is dead and lies with
your ancestors. She died in the peace of God my
informant said and knew nothing of what has
happened since you left. I sent money that
masses might be sung for her soul and in honor

of her charge who is a brave woman, well worthy of her proud name."

Luisa had thought herself prepared, but this news pierced like a knife to her heart. Marmoor, Dame Matilda, irrevocably gone. It was unbearable. She did not take in the last words Marcus said. She simply began to cry, great gulping sobs of loss. Once started there was no stopping and she began to shake.

Marcus pulled her face to his shoulder as he patted her back and made soothing sounds. Then he picked her up and sat down on the rug with her in his lap while he waited for the storm to subside. Luisa tried to regain control but the shattering events of the past days and months took their toll. Release had to come. In these moments he was not the man who held her fate, nor her onetime lover, nor yet the stranger who accused her of spying. He was a person who offered some measure of comfort.

He set her down gently, rose, and went to get the leather flask Ian had had earlier. He thrust it into her hands. "Drink. I don't suppose it'll be very good ale but maybe you'll feel better."

She obeyed but the tears continued to stream. The power of speech seemed to have failed her utterly. She could see nothing but her overwhelming loss. Marmoor lost forever. Dame Matilda dead. She a prisoner in Wales and possibly with an English price on her head if Father Sebastian possessed half the power he believed he had. Her old formula and talisman buzzed in her mind. *I am still Luisa Marmoor.* It was no use. The coil of her life appeared broken.

"Listen to me, Luisa." Marcus was so close to her that the intense blue of his eyes surrounded her. The carved face held harsh lines and his high-bridged nose flared. "Once I, too, faced the end of my world and all that mattered. I sought death in the ranks but it never comes to those who seek it." He paused, clenching his hands together in hard fists. He seldom spoke of his past to anyone. It festered inside him but the pain of reliving those memories was too painful. Luisa's hurt was suddenly one with his. He wanted only to comfort her in her travail. Marcus spared a wry thought. He could not remember a time when he had felt so about a woman. "Things are different for a woman, of course . . ."

"Yes, harder." Luisa gulped the words out, her attention captured by the bleakness in his voice.

"Do you truly think so?" One corner of his mouth lifted in what might have been an effort at a smile. "I once fought with Henry of Lancaster, father of the present king, in order to depose King Richard. I was very young and impressionable. I really believed in impartial justice. Henry had been cruelly exiled, his lands sequestered, and his son held hostage. Richard was my king but I truly sympathized with Henry."

Luisa sat back on her heels and looked up at Marcus. Instinctively she understood that he dredged in his own depths of pain to help her through this time. He was not a man who allowed others to penetrate his defenses. Speech must give him relief as it had for her the other day on the mountain. His eyes stared inward as he continued.

"How did my ruin come about? So easily. I was newly at court, ready to serve King Richard, and full of myself. I spoke my opinions—nothing had broken into the open at this time—and the king himself asked what I thought. Fool that I was, I could only be honest. Richard of Bordeaux was like that, charming in one instant, savage the next. Several casual sentences on his part and my family was ruined although we had served the Crown loyally for centuries. He sent me away in disgrace just months after the sentence of exile was brought against Henry of Lancaster, his own cousin."

A spout of rain came through the hole in the cave roof just then and spattered the fire's edges. Smoke rose from the ashes and they began to cough. Marcus stood up, reaching down to pull her to her feet.

"Do you feel well enough to come over to my quarters, Luisa? There's wine and brandy, better fires, and you can tell me about Marmoor if it will ease your pain." His fingers were warm on her wrist as he scanned her features, but the loss of the past was still stamped on his face.

"You know enough about my loss. Tell me about yours." She was proud that her composure was returning although what had happened at Marmoor did not bear consideration now. She wanted to get as far away from her hurt as she could. "And, yes, let's go. I'll be glad to get out of here."

They dashed out in the storm and ran, holding hands, over the slippery rocks and mud. No one was about except for the guards who always watched the camp. Thunder rumbled and a flash of lightning ripped down the dark sky. Luisa and Marcus were wet to the skin from the first step they took. She was glad for the weather; it seemed to express her feelings perfectly.

It was a relief to reach Marcus's private cave and find the fire well prepared, and drink set out along with several kinds of meat and fresh bread. He stood, wet as he was, to drink from the brandy jug and passed it to Luisa, who did the same. The powerful swallow spread through her body like a flame.

"Get out of those wet clothes." Marcus reached into a chest and pulled out a woman's thin gown of golden silk. "This ought to do." He added a cloak of gleaming brown fur.

Luisa took them, wondering if he kept such things for Talwis and other women. She went to the corner he had indicated and changed quickly. He had retreated into another area to do the same. It was a blessed relief to be warm, dry, and in the company of this man. For the moment it was enough.

"Better?" Marcus wore a short robe of blue velvet which was the exact shade of his eyes and clung to his muscular body as though tailored to its exact measurements.

"Very much so." Luisa was beginning to feel more oriented. The heaviness of the blow she had suffered was relieved by the torrent of tears.

Marcus settled himself on the wide rug and

indicated that she should sit. The gown emphasized the curves of her bosom and waist, made her skin glow and her eyes shine. Her heavy hair cascaded over the cloak which framed her face. She shifted from his scrutiny, turning to pour some of the sweet wine into a waiting cup.

"Good." He took up his tale again with apparent ease, but she saw his mouth tighten and the lines of tension come up as they had earlier.

"My friend David and I were very close in those long ago days. Our lands ran together as did our interests and convictions. I remember we even wanted to marry sisters. That next summer when Henry Bolingbroke landed, saying that he came only for his ancestral lands and not to seek the throne, we were in a dilemma. Richard had taken my family's lands and smirched our name because he doubted our loyalty. He trusted no one in those last days. My father and I lived on the charity of David's family. They were true servants of Richard but took great risk for us out of friendship. I wanted David to go with me to fight for Bolingbroke and I was very persuasive. My father was harsh, saying that it showed evil ambition to return and muster troops just when the true king, Richard, was in Ireland. I should stand ready to fight for Richard if it came to that. Fight for the man who had ruined him! He is the king, God's anointed, declared my father. I saw a man as other men, and a lesser one than many!" Fury swelled Marcus's face as twin veins stood out in his bronzed neck. He was oblivious to Luisa's presence, needing to rush on with his story of the events that had shaped him.

Luisa was in his spell also. She could see him, younger than she was now, eager and ready to fight for what he considered the right. Just as Luisa Marmoor would have done if she had been born a man. In this way they were alike.

"I was eloquent, you can believe that. Simple justice, his lands and his family—that was all Bolingbroke wanted! I really believed it. My father declared me no longer his son and left the castle of David's family. David went with me to stand with Bolingbroke. We heard his vows and protestations again and trusted him to come in peace. Every child knows what happened. Word of his return spread, he was honored, Richard came back from Ireland, and Bolingbroke gave challenge for the Crown. David was killed in a minor scuffle, not even a battle. I was untouched. Richard was soon forced to abdicate and later killed. He was a bad king but he could have been controlled. I and many others had no reverence for him, but we did not want him torn from the throne. Bolingbroke took it by lies, treachery, and murder. The house of Lancaster, his house, was unopposed. Usurpation was a fact. My father died soon after this. They said he fell into a fit the day I left and never spoke again. My sister entered an enclosed nunnery for her own protection. David's family declared blood feud against me. The girl I thought to wed before my lands were taken had just given birth to twin sons for the man she was glad to have rather than stand by me."

Marcus was striding back and forth, his body taut and rigid. It was an effort for him to continue but Luisa saw he must. He might have begun this recitation for her sake, to distract her mind; now it went on because such feelings had to have an outlet.

"Bolingbroke, now styled King Henry Plantagenet, fourth of the name, summoned his supporters to reward and congratulate them. I did not come to London and he sent to ask why. I was brought to his court by express order. That was probably the only time he ever heard the complete truth about his dealings. Usurper, murderer, destroyer of ideals. I called him all that in front of his sycophants. I was half-mad with my losses and that alone saved my life. Within twelve hours I was on a ship bound for the Continent and forbidden to return to England. Lifelong exile."

He was silent for a long time, staring into the fire, his face grim and set. Luisa dared ask, "How did you come to be outlaw in Wales?"

The blue gaze was on and through her. His powerful body heaved as he jerked the words out. "I debauched myself in the stews of Paris. The ruler of France is mad and his wife a harlot. Bolingbroke would have been right at home. I wandered in the Holy Land and found it bare of meaning. In Italy I fought in numerous battles of the city-states. Never a scratch. Nothing had meaning. I woke daily and hoped for my death. A friend I made while in France invited me to go with him on what he thought could turn out to be an amusing expedition—some not so secret help to Owen Glendower, the Welsh Prince of Wales. Owen had just risen against the English, the new king would have problems enough, and this was a very desirable state of affairs for France. England, you know, has called title to France for many years."

He sighed and the final words came in a great rush. "We came here and I was fascinated by the odds. The might of England's arms, the very rule of Lancaster and his whelps challenged, Wales wanting only to go its own way—these things lured me. When I met Glendower and began to know him, I found him to be that rarity, a man of honor. When my friend returned to France to see about money for Wales, I remained. Glendower saw the open wound in me and gave me his cause to espouse until I could care on my own. The cause of Welsh freedom came to be what I lived for. I and my men strike where we will do the most good. We are in constant danger and use any method that will help. The English call me Proteus, for I have many guises; you, Luisa, have seen a few of them. For his own reasons, Glendower has retired from the active fray after years of fighting Prince Henry at the border. So long as Lancaster rules and until Wales is free, I will fight. Having nothing, I needed nothing. The battle has been all."

Exhausted with the passion of his story, Marcus leaned back against the furs that cushioned him and closed his eyes. Luisa could hear the howling storm outside and the distant crack of a tree trunk as it fell before the wind.

"Marcus." Her voice was soft in the quiet room. "Your pain helps me bear my own. I, too, have been wronged by Lancaster and would have revenge." She did not want to suggest that they join forces; it was too soon as yet but the course was logical. The outlaws might offer safety for her but what had she to give in return? Luisa Marmoor was not a camp follower.

The atmosphere was suddenly charged between them as Marcus opened his eyes. He watched her from under dark-lashed eyes, the blue gaze intense. His long, powerful body stretched as a beautiful animal might. The arrogant certainty of the man had returned in full measure. The firm, lean jaw was set purposefully.

"That was long ago, my dear. I was a boy, with a boy's idealism."

Luisa leaned forward, well aware that the golden gown was slipping off her smooth shoulder. Her chestnut hair flowed down her back and rippled in the candlelight. "And now? What of now?" She was tense, her very being hungering for the feel of him.

"Now I am a man who wants Luisa Marmoor very much." The lazy smile caressed her.

"I want you," she answered and reached out toward him.

A moment later they were in each other's arms.

Chapter Thirteen
LOVE'S COURT

"Do you plan to sleep all day, my dear Lady Marmoor? If so, I suggest you make arrangements beforehand. Otherwise that most faithful servant, Marcus Lenley, will simply fall upon and devour your delectable body. He is improperly trained, you see."

Luisa sat upright to see Marcus kneeling beside her, a wooden tray in both hands, a mischievous smile on his lips. He might have slept for twelve uninterrupted hours had she not known better. The bronzed skin was fresh and smooth, the blue eyes merry. He wore a loose pair of white breeches which emphasized his lean body and powerful shoulders.

"Marcus! What hour is it?" Even more than his presence, Luisa was interested in the contents of the tray. "I'm starving!"

He could not resist. "For me? I must confess to being flattered." He put the burden down and started to reach for her. "The food will be cold later but surely love is all."

Luisa looked at him. His face was grave as he examined every line of her slim, nude body which was covered only by her tumbling hair. Her full breasts were only partially hidden; their nipples were rosy and faintly upturned. Her flat stomach, hips, and thighs flowed into each other in a soft roundness that made his manhood shift and rise. Luisa saw it and smiled.

"Feed me first!"

"Alas, for romance." They laughed together and settled down to the riches of breakfast.

There was fresh, warm bread to be spread with rich butter, roasted hare, spicy jam, cool milk, goat cheese and a mild ale. When Luisa expressed wonder at the variety, Marcus said, "We keep animals in the high pastures and some are always in our vicinity, tended by those of us who know such things. Then, too, if the English should penetrate into these fastnesses, we can appear to be simple cave dwellers eking out a meager living. We aren't totally a band of raiders. Some farm, pursue trades, work as scholars, carry on all the businesses of life. We are all ready to fight when we must—that's the only difference."

"There are many women among you?" Luisa could not resist the question even though she knew she ran the risk of being thought jealous. How was Talwis taking what all the camp must know?

"Many. Children, too." He did not elaborate and the laughter did not return to his eyes.

They were silent after that as the food vanished. Luisa could not recall being so hungry for many weeks. She had pulled the fur cloak over her body and soon grew conscious of the chill in the spacious cave. It was still raining steadily for she could hear the drumming sounds and see a tiny portion of the gray sky at the edge of the ceiling. Marcus stoked the fire so that it roared up. She stretched her hands to it gratefully and he came to kneel beside her. Pushing back the curls at her ear, he kissed her softly, the merest touch.

"Do you think me shocking to consider this just after breakfast?" He ran one finger down the side of her neck and around to her collarbone before putting his mouth to her pulse.

Luisa looked at his bent head and the soft dark curls there. She let her hand drift among them and, when he lifted his face to meet her gaze, was faintly astonished to see the expected passion but also a tenderness of such depth it made her tremble.

"I'd not consider it shocking even before breakfast." This was time out of time. She would not quibble about emotions but take what she found and worry later if that must be. "Oh, Marcus, I wish . . ." She did not know what she wished but the poignance of the instant was nearly unbearable. Love was not a word Luisa Marmoor used easily; she had said it to only one or two people in all her twenty years, but she came very close to saying it to Marcus Lenley just then.

He caught her wrist and his full mouth tightened. "No words, Luisa. One can drown in words and their possible meanings. Kiss me."

She put her arms around him, opened her mouth to his, and lay back when he urged it. Her body and flesh were his; her mind and inner spirit were held in abeyance even as Marcus kept his own. Their sharing was more than most people ever had, Luisa thought, as he entered her and the joyous rhythm swept them to completion.

Later, when they lay lazily watching the flickering fire and caressing each other slowly,

Marcus said, "Did you enjoy the Boccaccio I sent you?"

"Very much. I didn't know you sent it. I thought Talwis simply brought it. How did you know I enjoyed such things? Or that I could read at all? Dame Matilda denied that learning for women had any value at all." Luisa turned her head to look up at him.

He gave a devilish grin. "I knew you for a learned lady when we met. Little happens in this camp that I don't know, Luisa. Talwis does what she is told. Those who serve with me do."

"But I'm your prisoner. Does that entitle me to thoughts of my own?" She spoke lightly but there was an undercurrent of seriousness in her tone. Whatever the physical circumstances, she must remain her own person. Had he ordered Talwis to be his mistress? No, no more so than Luisa herself. Women naturally came to so handsome and virile a man as Marcus Lenley.

"Sweet prisoner," he agreed, bending his head to sample her lips and touch her soft breasts.

In a few minutes he rose and walked over to a metal-bound chest. Luisa sat up to watch and was surprised to find it filled with books, a true treasure at any time but even more odd in an outlaw camp. At Marmoor she had counted herself wealthy beyond all reason to have six books; Marcus must have twenty or more.

He came back to sit beside her. A volume of many thick pages in rather bad handwriting was carefully put down on the fur rug. "You have heard of Geoffrey Chaucer, perhaps?"

"Only a little and that in Dame Matilda's talk of the court. He's supposed to have admired John of Gaunt's wife, Blanche, and written a poem about her in English. An admirer of the royal line, I think?" Luisa bent forward to look at the pages, but her mind was on the clean lines of her lover's body as he searched for what had captured his fancy.

"And I thought you a learned lady! Shocking!" He appeared quite earnest as he waved the book toward her. "Remember your experiences on the pilgrimage? Well, listen."

For the next hour Marcus read to Luisa of the pilgrims on journey to Canterbury, of the Knight and his lordly tale, the good wife and her husbands, the cruel husband and his obedient, long-suffering wife, and others of the company. The book from which he read was a hodgepodge of French, plain English, and some Latin for it was an attempted translation that had gone awry. Luisa was delighted and told Marcus so.

"There's so much I don't know about you." She stretched, sighing with contentment.

"Also much you shouldn't know, Luisa." He stared darkly into the fire in one of the mood swings she was beginning to learn he was subject to.

She slipped closer, running her hand through his hair. "Love me." Her instincts told her that this time was precious; she must drain the cup of pleasure while she could. She dared not admit the fact her heart understood all too well: her love for Marcus Lenley was becoming a reality.

His mouth claimed hers for a tantalizing moment before he lifted her chin and looked tenderly into her eyes. "Fairest of women! And the most unpredictable!" When she started to protest, he stopped her with kisses and there was only one reality for them.

They remained in the cave when the rainstorm did not abate, and it added to the feeling of delicious seclusion Luisa felt. Marcus conferred briefly at the door several times but showed no desire to leave. Food, wood for the fire, water for washing, and wine were brought in; except for these minor interruptions they might have existed in a separate world. Their lovemaking was by turns gentle, frenzied, slow paced, and hungry. Each time was a revelation for Luisa and, she sometimes thought, for Marcus as well.

It was during this time that Luisa gained an understanding of what true companionship could be. She and Marcus delved into his books—Greek and Latin texts, theological treatises, romantic poetry, and Welsh folktales—all laboriously copied out by some scholar and carefully kept since. The breadth and scope of her lover's knowledge fascinated Luisa, who knew herself to be educated far beyond the standards of most men. They were not always serious, often playing games, rolling and tumbling like puppies on the fur robes. Music was part of their pleasure when Marcus produced a lute and they sang rollicking ballads, bawdy ditties, love songs. They danced together in the stately movements of an old court pattern and capered in country frolics. Luisa believed she could know Marcus for a lifetime and still be able to discover something new. She hoped he felt the same toward her.

Marcus taught her some of the skills learned from Saracen women during his travels in Outre Mer, as the men of the Lion-Heart's day called those lands. Their experimentation and adaptations sent them into frenzies of laughter and also stirred their passions. Luisa came to a deeper understanding of her feelings for Marcus during the time of their closeness, but she was always conscious of the fact that their idyll must soon end.

Chapter Fourteen
LADY LIONESS

LUISA WOKE AGAIN to find Marcus standing over her, fully dressed in dark green breeches and shirt, dark hair mussed, white teeth flashing in a tantalizing grin. He appeared to be up to some mischief. The hand that was behind his back came to the front and dropped a homespun gown of a tawny, pale shade before her.

"Put this on. I hope it fits. We need to hurry. I'm taking you to the overlook. The rain has stopped and it will be beautiful there."

She moved voluptuously, letting the fur cloak drop from her long, sleek legs. "At this hour?" She could tell it was early. She had hoped the

idyll could continue another few hours, even
another day. She bantered, "It will take me some
time to remove the aches and pains that you
have inflicted upon my body."

"Me? I suppose you had nothing to do with
any of this? You simply endured?" The blue eyes
blazed with laughter, their shadows completely
gone.

"Well . . .," she began to admit, and looked
deeply into his blue eyes.

But he was not to be put off. "Ah, no, seductress. Get up." He pulled her up and dropped
the gown over her head. "That's awful. It must
have been made for someone twice as large as
you."

"You're quite right. I do much better without
it." Luisa made as if to yank it off but he stopped
her with a brief kiss and handed her a length of
cord to go around her waist.

"Hurry, now." Marcus took her hand and
rushed her out into the gray light of the early
morning.

People were abroad in the camp already and
they greeted Marcus with smiles but showed no
interest in Luisa. She smelled cooking meat and
saw some men carrying wood to the fires and
lively children shaking wet branches at each
other. It was foggy and shapes swam up out of
the distance as she looked about. The cool air
was refreshing but Luisa wanted nothing more
than to retreat to the cave once more.

Marcus took another, shorter route to the
overlook. Luisa's leather slippers were too large,
forcing her to go more slowly over the wet rocks

and slippery grass. They kept up a lively banter
as they went. Marcus helped her over the rough
places, his hands lingering at her slender waist
and rising to her uncontained breasts.

It was full morning when they reached their
destination and stood under the spreading
leaves of the huge tree. Marcus spread his cloak
close to the trunk, where the ground was least
wet. Then he led Luisa out onto the overlook.
She gasped at the panorama before them while
he looked at her face and his country by turns.

The great red sun was poised just above the
horizon. The distant mountains gleamed almost
black in their mantles of heavy green. Birds
trilled in the stillness and circled high over them.
Droplets of water on the trees and bushes
flashed rainbow prisms in the brilliance. Pink
and golden flowers wakened to life at their feet.
Wales stretched for miles beyond, through lake
and waterfall and meadow and forest, to the
mountains and the sea.

Marcus pulled Luisa into his arms, kissing her
so fervently her legs went weak and she clung to
him, overwhelmed by his passion and the
beauty around them. Their bodies molded to
each other while their mouths locked. The
heady, sweet fire came more strongly upon
them. Marcus swung Luisa up in his strong,
powerful embrace; seconds later they were
bound together with a passion that grew with
every touch.

"We have celebrated ourselves in front of all
Wales," said Luisa fancifully as she shifted Marcus's head to a comfortable place on her naked

thighs. When she leaned over her breasts bobbed, white and enticing, just out of reach of his mouth.

He captured one of her hands in his big brown one. The tender intensity in his voice made her search his face as he smiled up at her. "Aye, love, so we have. Do you think Aphrodite haunts these glens? Or are you she in mortal guise?"

Luisa was silent. She wanted to fling herself into the cradle of his embrace, vow her love, and hear him declare his. When she looked down at him much of her thoughts stood revealed. She understood this and tried to turn away but his words held her.

"Luisa. There's so very little I can do about the way things are. You deserve all that is good and worthy."

He would say no more but the spell was broken. Luisa, recalling Eve in the garden, drew her gown over her bare flesh while Marcus busied himself with an inspection of the area around the overlook.

Playful banter was safe. Marcus turned, surveyed her minutely, remarking, "I tell you, seductress, that I have had Talwis prepare some gowns for you which will become you far more than the one you now grace. You must wear the thinnest, most low cut of all when we dine together tonight. Who can tell what effect you may have on me?" He gave a low laugh as if to tease her again.

She too could play the game. "You do me great honor, sir. I cannot think what I have done to rise so high in your regard." She reconsidered. "Or perhaps I can."

Marcus picked up a flowering branch, swirled it in her direction, and drew back as she reached for it. Laughing, Luisa caught him by the shoulders and they spun about as children did. Then once more they fused into a hungry embrace, their desire growing until all else faded for them. The poignance of this time left its mark. They worshiped each other while the deepening sunlight dappled their bodies in gold.

Marcus kept Luisa constantly with him in the week that followed. She saw nothing of Edra and Ian but Talwis, cool and correct, fitted her with several gowns of green, tawny, and white. It was Talwis who showed Luisa the stream where the women went to bathe and stayed with her while she did so. She saw to Luisa's needs and never gave another hint of caring about Marcus. Luisa felt with a heightened certainty that Marcus and Talwis had loved in the not-so-distant past. She did not often think about it. Everything paled into insignificance beside the brilliance of her growing feelings for Marcus.

She tramped the woods with him when he went on patrol, waited nearby when he was in council, dined alone with him, swam and hunted and fished in his company. They made love as many times as opportunity presented and still Luisa's bones shivered when she saw him stride toward her. Neither spoke of the future nor its expectations and contradictions.

Now and then Luisa would catch the quizzical eyes of some of the men who conferred with him and fancied she saw hostility there. She would smile and nod in greeting; such gestures were returned with a rectitude unexpected of a band of wilderness raiders. The other women and few children stayed to themselves, content with side glances as well as a few outright stares. Marcus was her enclosed world at this time; she felt so bound to him that he must, of necessity, be so to her.

Early one morning Luisa was walking with Marcus around the periphery of the camp toward the stream. They were going to fish and she would prepare whatever they caught. If nothing bit, they would go hunting after a council meeting he must attend.

"Marcus!" One of his men hailed him. "There is news! The messengers await you and the matter is urgent."

He dropped Luisa's hand. "Damn! I'll have to go." The blue eyes burned into hers. "I'll have to be the warrior again." The carved lips were very near hers but he would not kiss her in the open this way. His face held the look of youth that was so often there since she had come.

"Go and hurry back. I'd not take you from your duty." She was serious, hoping he did not know she would go in her shift through a blasted and burning Wales if he asked.

He smiled. "You are an understanding lady, Luisa."

Luisa stood watching him as he moved away, his tall body fluid and graceful under the blue surcoat and high boots. She knew she had loved him from the beginning, perhaps in an ideal way

as might a maiden, but now she loved with all
the newly awakened passion she possessed.
They had made love only a few hours ago, and
now she wanted him again. Perhaps they would
not fish but just retreat to his cave and explore
their own world of desire, which was always
new and fulfilling. Some part of her mind stood
aside to question the fact that Luisa Marmoor,
the independent and free spirited, whose concern for her estate and the life she had known
was once overwhelming, could so easily be distracted by desire and companionship. Restlessly
she put the thought aside and went back to his
quarters, noticing again that it was as if she were
a shadow for all the attention she was paid.

Edra waited there for her, the brown eyes
alight with pleasure, a heap of delicate silks in
one hand. "I was hoping you'd come soon. Do
you like these colors?" She spread out an irides-
cent rainbow. "We can sew gowns together if
you like. Ian and I have missed you."

"I was with Marcus." Luisa found the idea of
stitching away in the outlaw camp faintly amusing. She had never been good with her needle
and did not care to be. But it would provide an
opportunity for chatter and renewal of their
friendship.

"He's different these past days," Edra later
said guilelessly as she held up several shades of
blue to Luisa's face. "Naturally there have always been women; a man must have them." The
color suffused her smooth skin and one hand
went to her mouth. "Luisa, I didn't mean . . ."

Luisa suddenly felt considerably older than

Edra. "Of course you didn't. Now, how do you think I'd look in red?"

Neither heard the door swing open, but when Marcus spoke Edra's name they both jumped. Luisa started toward him with a little cry of delight. When she saw the hard look on his bronzed face she stopped where she stood. His mouth bore a cynical smile and his eyes were empty.

"What is it, Marcus?" Luisa wondered what could have changed him so within the space of an hour.

"Edra, leave us. I must speak to Lady Marmoor." He gazed beyond Luisa as he made an impatient gesture at Edra.

The other girl dashed past them, forgetting her silks. Marcus fixed his eyes at the lobe of Luisa's ear as he spoke in a flat tone, devoid of all emotion. He might have been reciting a list.

"Urgent messages have arrived from London. Your betrothed offers to pay whatever ransom is asked so long as you are not harmed. He does not demand any assurances about your virgin state. He declares that even though the English are sending forces to further invade Wales, he will do what he can to hold them back until you are set free. Nothing, he states boldly, must place the life of his future wife in jeopardy. Such is his feeling for you that he takes you without dowry. By the Blessed Virgin, you are fortunate in such a man, madam."

"Betrothed? Me?" Luisa was stunned.

"Can you have forgotten so quickly? I have often had occasion to wonder at the memories of womankind. Sir Adam of Wenlock, of course. You didn't mention him to me." The cold gaze locked with hers.

"Marcus, I can explain." She had mentioned Arban and her flight but such had been her repulsion at the thought of his friend and then Father Sebastian's interest in her that she had not spoken of them by name. She had so badly wanted this time apart with Marcus and now it appeared to be her undoing. Eagerly she launched into the tale, the words tumbling over themselves in her haste to make him understand.

Luisa was so intent on what she was saying and the face of Arban returned so vividly to her that it was some few minutes before she realized Marcus had shifted position several times as well as glanced at the door impatiently. She cried, "You're not listening!"

"Of course I am. You have explained yourself at great length. Surely you don't expect me to recite every word back to you?"

"Why have you changed so?" Luisa went toward him, both hands held out in appeal. She could not help herself. "I've never seen Adam of Wenlock! He's nothing!"

"That, at least, is correct." The flat, blue gaze revealed nothing and his tone was almost bored. "You lied by omission, madam. You have associated with dangerous persons in high places. Arban, as you know, is a spymaster for the king. Father Sebastian seeks heretics and has a royal decree to burn them. Lady Barthampton would have a plot while she breathes and even Queen

Joanna is embroiled in them. Your betrothed is of their stamp."

"I have nothing to do with those people!" She heard the anguished entreaty in her voice and knew the bitterness of this terrible moment.

Marcus started toward the door, then turned back. For her he had laid himself bare, but now he knew he could never let her know how very much he cared at times; that would be his sure undoing. His resolve strengthened. No woman must be allowed to deflect him from the Welsh cause. "Your betrothed wants you but he also desires our deaths. We have word that he is urging King Henry to savage measures in retaliation for what was done to Lady Barthampton and her entourage. He hopes to trade with us for you, thinking we'll remain here. The army is assembled close to the border and has gathered there while I tarried with you!"

Luisa's head went up. She spoke as coldly as he. "What will you do now that you are convinced of my perfidy?"

"My men say that I have had the pleasure of you. I should take the ransom, kill you, and send your body in pieces to Adam of Wenlock. Then we can do as Welshmen have always done against the invader—fight and retreat to the mountains." One corner of his mouth turned up in a cynical grin.

"Try it and be damned, Marcus Lenley. I doubt not that you have slain many women! You'll not find it easy to conquer Luisa Marmoor, I can tell you!" Courage and anger whipped her color high; the Marmoor temper returned in full measure. Her own proud heritage rang in her voice as she challenged him.

Marcus smiled in what appeared to be genuine amusement. "But I have, madam. I have. Did you not lie near to weeping in my arms a short while past as you wanted more of my kisses? Swords can be redundant, can't they?" He went to the door and called for the guard. "Watch her closely. She is not to leave this area."

They stared at each other across the ashes of their passion and for both there was no leavening.

Chapter Fifteen
DECREE OF THE COUNCIL

LUISA LOOKED AROUND the ring of grim faces and saw no mercy there. The partially covered fire threw long shadows over them while the encircling rock walls pressed down. Overhead the night sky was overcast. The breeze was chilly, bringing with it scents of more rain. Distant noises from the rest of the camp filtered over the ridge to her ears. Marcus stood apart from the eleven men of his council, his dark visage impassive and his eyes sweeping past her as though she were not present. A black-robed priest stood beside him. She felt her legs shake. Did they mean to dispatch her this night?

It had been a long, agonizing night and day since Marcus had changed toward her. No person had entered the quarters since his departure. Some food and drink were left at the door but she could not bring herself to eat. At first she had wanted to fling herself down in a storm of tears but if she did so it would be impossible to stop. Her very life was at stake, she thought painfully, and all she could think about was Marcus. She did not believe she had done anything so awful in what she had failed to tell him. How he had come to alter so drastically within the space of an hour with neither reason nor justification she could not understand. Perhaps their time together had been only a dalliance to him, all the more pleasurable because she was a virgin and easily cozened. Reason and speculation went round in her head until madness seemed preferable. Marcus haunted her nightmares during the brief time she managed to nap.

In the slow, dragging hours of the night Luisa's core of strength asserted itself. Her passionate interlude with Marcus was over and now she must try to survive. Her heart might be torn but she had her wits, a sharp mind, and powerful will. She must use them. With that decision her hurt abated a little and she was able to think, even if her flesh did not cease to ache for the man she had once believed she loved.

"Woman, you are summoned!"

The harsh call brought Luisa back to the moment. The white-bearded old man in his long dark robes seemed like a druid out of an ancient ritual as he paced slowly toward her. She did not move, allowing him to come the short distance. His fellows muttered among themselves and watched her all the more keenly.

"You have been summoned here to hear the sentence and command of this council. After it has been passed the holy father yonder will hear your confession. You are judged to be a menace to our plans. If kept prisoner you would impede us; if released you would tell all you know to the English. There is no choice as regards our ruling. The matter is clear."

"Not so, Lord Councillor." Luisa's clear voice sliced through his as she stepped forward so that she stood directly in front of him. The wind moved the silken draperies of her red gown over her slender body and molded them to her. She had bound her chestnut hair in a coronet of braids around her head and left it bare. She knew her profile was pure in the flickering light. "Surely the persecuted do not seek to persecute! Are you men of England, with perfidious English ways, or are you true, honorable men of Wales? The justice you offer is not justice but savagery!"

"Silence the woman!"

"Give the sentence and let it be carried out!"

"Get on with it, Drar!"

The cries circled Luisa. Drar reached out a hand to take her but she spread both arms, well knowing how the full sleeves fell back from her rounded flesh in the gesture. "Hear me, Welshmen! You have already spent much time in debate! Let Luisa Marmoor, a victim of King Henry V and his policies, speak!'' She paused and looked at them in turn. ''What is there to lose?''

Luisa looked toward Marcus but he was gone. Had he known what was to happen to her and departed, unable to face an act he might have stopped? The priest was there, his face a pale wedge in the darkness. She ordered herself to forget everything else except the dangerous drama that must be played out.

''What, indeed?''

''Let her get it over with.''

These and other grumblings came to Luisa, who did not move or bend before those who glared accusingly at her. ''A modicum of justice, men of Wales!'' Her voice, trained in song at the convent, had never been able to carry tunes to any degree, but it was strong and she could project it, mimic people and animals, and lower it to deep softness. She did so now and every man heard the planned tremble as she said, ''Drar? Surely you have doubts as to the wisdom of this?''

The old man looked at the young woman in all her fearful pride. ''Speak and be quick about it! We'll not tolerate ramblings and tears!''

Luisa, who had wept more in this camp in a few days than she had in years at Marmoor, spoke scornfully. ''We of the Marmoor line—I am the last—do not weep. We act!''

She wanted these men to see her as a person, a proud bearer of a once-great name, who suffered even as they did. Not a useless hostage or erstwhile mistress of their leader, nor yet an insignificant woman, but an Englishwoman imperiled and fighting. If she could make one or two doubt, some time was bought. She had no idea of what to do beyond delaying tactics and a hope that Marcus would intervene. Yet, if that were his intention he surely would have done so before now. She would not submit blindly to fate; it was possible that her scheme had some remote possibility of success. Chin lifted, with no sign of the fear she felt, Luisa began her struggle.

"My estate, my Marmoor, was won in battle and honor on the fields of the Crusade when my ancestor pleased the Lion-Heart and received it as a token of the royal favor." Her words rang out with all the sincerity and power she possessed. To lose their interest would be fatal. For those who cared little for rights and wanted only to get the unsavory business over, Luisa moved back and forth, using the motion of her body to hold their attention. Marmoor's story unfolded and with it a picture of England and her people who, much like these men, were honest and decent folk who tried to live and carry on their ways without interference.

Although the winds were cool, the palms of her hands were damp and there were beads of sweat on her upper lip as well as her hairline. A pale moon was slipping down the sky. There was a rumble of thunder in the east as lightning flickered faintly.

"You think, you who sit out in the council and pass judgment on me, that what has happened to Marmoor and those who have loved it, has nothing to do with Wales and the struggle here! It is everything! If tyranny is endured one place, will it not flourish in another? It is better to stand and fight!"

Luisa's battling words conveyed her true feelings and the council's men reacted to the tale of the dwindling estate, the efforts to hold what was hers, the determination of the king's men to take it, and, briefly, her own escape and the final fate of Marmoor. It was the violation of the ancient right of the landholder, the possession of the earth, which outraged these men and Luisa's words touched many of them.

At the end Luisa stood very still, the wind moving in her silken clothes, the pain and loss apparent for all to hear, and spoke, not in flaming words but in the simplest ones of all. "I was reared there. I love it with all that is within me. It was taken from me. My body and my life were to be placed at barter. Who among us would kneel to ask for more of the same? If all this has rendered me worthy of injustice by king or outlaws or even God in His heaven then, by all things holy, His very word is misinterpreted!"

The sound of her voice died away on the breeze. They were not to know that the loss of Marcus was intermingled in her pain. Love was a rare enough thing to most people, she knew, and marriage was no more than a practical business. Some form of love had touched her; it might be all she would ever know, particularly since her very life was in the hands of the men before her.

The time of their decision was upon her. Drar approached, his face unreadable in the shifting light. Her gaze went round the circle and saw the others were equally impassive. Where was Marcus? How long had she held the outlaws by her tale?

"You are eloquent, madam. Many in this land have died, been burned out, seen their families slaughtered. Do you really think we mean to risk bringing down the full might of the English upon us before we are fully prepared for a war? We delay and delay again. By the time they find you have paid the price, we shall have some of their gold and know their plans." He whirled to face the others. "Let us proceed!"

Luisa cried, "I have not finished! You have women in your band; let me join you! I can write to Sir Adam of Wenlock, tell him I am safe and well and I have chosen this life of my own accord!" She thought wildly that this was a mad thing to say. That would surely not stop him. And how could she exist around Marcus after what had happened between them? He had made life bloom for her; she was in his debt for that. But she wanted to buy time, divide the council if possible, and beyond, to keep her very existence.

"Madness!"

"What she says has truth in it!"

"Adam of Wenlock will destroy us all! Word has it that he raises an army equal to that of the king himself!"

Luisa forced herself to remain quiet as the men huddled together, more to keep her from hearing what was going on than because of any real disagreement. She saw the priest look around and then go behind the tall rock. Drar's voice rose up over all the others, "No! It is devil spawned! I will not allow it." Someone younger spoke in Welsh and again in English. "No!" the babble of cries went higher. Luisa knew she had cause to be thankful for the power she had temporarily exercised over them. Surely they would not proceed against her without the full consent of all?

The priest appeared suddenly at the edge of the fire and held out his hands for silence. He was a tall, imposing man with black hair touched with white, his tonsure gleaming in the light. His shoulders were broad although one sloped slightly on the left. He carried a long stave in one hand.

"Men of the council! You cannot agree, therefore your past decision is invalid. Lady Marmoor, I have heard your words and know that you wish to live most dearly. We of this band committed to Welsh freedom must follow the course ordained for us. I, Father Peter, ask you this question: Will you obey the directions given you?" The deep voice rang across the others and halted them completely. Faces turned to watch him while heads nodded.

"I will. I swear it before Mary, Mother of God, the saints, and the Lord Christ, even to the Father Almighty." It was a great oath and Luisa crossed herself as she said it. Life held a high price.

"Is this agreeable to you?" He faced the council.

Only Drar hesitated and glanced about. Some of them nodded as the priest continued. Luisa watched avidly, thankful for the decisive voice which had finally emerged. He addressed them all.

"This woman will write the letter to Sir Adam of Wenlock as she has said. We will go deeper into the mountains and wait as Glendower taught us. But, and this is the most important, so that no pursuit may be undertaken due to the possibility of the lady being under duress, a marriage will take place this night before us all between Luisa Marmoor and Marcus Lenley. Word will be circulated of this in Wenlock's territory and in London. Another priest will perform the ceremony here and testify to its validity before Wenlock. Further, when the Lady Marmoor writes to Sir Adam, her happiness will be of sufficient detail to convince him."

There was total silence in the council. Luisa was dumbfounded. She had thought of marriage as bondage when Arban made his hideous proposal. Later she had foolishly dreamed of Marcus in that status, thinking of them both as deeply loving and ready to share themselves with each other. She was now ashamed of the glorious delight which had lifted momentarily in her heart. Proud Luisa Marmoor yearning to remain with and even wed a man who scorned her? Yes, she decided, if that were the means to continue living.

Drar said, "Is this the will of Marcus? Why do you speak for him, priest? Let us hear from him in the matter!"

Almost as if he had been waiting for the right moment, Marcus came toward them. Another priest, small and pale, walked by his side. Luisa was careful to keep her own face impassive as she looked at them. Marcus was scowling; his dark, bronzed countenance bore deep lines of bitterness. He did not do this willingly. It was something necessary in order to keep the faith of his men, serve his cause, and whatever else might plague the soul of this leader who had faced a hard battle just now. Luisa had battled for her life against nearly overwhelming odds and she had won. Only a fool would doubt it had been worth it.

Marcus said, "It is my will. Lady Marmoor has stated that she is willing. Let us get to the business. I have much work and little time in which to do it." His tones were flat and hard. His eyes were deep set and sunken. He was tightly reined, his control rigidly held. She must not know the power of his feeling for her. He did not trust her and he knew he didn't trust himself where she was concerned.

There was no personal word for Luisa, no glance of recognition. She could have been anyone, a stranger, a bare acquaintance, an alien. The small priest stared around at the glowering council, which now knew better than to question Marcus and motioned for him to stand near Luisa. Marcus moved as though in a deep sleep and, at a whispered instruction, took her cold hand in his. She attempted a half smile and was horrified at his response. The glittering gaze held unfathomable hatred.

The priest gabbled hurriedly in Latin. Luisa knew the language, of course, as every educated person did, but she barely understood the holy words because of his speed. When he paused in one place she made the response of willingness and Marcus did the same. In another breath, they were wed. Marcus now held complete power over her life.

"Summon the camp. I will meet them with my bride. They may rejoice this night. Tomorrow we move on." Marcus snapped the orders out. "Come, wife. We have much to celebrate." His grin was wolfish, his grip iron hard on her arm.

Luisa said, "That is true, my lord husband." She saw the grin widen and knew that her bondage had begun. She was Luisa Marmoor still and she would survive.

Chapter Sixteen
DAILY BREAD

"YOU CANNOT BLAME me for what has happened, Marcus." Luisa faced him in their quarters, her eyes bright with unshed tears. He had not spoken a direct word to her since they left the council meeting but had pulled her along as though she were a prisoner desirous of escape. After the men had assembled as he had ordered, he announced the fact of his marriage. The priest was to depart to see Adam of Wenlock the next morning. Their own camp was to be abandoned soon afterward. Then he had stalked away, Luisa in his wake, the excited, curious, and hostile voices of his men in their ears. Now they stood poised on the edge of their own battle in a place which had once held such happiness.

"I do not blame you. Certain measures were needed." He stood before her, unfastening the lacings of his shirt with a casual manner. He clipped off his words precisely. "Come." One hand reached out to her shoulder, missed, and slipped down the silken sleeve. Angered, he jerked his arm and the whole gown ripped free.

Luisa cried, "There's no need to act this way! I don't believe I was unreceptive to you in times past!"

Her words were choked off as he seized her wrist in a firm grip and drew her to him. The brilliant blue eyes were nearly slate gray with repressed fury. His black brows winged upward and his scowl was ferocious. Not a trace remained of the once-gentle lover; this was a man she had never known. She thought fleetingly of the scriptural injunction against demons. One seemed to occupy his body now! Her own anger flared.

"You're hurting me! Why must you behave so? One would think you an ignorant clod!"

The stinging words made one corner of the mobile mouth turn upward in a travesty of amusement. His lips pulled back from his white teeth, an oddly feral expression. "Not another word. I have had my fill of emotions. You have one use and one only. Let us get to it." Marcus hoped she would fight him. He fought himself and something in him wanted to blame her. Love and hate struggled in his mind every time he saw her. Luisa was not a person to show fear, but he wanted to make her afraid. He wanted to care for her freely. She was his wife, bound to him now. Perhaps that would put an end to their conflict. The old frustrating anger battled with tenderness as he reached for her with demanding fingers.

Luisa opened her mouth to speak despite his order, but he pushed her to the floor, pulled the shift from her, and then performed the act of possession as casually as though she were a doxy from the street. He simply released his feeling in one forceful act and stood up to leave. Luisa lay before him; she was temporarily battered down in loss and humiliation. Wisdom told her that his reaction was far more complicated than she knew; it was not Luisa herself but events and emotions far greater. She was only the catalyst. With this realization, Luisa understood that submission was the role she had to play this night. The latent savagery in Marcus was rising and his pain must have an outlet.

"You know your master, is that it?" He bent over her, as if daring her to challenge him.

Every nerve within her readied itself for response but she resisted and remained still, her slim body smooth and supple on the pallet. When Luisa thought of the earlier tenderness they had shared and the terrible finality of the act he had just accomplished, she wanted to scream aloud. She was far from tears, though; she was alive and at the present that was enough. Now pride was not so important. She said nothing.

"Well." His repetition was itself an insult. "This may turn out to be a singularly dull marriage." His voice sharpened derisively on the last word. He stood again, adjusted his clothes, gave her one final stare, and strode to the door, slamming it behind him.

Luisa thanked the instinct that had protected her from violent expression. Marcus was near to murder. Pity for him twisted in her. What she felt was far from the consuming emotion in their halcyon days so short a time ago, but feeling lingered on and it would take little to stir it again.

She rose, unutterably weary, pulled a fur cloak over herself, and tumbled down on the couch where they had so often loved. Nightmares stalked her sleep.

When Luisa woke it was with a sense of heaviness and foreboding. She told herself sternly that her life had been given back, largely due to her own efforts, and she must now accept whatever came until some plan for the future presented itself. Acceptance of her situation must include extreme care with Marcus as well. She sat up, shifting her heavy hair back, and wondered what she could wear. A rumble in her stomach reminded her that it had been long since she had eaten.

Just then the door was thrust open and Talwis came in. She had a subdued look on her face and her eyelids were puffy. "You are to sign this letter immediately. After that is done clothing will be provided for you. We move out within the hour. You must be ready."

Luisa said, "We go into the depths of the mountains?"

"Yes." She shot Luisa a cold stare. "I go to another village."

Luisa wondered if Marcus had given specific orders for Talwis because she had been his mistress and he now intended to indulge in joyless demands on the wife he had taken so unwillingly. Why had he done so if he cared so little? She had no illusions about the treatment a lone woman would receive at the hands of a band of outlaws, but she did not think they were disobedient to a leader's expressed command.

It was time to assert herself. She drew the furred cloak over her bare shoulders and rose. "I will read the letter now. Where is it? Also I am very hungry. Is there food?" She was slightly ashamed of her haughty tone, but she understood quite well that Talwis was disgruntled, meaning to say things to Luisa she dared not to Marcus.

"I will get food but you will not read the letter." Faint incredulity was in her voice as her eyes swept up and down Luisa's form, not missing the shadows under her eyes and bruises at her neck. "There is no need. The messenger awaits and Marcus has already decreed the contents."

"Bring it." Luisa's chin went up. "I must see if

the words are properly chosen. I believe I have more knowledge of these matters than some." Let Talwis tell Marcus what she had said! She would assert herself as best she could.

Talwis met her stare coolly, then reached into the bag she carried and brought out the parchment. Writing materials followed. Luisa ignored her as she began to read. A moment later the door closed heavily.

"I, Luisa Marmoor, choosing this life and the course of my own will, do this day declare that I am the wife of Marcus Lenley of England and Wales and repudiate . . ." The sentences ran on in declaration, explanation, and flat determination. No man alive would believe it had been written by a woman following her heart, a woman giving up what must be considered an illustrious marriage for love. Sir Adam of Wenlock, unless he were very much a fool, would surely think she wrote under duress and be all the more angered against the Welsh and their supporters.

She crumpled the sheet and threw it down. Then, thinking better of it, she began to unfold it and shaped her own thoughts in swift phrases which might buy them all a little time.

"Here is food and the other things you need. Have you signed?" Talwis entered and gasped as she saw what Luisa was doing. "You cannot!"

Luisa glanced up. "Please bring more parchment. I am rewriting this letter."

Talwis ran out as Luisa started for the meat pasties, brown bread, and weak ale. She was surprised at how good the food tasted. Her brief show of independence made her feel much better; she knew she was right in her objectons and as soon as Talwis returned with the parchment she would work out a far better version.

The girl seemed to be taking a long time, and Luisa could do little more until she had writing materials so she washed her face in the water provided and wound her hair back on her neck in a coil of braids. Crude leather shoes, suitable for hard walking, and a coarse shift as well as a dark green gown of homespun had been furnished. There was even a brown cloak. These were nothing like the silks and delicate fabrics over which she and Edra had rejoiced but that had been in another life.

"Just what do you think you are doing, madam?" The freezing voice rang out, making her jump. Marcus, clad all in brown, a bow on his back and a heavy knife at his side, the cold blue eyes savage, strode in and stood close to her. "How dare you send such a message? I have given orders. You will not flout them, do you hear? Or can it be that you think you stand high in this band? Do you, perhaps, believe you can render leadership? Must I take valuable time to give you a lesson in obedience before taking you into the interior of Wales and leaving you in a remote village with guards?" His bronzed fingers clenched with his effort to hold still.

Luisa did not move. "Marcus, the feeling you have toward me should be no part of this. The letter to Sir Adam is a Welsh defense which anyone might say had been dictated to a frightened girl. I doubt Arban would have told him of my hatred of such a marriage." She shook her head at his cynical glare. "Nor does it matter if you believe me. I know the truth. Better to let Wenlock think I was abducted and fell in love and am silly over it. He will be the more angered, of course, but will think of ways to tend his vanity before setting out to war. That gives us more time."

"Us?" He said the word with suspicion.

"Yes, whether you like it or not." How was he taking her boldness? She must not fight him over matters of the flesh but what of policy? He was a dangerous man but he had saved her life in the end. She was right and she knew it. Could he be convinced? She bent and held out the beginnings of her letter. "Read and then judge."

Marcus gave her a scorching glance but did as she suggested. *Although greatly mindful of the overwhelming honor you have offered me in the gift of your most noble name and person, yet am I torn with pain beyond all telling when I say that all the loves of the ballads are nothing in comparison to what I now feel for the man who is my husband. I pray you in your Christian charity and much-vaunted generosity to pursue no longer the course once set for the seal set upon me and my husband is not to be broken by God's law.* . . . His mouth quirked downward. "By all the saints, madam, it says nothing! This is the babble of a romantic girl!"

"Exactly." Luisa leaned toward him earnestly. "That is what Wenlock, too, will think. He is rejected for an outlaw chieftain. It is a personal thing. Nothing can keep him from seeking revenge, but his vanity, as I have said, will need flourishing first. Your letter was a manifesto. Mine is a girl's letter and therefore to be believed."

Marcus looked at her and down at the letter again. There was no expression on his face. "You shall write as you wish. I also. The versions shall be compared and the best sent. Do not attempt to advise me, madam. No woman rules here."

Luisa wanted to make a quick retort but something warned her that this was unwise. Palpable anger pulsed from him although he tried to hide it.

He said, "You have met Wenlock or are his spy. I think you will tell me the truth in the not-so-distant future when I have time to deal with you properly. Can you be so lacking in sense as to think I would follow instructions you give?"

Luisa felt as though he had slapped her face, but the pride of the Marmoors held her steady. "Then consult with your council. They will tell you."

Red stained his cheeks and receded, leaving him white under the bronzed tan. "I have no more to say, madam. You are yet prisoner here and, as you ought to know, serve only a woman's purpose." He lifted a questioning eyebrow and gave her a cruel smile.

"The letter is policy. It has nothing to do with you and me." She did not intend to acknowledge his cruelty although the pain twisted deep inside her heart and mind. Had he come to hate her? Her own resolve hardened and with it came determination to survive even his hatred.

He laughed, a sharp bark that barely moved the corners of his mouth. "Women are all emotion. Spare me more of yours lest I drown in it." He went out as quickly as he had entered.

Luisa was left to wait. She had no regrets for what she had done and she now must try to think of strategy for the future. There was no illusion left for her, only bleak reality.

A short while later the door opened again and a burly, dark-haired man leaned in. "Come, Mistress. It is time to go. The camp is breaking up. I'll be near you as we march." He waited for her to pass.

Luisa knew this was one of her guards. She gave him a gracious smile and went out into the cloudy, damp morning. The camp was bustling about and columns of men stood waiting, poised in three directions. Some of the women were still gathering supplies, loading them on pack animals. The looks that drifted over were incurious and dismissing.

She saw Talwis approaching and maintained the smile. It should not be said she was ungracious or sullen. The other woman's face was calm as always but her eyes held surprise.

"Here is the letter. Sign, if you will." She handed Luisa the rolled parchment, retaining the quill until it should be required.

Luisa scanned the ponderous phrases which must have been penned by Marcus. They contained most of what she had written but the words were scattered around in such a way that they could not possibly represent a cipher or give a secret message of any type. Sir Adam would be confounded by the respect and admiration she seemed to have. A grin came to her mouth as she signed with a flourish. Marcus had given heed to her advice. What might she next win?

"Lady." Talwis was now so close to her that Luisa could see the bewildered loss in her face and the fine lines under her eyes, which had not been there at first. "I would ask a favor."

"Of me?" Luisa was startled. "How can I do anything for you?"

The damp wind made them both shiver. A child began to cry piteously close by. The tramp of marching feet began and Luisa's guard shifted from one foot to another as he watched the women.

"It is not for myself. Rather, for Marcus. Be gentle, I beg you, wth his heart." She stared earnestly at Luisa.

Luisa did not pretend to misunderstand. "I do not have any portion of his caring, Talwis. His pleasure is in cruelty now."

"Love and hate are always mixed in him. Do not allow hate to triumph or it will destroy him utterly." Her pain was wrenching to see.

Luisa put out her hand. "I will have a care for him. I promise."

Talwis did not take it but tears welled into her eyes. An instant later she dashed away, leaving Luisa to wonder at their strange encounter.

Chapter Seventeen

HEARTLAND

LUISA DUG HER fingers into the rock crevices, moved her toes to another, and dared to look down. The tiny trail was nearly invisible as it twisted among bushes, flowers, and rocks covering the mountainside. A faint cloud of mist floated to one side and purple peaks glittered in the distance. She saw movement far below; it was a shepherd tending some sheep. When she tilted her head, she could see the huge outcroppings of dark rock above. They had been climbing for hours and her arms were aching, but a powerful, exhilarating feeling came over her as she tested her body and won. She held her own on the wilderness trails, slept in the open, and ate their often-coarse food without faltering. She had been the recipient of stares at many times and had thought how curious they might be if they knew how much of this march was ease itself compared to her life at Marmoor. She felt the perspiration drip down her back and wondered how long before they paused for the early meal.

Luisa moved on slowly as the woman behind her took her own place. They had been traveling for four days and nights. She felt all the more strange because there had been no contact with Marcus; perhaps he did not even move with this particular branch of the outlaws. She remembered the indignity of their last bedding and tried to convince herself she did not care. It was little use. These days she was ignored by everyone except for Huw, the guard who stayed close always. Luisa was beginning to realize that although she missed the passion and delight of her earlier relationship with Marcus, she also missed even more strongly the friendship they had shared. She had never been able to speak casually with the people of Marmoor and the village, nor even to exchange badinage with the pilgrims. She had won her life with the council but these people left her severely alone. Efforts to talk to Huw had resulted in some comments in Welsh and a deal of head shaking. She felt he secretly understood her English but Luisa did not press the issue.

They finally reached the surface of the mountain and took shelter in the copse on top. Luisa pushed her hair back from her face, wondering how far they were going and what her own destination was to be. As she nibbled on black bread and knelt to sip from the tiny spurting stream that tumbled on down the mountain, she knew she must begin to make a place for herself with the people. She often thought of how deeply she longed for the friendship that had begun with Edra and Ian but when she asked Huw about them, he simply shrugged and walked on.

She began to revel in the cold morning mists, the burning heat of noon when the brilliant skies seemed to press close, the peaks and gorges and icy streams, flowering hills, and secret paths. Marmoor was lost and England no longer her country. Wales and its freedom became more and more a symbol to Luisa. She must believe in something. This was a good cause and certainly a reasonable one.

Several more days passed. During this time they were joined by Huw's wife, Elmina, whose rotund body and sharp black eyes nearly matched his. Luisa asked her about Ian and Edra but she merely shrugged. These two were constantly about Luisa and she thought of protesting but to whom? In the end she bided her time with grace.

When the band divided for a final time, Luisa was among those who went deep into the woods of the high mountains where a small village lay. There were rude huts with walls of wood and clay, and a few of stone. She was given one slightly apart. Huw remained outside and Elmina brought her a bed of branches and food. Her expression never changed as she served Luisa.

Each day some of the men went out in a party, leaving early and returning late. Luisa envied them their freedom but by now she would have found any work welcome. The few women were always baking, cooking, spinning, and seeing to the weapons of their men. She had offered help but they looked past her. Even the children dashed away. Was she possessed of the evil eye? When she tired of sitting outside the hut or lying inside recalling the happy times with Marcus, she walked in the area around the village with Huw close behind. He never challenged her but those hard eyes were as good as a knife at her back.

Marcus had not appeared since the day of their departure. She tried to tell herself she was glad, but her heart still yearned for the sight of him. Was this virtual imprisonment and isolation his punishment for failing to tell him of Arban, for daring to try to save her own life? If this was to be her fate in the future, Luisa determined again that she would not be treated lke an outsider or a weak woman. The women of the outlaws were few but she saw they were self-sufficient, well able to ride, hunt, defend themselves, and watch a trail. They practiced these things daily in addition to the womanly work they did. Why should Luisa Marmoor not do this and more?

"I know you understand me, Huw. Doubtless you have reasons for your silence. Be that as it may I have nothing to do, as you well know. I know something of weaponry and I want to learn more. Ask among the men for me so that one may be found to teach me." She walked up to him and planted her fists on her hips. Green eyes met black ones and neither yielded. "I will demand this until you do as I wish. And I have another wish. I wish to increase my knowledge of Welsh. Find someone to do that."

He shifted uneasily, looking beyond her. She moved in front of his gaze and stayed there. He made as if to walk away and she strode with him.

"Answer me!" The roar was the same that had once made the villagers of Marmoor rush to obey. Even now people were looking up curiously.

"You are safe here. No need to do anything." He bit the words out, flushing as he did so.

Elmina had come up, her heavy features working, one hand raised in what might have been a threatening gesture. She looked at Huw commandingly but said nothing.

Luisa thought they had been given their orders by Marcus. She was to be ostracized, allowed to languish in boredom and loneliness. But Luisa Marmoor was not one to live that way. Her boldness had worked once; now she would see if it worked again. If so, well and good. Even failure would bring a cessation of boredom.

"A band such as this cannot afford to have one person who does nothing. Each person must be prepared to defend the others. The day is not far when Wales will need all those who care about freedom! The time when the sword is once more lifted against Lancaster cannot be far away. All know my history, I believe. My native land took everything from me and pursued me when I rebelled. I do not ask this in the name of your leader who made me his wife. I ask this most simple thing in the name of us all!" Her clear voice rang out over them as she stood, hands held in front of her, old brown gown swinging around her ankles, chestnut hair tumbling over her shoulders. She had invoked Marcus and Wales and curiosity. What was left? Challenge! "Let one come forward who will teach me the skills of survival in these mountains! Let him or her come to me in my hut!" She turned from the fairly small group that had begun to gather and strode toward that sanctuary.

It seemed a very long time until Elmina thrust her head in the curtain which served as a door and remarked ungraciously in excellent English, "On the morrow at five of the clock under the oak."

Luisa's voice was cool as she said, "I thank you." Their eyes met and clashed before the older woman turned away.

That night she tossed on her bed, and try as she might to turn her mind away from Marcus she could not. In the daylight hours it was easy enough to marshal her defenses and stoke her anger at the way she had been treated. At times in the dark stillness she wept into her hands and recalled the words of Talwis. Evidently Marcus had revealed something of himself to her; Luisa knew her concern for him was utterly sincere. Yet he had callously sent Talwis elsewhere after flaunting his new woman before her and making her a serving maid. Wife or not, Luisa vowed he would never do that to her. She struggled against vulnerability, the recollected passion, and was determined on her course.

"I am Walter and my time is extremely valuable." The tall, slender man was in his early forties. Expressive dark eyes checked Luisa and found her wanting. "Have you nothing suitable to wear? How do you expect to work in that garb?" His resentment at teaching her was plain.

Luisa had wondered the same thing but she did not want to push Elmina too far. Later today if this went well she would ask for boy's clothes. For now she simply pulled the skirt of her dress through her legs and fastened it at her belt. She rolled the sleeves high and glanced at Walter. His face was red but something approaching laughter was in his dark gaze.

"Will this do?" She spoke in English as he did. Did everyone here speak her native tongue? Marcus must have cautioned them well against any dealings with her. It was surprising they disobeyed him even to this extent.

Walter strode toward her and handed over a light sword of a material that could be none other than Damascus steel. The handle and grip were of pure gold. "My lady is bored and must be accommodated, is that it? I was told you have a smooth tongue. Does it extend to your sword hand?" He lifted his own heavier sword and smiled goadingly.

"I come to learn, sir. Somehow I think you must be a master." Luisa Marmoor could be charming when she chose and her own smile caressed him softly. "I want to be able to defend myself and others when the need comes. Does that speak of a bored lady in her solar?"

His answer was a swift movement of the sword so that it rested on her chest. Her motion was as quick as his when she whirled, moving toward his face with her blade.

"*En garde*, Walter!"

"Just so, madam!"

So began some of the most grueling days of Luisa's life.

She learned the art of swordsmanship, the use of the dagger, and much of archery as well as all the abilities required for twisting, tumbling, and enduring. At first she told herself she did all this to remove her mind from her essential predicament, but she soon came to realize that all the cajolery of her speech had been true and remained so. What was left for her but this band? The strain of pulled muscles, an aching back, and a throbbing head were most effective in banishing any thoughts of passion.

Walter came from his first reluctance to work with her into an acceptance that never took verbal form. He found more and more for her to do, setting exercises and feats to be performed endlessly until he deemed them correct enough for one day. Each day her arrows came closer to the bull's-eye, her use of various daggers became smoother, and her swordplay easier. Summer day poured into summer day as Luisa found release in physical action, forgetting all else.

Walter set her tasks of running and climbing, ordering her about as freely as he might any apprentice in some other existence. An older man curiously like him called Ned often watched and spoke to her, first in English, then Welsh. He never seemed to tire of correcting her pronunciations, growing gleeful when her tongue would not curve around the words. He and Walter were giving her invaluable lessons in survival but she found herself longing for friendship. They never exchanged a trivial word with her; all was concerned with the business at hand.

One afternoon at twilight Luisa pulled her exhausted body onto her bed and found there a folded, sealed parchment. It appeared unopened. She knew questions to Elmina or Huw would prove useless. Slowly she opened the sheet and read in the rounded, uncertain handwriting more hope of a future than she had considered possible a few scant weeks before.

*Luisa, I do not believe all the tales that are
going around about you and neither does Ian. He
and I won't be separated so we are going to join
a section of the band that travels deeper into the
hills. We're certain to see you. It is said you wed
Marcus by tricks, that you're a witch, a spy, and
not a true convert to Welsh liberty. We're eager
to see and talk with you. This note is sent by a
friend whom you will not see. Soon, our friend.*

Edra's name was slashed down the rest of the
page.

Luisa was unashamed of the tears that
filmed her eyes. The loneliness she had experienced since coming to the Welsh land lay more
heavily on her than she had ever imagined. At
Marmoor she had had Dame Matilda, who
lived in the past a great deal but was always
ready to explain the ways of a proper maiden
to Luisa. And there were always people to exchange an idle word or to laugh with, a dog or
a child with whom to play, the beloved acres
to watch and worry over. If she had been Luisa
Marmoor, lady and chatelaine, heiress of a
powerful family, she had also been friend and
worker to those few directly involved in her
estate. Now she felt truly alone.

She shook her head impatiently, rose, and
walked outside the hut in the misty near-dark-
ness. Huw looked up alertly and sank back down
to continue his low-voiced conversation with Elmina. Small fires burned before several of the
other dwellings. Men hunched down murmuring as a woman or two passed by. She heard the

ring of sword on sword from several directions. These outlaws never missed a chance to work on their skills. Luisa admired this for their lives were continually in danger. Hers was also, she supposed, but in some ways her fate was worse. Her body was not even her own in the eyes of the English officials.

There was a flash of flame and gold across the evening sky just where the brilliant first star had begun to glow. It was almost answered by another, which crisscrossed the lower end. Luisa wondered if these were signals or warnings. The air was charged with heat and power, giving off the feeling that came before a thunderstorm. Another rose again in the west and this time one of the men called out an excited question in Welsh to one of his neighbors. Luisa could not understand the answer, but the note of heaviness in it weighed on her heart.

Loss and self-pity and uncertainty for the future made her do a thing she seldom did. Approaching Huw and Elmina, she demanded abruptly in the voice Lady Luisa Marmoor had used to the king's officials, "What was that? What is happening? Tell me."

Elmina spoke in a high, shaky rush of sound very different from her usual matter-of-fact monosyllables. "The seer comes soon! He knows the future. He can tell it!"

The three stared at each other. Superstition it might be, but Luisa felt the goose pimples slip over her flesh while the darkness came down and another flare tore the sky.

Chapter Eighteen
DREAM SLAYER

"Now we shall see what you have learned."
Walter rested the tip of his sword lightly on the
ground and fastened his dark eyes on Luisa's
perspiring face. The midmorning sun blazed
down on them. There was no hint of a breeze in
the green clearing where they stood.

Luisa's body felt heavy and clumsy as she
mopped her forehead. They had been working
since dawn with the pattern of exercises Walter
set for her. She did them over and over again—
push, thrust, feint, jab, turn, and continue. The
repetition was wearing; she had made some mis-
takes and Walter swore at her in Welsh. Luisa
was pleased that she not only understood but
could answer in kind. His expression never altered but the commands continued. In the few
days since the flares in the sky he had pushed
her unmercifully and the work fed her feelings
of unease.

"What do you mean?" she asked after a particularly sharp rebuke. Had he not been watching her all morning? She was looking forward to
the cool ale in a flask under the shade tree.

"This and this and this!" The point of his
sword was all around her in a moment, flicking
at her shoulder, bringing blood on the side of
her neck, ripping at her mended breeches, tearing the flesh of her sword hand. "Will you not
defend yourself?" He allowed himself a pause as

she backed away. "Or is this a sort of game we play?"

"Game, you say?" Luisa came belatedly aware to the fact that she must defend herself or he would literally slice her up. Her tiredness and thirst faded as her sword lifted to counter his. "Perhaps the teacher must defend himself?" She drove forward in attack and was inordinately pleased to see him move backward, surprise on his face.

The battle was nothing like the stylized sword-play she had read about or the tourneys Dame Matilda had described. Here were no salutes, courtly good wishes, and gestures of gallantry. They rushed at each other, clanged blades, twisted, whirled, moved delicately away, and came together again. Metal rang against metal as Luisa fought to turn his blade from her and gain the advantage. More than once she felt watched from all sides but did not dare turn to look. What if the whole camp were here? What might be more easy than to kill her this way and say she was slain in battle? Who cared enough to ask questions?

Then she had no time for thought. Walter's sword wove an impenetrable net about him as he tormented her from its confines. Back and forth they went across the clearing, now in one direction, now in another, blades clashing, their own breath hissing in and out. He made a mis-calculation once, her sword drove into his upper arm, and the blood poured out. He lunged forward past her attempted defense and flicked the weapon from her hand, holding his own point at her throat while he grinned wolfishly in the first true emotion she had ever seen from him.

Luisa took an involuntary step backward as if in shock. Then she threw herself down at his legs, catching him off balance. He fell clumsily but his hand jerked out his dagger as the other reached for her ankle. They tangled together, wrestling briefly. Then Luisa kicked out, tensed, and rolled free. She jumped to her feet, caught up the nearest sword, and put it to his throat as he lay prone. She grinned as he had done, feeling the triumph heady and sweet in every part of her body.

"Now, Walter, what will you say?" No wonder men enjoyed this sort of thing! Her physical hurts had vanished. The foe lay at her feet. Did generations of Marmoors look down from some sort of Valhalla at the fierce daughter of their race? "Do you yield?"

For answer he threw a pile of leaves clutched in one hand directly at her face, gathered himself, and rolled free of the point. Startled, Luisa moved back to brace herself to meet his attack but it was too late. Walter had her by the throat with both hands and the face of murder looked down into hers. She kicked once only; the world swung toward darkness and she lay still.

"Now I will ask you as you did me. Do you yield?" The voice was hard and grating.

Luisa tried to struggle but it was useless. How could she have been so sure of herself? If she lived that must not happen again.

"There's no disgrace, girl! Say it! Do you yield?" Walter's voice came from far away. There was a strange note of anxiety in it as the black eyes fused into one whole.

"Yes." She was unable to say anything else.

"Good." He rolled away from her and walked away. Then he was holding the ale flask to her mouth and pouring the life-giving fluid down her throat. Luisa sat up painfully, now drinking on her own. He fastened his black gaze on hers, and she saw that he was as hot and bloody as she. "In combat I should not mind if you stood at my shoulder."

Luisa tried to speak but only managed a whisper from her bruised throat. "I am fortunate in my teacher, Walter."

Later they sat in the clearing drinking ale while he took the battle apart in detail, explaining what action should have followed each move and why. He added, "This will be a part of the regular training from now on. You are learning." The accolade made Luisa smile with pride. She realized that she had not thought of Marcus in several hours. Any activity capable of driving him from her mind was to be greatly encouraged.

Walter's manner toward her did not change perceptibly after that, but she sensed he no longer disapproved of her. He never offered another compliment but such was not his way. Luisa found herself growing more lean and supple, her body sharpened for the hunt, the ability to sit unmoving for hours on watch now a natural thing. She found she depended more on her own native powers and less upon circumstances or feelings. She had entered a world where she was unwelcome and was beginning to prove herself by will and determination, just as long ago in the fields of Marmoor she had done what had to be done. It was likely she would always remain apart from people in this new life, but now battle and struggle would replace her memories of companionship.

A fortnight had passed with no word of the seer. In the days since Luisa had seen faint flares in the late nights and felt the excitement of the camp. Elmina and Huw spoke no more of him. Her pride allowed no further queries. She was most content when she worked with Walter or performed the duties he set out for her; the harder the task, the more eager she was for it. Walking alone on the high trails reminded her of Marcus and the overlook. Too much introspection, however, was too painful.

Early one hot afternoon Luisa was walking toward the butts to practice archery. Skill was essential and she found it difficult. "English bowmen are famed over all of Europe," Walter told her. "Rightly so. Where would we have been without them at Crécy and Poitiers, the great battles of the Black Prince?" Walter apparently knew the history of every battle ever fought and could tailor his remarks to match. Luisa was determined to improve.

Suddenly people were running past her, jostling together and calling out. She understood enough to know the anticipated moment had arrived. "He is here!" "John!" "Now we'll know!" "He'll give the sign!" Others seemed less eager as they clumped in knots, gesticulating and whispering. She saw sharp eyes on her and wondered if they found her changed in her brown breeches and shirt, thin sandals such as all wore, and chestnut braids wound to make a long one down her back. Was she a prisoner or the wife of their leader?

Luisa followed the others. She meant to insert herself into every area of camp life without being too forceful about it. Huw and Elmina materialized not far away; she assumed they watched her while dueling with Walter and that their eyes remained on her at all times.

Although it was very warm and a soft, flower-scented breeze was blowing over the forest and clearings where they gathered, a great fire had been kindled. Deer haunches were already being roasted and flasks of ale went from hand to hand. The sky was lightly dotted with small clouds that seemed to touch the crags above. Birds soared in the wind, rising and falling with a sure ease. Laughter and talk rose among the people. Anticipation was keen but Luisa's eye picked out many who still murmured gloomily. She did not miss the watchful looks she was given. Head held high she walked to a place aside and sat down to watch.

"He comes!"

"Here, make way!"

The cries went from mouth to mouth, the people bending like trees before the wind as they repeated the same words. The tall man who moved slowly into view as he leaned on his cane was immensely old. His wrinkles folded into each other, white hair and whiter beard streamed to his waist and melted into the white robe. Blind eyes stared out at an unseen world. One hand was twisted so out of shape that the fingers lay back on his wrist. His steps did not falter nor did he allow any to help him as he mounted one of the huge rocks which lay at the center of the camp.

He began to chant, his ancient voice full and vibrant as that of a young singer. It rose over the complete silence of the crowd, carried into the crags and treetops, over the circling birds, and into the valleys beyond. It entered Luisa as well as the others and possessed them utterly. This was a bard of the old wandering tradition, a teller of tales from out of time going back to the days when giants ruled the earth.

Luisa caught enough of what he was saying to know that he retold the tale of Taliesin as god and hero and poet, a tale every Welsh minstrel knew. He was the participator in all things, the end as much as he was the beginning, the teller of the secret wisdom—legend incarnate. She thrust aside the tearing memory of the night Marcus had held her in passion's aftermath and spoke to her of Taliesin. John's voice shifted, rose and fell in power, and held all captive to his artistry. The golden day paused, his was the only life, the only reality.

When the silence came it was so complete that no one stirred. Even the children remained still. The hairs rose on Luisa's arms. A primeval fear pulled at her vitals although she sat in the full light, surrounded by others, and felt her legs cramp from sitting on them for so long. Neither she nor any of the people shifted their gaze from the seer.

He spoke in English, the music gone from his voice. Now he spoke as might the last man alive on a blood red earth. Luisa could not push the thought from her mind; it was the purest reality.

"The sun of our land is set. The day of our prince is done. I have seen the vision of war and death. We walk no more under the banners but are devoured by the lion. The dragon is slain. Let it be done here. I have seen the beginning and the end. They are the same."

He stood for a moment, seeming to gaze over them all. The cooking fires blazed up in the freshening wind, which drove white clouds over the sun. John shook his head, set his staff more firmly in his good hand and strode away. No one followed.

Luisa risked rebuff as she leaned toward a young man who sat as though stunned beside an older man stretched out on the ground. She had to know if her suspicions were correct. "Forgive me, what did the seer mean by his last words?"

The older man sat up, tears gleaming in his eyes. His tone was dull and flat; he might have been speaking from a far distance. "Wales will never be free. Lancaster will rule. There is no hope. John has seen it."

"John has seen it." The younger man spoke the last words with a horrified reverence that evinced utter belief.

All that was hard and practical in Luisa Marmoor rose up in denial of the idea that a blind ancient could stop a war for freedom and destroy a dream. She cried, "He speaks the language of poetry, not of freedom!" She might have said more but her clear voice carried and several men turned toward her, threats plain in their movements.

Almost blindly she stepped aside and took the nearest path away from the camp. The hubbub that arose was in Welsh; for once she did not try to piece the words together. She walked swiftly, trying to put all thoughts out of her mind. The undergrowth made it slow going and tiny vines reached out for her face so that she had to slap them back. The cool lush scents of the woods drifted to her nostrils and soothed her. Birds rustled in the thickets while insects made raucous sounds. Then everything went still as an owl called. Luisa stopped to listen, thinking it was an ill omen indeed. Surely she had been mistaken.

Overwhelming dread came over her just as it had earlier. The forest walls around her faded and she saw a green slope in the light of day which was reddened with blood and littered with corpses. If she were closer she would know some of those who lay dead. They were women and children, all ravished and torn. Several figures walked among the carnage and one laughed. Luisa saw these things as clearly as she had seen anything in her life. A sorrow fierce and powerful bent her down. Salt tears ran into her mouth.

The owl hooted again. Luisa turned her head from the death scene in front of her and saw the seer standing in the copse near her. His face was turned toward what she had just seen, and it bore the horror of the vision just as she knew her own face did. His expression was contorted with pain beyond tears. Luisa understood that in some strange manner she had seen part of his vision of the future, the immense sorrow that was his. As he paced slowly by she caught a final glimpse of the shared perception. This time it was of towers, pacing clergy, and the faded dragon banner draped over a pile of stone while the sound of weeping poured over the world. *"The dragon is slain."* The words hammered in her head until she thought it would burst but she could not move.

Then as though a cord had snapped, Luisa was free. Her forehead was damp as were her hands. Her clothes were sticking to her body and she felt feverish. Her dark hut and bed of branches seemed the most desirable thing in all the earth. She was conscious only of the need to get there as quickly as possible.

She had run a short way when a tall figure loomed up in her path. She tried to dash around but it stepped in front of her. Exhaustion made her rash as she snapped, "Let me pass. There is enough room for two."

"I don't think so, Mistress Lenley." The voice was drawling.

"Marcus!"

The filtered sunlight fell on his bronzed face and outlined his stern mouth. The blue eyes might have been looking at a disliked stranger. His tone was baiting. "I've heard tales that ill become a wedded wife. Discipline is in order. I assume you've been hugging with a lover while that meeting was going on?''

Luisa was suddenly weary to death of their verbal sparring. She looked on Marcus and was unmoved. The familiar craving did not rise. No longing for what might have been stirred in her. Out of that blessed relief she heard herself saying, "Think what you please. Just don't come near me with it.''

As she passed by him unopposed she heard his mocking laughter. "Don't worry, wife. I've already chosen an eager wench for the night.''

She felt as though she walked in a nightmare. Perhaps the vision had been part of it. Marcus would laugh savagely if she tried to speak of it. Let be. She rushed toward the haven of her hut.

Chapter Nineteen
DEATH'S PROPHECY

LUISA LAY WAKEFUL during the rest of that long afternoon and night. She heard Marcus roaring at intervals, sometimes in anger and others in cajolery. He was answered by fearful cries and anger to match his own. She did not understand what was going on, but wanted only to slide down into the peace of sleep and escape the weariness that dragged her down. Her limbs felt as if they were weighted with rocks. Her head unceasingly ached, and in the warmth of the night, she shuddered feverishly. She fell into a fitful sleep.

She woke refreshed in midmorning. Luisa rejoiced in the suppleness of her body and the renewed feeling of life, the cessation of discomfort and outright pain, the sheer pleasure of health restored. She did not doubt that she had actually shared in John's burdens the night before, but whether her difficulties had come from a true vision or merely sympathy with him was unknown.

She dressed hurriedly as she was eager to find out what was happening in the camp. She heard marching feet, the clatter of weapons, orders being given, loud arguments, and a rush of activity. After yesterday and John's prophecy she would have expected gloom and despair. Had Marcus heard and believed? She did not think anything could dim the bright edge of his hatred for Lancaster and his minions. She wondered also who he had taken to his couch last night. Luisa clenched her fists and jumped up. There was no time for thoughts such as those.

She scrambled into her boy's garb of green homespun which Elmina had unwillingly altered to fit her, thrust her feet into sandals, and strapped the sword Walter had given her at her waist. Her skin tingled to the dash of cold water she gave it. She braided her hair and twisted it around the top of her head, securing it tightly with wooden pins. When she was ready she looked down at her hands, browned by the sum-

mer sun and hardened by lessons of war. Dame
Matilda would have been horrified at her
charge's appearance but Luisa was proud of her
recent accomplishments. The thought of battle
was terrifying, yet she would be doing something for her own destiny, striking a blow in
retaliation and for a just cause. "I am not as I
was." That was the simple truth. For all her
courage and devious ways, Luisa knew she had
been an idealistic girl with a heart of dreams
before leaving Marmoor. Now she was a woman
who had known passion and the bitter aftermath, a wilderness woman well taught in the
martial arts, one who believed in her own abilities and was ready to face what she must.

Luisa knew she was wasting time. She pulled
the curtain aside and rushed to the center of the
camp. She had interpreted the sounds outside
her tent correctly—the outlaws were going to
battle and she was being left behind. It was a
bright day with no wind. Good fighting weather,
she thought and then recoiled from the ardor for
violence that had possessed her of late.

Many of the men had already departed.
Only two rather straggly columns were left and
they were gathering supplies, looking to their
weapons, and bidding farewell to the few who
were to be left behind. Luisa ran back into her
hut, snatched up her dagger and bow with the
full quiver of arrows, and sped to join the
nearest column. Several of the men stared
questioningly at her but she met their eyes until they fell.

"Just what do you think you're doing?"

The angry shout made Luisa jump in spite of her effort to remain calm. Marcus was striding toward her across the clearing, his dark face furious, the brilliant eyes flaring with a barely contained rage. He was dressed completely in brown of a shade that would merge with the tree trunks. His hair was a riot of dark curls he had tried unsuccessfully to slick back with water. The droplets still clung to his forehead. He was fully armed, his broad shoulders, slim waist, and powerful body accentuated by the weapons.

Luisa kept her voice cool. "We go into battle. I am ready."

Someone gave a bark of laughter, quickly hushed, and avid faces turned to watch this interesting encounter. The remaining women dashed off to fetch others and children sank down to stare.

Marcus came close and said, "You are right on the first and wrong on the second. Go back to your quarters."

Luisa tried another tactic. The muscles in his left cheek were jumping. While he held his voice low, she heard the rising fury and knew it must soon break out. "What has happened?"

"Soldiers have been sighted even deeper in Wales than they usually dare venture. They may belong to the king or to Adam of Wenlock. In any case they must be driven back. This may be a full offensive. Now go back, Luisa. This is not your place." He tried to speak reasonably but it came out as a command. Turning his back to her, he ordered, "Men, let us go. We must hurry to catch up with the others."

Generations of Marmoors rang in Luisa's voice as she cried, "I am trained in weaponry and I have a grudge against Lancaster! I am going to fight with you!"

"No," he said firmly as he turned to face her.

Both were oblivious to the watchers and to everything except the personal struggle raging between them. The circle of watchers grew larger and began to whisper. Some of the men in the columns sat down, prepared for a fascinating delay.

Luisa was tempted to try the lively brand of oratory that had helped inflame these volatile people before in her favor, but one look at the white lines around Marcus's mouth told her that he would not allow her to go that far if he could possibly prevent it.

"It is my right." She kept her voice muted.

"You have no rights in this land." His blue eyes bore into hers. "I wed you and saved your life, have you forgotten that? By the Rood, I should have left you to your fate!" He tried to stifle his fear by fury. What if something happened to her? He could not bear to think of that possibility. He must not allow himself to continue thinking of Luisa at all.

Luisa lost her temper suddenly and completely. The celebrated Marmoor rage, second some said only to that of the Plantagenets themselves, swept over her. She stalked toward Marcus, one hand on her sword, unaware that her teeth glittered where her lips were pulled back and her eyes blazed. He did not move but some of the watchers crossed themselves while others gaped in admiration.

"I curse the day I saw you, Marcus Lenley! This is a matter of honor, a thing I should have thought you understood! I thank you for my life but you ought to recall that I also saved yours at the pilgrimage. I pray for the day our bond may be safely dissolved! I am partially responsible for the perils in which your people now find themselves. I have vowed to fight for that and also for myself! Count me as a soldier in your ranks and if I fall, I fall!"

Marcus said, "We are wasting time. You have said it, if you fall there you will remain." He shrugged as if he had lost interest. Only his stance and expression revealed the raking fury within him. His manner was mild, deceptively so. "We leave this minute!" he shouted.

Luisa took her place at the end of the line while Marcus went far ahead. One of the men, a short stocky individual who must have been nearing sixty, gave her a cocky smile and said under his breath, "Heard you've been making Walter work for a change. Glad you're back here with me!"

It was a welcome greeting. Several of the others looked warmly at her, not daring to laugh outright at his words. Luisa felt a surge of gratitude as she said, "So am I!"

They began to move, Luisa walking in the ranks as though there had never been any doubt about her rightful place there. The glances she received from the men were no longer surly and, best of all, no longer went through her as if she were invisible. When they were well in stride she turned to the stocky man, whose name was Gilbert. "How far are we going? Do you have any idea?"

"We're going to join up with another section of our band in a valley about two day's march from here. We'll take care of those English soldiers, then come back and have a celebration feast. A good victory will make those worriers get ready to fight again. John's an old man, Marcus is right to honor him, but it's been long since he lifted the dragon standard." Gilbert appeared ready to explain the entire political situation not only to Luisa but the company at large.

Luisa dared not ask anything else lest Marcus hear and take exception to it. She smiled and quickened her pace, deliberately taking long strides as if to maintain speed. Had Wenlock received her letter? Did he believe it? Surely if these soldiers were his their subterfuge had done no good. Did Marcus think the letter had brought them all the more quickly? She wished she could talk with him rationally and put the past behind them, but their shared anger made this impossible.

They paused in the late afternoon for a hasty meal of bread and cheese. Luisa bent over a stream to drink and wash her hot face. As she stood up she saw Marcus reflected in the water next to her. He brought his big body close to hers and she felt her treacherous senses leap in gladness and longing. Her flesh was still in thrall to him.

"I advise you not to cross me in such a manner as you did this morning. We take our wars seriously, we of Wales, and your playacting is only foolishness. Your pleasure was evident. You won't find battle to your liking. You had best beware, madam, for when I find out your true ties with Wenlock, Arban, and the rest of the scurvy bunch, nothing will save you." He spoke softly but every word was piercing. He felt his passion rising at their closeness. Why was she so utterly stubborn and determined to flout him at every turn? She would laugh at any appeal he made. He knew that. She would not have the satisfaction of seeing him plead with her.

Luisa said earnestly, "I wish you could believe me, Marcus. I am just a victim of Lancaster who is now devoted to this cause as a means to bring him down." How had all that they had shared vanished into cruelty and distaste? Her feelings were evident in her eyes and Marcus momentarily hesitated, his own gaze softening into gentleness.

Then his face was again blank and cold, his voice flat. "We are what we are, madam. Obey me in the future and behave as a woman should or you will find yourself back in camp with strict guards set about you."

Luisa heard a voice say in memory, "Ah, seductress, you have bewitched me with desire." Desire, yes, but no tenderness was left, and still his mistress had asked Luisa to have a care for Marcus's heart! There he was, rising to his full height after having given his edict. Fury swept Luisa as she jumped to her feet and cried, "May the devil fly away with you!"

The men close enough to hear burst into laughter. Marcus gave Luisa a murderous glare and roared out a command which brought them all to their feet.

No one ventured a comment to Luisa after that. The pace Marcus set was intended to leave no time for slack. They stopped for the night only when it was well after dark and the full moon high in the sky. Luisa's sleep was again fitful; she was unable to get comfortable and dreams of bloody battles haunted her. She tossed and turned in heated struggles, waking to the hammering in her head and aching in her bones.

It was noon of the next day when they reached a circle of rolling hills that gave onto the valley where they were to meet the other band of warriors. The marchers went rapidly and a bit carelessly, talking now and then. Their own people must have first spied out the land, Luisa thought, and Marcus posted his own watchers. The warm day had a clarity and sparkle which raised her spirits. She pursed her lips in a tuneless whistle, wondering if Edra and Ian would be among those they were shortly to see.

Suddenly Gilbert choked on his laughter and fell forward, an arrow protruding from his back. At the same time a rush of arrows came down on them, many finding their mark. Luisa had no clear memory of dodging back, but she and some of the men sheltered under an outcropping for a few minutes. They were caught between two forces of the enemy which came at them from alternate sides. Marcus was rallying the men, shouting encouragement and curses. They rushed back to join him, Luisa swept along in her first battle, forgetting the savage fear of her dreams.

A huge bearded man engaged her almost instantly, pinning her against a rock so she could not use her sword. Her hand grappled for the dagger even as he put his fingers on her windpipe. She pushed the blade into his stomach with all her power and twisted it. He howled, gurgled, and collapsed in his own spurting blood. Sickened, Luisa looked down at him and wanted to vomit.

A trumpet call rang out and was followed by another. Their assailants tried to withdraw but many were cut down as they did so. The ambush was foiled by the sheer ferocity of the Welsh. A final clatter of hooves, running feet, and one last flood of arrows signaled the departure of the foe. Luisa saw that the bearded man's blood had stained her entire body. She was wet with her own sweat and her lower lip was swollen where she had chewed it. Faintness swam at her but she fought it off, then bent to wrench her dagger from the body.

Marcus appeared at the head of the trail, his eyes going quickly to her. He called, "Hurry down into the valley! Those men knew we were expected. They chose just the right place to wait. We'll come back for the dead."

They went stealthily over the trail, weapons poised. Luisa felt as if she had been doing this forever; over her gladness at the fact Marcus still lived was her pain for those who died. Her head hammered with concentration even as her eyes swung watchfully back and forth for the slightest suspicious movement.

Finally they rounded the last turn into the valley and Luisa was met with a familiar sight. In this valley the green slopes of the mountains shimmered in the light of the westering sun and a hot red light reflected bloodily. Here the bodies lay crumpled as they had fallen, arrow shafts protruding back and front. The entire band had been slaughtered and more. Men, women, and children had been decapitated, hacked until they seemed no longer human. The shelters were smashed and gutted, the cooking pots shattered. The women had been raped and disemboweled. Edra lay among them, her body savaged and her throat cut. It was not hard to guess what had come first.

Luisa stood dry-eyed beside her friend. This was the seer's vision come dreadfully true.

Chapter Twenty
I WILL REPAY

"YOUR KILLER SHALL die by my own hand. He shall die as lingeringly as you did. I swear it by your blood and mine, which calls out for vengeance. I swear it." Luisa knelt beside Edra as if in prayer, but she whispered the oath over and over again. This was to be her mission, a reason for all existence. She knew whose men had done this. If only she had told Marcus about John's vision the company might well have chosen another way or sent warning. She had known it for a true prophesy. Why also had she not told

Marcus of Adam of Wenlock to begin with? She cruelly blamed herself, not heeding the voice of sanity which told her she could have done little to alter present circumstances. Blood revenge was the only thing to free her now.

There was no time to mourn or weep or place blame. These deaths were so fresh that the blood had barely congealed on the corpses. The killers could not be far away. Marcus's face was like those of the others, white and shuddering with shock, but he rapped out orders. "Send scouts ahead, the swiftest we have. Locate the English and return as quickly as you can. They may think the ambush attended to most of us. The rest of you post guards and get what weapons you can from what is left. Hold yourselves in readiness to march. I don't think they'll be back but if they come we'll tear them apart. Now we must bury our dead"

Luisa toiled with all the people, scrabbling at the yielding earth with her bare hands when sticks failed, until the mass grave was hollowed out at the foot of one of the green slopes. The brilliant day shone down undisturbed at this horror. She let the tears run into her mouth and eyes; she was not the only one. They did not speak for there was nothing to say. Luisa looked up once to see Marcus staring at her, a flat, cold blaze in his look which sent a frigid warning to her heart. Did he blame her for this? She looked down and again blamed herself.

The sun was still high when the last bit of ground filled the grave of more than fifty persons who had been alive that bright morning. A man who had been in holy orders at one time spoke the gentle words consigning the dead to the care of the God who had shown them no mercy in this life. Marcus came to stand by the head of the grave. He looked around at the sickened faces before him, then up to the guards posted at the rim of the valley in all directions and back to the unsheathed sword in his hand.

"I can only swear that those who did this shall be punished! Our enemies will say we have done such and more, but we know that to be false. This was slaughter! Our cause still lives although our comrades lie dead. Who can doubt that this was the hand of Lancaster? When he lies dead our revenge will have just begun. Remember that when you slay one of the enemy, the blood of our friends calls out for more and more!"

The echo of his words rang out and back. Marcus, the imperturbable, the bold leader, wept as he faced them all and none thought him the less for it.

Luisa watched all this, though all feeling had left her. In memory she walked with Edra to the overlook, talked of the Welsh legends, splashed in the cold stream, and laughed in the delight of the moment. Was Ian slain also? Her fingers clenched convulsively as she remembered the man she had killed and whose blood even now stiffened her clothes. With what joy and pleasure would she slay Adam of Wenlock? Some intuitive knowledge told her it was he and his men who had done this thing. What could one woman do against the power he must hold?

"Make ready! They go to the east!" The cry

rang over the band and galvanized them. Marcus was pacing up and down the long length of the grave site, his profile carved and hard in the light, the emotion drained from him. It was strange that one of the scouts had returned so quickly and yet it must have been hours. Surely it was dangerous to linger here!

"Do you recognize this?"

Luisa whirled to see Marcus at her elbow. She had been so deep in thought that she had not seen him approach. Now she looked down at the torn badge in his extended hand. The yellow cloth bore a wheel and part of a charging animal. Memory whirled backward and she saw it once more at the convent in London where men watched the gates.

"I think it might be Adam of Wenlock's." She explained the possibility to the stonelike, ravaged face of this man who was a stranger.

"Think! This is the badge of the murderer and it is you who have brought him among us! Would God I had slain you the first time I saw you!" His cry rang out in an agony of self-loathing. At that moment he wanted to convince himself that he spoke the truth.

"That is unfair. I have told you everything and even then I tried to keep him from coming into Wales. You cannot suspect me! You cannot!" Luisa felt she could endure no more. His attack here on the field of the dead was beyond her comprehension. "You look for a scapegoat! What manner of man are you, Marcus Lenley, to blame one woman for all that has happened? Examine your own faults first!"

He might not have heard her as he continued. "Wenlock is a man who delights in cruelty. Your letter must have inflamed him. Perhaps you planned it so! You are their tool, Luisa Marmor, and I have protected you."

She saw that he utterly believed what he had just said. Moreover, those around him were nodding their heads in agreement. Anger left her and she was swamped with self-pity. He blamed himself and she felt responsible and his very fury was channeled against her. The coil was unbearable. With no other thought than to spare them both, she cried, "This was foretold! Listen! Marcus, hear me!"

She now launched into the vision she had shared with the seer. "Maybe he did see the future. Possibly this was ordained by a savage God! How can we know?"

"And you told no one of this?" Marcus spoke very softly but he was bone white. His men drew closer; they were nearly as pale as he.

Luisa said, "I thought it an illusion, but now I'm not so sure." Was that some small comfort for the slaughter? Was it better to believe in the savagery of God or of men?

Luisa saw Marcus's hand tighten at his side, and he grated out a rush of words. "Had we known . . . any warning . . ." His hand came slamming down onto his other palm. Marcus knew that he was being unfair to her. He would not have believed her vision even if she had told him every detail. But the agony over this slaughter tore at him. He blamed himself bitterly and that was unbearable. He cried out against Luisa and that hurt even more. Only battle could give expiation now. Perhaps there he could forget this woman.

They stood staring at each other in that place of death and horror. She knew Marcus was beginning to believe the vision and the words of John. Against all the strength of his will Marcus thought the dragon was indeed slain and his people doomed to be hunted out of the hills and mountains in the name of Lancaster's justice. Luisa stood at the bar of her own justice, wondering if her determination to remain with this band had helped to bring about such dissolution. She had sworn a blood oath and that must be served, but there was one other thing she might do in expiation. It seemed very fitting that the last sight she was to have of this contradictory man who had taught her the beginnings of love was his face twisted in rage and pain as she struggled to keep his hands from her throat.

"I can't bear this! I can't!" She sank to the ground, put her head in her hands, and burst into all the sounds of tears, but her eyes were dry. She felt she would never weep again, never release the agony which now raked her. She shook and trembled with the power of her sorrow, a pain she felt would never abate.

"For God's sake!" Marcus moved away and shouted at his men. "We've wasted enough time with all this! We'll weep for the dead when Lancaster and Wenlock and all their minions hang before us for the villains they are. Come on, my sword shall be my prophecy!"

A wavering cry of enthusiasm answered him.

Luisa threw herself full length on the earth and buried her face in her tumbling hair. She sounded hysterical and wished she were. Now someone was bending over her and pulling at her shoulders.

"Lady, we have to leave. Get up and come. You have to."

"No! No! No!" With each word she wailed the louder, hammering her fists as she did so.

"Lady. Please!" The voice was despairing.

Luisa rolled over a little so that she could see what was going on. The band was ready to go, already formed purposefully into rows, the sun glittering on their weapons and grim faces. She could not see Marcus but surely, feeling about her as he did, he would leave her behind and she would be free to do what was becoming an obsession.

"Come on." The face above was twisted on one side with the effects of an old sword cut, thickly bearded, and burned by many suns. He looked as if he ought to be sitting by a village fire reciting tales to eager boys, not battling in the mountains.

She wanted to scream at him, at them all, to leave but knew she must not. "I have to rest for a few moments. I can't move." Dry sobs tore at her voice.

Marcus called out harshly, the tones holding resignation and contempt. "Richard, we must go. Let her calm down, then take her over the mountain and into the first village you see. Explain matters, tell them she must be kept prisoner until we return, and rejoin us at the border. There's nothing else to do."

"But, Marcus . . ." He started to protest and was cut off with a roar.

"I command it! Would you rather I slit her throat and left her here?"

Luisa cried, "Go! Do what you have to!" Then she let her body go in a simulated faint. The grass tickled her nose; she struggled to hold her body still.

"I have commanded you, Richard."

"I obey you, Marcus. She has simply collapsed after the way of women. Don't worry." Richard apparently had seen something in Marcus's face that Luisa knew nothing about for his anger at being left behind appeared to be easing.

"Hurry to us, Richard." Marcus spoke more calmly now. "Watch the woman. She is a deceiver." His voice went low. "Aye, a deceiver." She had led him from his dreams of a free Wales. For her sake he had dared to think of love, had almost allowed himself to trust again, and had even begun to move away from his shield of protective anger. Marcus shook his head. It was bitter to leave her but there was no choice. His life belonged to Wales, to Owen Glendower who had commanded his first true allegiance. Of course Luisa was a deceiver who played with his heart and mind. He had to believe that or he would go mad.

Luisa nearly raised her head. There was an odd note of tenderness in his pronunciation of "deceiver." She could hear him whispering "sorceress" and "seductress" in her ear back in the cave when it had seemed they were truly united. She knew he did what he had to do; in some dark, mysterious part of his mind it was reasonable that he believe her capable of spying, lies, and complete deception. He was marked with the dark stains of hatred and who knew if anything might free him? He was now blinded to the richness of emotion they had shared. Luisa lay with her face in the dirt, her body sprawled and limp.

I will never see him again. The thought rang in Luisa's mind over and over again as she heard the men departing and the valley of the dead growing silent. Knowing herself foolish, she let her memory range over all their association and regretted the loss all the more. If her plan worked, she would have little enough time for recollection in the future. For the time being she was buying precious time toward the realization of the personal revenge she, Luisa Marmoor, intended to exact.

Suddenly she heard footsteps coming close and could not prevent herself from tensing. Then cold water poured with icy force over her neck and back, running into her ears, making her shiver. A strong hand pulled her up, turned her face toward the light, and poured ale into her unresisting mouth all in one motion.

Richard stared down at her. "That'll wake you up. Always works. See if you aren't better now." He was half grinning.

She pushed her hair back weakly and sighed, recalling the role she had to play. Her skills at mimicry had helped to save Marmoor for a time. They had worked just now with Marcus and must continue to do so with Richard. "What has

happened?" she asked. "Why is it so quiet? I'm
so very tired. Do you think I could just lie down
and sleep for a while? Surely some place is safe
around here?" She loathed playing the part of
the weak female, but Marcus would never have
allowed her to continue on with the band nor
would he have given any form of sanction to the
sort of revenge she planned for Adam of Wenlock. She had made a vow to Edra, a vow she
intended to keep.

"Do you remember what happened here?"
Richard helped her to her feet, letting her lean
on him as he steered her away from the valley
floor and toward a secluded grove of trees.

She whispered, "Yes, but I want to forget. I
can't think about it. I won't."

Marcus had chosen her keeper well. His touch
was respectful but firm, his manner agreeable.
Richard would never improperly touch the wife
of his leader. She knew she was not above se-
duction if it became necessary for her freedom,
but there was no need. He settled her down on
his own cloak, suggested more ale, and placed
himself nearby with his sword drawn.

"You might be a guardian at the door of par-
adise in other circumstances!" She gave a giggle.
Let him think her a fool. He was more likely to
be less watchful.

He coughed. "Marcus bade me see to you and
so I shall. Rest easily, my lady, and the morning
will see you as safe as you can be in Wales."

Was she about to be hysterical after all? That
seemed funnier than any joke she had heard.
Her shredded nerves struggled for composure

and she turned her head into her arms as though suddenly overcome with weariness. He was his master's good servant. She wished she might do better by him.

The night was very dark and still, the moon a shadow in the sky, when she slipped from the bed and picked up her weapons from the rock where he had placed them. The snores of an exhausted Richard resounded over the area as she moved away. An invading army would have been hard put to waken him. He had given her his cloak and she had pulled it high over the piled branches and grasses of the bed he had made for her. She hoped it would fool him for a while.

As she turned for one last glimpse of the valley of horror, Luisa made the sign of the cross for Edra and all who lay there. She did not invoke the Christian God for herself; the blood savagery of an older race must suffice.

Luisa Marmoor walked into the wilderness determinedly. She was going to kill Adam of Wenlock.

Chapter Twenty-one
DEBTORS

GOLDEN LIGHT BLAZED into Luisa's eyes and dissolved into dizzying shades of green as she walked through the forest. She lifted one hand to her face but pulled it back when she saw the red trickles. Her breath came so heavily that she thought it must surely stop. She heard a small voice as though in a daze.

"Only a little more. Don't worry, we'll soon be there," said the voice.

"Where?" The one word cost her such effort. She felt confused and disoriented. She stumbled. Hands supported her, holding her upright, and guided her faltering steps.

The thin, worried face of a boy held back her darkness.

"The village isn't far. We'll go to the witch who lives just outside. She has a fearful look but I think she'll help one who has walked with the outlaws of Wales."

That struck her as funny. "Outlaws and witches." This was the stuff of Welsh legends. She laughed and that was a mistake for she began to cough and shake. She was suddenly both hot and cold. Fever burned in her veins and she descended into the maelstrom where life and death merged into nothingness.

For a long time Luisa walked the ways of hell, which mingled with the more familiar ones of earth. Demons leered and pinched, ghostly figures took counsel of skeletons; she burned and froze alternately while fingers scorched her skin and voices muttered. Long teeth sank into her body. Awful faces floated under her closed lids. Edra's death and the repudiation by Marcus replayed endlessly in her mind. Finally she drifted to the bottom of a cold lake, colder than any she had ever imagined. Drifted and rose to the soft dawn and flower smells.

She lay on a bed of rushes and branches covered with an old, soft mantle. A spray of blooming flowers stood close by her head. When she started to turn over, her head whirled once more and she was forced to lie back down. A kettle rattled in the background of the small hut where she was, and one of the faces of her dreams bent over her. A gnarled hand caught her head and lifted it. A cup of meat broth was put to her mouth. She drank because there was no other choice and warmth poured over her. Speech was now possible where it had not been previously.

"How long? What place is this?"

The woman who looked at her was ages old. She had scraggly white tufts on her head, one eye, and no teeth. Her hands were horn hard, her face so wrinkled and seamed that it was impossible to tell if she smiled or grimaced. Her voice was deep and cultured, the French accent pronounced.

"You were brought here yesterday. Your illness is the ague and will be quickly over. Don't worry, you're safe here. The boy who found you wandering in the forest and brought you here, Rob, is gathering wood for the fire. You may call me Mag."

Luisa tried to frame more questions but the soft dawn was growing brighter and her eyes hurt. Healing sleep whirled over her once more. This time the dreams were sharper, more real than the stuff of nightmares. They told her she had failed to save Marmoor, herself, even her honor with the vow. Sir Adam, who murdered Edra, still walked the earth. And the horror of it was that she did not greatly care. Apathy was comforting.

When she roused herself later in the day the mantle of unconcern was still with her. Mag's potions and watchful concern and the element of safety here—nothing seemed to really interest her. She only wanted to burrow down in her bed by the door and forget the world. Even when Mag heated water for her to bathe several times, it did not really matter. She looked at her reflection and saw that her body was still firm and shapely, honed by the training in the mountains, her hair a cloud over her shoulders and her face a little thinner and whiter but fair with a woman's loveliness. She shrugged and turned away from the steel mirror, uncaring.

Mag said sharply, "I dare not harbor you two past tomorrow. You will heal rapidly and the fresh air will be good for you. It seems there are many searching for you. It is dangerous for all of us here. Rob wishes to join the outlaws in the mountains not far from here. They will welcome help. There are said to be great plans. He is old enough to fight and women can as well."

"He can't be more than twelve!" An image of

a slight boy with black hair and gray eyes flashed in her mind.

Mag looked at Luisa, seeing the shadows under the dulled eyes and the too-pointed face. "It is what he wants and he can choose. The man called Marcus has sent out for recruits. All are welcome. Go to them."

The accent was very much as that of Marcus when they first met. Luisa was drawn out of her retreat sufficiently to say, "You are of France, are you not? How is it that you are here and in such guise?"

Mag's voice was wearily bitter. "Yes. Once I was as fair as you, if that can be believed. I loved an Englishman who traveled in France between the wars. We were wed only a short time when he died of a simple scratch. I cursed the God who let it happen. The zealous servants of the church heard me; I was punished and now am as you see. I came north and have remained here. But all this was long ago. Will you do as I suggest and go to the outlaws?"

"No." Luisa lifted her hands. "These will do me good service. Nothing matters. I just don't care."

"Listen to me, girl!" Mag in repose was a bad enough sight but Mag angry was truly fearful to see. "You are tormented, I know, and retreat from it. Your wound is of the spirit. Talk to me about it."

"No." The word hung on the still air.

"Marcus leads the outlaws. His name was constantly on your lips. Is there hatred between you now? What have you done that you must blame yourself night and day as I have heard you do while you slept? You love this man." The last was not a question.

"It is not true!" Luisa sprang up, hair swirling around her in a silken skein. Anger roused her from her comfortable, apathetic state.

Mag's hand was hard on her shoulder as she turned Luisa to face her. "Tell me." Her eyes commanded. "Exposed wounds heal the better."

Luisa stared into the implacable face, opened her mouth, shut it, and tried to will her mind back. She could not. There was no retreat. She had shared her heart long ago with Marcus and it had been torn asunder. Begin with him and not with Marmoor.

"I felt passion for the outlaw—no more. He took me prisoner." Once begun, the tale spurted out swiftly. Her voice rose and fell with pain, passion, recrimination, and loss, but no tears. Those had dried up long ago, spent in her body's hurt, lost in nightmares of waking. She spared herself nothing in the telling.

The stream of words poured on with only momentary pauses while Luisa gulped thin ale to ease her throat. When she faltered, Mag fixed Luisa with her one good eye and said, "Continue." The massacre rose before her so clearly that she had to close her eyes only to find it more vivid in her mind. She told of its horror several times, blaming herself. Mag asked about Marcus again. "He has repudiated me and I him!" Thus it continued as the light faded and time spiraled down to the cessation of her tale.

Luisa noticed as if from afar that the tenseness

was going from her body and her hands now ceased to twist. There had been a constricting heaviness in her chest and lower back which was easing. Her vision narrowed down to the sight of her bed, which would provide the rest she so urgently needed. There was no past, no future, only this quiet meager hut and the great piercing eye of this woman who ordered and received obedience. Her voice slowed and quieted. For the first time in hours there was total silence in the room.

Mag rose and came to Luisa, who stared at her thinking suddenly of great Odin, who had given his own eye for wisdom. "Luisa, hear me well. You have condemned yourself. You alone have passed judgement. No one else can do so. From what you have said of your Marcus, he battles his own feelings. He had to blame you for them as he cannot fully deal with either what happened or his reactions." She slapped her breast. "I know about guilt. After my husband died I blamed myself for loving him, for coming to England with him, for living at all. I think I even welcomed the torturers for my expiation. Is that not perhaps why you sought Sir Adam out in such a mission of death? For Luisa Marmoor? Not for Edra who is dead? You still live. Marcus is a good leader, whatever his difficulties. If there is no resolution for you and him then do not be shackled by his thoughts of you nor what you expect he thinks. You have been your own vengeful god, Luisa. There is still this world and it is sweet beyond the telling."

Luisa stared at the bent, twisted old woman

who must live like an outcast, feared, barely tolerated, possessed of hideous memories, and bearing the marks of torment on her flesh and bones. If it were known she sheltered the fugitives, retaliation would be swift and savage. The church was merciless with those who avoided its ministrations. Mag could not survive another brush with it. What would she, Luisa Marmoor, have done if faced with the cruelty meted out to heretics?

Out of compassion and an endless gratitude, Luisa gathered all her strength and said, "I can never repay you. I have been my own judge, I understand that. But I simply wanted to go my own way and all the forces of the kingdom mitigated against it."

"And will always do so. You must make your own way as best you can." Mag rose to light the one bit of candle on the table. Her shadow rose long in the feeble glow it gave. "As I did."

Luisa thought of her own youth, comeliness, abilities of body and mind, the passion with Marcus who had taught her much, of the young boy, Rob, and Mag herself. What right did she have to sink back, tangling herself in useless pain? The world provided enough of that; she did not need to add to it. If Mag found the essence of life sweet in her bitter circumstances, how much more might Luisa Marmoor do so? Resignation was not her way but much had to be accepted. She looked up at Mag to convey all she felt and saw there was no need; the old woman understood.

"You are better. I can see it." Mag held out an

old, intricately carved flask. "This is the best of French brandy. One of my guests left it not long ago. You will join me, I hope?" She poured some out into a battered cup and held it toward Luisa, who sniffed the aroma appreciatively.

"Yes, of course." She drank a little, thinking it tasted of crushed flowers on a summer day. It was strange, she thought as she and Mag smiled at each other in sharing, how the need for sleep had receded. She felt alive as she had not felt in many days. The inward battering had lessened already. She would always hate Sir Adam, but the blind urge to kill him was no longer her total motivation. Reason told her she had been only a minor—a very minor—part of his military excursion against the Welsh. Outlaws and English alike harried the border. Had she actually sought death in return for her sins? So it appeared. She voiced this to Mag, who merely smiled and sipped.

"I want some, too." Rob materialized in the doorway and stood grinning at them. "Glad you're better, Luisa. Your face is brighter. Mag, I'm starving!" He seemed so familiar with her and she wondered if this was so because she had babbled during her illness.

"There's bread and meat over there. Bring a cup for the brandy and then go look around outside. We don't want anyone sneaking up on us." Mag glanced fondly at Rob and back to Luisa. "Hurry back."

In the manner he had of behaving as a young boy one moment and a gallant gentleman the next, he gave her a half bow, which included

Luisa as well. "I'm just back from the woods but I obey the ladies. I'll take the food with me!" He grabbed it and dashed out.

Mag said, "I have a friend who wanders about freely; he's thought to be half-witted but no one knows how clever he truly is. He can guide you both to the outlaws. If you cannot bear to be around Marcus, there are other sections of their army where you can serve. There will be a measure of safety and you can strike a blow for Welsh freedom. I think this is best for you and for Rob."

Luisa tilted back her head and sat looking into the candlelight. "No, Mag. I'll go with Rob to the outlaws and see that he is safe. There's no need to see Marcus. None at all. Then, as I planned before, I'll go elsewhere and earn my keep, wander around a bit, see the country, maybe even go to France. I can mimic, quote, teach, and work in the fields. How many people can do all that?" She gave a short laugh. "This isn't flight or evasion, Mag. Just a reasoned choice."

"You're different already. You're sure this is what you want?" They were equals now, no longer wisewoman and confused patient.

"Quite sure." Luisa would have said she was truly herself again but that would not have been totally correct. In part she was altered from rebelling girl, hungry lover, and instrument of revenge; she was a woman who now knew when to accept and when to fight. She was tempered in the crucible and so forever changed.

"I will send word to my friend, Clau. He will make sure the outlaws are told of your coming."

"Thank you, Mag." Because there were really

no words for what she felt, Luisa lifted her cup toward the old woman in homage and salute.

Chapter Twenty-two
CALL TO ARMS

THEY STOOD IN the earliest dawn light to say farewell. Luisa wore a reasonably well-fitted suit of boy's clothes, as did Rob. A sheen of tears was in Mag's eye and the villainous-looking old Clau stood studying the horizon. Mag had insisted they rest another day; Luisa felt fully restored now and far more herself than at any time since the massacre.

She kissed Mag on the cheek, then took both of the old woman's hands. "I will remember all you have taught me. Bless you forever."

She was brusque. "See that you rule yourself with reason and not so much feeling. Peace." She tousled Rob's hair and winked fiercely with a savage face. "Take care of each other. If you see a demon who looks as I do, think I have come to help you."

They laughed as they were meant to do and Rob devotedly said, "Luisa is my lady. I will have a good care for her always." Chivalry rang in his tones and Luisa spared a thought to wonder once more how he had come by it.

Clau snorted. "Better move on while we can. Hurry up."

They gathered up the extra food and warm cloaks Mag had procured for them along with a pair of keen daggers, waved once, and followed him over the hill and around the curve that led upward into the mountains.

As the day went on, Luisa walked briskly, swinging her arms and feeling her whole body respond to the cool, fresh air. She might never be really whole again but she was no longer ravaged of heart. If I do happen to meet Marcus, she told herself, I'll just say I have come to see Rob and leave again. He couldn't make much of that. Rob seemed to regard her as his family now. She did not know how to tell him she did not intend to remain with him and it was not going to be possible to slip away.

They went upward along the changing face of the crags and into the little valleys which lay like jewels among them. Clau was constantly watchful, saying nothing beyond the bare civilities. Luisa and Rob chattered, laughed, and sang songs. He told her of his life.

"Robert Black is my full name. My father was killed fighting the English, my sisters and brothers died in a raid, and my mother ran off with a tinker last year. I've been wandering a bit, but now I am going to join and fight against those who destroyed my family!"

Luisa tried not to think of Rob's sad little tale and asked him about his good manners.

"I think I was taught to read fairly early on; anyway, I can and it helps. I was told stories about knights and fair ladies, too. Now I will fight and you can be the maiden I battle for!"

Rob grinned as they walked rapidly along. "Fighting's the important thing, Luisa. I'll do it for us both! Every night I'll come and describe the battle for you. And one day ballads will be made about the great warrior, Robert the Black!"

"Doubtless the outlaws will set you to gathering firewood or minding the animals, mighty one!" They laughed together and went on.

Several days after leaving Mag, the party came to a high place in the trail where two crags nearly joined. The slopes of the far mountain shone brilliantly in the now-cool air. Clouds scudded overhead and the scent of rain was omnipresent. The woodland green about them was faintly touched with yellow and red. Autumn was not far away.

Clau lifted one arm and gave a long whistle. It was answered by a birdcall. He turned to them. "I go no further. All that I promised Mag is done. I will wait here for you for two days and nights. If you do not return by then, I go."

Rob had not heard the last of that exchange for his whole attention was centered on the two men walking toward them, bows at the ready, eyes scanning the trail before and behind.

"I will join you. Be sure of it." She was grateful to Mag once more for her concern that Luisa not travel in the mountains alone.

Clau spat and walked away. He would do as he had been asked.

When the men came closer, dark bearded and dour of manner, Luisa drew Rob near and called, "We are quite alone. I ask assistance for the boy."

One of the them looked carefully at both Rob and Luisa before remarking, "It is several hours' journey yet to the camp. We must move rapidly. The matter can be discussed when we arrive."

"I thought messages were sent about our coming." Her voice was sharp and Rob turned a puzzled stare on her face.

"Aye." The outlaw said no more but placed himself ahead of them, walking so rapidly speech was impossible. The other brought up the rear and it was no accident their fingers hung near the daggers at their belts at all times.

The land grew wilder, the paths more devious. Luisa was conscious of watching eyes as they moved along. The air of urgency in the men affected Rob so that he asked no questions, moving sturdily in her wake, glancing around with excited eyes at this legendary land of the Welsh resistance. Trees stood golden on the crags and once they passed a waterfall through which the fading light cast rainbows. Luisa's heart responded to the beauty of the land and excitement began to beat in her. She tried to tell herself it was not because she might see Marcus, but she had learned not to lie. She must hope for restraint; let pride be her gauge.

The camp lay within the woodland confines and was bordered on one side by a wide stream which rushed between high-set rocks. A steep crag rose behind it, bushes growing from the crevices. A great fire was laid and women were carrying more wood to place on it. Meat roasted from spits and jugs of ale were passed about among the many people there. This had to be one of the more remote hideaways but guards were everywhere.

One spoke to their escort briefly, then addressed Luisa in clear English. "Our leader will speak when all are assembled. He will have no time for you until that is done, nor on the morrow either. But afterward he will want to talk with you and see what sort of information you bring. You are to be set apart for now; your stories checked to make sure no spies come among us. If true, you will be welcomed to our banner. If not . . ." Menace hung in the air.

Luisa cried out, "I must not stay. I have to go." She knew she could get back to Clau if she left very soon and doubtless the outlaws would give an escort, but he'd not wait past his time and the going was likely to be slow, especially if they took her by another route. She forgot to lower her voice and the outlaw took a menacing step forward.

Rob was gazing incredulously at her. "Luisa, you cannot leave! We're comrades!"

"They didn't mention a woman!" the outlaw snapped. "What plot is this? No matter, here you will remain until our plans are prepared. There'll be no treachery this time!"

She protested but it was no use. She could not imagine why Clau had left the problem of her sex to be discovered; naturally they were suspicious. Rob's face was averted, his back stiff and unyielding. The guard was joined by another who looked equally doubtful. Their escort was fingering his dagger and now they were beginning to draw more attention.

Someone called out in Welsh just then and there was a flare of torches in the distance. The first guard said, "Sit under that tree over there and don't think of leaving it. This will have to be taken higher." He waved three of the onlookers to remain with them and strode purposefully away. They were prisoners again.

As the night deepened and a full moon rose, Luisa tried to make Rob understand but it was hopeless. There was much that could not be satisfactorily explained to herself, much less to a boy of twelve. Finally, past the lump in her throat, she said, "I have to leave and that's all. Our paths are set in different ways."

His chin trembled. "We were comrades. Or I thought we were." He moved away from her and stared out over the glen. They did not speak again.

The fire was higher now, the company expectant, nearly silent. Luisa felt a sick anticipation lift in her. The guards drew closer, watching eagerly. A man strode into the light and lifted his arms as he began to intone Welsh phrases. Luisa knew he was a bard and that he recounted one of the endless legends of this region. A strange excitement lit the rhythmic, often harsh words as the bard moved about in the orange and blue flames, the crag and wood a backdrop behind him. The people swayed back and forth, sometimes calling out words as he said them. She understood some of the language, much of it battle terms and calls for freedom. Apparently she had learned more than she thought.

He finished and stood aside as they cried honor

to him. A woman pressed a cup into his hand. He
held it up and cried, "Wales!" Luisa and Rob
stood and shouted with the others, all barriers
down. "Wales!" "Freedom!" The cries came
again in English and French. "The dragon!"

She knew the tall figure who moved from the
shadows even before someone called his name
and it was taken up. "Marcus!" He moved with
a lithe sureness and the controlled power she
remembered so well. The broad shoulders, tapering waist, and strong legs were well outlined
by his dark shirt and breeches. His white teeth
flashed as he exchanged greetings and comments with those nearest to him. The carved
profile was perfect in the reflected firelight. His
black hair tumbled riotously over the high forehead as he brushed it back in a quick, impatient
gesture. Luisa felt the blood hammer in her temples. Nothing was altered. She still wanted him
passionately, wanted also to share in his mind
and heart, to be with him in all things. She was
herself, but she longed to be part of him as well.
Marcus Lenley, her husband by duress and co-
ercion, was also the man she loved. She could
not deny it any longer, well understanding nothing was ever very likely to come of it. It was
vitally necessary for her to leave this place. If her
own sanity were to be preserved she must make
a life elsewhere. Luisa Marmoor was not one to
hang about a man who disliked her, whether he
might want her body or not. Marmoor was lost
for now; who was to say such an untenable situation could not be altered. Kings were often not
long for the throne. If she must have a cause

then let her find those disaffected ones who objected to the present king and work with them. The restoration of Marmoor was all she had ever really wanted, she told herself.

Marcus was speaking now, his voice steady and strong in the silence of the camp. Luisa listened and her whole life seemed to come down to this instant in time, to this place in the remote Welsh mountains where a throne might be toppled. She was no longer herself but one of the crowd of hearers who would have died had he given the signal.

"The time is now. Messages came from London today. Sir Adam of Wenlock, he who tortured and harried our people, is detained in London by direct order of the king to answer charges of venality and misuse of power. Likely he grew too powerful for Lancaster's desires! There is no other concentration of power along our border at this time. Others will join with us. Listen! King Henry has imprisoned his close friend Sir John Oldcastle, a Lollard, for heresy and will move against all Lollards. Surely they will rise against the regime in turn! Some of us have been among them and believe it so. Also, many of the English now believe Lancaster wrongfully reigns, that Richard's heirs should rule and his murder should be avenged!"

Cheers swept the glen and reverberated on the crags. Luisa and Rob shouted as loudly as any of the others. She turned around to look further and saw a familiar bearded figure at the outermost section of the crowd. It was the seer, John, standing quietly, making no move, ignored by those near him. Marcus commanded all the attention.

"All Wales remembers the hand of the king when he fought here as prince. It is rumored in London that he plans some great undertaking which will make him known throughout Christendom. Perhaps he plans to go on a Crusade to the Holy Land. In that case he cannot mount full-scale war on us." Marcus raised both arms and his deep voice rang with conviction. "Join with me, people of Wales! Word of our gathering goes out to all I have named and any other disaffected! We have every chance of success! I have received word from France that aid may well come in force if we show ourselves strong. The battle may be won before Lancaster knows what is happening!"

He leaned forward, the fire flickering on his bronzed features and throwing his sharply chiseled mouth into relief. The bard moved up beside him and the assemblage held its collective breath.

"Are you with me? Fight for Wales! Death to the usurper! Are you with me?"

"Yes! Yes! Yes!" The mountains rang with their acceptance and delight. The bard was chanting in Welsh, whereas Marcus had spoken in English. Now Marcus chanted with him while the people shouted. Tears were running down Rob's face and Luisa's palms were wet.

"Hold!" John, the seer, brandished his stick and made his way toward Marcus. A boy went at his elbow to guide him unobtrusively.

Marcus came to meet him. "You are thrice welcome among us at such a time, John."

The seer ignored Marcus as he turned to face the company. "Men of Wales, you must not listen. I have seen the shape of the future and the time is wrong." He spoke slowly, the words coming in a ringing undertone.

Marcus cried, "Everything meshes together for us, John! It is our time, the time for Wales!"

"Yes! Yes! Yes!" The deep-throated cry of the people was not to be halted. Luisa screamed with them, forgetful of anything else.

John raised his hand and spoke into the quiet. "Lancaster's glory is near and that house will fall in blood but not yet nor for years to come. If you pursue this course, death and imprisonment will be your lot. Do not nourish false dreams. I will come no more among you." He began to move away and the people parted ranks for him.

A hum of speculation rose. There were angry outcries and mutters as people began to argue. Marcus faced them and lifted his arms for silence. Rob leaned forward to hear his words, his young face ashen under his tan.

"John is honored amongst us all. His visions have been proved over and over again. I believe we must take this opportunity and fight. The time is ripe for our cause. I am a man of battle, my own choice is made. We are free men here. Think of all I have said, on the knowledge and experience I bring with me as your leader, chosen by you. Ponder these matters well and we will vote on the course to be taken. I have made my own choice. I shall lead those who wish to fight, whether they be a host or several or myself alone." He paused and stared at them all, his face grim.

"I go with you! I will fight and kill many Englishmen!" The clear treble rang piercingly as Rob jerked away from Luisa's restraining hand and ran down the hill toward Marcus.

Chapter Twenty-three
OWEN GLENDOWER, PRINCE OF WALES

"I CAN FIGHT! Wait for me!" The passionate young voice caught the attention of many and they turned to watch Rob as he ran. Luisa knew she had no hope of catching him now; she slowed and followed more calmly. He stopped just short of where Marcus was approaching and looked eagerly at him. "Take me!"

Marcus's mouth lifted in a smile that was at once bitter and longing. His eyes were bleak. "Thank you for your dedication and determination, young sir. With an army of men such as you we could sweep all before us!" He held out one long-fingered hand to Rob, then looked behind him and saw Luisa.

She had removed her hood and her chestnut plaits had fallen down to frame her face. Shadows danced across her face as his gaze locked with hers. In the instant before his brilliant blue eyes became passive, Luisa saw the utter gladness there. Then his face hardened and he spoke without inflection.

"Madam, I had thought you far from here. Why have you come?" It took all Marcus's strength to maintain his control. He had implored God and all the saints for her safety, worried through endless days and nights, thought of her when he should have concentrated on battle plans, and remembered their lovemaking. She would never leave his mind and heart. He knew that now. But he had come to terms with himself; Luisa Marmoor would not be allowed to come between his feelings and his duty.

Luisa decided her longing imagination had run away with her. She matched his tone. "I brought him here, a recruit for your banner." Her hand motioned toward the gaping Rob. "When I wished to leave I was detained by your men who stated you wished to speak with any who came. I'll not remain to trouble you, be certain of that."

Some of his men were surrounding him, talking in English and Welsh, urging him to speak again. He said, "You cannot leave until our course for battle is settled. No one must alert the English. Afterward, you shall have escort to the border and beyond." He turned to Rob. "Come with me, lad."

Rob looked at Luisa, who nodded. The smile he gave her was brilliant. She said, "I am grateful, sir. Is there some place where I might rest?" She had to get away from him; longing and pain and resentment were about to take their toll.

He snapped his fingers at several women lingering close by and. snapped some orders in Welsh. They came up and she followed obediently. Marcus did not look back, nor did she. Her course was set.

It was raining when Luisa woke the next morning in the crude shelter formed by an overhang of rock and bound-together branches. She had tossed aside her heavy cloak in the night and now reached for it gratefully. Her stomach lurched alarmingly, and more sleep was impossible. Was it too early for food? She had rested well. Marcus's very coldness had given her support; she had expected to weep and yearn over him, but exhaustion's bludgeon had tended to that. There were neither tears nor dreams.

She wound her plaits around her head and, muffled in her cloak's warmth, went in search of breakfast. A fire burned dispiritedly in a shallow opening under another ledge. Cook pots were set about and cups for dipping stood ready. Men and women sat together talking or walked in groups, disputing in three languages. Guards patrolled, appearing not to notice the steady rain which bore leaves to the ground and whipped among the nearly stripped trees.

Dipping a cup in the stew, she stretched out the other hand to the fire and delighted in the warmth while she stared into the gray day. She had lost Rob to the outlaws; it was what he wanted and Marcus would surely see to him. A pang touched her for she was very fond of the boy. Just then she saw Marcus walking with several men, speaking emphatically as they moved. One put his hand to his dagger and offered the other to Marcus, who took it fervently. The others crowded around eagerly. He must be speaking to everyone personally. There was likely little doubt which way the vote was to go when finally taken.

She sat down by the fire, thinking the stew was good if awful in appearance. Her own decision was made. All she had to do was wait to be taken to the border, out of Wales, away from Marcus. The wind shifted, spattering raindrops near her and bringing the scents of earth and freshness with it. She yawned and stretched lazily.

The voice broke into her calm. "Mistress! Mistress! Come with me. Do hurry!" It was one of the young guards, nearly clanking with all the weapons he wore, his face urgent.

"What is it?" Was Rob hurt? She jumped up, wrapped the cloak more securely over her shoulders, and stared at him.

"Come." He was already running and she had no choice but to follow as fast as she could.

They went toward the crag, off to the side where a trail branched off to lead upward into a pile of high rocks overlooking the foaming stream. A figure stood there, well muffled in cloak and hood. She would know Marcus in whatever guise.

As she watched he threw back the hood to reveal a pale face with down-cutting lines and somber eyes sunk deep under the dark brows. The mockery that always lingered in his stance and gaze was gone. This was a man who might have recently seen death. He waved a hand at the guard, who fixed worshipful eyes on him.

"Go back. Postpone all the meetings. Say that

I am in council, that I meditate, pray, anything. Give no hint of what has occurred."

"I swear it by the holy cross." He vanished around the bend.

Marcus said, "I am sorry to disturb you. I had not thought it necessary to see or speak with you again, but we are summoned."

Luisa was not ready for the bitter pang she felt at his words. There was nothing between them, surely. Why did she feel as though she had been stabbed? She could be cool in her turn. "Who does so and why?"

"The message came only an hour ago, borne by a trusted servant who moved so swiftly he now lies exhausted. I and my wife must travel at all speed for the very weal of our land is at stake. The wording is correct for it was committed to memory. My wife, it said. You are that, by one way and another, so you must come."

"Who commands Marcus Lenley?" Sarcasm rang in her voice. "And who can command me? I am not of you."

"He who has the power to command all of us. Owen Glendower, true and rightful Prince of Wales."

Luisa gasped in astonishment, her eyes growing huge as she looked at Marcus. The very name brought back memories of the conflict years ago which had brought news and gossip even to remote Marmoor. Glendower, once an English gentleman though truly Welsh, now a legend for centuries to come, had fought both Henry IV and Prince Hal to a standstill only to have the tides of battle and freedom turn from him. Once all Wales had rung with his glory and deeds.

"He is dead, they say. Or in France, or the Holy Land."

Marcus spoke flatly. "Glendower lives and we are summoned. If he gives his sanction to our battle and the rising of Wales, there can be no question of a great following both here and in England itself. Even the French will come."

"And if he does not?" She shifted position uneasily. "And why has he asked me to come?"

Marcus pulled his hood up against the increasing rain. "He *commands* and you of all people will ask no questions. And he cannot refuse our battle. He is Wales. Now come, we must not waste time."

Questions pounded in Luisa's mind but she would not voice them. She followed Marcus to the horses, which stood ready. The rain had begun once more and they were soon soaked to the skin. The trail grew so narrow that they had to pick their way with care; one moment they looked into the depths of a gorge, another at a taller crag. Marcus was sunk in his own thoughts and Luisa thought mainly of her discomforts; her wet, cold clothes and the chafing rash on her back and legs. They wound endlessly through great rocks, valleys, flat spaces, caverns, and trees. The rain settled in, a drenching downpour which made them go all the more slowly.

At one point Luisa thought uneasily of her recent illness and asked, "How far is it? I had the ague not long ago. . . ."

Marcus turned to face her, his face furious.

"You will continue even on your very deathbed, madam! Now be silent!"

The time was long past when Luisa would endure such nonsense in hope of peace from Marcus. She gave him a level stare. "One sentence in half a day is not overmuch conversation, sir. I begin to think your wits are addled before your battle even begins."

He reddened and clucked to his horse to move on. Over his shoulder he said, "It is far."

Luisa had cause to believe it. No words passed between them although he did pause just as gray day faded into wet darkness and handed her a flask of brandy. She drank deeply just as he did. It gave them both needed strength for continuing the journey in the rain and cold. They had to exercise much more care in travel now because the footing was high and slippery. Night came down heavily, hours dragged, and still they went on.

The birdcall split the air close to Luisa's drooping head and she jumped. Marcus caught her bridle, reining in both horses. He gave a low owl hoot which was immediately followed by another. A shrouded figure stepped from some bushes and held up one hand. Marcus greeted him in Welsh, was answered, and dismounted. Luisa did likewise, her muscles protesting as she moved.

"He awaits you." Their escort took their horses and urged them forward onto the dark and slippery trail.

Marcus nodded and went ahead, his stride eager. Luisa saw that he was familiar with this place and did not fear to make a misstep. Another man moved out to join them, hand ready on his dagger. Glendower's men took no chances.

They walked in the rain for nearly another hour. It was an endless time for Luisa, who thought she would never be dry again. Words were beyond her; she could only put one foot in front of the other and pray that the distance lessened. Now and then she heard steps and saw motion in the bushes near them. They were watched all the long way.

Luisa first saw the stone house through sheets of rain as it sat poised on the crag overlooking what appeared to be a deep drop into a ravine. Firelight blazed through one of the openings in the living rock, and branches whipped back and forth with the rising wind. The dwelling looked enormous, a veritable stronghold. They came to it rapidly and now she could see figures moving around inside. They had come to their journey's end.

Luisa and Marcus entered a large room which was nearly bare of furniture but crowded with arms of all sorts, furs, chests, and trophies of the hunt. A pale girl held out two thick fur cloaks and said, "He will see you now. Hurry."

Luisa pulled the warm fur tightly about her and pushed the hood aside. Her shoes squelched with water so she kicked them away. Marcus stared at her in surprise, then led the way into another area entirely different from the first.

A great fire crackled along one wall. Tapestries depicted heroic scenes from mythology and the Bible. Books were carefully stacked on an ornate chest and another lay open on an inlaid table. A sword of Damascus steel was ready to hand, a horn and dagger close by. A lute was ready for use as was a harp. But it was the occupant of the room who drew Luisa's undivided attention. He sat in a tall wooden chair piled with cushions and rested his feet on another pile; his appearance was like none she had seen before.

The white hair and beard mingled together and were carefully tended. He had long hands and feet, piercing gray eyes that held a touch of topaz in their depths, a high forehead, and aquiline nose. One corner of his mouth turned down and twisted. A white eyebrow pulled permanently upward to give him a look of query. Both hands shook as with the palsy and a tall, carved stick lay across his knees, which trembled also. He wore unrelieved black, a shade to emphasize his impressive stature. Luisa thought this was how Moses must have looked on the mountain when he spoke with God.

He said, "You came swiftly to my call, Marcus." His voice was shaky but still strong as he spaced his words carefully. The assessing gaze went to Luisa. "Mistress Lenley, I give you God's greeting. I am Owen Glendower."

Marcus bent at the knee and Luisa swept him the curtsy Dame Matilda had taught her long ago. Then she said, "I give a vassal's homage to the true Prince of Wales, my lord. It is wonder indeed to stand before a legend."

"Fair spoken, lady." He leaned his head back and seemed to struggle for breath. Instantly the pale girl was at his side with a cup of some steaming brew. He drank sparingly and waved his hand to include Marcus and Luisa. "This will pass. Sit on those stools yonder. Marion will bring food and drink."

Marcus's words came in a rush. "I do not wish to be abrupt, sir, but you must hoard your strength. I think I know why you called me here. Our cause is ready to prosper and you want the details. When I return with your words of inspiration and sanction—oh, I know you desire secrecy and I would never reveal your life or whereabouts—I shall have such fire to lead—"

"I do not give it." The words fell as cleanly as a drawn sword between them.

"Sir?" Marcus was puzzled, the dark brows drawn together in a frown.

"I no longer give sanction to war."

Marcus went so white that Luisa took an involuntary step toward him. He motioned her back with a sharp gesture. "Sir, you are still ill. Please don't excite yourself. We can speak of this tomorrow."

Glendower's voice was that of a dragon's. "You will wage war no longer! I have said it!" He spoke with all the authority of the prince he was. "I knew King Henry in war when he was but a lad; he has much honor. When he is free of the plots and machinations of others, he will give England a just rule and Wales as well. We could not win against him in the days when victory was so close; now there is no chance." He paused for breath and Luisa saw the ashen look on his face, the great pulse leaping at brow and throat.

Glendower was not an old man, but his health and energy had been sapped by the long years of war as well as the hard life of the mountains, where he had been trapped for some time. If the English could not enter Wales safely, neither could Glendower live freely. Luisa recalled the tales she had heard of his exploits and wondered how he could sanction such a mild course now. Denial rose in her but that must come from Marcus.

Glendower was nearly whispering now. "Marcus, you brought courage and zest to our cause. I have rejoiced in your friendship. I heard of your marriage. Strange circumstances but you were ever impetuous. I sought to see your lady wife so I may know that you comfort each other. I see there is love between you; may it give you peace."

Luisa stared at Marcus, who hurriedly masked an incredulous look. How could the prince know of her feelings when she barely knew of them herself?

Chapter Twenty-four
HONOR'S DECEPTION

"We are alike, Luisa and I." Marcus spoke wryly. "I thank the prince for his concern for us." The formal words stopped and became pleading. "Sir, we can arrange for you to take ship to France and our friends there. Your illness could be treated and you could live in warmth. When your health is regained in that fair climate, you can return to lead us again. Only if we of Wales show ourselves strong and united, powerful in battle, will there be any dealings with Lancaster. This is what you taught me long ago." He paced back and forth in front of Glendower's chair.

"I will die in these mountains. King Henry offered me free pardon if I would come to London. I refused. I will never leave Wales now that this shaking sickness has come upon me. Many believe me dead and it is better so." The soft voice rose to become that of the commander. "Marcus, I ask one last thing of you. I ask it in the name of the love you have borne Owen Glendower and Wales. Promise that you will no longer lead Wales in battle, that you will not raise the dragon standard in war again. Your word, sir!"

Blue eyes met gray ones as Marcus gazed at the man he had loved and served, who had taught him how to believe in something greater than himself, the man who had always meant honor and truth to him. Luisa felt her heart twist with utter sadness for them both. What would happen to Marcus now that his cause lay snuffed out at Glendower's feet?

Marcus went to one knee and stretched out his hand in the vassal's oath. The words were wrung from him in a transcendent bitterness. "I swear. I swear it by the Prince of Wales."

Luisa felt tears come to her eyes and then the commanding stare was on her face. She was reminded of the soaring eagle. The presence of this man! How had Wales lost when such as he commanded?

"Will you so swear, Mistress Lenley?"

Marcus cried, "She has nothing to do with this!"

"It is needful that she swear also." Glendower's eyes never moved from Luisa. "Mistress?"

"I give you my oath, Lord Prince."

Glendower leaned back in his chair and the firelight reflected on his white hair, smoothing his seamed face. His hands shook but his voice was rock steady. "The fate of Lancaster will be in the blood by which it rose to the throne. John the seer has said it; I know nothing of prophecy but it may help you to become reconciled to my command."

Marcus's face flushed red. He started to speak but Luisa broke in.

"Sir, you would not consider France? These mountains are so cold, the winds so piercing." Her voice was light and inquisitive. Beside her, Marcus snorted in anger.

Glendower said, "If I could not accept free pardon from my honorable enemy, then I could not flee. I belong in these very mountains and here I will die."

Luisa's practical brain noted that he repeated himself with an oratorical flourish which must have served him well once. Marcus was like him in speech. The obvious weakness of the prince was more evident now and the girl hovered nearby. Marcus was in an agony of his own.

She was never to know what came over her but suddenly she began to speak with intimacy and a kind of authority to this man who appeared so near death. "You will live wherever Welsh hearts meet and freedom is sought. Your name will survive in these mountains and the bardic legends for a thousand years. Owen Glendower is the very golden dragon of Wales." She stopped, flushing at her own temerity.

For one last time that night, Owen of Wales sat erect in his chair. "I thank you for your words, Mistress Lenley. They mean much to me. Marcus, I will say farewell. Remember all that I have said. We shall not meet again in this life. God's blessing on you both now and forever."

They knelt to feel the shaking hands on their heads, bending minds and bodies before the last true Prince of Wales. Marcus reached out and took Luisa's hand in an iron grip. She heard Glendower murmur in approbation and then he was gone from them.

In the aftermath of her powerful emotions Luisa was beginning to shiver, despite the warm fur and the distant fire. What had made her speak so to the prince? She, an Englishwoman! Marcus released her and spoke in an angry whisper. She saw that he, too, shivered, his powerful shoulders heaving with chills.

"You gave the prince pretty words. Has no one taught you the place of a woman is to be silent before her betters?"

She understood his pain, understanding he was trying to release it on her, and her voice became soft. "I was overcome with awe, Marcus. The greatness of Glendower has rung in my ears since childhood."

He fairly hissed the next words. "Keep your tongue off him! You are not worthy!"

A sound at the door brought them back to their surroundings. It was a servant bearing a torch. Her face was impassive; it was possible she had not heard them. "If you will come with me. Lodgings are prepared for my lord's guests." She turned and waited for them to follow.

After a short trip through dank corridors, they came to a massive door which opened onto a chamber filled with light and warmth. Candles were everywhere, the fireplace roared with heat, scented herbs and rushes lay on the floor. Several clothes chests lay open for inspection, rich garments spilling out. Tall screens partitioned off sections of the large room, but there was no missing the enormous wooden bed piled with cushions and bright covers. Trays of roasted meats, breads, and sweets stood ready. Flagons of sparkling wines were beside them. Everything waited for the delectation of husband and wife.

A young girl came toward Luisa and a man at Marcus. They spoke nearly in unison. "We are to help you prepare for rest and comfort. We stand at your disposal." Just then the soft music of a lute was heard and a man began to sing of love in French. It seemed to come from behind one of the screens.

"Leave us. We are fighters and need nothing of this." Marcus gave one of his most fearsome scowls.

The servants ignored him. The girl said, "We are commanded only by Prince Owen, who has given his orders." She put out a hand to Luisa. "Come, lady, and bathe in the water we have prepared."

Luisa decided all battles could wait until she was warm and dry. She followed without another glance at Marcus, who was still resisting. The bath was flower scented, marvelously hot, and relaxing. The girl said no more but soaped her skin, washed and rinsed her hair, and perfumed her with petals of a rose. When she brought wine, Luisa gulped it down eagerly and almost choked on the power of the brew. Her hair was spread out and brushed until it shone. A white chemise of the most gauzy material she had ever seen was slipped over her shoulders and a soft cloak of pure white velvet followed. Both were low cut so that the swell of her breasts showed. Luisa stared at herself in the half-length mirror provided and saw a woman ready for love. Her eyes were sea green with mysterious depths and had the slanting look she had so often deplored in her youth. Her small, square chin was balanced by the new maturity in her face and in the hollow spaces under her prominent cheekbones. Her dark brows winged upward in contrast to the tumble of chestnut brilliance that was her hair.

"My lady is fair." The young girl smiled wistfully and folded back the screen to take her to Marcus, her unwilling husband.

He was already seated by the fire, a tankard in hand, and had been drinking for some time because his words were just slightly slurred as he greeted her in a tone that only she would recognize as sardonic. Outside the minstrel sang a

Latin love song about the coming of spring to lovers.

"Ah, you are robed and elegant, I see. And to what dare I attribute such a show?" His grin was bitter, his eyes icy with pain.

"You, too, are comely, sir." Luisa was determined to give him no opening for a quarrel.

He tilted his tankard and waved the servants away. This time they went without question, duty done. Luisa looked at Marcus and thought again how much he must resemble one of those Greek statues of Apollo she had read about. He wore a loose robe of blue silk with long loose sleeves which fell back to show his bronzed arms. He had belted it only loosely and his muscular, lean strength showed with every motion. His dark curls were damp and curled over his high forehead, several nearly touching his dark eyebrows. The arrogant nose and smooth planes of his face along with his brilliant eyes might have contemplated the world for thousands of years past. To her, in that instant of time, he was all things desirable and she shook with the need to feel those long hands on her smooth skin.

"Did you hear me?" Luisa was jarred out of her musings. There was a sharp note of irritation in his voice as he tried to keep it low. "Listen to me, if your wits are still within you to do so." He leaned toward her as he spoke and she caught the scent of sandalwood.

Contradictions swept over her; she wanted to slap and kiss him in the same movement. "I don't want to quarrel, Marcus. Save it for the trail."

The minstrel now sang of unrequited love, passion beyond the grave, and united lovers in a pagan heaven. The fire crackled and snapped. Marcus drank deep, watching her with veiled eyes.

"Owen is a sick man; I hadn't realized how sick. We mustn't quarrel or upset him. Therefore, my dear wife, we'll act as though matters were fine between us until we leave here. Then it will be possible to go our separate ways. I wouldn't put it past some of those servants to keep watch on us and report back to him. So tonight you'll serve a woman's function."

Luisa instinctively drew back. Angry flames burned in his eyes and his full mouth was white around the edges. "I, no less than you, wouldn't want to disturb the prince." She spoke softly.

He grinned with no amusement, his teeth white against his bronzed skin. One hand curled convulsively around the tankard and she saw the silver bend. "Fetch food to me and more drink. A good wife waits on her husband's every wish and you will want to be that, won't you?"

"As my lord wishes." She could play the role as it came. She went to the array of food, piled a dish high, and brought it back to him. After putting it at his elbow, she brought the wine and held it ready. He looked at her, making no move to take anything, and one corner of his lip rose.

"You've not chosen my preference. Take it all back." He would not have spoken so to his least-favored servant.

"Pick what you want. I'm hungry myself." Luisa put the flagon at his feet and started away.

Marcus leaped from the chair and whirled her

to face him. The fury in his face was the anger he could not show Glendower. He raised one hand to slap her; it was his sword hand and somehow she knew all his power would be behind it.

"By God, you'll obey me or suffer the consequences!" His voice rose and he forgot his own recent edict of quietness.

Luisa caught his madness and used it in her turn. She dodged back from him, picked up the flagon, and threw it at him. It was open and the wine poured over his body, face, and the floor. The container clanged on the stone floor, rolled, and stopped. Marcus cursed under his breath, grabbed Luisa, and pulled her to him with every intent—or so it seemed to her—of strangling her at that instant.

"What is it? What has happened?" The head which poked around the door was that of a young man, probably less than twenty, with wide, incredulous brown eyes. He held a beribboned lute in one hand.

Marcus seemed incapable of speech but Luisa turned as well as she could in his grasp and fairly spat the words out. "Leave us, do you hear? Have you never seen husband and wife together? Get out! Get out! Sing one song to cover the noise and go! Do you hear me?"

"Yes, my lady. Yes, yes, of course. Immediately. What would you like to hear? Oh, I'm going." The door slammed emphatically and he began to play a love song of the Amazon queen who renounced all for love only to find that men feared her.

Luisa burst into laughter, and after a second

Marcus did also. He released her, went to the table, and filled his platter. She did the same and they satisfied hunger and thirst without comment while the minstrel went through what must have been ten verses of the song.

"Women have another function, madam." Marcus's voice was bitter and hard, but the glitter in his eyes had been replaced by another type of hunger. "I've not been satisfied in several days now."

"I'm not your doxy and you know our marriage was one of expedience only." Luisa tried not to show her hurt at his words.

Marcus tossed aside the wine-soaked robe and stood completely revealed to her. The long lines of his muscular body flowed into each other just as the music outside their door did. He could have been a reckless devil, a bright image in another life. Points of blue light shone in his gaze as he reached for her.

"Expedience. You have named it." One day, he thought, he might actually believe that was all it was.

"So I have. Women have needs as well and you are here. Why not?" It seemed they had never loved each other tenderly and caringly.

She tossed the velvet robe aside and loosened her shift so that she stood naked before him. There was no sign of any reaction as she walked up and put both hands on his shoulders, raising her face for his kiss. He pulled her to him in one swift gesture and his mouth came down on hers hard and demanding.

His arms were bands of iron, his hunger a

ravager, gentleness a thing forgotten. They
fought together and separately as they twisted,
struggled, caressed, and burned. Luisa's lips
drew hungrily on him as her fingers moved over
his body. His hands locked on her breasts,
slipped over her shoulders, and traveled down
her back. Then he drew her to the floor and
plunged into her, loosing his power, drawing
back, and going deeper. His face over hers was
triumphant, aggressive.

She felt the volcano inside stir and burst forth.
There was no more control in her body than in
the winds. She held him and he her as their
mutual ravishment roared to culmination. This
was an elemental joining, the filling of a basic
need, as far from the tender passion they had
once shared as love from lust. Luisa had wanted
him and still did, but this was a mockery.

She stretched voluptuously, her smooth body
touched with perspiration, and said, "Very good
for you, Marcus. Now I will have my own satisfaction." She looked at him with sardonic eyes.

Chapter Twenty-five
BROKEN FAITH

LUISA'S MOUTH AND hands traveled slowly over his
strong body. She moved rapidly, hungrily, and
she heard him groan as he grew longer and
harder. In so short a time it appeared culmination was near and she had no wish for that as

yet. Her own loins began to burn once again. Her breasts felt hot and heavy; her breathing was almost as fast as his. She unexpectedly lay down on him as he sprawled full length on the white cloak beside the fire.

Before he could say anything she took his mouth with hers and they locked in a savage kiss even as his manhood sought her heat. Their arms wrapped together as they tried to fuse the mutual desire into culmination. Luisa was conscious of every inch of Marcus; every nerve end was on fire with urgency. She moaned slightly, trying to wrench free. He held her all the more strongly, his fingers reaching for secret places.

Luisa went limp against him for a second, shifted, and moved away. He stared into her face, annoyed and frustrated. She began to move around in a kind of dance, her long hair whipping over him, her eyes alight with eagerness. When he tried to catch her, she retreated and came closer in the same motion. Her rose-tipped breasts and slender body gleamed in the combined fire and candlelight just as his darker body shone as though a polished statue.

"Come here, damn you! You know you want me! I can tell." He heaved out the words as he followed her, swollen with his need for her.

She gave a little laugh. "Then you must catch me. You do want me, don't you, Marcus?"

He lunged for her and she allowed herself to be caught. But, as they tumbled to the rushes, she turned so that she was astride him, legs outward. He put both hands on her sides and took her mouth swiftly. They kissed deeply.

Then there was no longer any denial. She rode him hard and fast, fighting back her response as she strove for mastery. He did the same and it became a contest. Shudders racked them both. Luisa felt consumed; she was welded to him and he to her. The explosion of pent-up emotion nearly shattered them when it came, propelling both into near exhaustion.

Luisa lost count of love's war after that. They were insatiable as they came together again and again, attempting to make the other yield. No words were uttered, this language came of the body only. She felt sore in every joint. She throbbed with weariness and still she lifted her mouth to his, sought him with her hands, and stirred him to incoherent response with her supple flesh. In his turn, Marcus would gather her to him, pressing her closer to his body, draining her mouth with kisses that seemed to draw out her very soul. Her breasts and womanhood ached with his caresses. They hammered and molded one another until all that was left was the need for sleep. Then they lay apart.

When Luisa woke, Marcus was gone. She had no idea of the time but the fire had been replenished; water for washing was set near it along with a plate of food. She stretched, feeling her muscles ache with the strain. The longing for more sleep nearly overcame her, but she did not want to be found abed when Marcus returned. The clothes in which she had arrived lay at the foot of the bed. They had been newly washed and dried. She lost no time in scrambling into them and braiding her hair around her head.

With her face scrubbed, the boy's garb redonned, and her hair secured. Luisa felt more like her old self than the voluptuary of the night before.

Just as she opened the door and looked out, Marcus came striding down the corridor with the girl who had attended Glendower the day before, in his wake. He was slapping one fist into the palm of his hand and muttering low under his breath. He stopped when he saw her.

"Are you ready to leave? I am forbidden access to my lord Owen! I have left a message but this person will not even promise to deliver it!" His brows met in a long dark line and his face was flushed.

"The prince is ill and can see no one," the girl said. "He told me last night that he had said all that was needful to you and you have given your oath on the matter discussed. He trusts you to keep it. Go, Marcus Lenley, and do as you have been ordered by your prince."

Marcus shouted, "Who are you to speak so to me?"

"Keep your voice down. I am his daughter, Marion. He is also my prince. While he could still speak he told me of you and your wife. He is pleased that you have each other." Her voice was strong but it shook as she continued. "I have lived apart from him, thinking him unwise to remain here. They sent for me some days ago and I regret I did not come earlier."

Now Luisa could see the resemblance to Glendower in the set of the girl's eyes and the high forehead as well as her unyielding manner.

Marcus started to speak but Luisa said hurriedly, "We shall pray always for the Prince of Wales. Marcus loves him and does not mean to act this way. We take our leave now. God and His Mother be with you."

Marcus glowered but there was nothing he could say after that. Marion smiled faintly and gave them her blessing as well. Then one of the ubiquitous guards came up behind them and said, "Come, the horses are ready."

Marcus and Luisa did not speak as they quit Glendower's stronghold in the cool, gray morning. The guards saluted Marcus gravely and watched until he and Luisa were out of sight around the nearest curve. Even then they felt the unseen presence of his men all around them. Mists swirled in the trees and the wind was chilly. The crags loomed up bare and menacing as they rode. The trees swayed, spattering them with droplets of water. This was now an unwelcoming place and Luisa was glad to leave.

Marcus was sunk in his own thoughts, his straight back a barrier as he went ahead of her. She gave way to her own as she recalled the previous night. It had been a battle with no winner. All her senses were drained, leaving her parched and tired. Past and future were equidistant. She had been determined not to give way to him but in the end her passions had won out. Perhaps if they had not had those few early days together in the beginning, things might have been different; she might not have known how it could be when love and tenderness matched between two people. Her mouth turned downward with distaste. For almost the first time since she had known Marcus, she could look on him and not be excited by him.

"You have talent for speaking to the powerful ones, I note. Luisa before the Prince of Wales! You are bold. Perhaps that accounts for your continued survival."

She bit her tongue rather than spar with him in his pain. She was as good a fighter as many and surely braver than most. How many could have fought for Marmoor as she had? In an effort to think of something else, she turned her mind to Glendower and all he had said. The reviving anger began to burn now that she was out of his commanding presence. Were they all to obey with no protest? Were they to accept tamely the rule of the English king who wronged them, who wronged her, too? Her mind began to twist with an idea. As the hours fed into each other she put it aside and brought it back until she was satisfied and, in some degree, hopeful.

Kicking her slow horse into a fast movement, she caught up to Marcus and asked, "What will you and all the others do now?"

His tone was sharp, his gaze dull. "Now? You heard me give my word to the prince. Disband, of course. Those who wish to carry on the war will harry the border, pillage as best they can, attack those English foolish enough to enter Wales. I will probably go to France and see if they intend to challenge Lancaster. I am still an individual, free to fight where I choose. Why do you ask? You'll be taken to the city of your choice, given some money, and we'll find some way to break those vows we made. Duress is a good argument for annulment, a valid one in our case."

Luisa stifled the pangs of loss. More was at stake here than the personal issues. "Marcus, listen to me. Bear with me. Just what exactly did we promise Glendower?"

He snorted. For a long moment there was only the clomping sounds of the horses' hooves on the rocks of the trail and a raucous birdcall in the foggy distance. "You were there. You heard. You took active part. Do you seek to bait me?" The words were harsh and hostile.

"Tell me." She was goading him but to a purpose.

"God's blood, woman! You heard me swear never raise the dragon standard against England, that I would not lead men into battle!"

She pulled her horse around in front of him to block his passage. Her green eyes were lamps in the mist. "There are other ways to fight! Use them!"

He made a disgusted sound. "How could a woman be expected to understand the ways of honor? Move. We must travel on rapidly. I would rather enter the gates of hell than face the men I have led with this ill news, but it must be."

"Don't act the oaf, Marcus!" She did not move in spite of his efforts to get by. "Remember those people you mentioned? All those dissatisfied with the regime? Aren't they still? The Lollards, the followers of murdered Richard II, those disaffected with Lancaster, the French? Stir them all together, include the Welsh bands and the whole land of Wales will rise. You did not promise not to fight, Marcus! You promised not to lead! I swore it, too, but am I likely to lead? Think, Marcus!"

Luisa felt compunction as she thought of the hawk eyes of Owen Glendower and his passionate conviction that the time for war had passed. He and Prince Hal had engaged in gallant, chivalric combat, honoring each other in mutual esteem. Well enough for the great ones, but what of people such as Marcus and Luisa, Rob and Mag and all those like them who lived or died at a whim? What of Arban, who dealt out injustice in the name of his ruler? And she only one of many. What of Father Sebastian, who had license to burn, root out heretics, satisfy his lusts as he would? Multiply that over and over again while men prated of honor and an old warrior drew to meet his God and think of peace. Men could be such fools!

"I am bound by my oath!" Marcus twisted the reins in his hands and no longer tried to continue the journey. The blue eyes raked her face. "Who breaks a sworn oath breaks God's law."

"A thing you've never done before, of course! Go to London with a picked few. Assess the climate of the times. Messages can be sent, matters arranged. You played parts well once as I recall. Do it again. Stir the pot. There are other ways and the cause is certainly an honorable one. When Wales rises you can join the battle. Glendower may never know the real story of it."

He laughed harshly. "The end justifies the means, is that it?"

"Sometimes, yes."

"Come on before I leave you." He thrust past her and hurried on, too fast for the narrow trail. "Stay behind me. You sicken me." He sickened himself, too, for he always seemed to berate her for feelings and ideas he had as well. She, at least, was honest.

Luisa told herself the seeds were well planted. She had said what she had to; now let them bear fruit. There had to be some grain of practicality in Marcus.

Silence wrapped itself around them again. The mountain night was drawing on and the air grew chillier. Luisa had assumed they would ride throughout the night and had prepared herself with one of the heavier cloaks from Glendower's chests. It was very welcome now. The forest trails were wider, the bare crags jutted formidably, and the dark streams rushed fiercely along. It seemed they were the only two people in this forgotten world.

Marcus paused before one of the streams and dismounted. Bending over he splashed icy water in his face and then turned to Luisa, who was glad enough to rest her aching backside.

"You are right. The winning of this battle is greater than us all. My personal honor must not stand out against it. Glendower is my friend, the man who led me to a belief in something greater than myself. He does what he thinks is best. I could have done no other than give my word.

The breaking of it is on my own soul. I shall tell the men of the band what has happened. Each makes his own choice. I do what I must." His voice rang with conviction and the light had returned to his eyes. He started to get back on his horse but Luisa stopped him.

"I have a stake in this, too. This idea was mine. You know you would not have gone forward with the war alone. I want to be an active part now. I am skilled in disguise and can use weapons; I am familiar with several ways of life and can mimic others; and I believe most strongly in what you set out to do. I want to go to London with you and your party."

"No! Am I never to be free of you?" The anger and desperation in his voice were nearly equal. "Would God I had never seen you!" He told himself he really wished that were so. What had life been without this bold, defiant woman? He did not really remember.

Luisa forced herself to calm. Rationality was the key to everything here. "It is my battle also. You know that is true and you know I can be of great help." She went up to him and put both hands on his, ignoring his instant recoil. "Let's declare truce until this war is done and we are free to take up our separate lives again. We are soldiers and as such have no right to let personal feelings interfere."

He looked down at her with great weariness. "We cannot undo the past." His dark face was somber but his anger was gone. "Truce, Luisa. This is not the kind of war I would have chosen, but because of your idea I can fight at least. I do not respect the kind of mind that thought of it but we do what we must." He smiled at her suddenly and even in the gloom his blue eyes were brilliant as the skies of a remembered day. "Truce it is. Welcome to the ranks, Luisa."

She smiled in her turn, choosing to forget his harsh words. "Thank you, Marcus. We'll go to London." It was a statement of fact.

"Aye. We'll go to London."

They stared at each other and this moment of communication was more satisfying than any part of the previous night's malevolent reunion.

Chapter Twenty-six
ROAD OF ALL DESIRING

"LUISA! I COULDN'T think where you were! No one knew anything! I'm sorry I was so mad the other night. You won't go away again?" Rob grabbed her around the waist and hugged her without shame.

Luisa set her chin on the black head buried in her shoulder and returned the caress. What could she say to him that might not turn out to be a lie later? Who knew what the future held? Lies. She thought suddenly of Marcus's friend who died in Lancaster's service believing lies. She had lied to Marcus mostly by omission in what she felt to be a simple and private thing.

Much of their discord had come from this. Now matters were so twisted between them that there might never be a solution or real trust.

She tilted Rob's head back and said, "I don't know, love. None of us knows what may come about, but I'll try to tell you what I can. I had to do something special these last days. All right?"

The gray eyes were bright. "Sure!"

"Then come sit with me and tell me what's been going on."

He sank down on the rock with her and began to talk of the preparation of weapons, strategies planned, old battles reconsidered. As the wealth of detail and boyish excitement went on, Luisa wondered how Marcus was faring. He had left her early in the morning at this way station, a hut of wood and mud built next to a crag, which was less than two hours walk from the camp. A burly guard and Rob had arrived at noon. Marcus had said he would soon report what went on. She had to trust him to keep his word, that they were indeed soldiers together in a venture of deep concern to both. And yet he had seemed very willing to be turned from Glendower, whom he loved, to her, whom he did not. Did he mean to trick her? Was this simply an easy way to be rid of an unwelcome burden?

The long, slow day dribbled toward its end. Luisa talked and speculated with Rob, washed her hair in the cold stream near the hut, dried it in the feeble sun, paced up and down, and kept a sharp ear for Marcus's return. She could not conceal her trepidation from Rob, nor could she confide in him. The guard was one of the few who spoke only Welsh; of a dour nature, he replied only in monosyllables to Rob's questions and the boy finally gave up.

There was little sleep for any of them that first night. During the second day Luisa realized she must not give way to nerves so she and Rob went fishing, first with poles and then by simply walking about in the icy water trying to grab the slender darting shapes. They had enough success to fill their bellies at midday. They slept for a short time and rose to play the tumbling games Luisa had loved as a child. She was glad to find herself still able to contort herself into amazing shapes one minute and out the next. Rob was an excellent pupil and they shook with laughter over their efforts. Her sleep that night was tired and dreamless. Rob rested close beside her, his cloak tossed free. Her last waking thought was of how much she had come to love this boy. Parting would be so very painful.

"Will you sleep the day away? Is this my army relaxed and snoring? Have I come to the wrong place?"

Luisa sat up to see Marcus towering over them in the bright sunlight visible through the doorway. She pushed back her tumble of hair and rose. He was smiling although his eyes were shadowed and his dark curls were askew as though he had run his hands through them many times. Rob came to stand beside her.

Marcus said, "They have accepted the idea with many misgivings. The magic of Glendower's name held them from open rebellion. It is hard to be prepared and in high spirits and then be told you must wait indefinitely to strike a blow. They were angered and cried out against me, called me spineless and a traitor to our cause. As I feared, they said a woman's wiles lured me from my duty to Wales."

"Luisa is a bold fighter." Rob spread both feet wide and stood before Marcus loyally. "She knows what is important."

Luisa wanted to ask Marcus if he, too, thought she had lured him, but that was far too dangerous a canker to open up. "It was wise of you to leave me here."

"Far wiser had I taken you to the border and left you." Marcus spoke with complete sincerity but the bitterness was gone from his voice. He saw Rob start to speak and shook his head. "We do as we must, Luisa. Let us not tear at our wounds. God be thanked that the band and I are at least in partial agreement, though some denounced Glendower, saying he is old, in retreat, and no longer a warrior. And that I should lead them now." He thrust his hand through his hair once more as if in frustration. "At any rate I have one month to stir things up in and around London, another ten days to prepare and report back. If I do not succeed in this endeavor, the armies of Wales will march and I am no more of their following. None dissented in this vote."

"It is an ultimatum." Luisa thought of all he had endured, how deeply the breaking of his oath—in spirit if not in letter—affected him. Now he was greeted with mistrust from his own men.

"Yes." He was strangely accepting. "But I am

given time to get to London before the accounting begins. I forbade them to speak of you. I still have some authority, it appears. Your name was not mentioned again."

"Marcus, I want to go," Rob cried. "You have no idea how useful I can be. Luisa, too, of course."

Marcus put out a hand to him. "My young lieutenant. How could I function without you? Luisa goes, too; it is our bargain. Some of the men declared for me, vowing to stand with me no matter what. Those I have sent ahead with specific orders regarding whom to contact. We have arranged meetings in the city at various times. Others came with me here. We must begin to plot. Are you ready for disguise and mimicry, madam?" His eyes rested on Luisa, no emotion except unity in them. She was his confederate, a soldier in his army just as she had asked.

Luisa told herself sternly she must demand nothing. In time she and Marcus might be friends, but she wanted no more of the hating passion that had consumed them in Glendower's dwelling. All her hopes and ambitions must go now into the battle for Welsh freedom—which was, more simply, freedom for Luisa Marmoor, a freedom to choose her own life. Marcus was not for the taking; he pursued more than contentment or love, he sought the dark gods of revenge and blood.

The little procession that set out a day and a half later would not have caused surprise on any road in the kingdom. A woman, old and a bit crippled, clad in dusty homespun, shuffled along on the arm of a bearded hunchback whose eyes darted everywhere as he twisted his head back and forth. A tall, blue-eyed man with a lame shoulder limped beside a young boy who led him slowly. Both seemed dazed, even a bit simple, and had to be guided by two swarthy fellows beside them who laughed and babbled in some guttural dialect all their own. All were meanly dressed, a little fearful, and had obviously never been very far from wherever they came from.

The three men Marcus had chosen to accompany them—Mark, David, and Ned—had been long with the outlaws and were completely loyal to him. They fell into their roles with enthusiasm and a sense of flair that reminded Luisa of Rob although they were into the middle years. Since speed was essential, Marcus had arranged to have mules waiting for them near the border. He seemed to have connections everywhere and it was this as much as their fervor which made her feel the mission would win out. Rob tended to overact at first and Luisa argued with him.

He regarded her seriously. "I must practice very hard to be a foolish lad. It is hard."

They all roared with laughter and their way was made easier.

As they went toward London in the cooling days and chill nights, each member of the party listened and observed, assessing all they heard. No one knew just what might prove useful in the days to come. Luisa concentrated on dress and behavior, the idle scraps of gossip, the talk of men at their cups or food. An old woman was seldom noticed and little heeded. Marcus treated her much as he did Rob or the men. He was the commander but his manner was easy, a trifle cool, always casual. She sensed he had finally settled her in a role he could accept for now and this was sufficient for her as well.

One night they took shelter at an inn's stable by gracious permission of the expansive owner and were even allowed to peer inside the window at the great folk drinking there. A merchant and his entourage, all brilliantly clad and sparkling with jewels, were holding court. He, corpulent and verbose, became more so with good wine and venison. Slapping the table, he called for more drink and began to speak freely to his friend.

"The Lollards grow in power. I tell you, friend Charles, this is a time for stern measures. The country is alive with rumors and discontents of all sorts. The very kingdom is threatened. Old King Henry knew what to do with rebels and heretics."

The other man drank deeply before replying firmly. "But consider. Sir John Oldcastle is one of their leaders, own friend to the king, yet he lies condemned out of his own mouth and will be burned. That is the order from London and a stern action, I'd say. Thus the king sets himself firmly against heresy and will root it out."

Luisa felt her stomach churn at the complacency in his voice. He might have been talking about gathering the crop in. What real difference did the ruler make, she thought? Dame Matilda, staunch supporter of Richard of Bordeaux, had told her many tales of his cruelty balanced by others of kindness. Marcus had suffered bitterly under both reigns. You had to survive as best you could and hope for the best. But heresy! Who could hope to disprove that charge once it was brought?

The merchant shook his head. "What we need is a good war. That always unites people. The land is split into factions, you know that as well as I do. The king ought to stop dithering at his prayers, get married, and produce a son for his line. He needs to take firm command before someone else does!"

The innkeeper looked up in horror. The merchant's followers and the rest of the patrons fell silent. This so nearly bordered on treason as to make no difference. What if someone reported them? If one spoke ill of the king, he should do it at home behind locked doors and to the closest of friends.

The friend said, "Leave the matter to those who rule the realm. It is beyond us all. There are more pressing matters for us. Let's seek fair diversion tonight for our wives await us on the morrow, or had you forgotten that?"

His listeners howled with laughter. The innkeeper bawled, "Drink deeply of my good ale, masters. It'll dim the thoughts of your wives!"

The talk was muted now but Luisa heard comments and speculation still. Much of these centered around Oldcastle's trial. What sort of man could condemn a friend to death? The talkative merchant was beginning a song about the charms of a certain tavern wench and others were joining in, but it had not caught on yet.

"He denied the very sacrament of the Mass. Said the Lord Pope was the Antichrist."

"Fearful! A wonder the devil didn't snatch him away then. He deserves the fire!"

"It is said that the king himself pleaded with Oldcastle and expounded the scripture, even begged him to recant."

Luisa turned away, sickened by the near pleasure in the speaker's voice. So much thought for religion, so little for the freedom that made life worth living. They were learning the power of discontent and Lollardry in the land, however, and this was all to the good. It remained to see how matters stood in the capital. "He who holds London, holds the land." This had been said throughout the history of England and it was still true. English discontent with Lancaster was the key for the Welsh.

"The soul of the righteous is the seat of God. Who needs anything else?" The fervent words came from a slim, bearded man close to the door. His companion hushed him vehemently and sang the merchant's song loudly.

Luisa put her hand on Rob's shoulder, comforted by the closeness of him. The real danger was in fanaticism, whether from church, state, or individual. Now they were headed directly into the thick of it.

Chapter Twenty-seven
MANY SHAPES

AFTER THE SECLUSION of the mountains, London seemed huge and crowded to Luisa. As the myriad odors made themselves apparent, she thought longingly of the freshness of country air. Wales was a place apart; it was here that their mutual destinies would be decided. They were to stay at the house of Master Malcolm Brecont, a wool merchant, whose father had come to England with Philippa of Hainault, wife to great Edward, in the last century. The family had prospered, and his name was now honored and respected. None knew that his interest in Lollardry had become overwhelming.

The party entered the imposing house by a side gate and waited in the courtyard. There was nothing odd about the dispensation of charity; the church commanded it. Anyone watching would have considered this an example of the merchant's piety. Within his household, Master Brecont felt himself safe. It had been determined that as much secrecy as possible would be maintained, thus he had only been told that a party of fellow Lollards, including some Welsh, sought succor for a short time. He had known Marcus for many years and now, on this blowy, chill afternoon, greeted the party as old friends.

"Welcome. Welcome to my house." Balding and comfortable, his small paunch carried rather proudly before him, he introduced his wife, Eliz-

abeth; a daughter several years younger than
Luisa, Philippa; and the delight of the household, a five-year-old boy called Richard. They all
sat beside the great fire in the central hall and
were served an informal supper of roasted birds,
stew, pastries, and heady French wine while
Master Malcolm talked of the great matter most
recently occurring in the city.

"Things are in an uproar now. Oldcastle escaped from the Tower just a few days ago.
Priests had been at him night and day to recant.
He was sentenced to death by fire." His kind
face was somber at the thought of the risk he
courted to his family by service to this faith
which seemed to many to be the only one.

Marcus said, "We heard of it as we entered the
city. There's a great price on his head; it's only a
matter of time until he is captured." His brilliant
eyes swung toward Luisa and back to his host.

He started to speak further but Master Malcolm rushed on. "You've probably not heard the
latest. Rumor has it that King Henry himself
arranged for his friend's escape; preparations
were made for him to go abroad in safety. Oldcastle fled into the city instead and now seeks
the mountains, where he will encourage rebellion against his onetime friend, our king."

"Is this true?" Luisa's voice cracked across his.
Marcus looked as eager as she felt. This was
news indeed! Any hand was welcome to them so
long as it was against Lancaster. "Tell us
quickly!"

They had not told their host of the relation

ships between them and she saw he wondered, not only at her presence but at the note of command in her words.

"I believe it is true. Lancaster does not know tolerance but it is likely friendship still means something to him. Who knows?" Master Malcolm shrugged. "We are not allowed to worship as we must. What is one single man's life compared to that?"

Kind as he seemed to be, there was still the thread of fanaticism burning in him. Luisa supposed it was in her as well and certainly in Marcus. Who among them was capable of judging the others?

"Malcolm, there is a matter of the gravest urgency which must be discussed," Marcus began. "You have much to lose. I will understand if you refuse. It shall be between us alone." The firelight gleamed on the planes of his face and reflected over the serious ones of the company.

Master Malcolm drew himself up proudly, smoothed his blue velvet doublet, and proclaimed, "I know the truth, Marcus, and am well aware that our immortal souls are of more importance than this transient world. I, my family, and countless others will do much to rescue our fellows from the sin that now rules England." His voice rang up to the vaulted ceiling, over the carved furniture and richly hung walls. It was filled with pride.

In the silence Marcus reached across to clasp Malcolm's hand. "I knew you'd say no less."

The family and remainder of the company withdrew. Luisa followed a little maidservant to the small room she was told would be hers alone. She decided that Master Malcolm would probably bestow the fire for heretics on the Catholics with just as much fervor as they on him. What logic drove such people to think any replacement for the king might grant the freedom of religion they wanted for themselves?

Suddenly a deadly fear poured over Luisa. She wanted to see Marcus more than she wanted anything else in life just at this instant. Heedless of common sense or reason she dashed back down the corridor, across the hall, and along the stairs. Her heavy country shoes banged on the wood, alerting the two men who stood just at the door of an anteroom. Marcus and Malcolm had not yet entered to begin their talks. What could she say? What did she want to say! All she could do was look at Marcus, the lean jaw, proud chin, tumbling dark hair over the high forehead, and all the powerful symmetry of his body, and long for some word of caring from him. That feeling was so strong it nearly swamped her.

As if he could feel her gaze on him, he looked up. "Yes, did you forget something?" He was in darkness but she sensed the singlemindedness of his emotion. Nothing must interfere with this conference. His profile was sharp and strong, but the intensity in him went beyond all else. "What is it?"

Luisa wished she knew. At the risk of making a total fool of herself, she found nothing to say. "I thought I left something." She sounded feeble enough; he'd think she was taking leave of her senses.

Master Malcolm stepped up to Marcus's side. "Send the maid to look for whatever it is, my dear." He chuckled comfortably. "Everything's fine, you'll see."

"Of course." She wanted to cry out to Marcus to take care, but they were all in this together and equal care was taken for all. She lifted her chin. "Goodnight, gentlemen." She turned and ran back the way she had come before they could comment.

Back in the chamber the maidservant was waiting with jugs of warm water for bathing. She made no comment on Luisa's odd behavior, having doubtless seen much stranger. "I will help you now if you wish," she offered hesitantly. Luisa bade her go for she wanted this time to herself. What had made her act so? She took off her dusty clothing, tossed it aside, then shook out her hair. She had not had a warm bath in quite a while and it was heaven. The water swirled over her pink nipples and slim body. She had the firmness of the trained outdoor person, the coiled strength of resilient youth. When Luisa held the mirror up to her face she saw that the hollows under her cheekbones had begun to fill out, her eyes were deep green pools under the slanting brows and her newly washed hair gleamed with dark fire.

She looked around. Braziers provided warmth and the candles cast pools of soft light. A tapestry depicting David and Goliath hung across one wall; a basin and jug were on a table near the bed. A furred cloak was tossed across a stool. She slipped it over her nakedness and paused.

Was it so simple? The thought had come suddenly. She had been near Marcus so much in the past days; he had accepted her as a comrade, then retreated with Master Malcolm and she had feared being left out.

It had been so long since she slept in a proper bed that she tossed and twisted for a long time before sleep finally overcame her. Her dreams were filled with battles, glaring eyes, angry denunciations, and heretics endlessly burning. She woke once with tears on her cheeks. She dreamed she stood once more before Glendower and whispered, "There are other ways to fight." A sense of betrayal went with her into sleep.

"Mistress, the sun is high! My mother said you were to be left undisturbed, but surely you will wish to see what I have brought."

The high, light voice belonged to Philippa, the daughter of the house, whom Luisa had met briefly the night before. She had a merry, rosy face and sparkling brown eyes that laughed as Luisa sat up blearily and began to shiver at the chill of the room.

"Look, gowns I have worn only once or twice. Father says Henry, my betrothed, will not wish to wed me if I continue to grow in height. Henry says otherwise. You don't mind that I have roused you?"

Luisa looked into the innocent, happy face and wondered if she had ever been so. The heavy dreams of the night had laid their own burden on her. Her voice was soft as she said, "You and all your household are too kind, Mistress Brecont. I certainly don't mind."

"Call me Philippa. I intend to call you Luisa. I know there are great secrets afoot and I'm forbidden to ask questions. Let's be friends while you're here. Do try these on!"

Luisa responded to the girl's infectious gaiety and garments flew about as the girls absorbed themselves in velvet, silk, fur, and linen. Some of the clothes seemed unworn; she guessed Master Malcolm was an indulgent father. Finally she stood arrayed in a blue-green gown on which the shades shifted when the light touched it. Bands of fur ornamented the long trailing sleeves and skirt. Her narrow waist showed to advantage with the artfully worked belt. A coif of soft linen in the same color as the dress hid most of her hair and gave her face a pointed look under her slanting brows. Her eyes blazed green and her lips had a pink sheen. There was a cloak of velvet and fur to wear over the gown, as well as hose of silk and elegant leather shoes only a little too large.

"You look the great lady." Philippa smiled, her eyes dancing with the questions she must not ask. "I vow, Henry's eye will be quite taken with you." She spoke complacently, knowing full well her own gown of rose velvet set her apart as though she were a special jewel.

"Tell me about Henry," invited Luisa. "Was he chosen by your father or did you grow up with him, perhaps?"

"That's the enchanting part, Luisa. He is from Southampton and had business *with* Father, whom he'd never met. I happened to be in Father's office that very day he came by and we were drawn together. He offered for me just about the time Father decided it was a good match. Am I not fortunate?"

"You are indeed." Luisa felt a pang of uncharacteristic envy as she wondered how it would be to have a protective family, a betrothed who loved and chose you, a certain future. How sure was anything? This family was in real jeopardy; they would suffer upheaval no matter which way the rebellion went. On the whole she was glad to be Luisa Marmoor with schooling in the adverse ways of life. At least she knew something of the ways of survival.

"Come, Luisa. Mother wants you to sit with her but I want you to go with me and Henry when he comes. We're going out into the city."

Luisa smiled. "I'll have to go with the others who came with me but of course I'm only too happy to do what I can otherwise."

"But they . . . oh, well." Philippa hesitated, then caught Luisa's hand. "Hurry, I want Mother to see how you look now!"

They ran laughing into the solar where Dame Brecont sat at her work, her capable hands moving smoothly over the tapestry she was repairing. Philippa gave her mother greeting, adding, "Isn't she lovely in that gown? We'll take her shopping with us. She can be the chaperone. I will see you in a short while, Luisa!" She dashed away, singing as she went.

Dame Elizabeth motioned Luisa to a seat as she concentrated on placing a thread. The brilliant sun shone in to reflect the lights on their gowns. It was utterly peaceful here and Luisa felt welcome. Philippa's gay song rang through the house, helped along by little Richard's piping in bad French.

"My daughter likes you. You will be company for her in the next few days if you can abide her chatter." Dame Elizabeth smoothed her brown hair back and fixed soft blue eyes on her guest.

"Madam, I am agreeable but I must see my fellow travelers and take counsel with them. We have duties as I am sure you know. . . ." Luisa felt her stomach knot into a ball of unease as the older woman held up her hand.

"I am to tell you that Marcus and the men who came with you, even the boy, have gone to a meeting involving your special concerns. It will take several days and you are to bide here until they return." She gave her calm smile and waited.

"Why was I left behind? This is shameful treatment. Quick, do you know the section of the city where they went? Give me an idea! I'll find them!" She had not been so angry in a long time. The fury was sweeping over her, making her face flame and her heart hammer wildly.

"I was told nothing more, Luisa, and it is better that way. It is our custom for women to be obedient."

"Bah!" Luisa forgot all courtesy as she paced up and down. "Did Marcus sanction this? Is it some idea of your sect?"

"My dear girl, it was totally Marcus's idea. Even so, we of the Lollards are not so foolish that we do not understand the exigencies of battle plans. Your boy's clothes are very convincing, but you have no choice in this. Marcus would not have you roused. They left early. 'Keep her safe.' Those were his very words." Dame Elizabeth's placid brow was wrinkled with concern and she laid aside the tapestry to rise.

Luisa whirled like an angry tigress. *"How dare he?* This was my idea! I have fought and undergone perils, endured much, planned for us all, and then I am left behind like a bit of baggage! How dare he do this to me? By the saints he shall suffer for it! I'll plant my dagger right in the middle of that arrogant face!" She stopped for breath and found that tears were running down her cheeks.

Dame Elizabeth put one arm around her. "Do you love him so? I know you were wed under circumstances of duress and that the marriage will be set aside for you to go your separate ways. Marcus told us that much; he had to for we must be so very careful."

In this moment of loss twice over, in this house of content, Luisa could say it honestly. "I have loved him since the first time I saw him. I will do so always. He does not love me but I love him and will until I die."

"I do not envy you. I first saw Malcolm on our wedding day and I counted myself fortunate and blessed that he was not old or cruel or hideous. We are happy and have been. Perhaps I have not known heights or depths, but my life has been calm and happy. I pray Philippa's will be the same."

Luisa looked at her and knew she would change nothing. Loving Marcus was worth the price.

Chapter Twenty-eight
THE WINNOWING

DAME ELIZABETH MOVED away from Luisa to look out the solar window and to allow her guest to compose herself. She continued to speak soothingly but Luisa heard little of what she said. In the shock of being left behind, she had revealed feelings she wanted to bury and keep secret. There was no denying their truth, however; she loved Marcus with all the passionate fury of the Marmoors, who selected one mate and remained loyal. Was it not one of their legends that an ancestor had loved a Saracen woman who spurned him and he remained in Outre-Mer in hopeless suit for her until he died?

Luisa would do no such thing. She was a practical person, after all. One would survive as best one could. In the deepest part of her she knew that nothing mattered to her more than Marcus. She would gladly go into exile if she were asked. Even Marmoor, dearly as she loved it, paled before human love, and now both seemed lost to her. Marcus had not asked her to go with him, either into exile or on this mission. But, perhaps there yet remained hope for Marmoor. If the rebellion was successful it would be the most reasonable thing in the world to ask for her estate and even additional lands back.

She lifted her head, brushed away the tears, and said, "Forgive this unseemly display. When Marcus returns, the matter shall be discussed.

Until that time, I'll be more than happy to serve you in any way I can."

Dame Elizabeth felt the palpable withdrawal and honored the courage that produced it. "I have seen no breach. All that has been said here remains between us. Please believe me, Luisa. Malcolm tells me so little; it is safer for us all. Marcus wishes to protect you."

"I have no wish to be protected! There is no need. I fight my own battles!"

Dame Elizabeth sighed. "Very well. Go out now with Philippa and Henry. The fresh air will be good for you."

Luisa curtseyed and went out into the hall where the young girl waited with a young man of stocky build, pale gold hair, and suntanned skin. He looked at his betrothed with adoring eyes; it was easy to tell who would rule in that household. Philippa presented him with pride and gave Luisa's last name as Martin. Only their host and his wife knew her real status with Marcus and none knew her real name.

"I am honored, Mistress Martin. Will you be visiting long?"

"Only a few days, sir."

"Permit us to show you something of London as well as the shops my lady here will frequent. I shall have the fairest wife in all Southampton." His pale blue eyes shone with pleasure at the prospect of outings with a friend of Philippa's rather than a suspicious servant who might tell Master Malcolm of stolen caresses.

Luisa read this on his open face and in Philippa's guileless eyes. "I am delighted to join you. I envy Philippa so handsome a gentleman." They all laughed together and she was grateful for the uncomplicated friendship offered her. Just for a little while she would be a carefree visitor from the country enjoying exploring with her friends. All else should be forgotten.

The day held a touch of chill but the coming winter was nowhere in evidence. Swift movement brought color to their cheeks and the passing sights excited them to chatter and lively conversation. They went to ribbon stalls, where each seller vied in telling the glories of his wares, and to the lace maker's stall, where his cobwebby creations floated from their fingers. Materials were viewed for gowns, leather for shoes, and jewels and gold enchanted them anew. Parcels were sent back to Master Malcolm's house in increasing number. Philippa's faced blazed with increasing excitement and Henry's with alarm as he thought of his extravagant future wife. Then when he looked at her beauty and grace his expression changed back. She was worth it all. Luisa was charmed with the young couple and her laughter rang out with theirs.

They wandered out into the exuberant bustle around them. Wealthy lords and ladies, churchmen, merchants, apprentices, common folk from the villages, and all manner of people moved rapidly by. Tradesmen called out their wares as the crowds bought, bargained, chaffered. They walked along the streets lined with people selling corn, gold, cloth, and all manner of food. Taverners called out the delights of various wines while pie sellers bawled with equal vigor. A lively game of bowls took place on one of the narrow streets to the consternation of those walking there. The boys surged up and down, yelling and scrambling. A tumbler stopped in midspiral and ran before them before jumping to safety.

"There's no place like London, but I am glad we are going to live in Southampton." Henry was precise as he looked at the brawling scene.

"I am sure you are right." Philippa's tone was respectful but the wink she gave Luisa was filled with mischief. They were not likely to be buried in Southampton.

A troupe of several singers and a juggler had begun their act on a nearby corner. They sang of the May and love, of youth and joy, delight in the chosen of one's heart. Luisa felt her eyes mist and knew Philippa shared longing glances with her Henry. One of the girls in the troupe lifted her timbrel and began to dance, a merry capering that set the gathering crowd to laughing.

Suddenly trumpets blared and there was a clatter of hooves and marching feet. The people turned from one entertainment to watch another. Luisa, unused to trailing skirts after wearing boy's clothes for so long, felt hers trodden on and turned to lift it up. Someone pushed her and she found herself at the very edge of the street. She stared transfixed as the company approached.

The escort wore the leopards of England and the same banners flew brilliantly in the air. The small group of men riding behind were richly and extravagantly dressed in velvets and silk. The sun turned their jewels to liquid fire. They laughed and talked as they rode, sometimes waving and tossing coins to the shoving, staring populace.

The cry began in one throat and was taken up by them all. "The king! Look, the king himself!" They began to surge around the taller of two men, who rode more slowly behind the gaily clad ones and was in earnest conversation with another.

Luisa looked at this man who was only a few years older than herself. He was far more soberly dressed than any in his entourage. His face was ruddy and slightly elongated, his brown eyes surveyed the cheering throng, and the long Plantagenet nostrils flared with pleasure at this welcome. His hair was brown and thick with shimmering lights where the sun struck it. He had a cleft chin and his body was that of a fighter, long and lean. Three rings only shone on his supple fingers and his brown clothes were unadorned. His smile was warm and brilliant as he lifted his hand in salute.

He was the king of England, holder of a precarious throne, called usurper and the priest's prince by those who thought another should rule. All that Luisa had heard about him came back as she entertained for one wild moment the thought of stepping out in front of his horse and capturing his attention that way. If she had not been involved with the Welsh cause she would have. Now, however, too much hung in the balance. Any momentary interest of the king would be brushed away by those surrounding him at any rate. She looked at the full mouth and recollected he had once roistered in the stews with commoners and upheld their cases before the courts, daring the displeasures of his stern father. "Hal! Ho, Prince Hal!" One more daring than the rest called out the old name by which the Londoners had called him in those days and the rest took it up. He waved and inclined his head to his people in a gesture that was curiously like homage. Was this a second's exuberance? A fascination with whoever ruled and not Henry himself? They had cheered Richard many times but that had not saved his life.

"That's the king, missy! Why don't you greet him?" The high, cackling voice of an old woman, very like the one Luisa had impersonated, rang in her left ear and made her jump. Those around them noticed she had not waved and did not seem to share their excitement. Henry and Philippa were some distance back, no doubt envying her the vantage point. "Wave to Hal yonder!"

The slight tumult caught the roving glance of the monarch and his steady brown eyes rested briefly on Luisa's face. This was Lancaster, despoiler of Marmoor and Wales, he whose family had helped to shatter Marcus. She did not move. She would not salute Lancaster. Her green eyes blazed in her white face, looking directly into those of Henry V.

"A rose for my lord!" Someone threw a bunch of golden-headed roses at him and he caught them easily but his mettlesome horse shied so that he had to fight for control. The people surged closer, some of his guards mingled with them and the procession swept along.

Luisa took opportunity to slip further back into the crowd as she looked for Henry and Philippa.

She had the sensation of being watched just then and turned her head to look. She looked straight into the eyes of a horseman in the back of the procession. It was Charles Arban. His face did not change expression but she knew he recognized her for his eyes glittered in triumph.

"Did you see him? I vow, he smiled at me! I know he did. Henry doesn't think so, but I do." Philippa surged up to Luisa, caught her by the arm, and drew her along toward the back.

Luisa was thankful for the girl's appearance, especially for the frowning Henry behind her. Out of the corner of one eye she saw Arban riding on with a dozen or so drably attired men. A contingent of churchmen rode at their heels. It was not likely he could leave the king's train to pursue her. Maybe she still had a chance.

"Don't you, Luisa?"

She put a hand to her head. "What don't I?" She swayed a little in the crush of people. "My head, this air. I can't breathe too well, I'm afraid."

Henry took charge. "See, Philippa. I'm not the only one who has problems with the smells of London. We're going back to your house. This is enough for one day. Luisa's pale as it is; we don't want her to faint. Come on."

Was this the way a hunted animal felt? It could run and run, fade into the forest, mix with others of its kind and yet the hunter came on, ready for the slaughter in a predetermined outcome. Luisa's feet moved with those of the others. She answered their concerned questions, vowed she was all right and just needed a bit of rest, and all the time she saw those eyes preparing her fate.

Flight was her first thought. If only she could get a message to Marcus! She must ask Dame Elizabeth.

When they arrived at the house there was a guest who was being catered to and honored. Lady Travers was at least seventy-five, garrulous, and in no mind to lose any sort of audience. She reclined in the best chair in the solar and prepared to hold court, her old eyes snapping and her coif slightly awry.

"You look a bit pale, my lady," said Dame Elizabeth. "Do you feel faint? Perhaps we'd best leave."

"Stay here, all of you. I like to see young faces about me. Faint, indeed! Why, in my day we didn't know the meaning of the word! Elizabeth, this generation is too soft! Mark what I say!" She peered at Luisa until the others grew uncomfortable. "Your face is devilish familiar. Those slanting eye brows, those deep green eyes, even your nose. Who does it remind me of?"

They all sat drinking delicate wine and eating small cakes while the old lady chattered of times past. Dame Elizabeth continued to sew, murmuring appropriate responses now and then. Philippa's eyes glazed but she sat perfectly still, the very model of a proper young lady. Henry yawned once, then blushed bright red and assumed an attentive expression. Luisa could not avoid the scrutiny, but she retreated into an attempt to make plans for escaping Arban if it became necessary.

"I have it!" Lady Travers let her voice go up in delight. "Philip Marmoor, of course! The handsomest man at King Richard's court. Retired to his estates after his marriage and died soon after. His wife did, as well." Her whole spirit was in another time. "I talked to him a bit; he was a flatterer in those days. He kept wanting to get back to Marmoor, he who had the favor of that most capricious of all kings. I saw his bride once. She was lovely but not so vigorous as he. They died of the plague and I wept for them both." The easy tears of age collected in her eyes. "Your last name is Martin? A by-blow, I take it?"

"Margaret!" The shocked voice of Dame Elizabeth rang in the room, causing Henry to jerk to attention once more. "What a thing to say! Mistress Martin is most respectable, as are her parents!"

Luisa was fascinated by this intimate glimpse into the past. "I've heard tales of King Richard all my life, Lady Travers. Was he truly as they say?" Too late she caught Dame Elizabeth's imploring glance and realized she had encouraged the visitor to stay far past her welcome.

"All and more, my dear." Lady Travers forgot Philip Marmoor and launched upon tales of Richard's reign and intrigues without pausing for breath. For a time Luisa walked in that era when art and literature flourished: Chaucer's tales enlivened the court and England stood foremost in the arts. Scandal and cruelty had no measure in these times; death walked beside the smiling king who could charm and execute in nearly the same hour. "Ah, Richard of Bordeaux loved beauty more than his kingdom and he paid for it. Bolingbroke's son, devoid of imagination and caring only for the sword, rules in his stead as did his father. England has ever loved her warriors."

Luisa came back to the present briefly when she heard Dame Elizabeth give a soft order to a hovering servant. Outside, the afternoon was dimming into evening and the household would soon be hungry. Philippa wore a look of resignation before her mother's stern glare and quickly shifted it to a smile of interest. The old tales were bemusing to Luisa. People saw matters so differently. She knew Richard had been a dangerous tyrant for all the much-vaunted glory of his court, yet a scant few years later men were willing to die on the premise that his heirs might rule. A pox on all kings and banner waving!

"Will you have more wine, Lady Travers?" Dame Elizabeth was determined to show hospitality to the bitter end. Her own eyes had begun to glaze with a surfeit of the tales. "And you will remain to dine with us, of course?"

"Certainly." Lady Travers was prompt with her reply. She caught Luisa's grin and the puzzled expression drifted over her face again as she sipped her wine.

"Then if you will excuse my daughter and myself while we check the preparations?" They rose eagerly while Henry bowed, hiding his own boredom with a struggle. "Mistress Martin and my daughter's betrothed will keep you company."

Lady Travers pulled herself closer to the fire. Henry and Luisa were forced, out of politeness, to follow. She fixed Luisa with a piercing stare for what seemed the hundredth time that day. Henry might not have been in the room as the years clashed between them.

"I am never mistaken in these matters. You have the mark of them both. There was a child. A girl. They died of the plague as I said and the little girl was almost alone on that forsaken estate. When the lord of the neighboring lands came to investigate, he found her beside their bodies playing. They were clad all in their best clothes and jewels, and lay in their blood for the plague had nearly torn their bodies apart. One does not forget such horror, I think."

Luisa thought of the old dread she sometimes felt, the pool of spreading blood which sometimes invaded her dreams and the whirling about afterward. Dame Matilda had called it only a nightmare. She had not remembered it for many years, but now she did.

Chapter Twenty-nine
SEAL OF THE DAMNED

"LADY TRAVERS, YOU are clever beyond all imaginings. This is a coil, I'll admit, but it concerns a vow to Our Lady and must not be broken. When all is complete, you shall be the first to know, I promise it." Luisa allowed her eyes to go soft with entreaty and earnestness. She would dearly love to strangle the woman where she sat, but no inkling of this must show. "Please, both of you. Say nothing. It is my vow." Would so weak a ploy work?

"You are the Marmoor child?" Triumph burned in the old woman's face.

"Yes." Damned if she'd say anything more.

Henry was intent on chivalry and favor. "Luisa, I will keep silence in the face of your most sacred vow. Lady Travers will also, I am sure. I am honored."

"Swear to it, my lady." The easy authority of Luisa Marmoor came unbidden and Lady Travers gave an evil grin.

"His very voice! This will make a merry tale! I so swear but remember your promise!"

They swore, the three of them, to keep the faith and the silence. Past and present mingled until Luisa did not know which was which. If ever the time came when she was free of intrigue, she would most happily seek out this old gossip and learn more of her parents and their lives. Dame Matilda had always been general in her tales; that was understandable, she had not wanted to cloud her charge's life with the memory of her parents' deaths.

That evening was to stand out in Luisa's thoughts as a bastion of peace after tribulation. They dined merrily on fish and venison, various sweets, and several kinds of cheese and wines. Lady Travers told a few slightly bawdy stories and their laughter was real. They diced for absurd penalties, exacted wagers, sang a few lively ballads, made up foolish tales for young Richard, and played chess with lovely chessmen which had been in the family for generations. The company was welded together in some strange way that was all the more odd considering the way they had begun.

Luisa had a passion for Chaucer. She recalled that it was something she and Marcus shared in those early days of amity. Now she acted out the Wife of Bath, dealing firmly with her husbands. They laughed most heartily as the wife grew more and more furious with her fifth husband while he read his books constantly.

"Luisa, I vow you are as good as a troupe of players by yourself!" Philippa cried.

Lady Travers had known the poet and she regaled them with tales of his various works and how they had been received. She ended by saying, "I have always preferred works in the Latin and French, but somehow our good English is the only language for this Geoffrey."

She thought of Marcus and his love for that land. The English loved Welsh music. It seemed completely proper to end the evening with a recitation of Welsh verse. Luisa had no actual ear for music but somehow the tongue-defying words had partially remained with her. There was no real translation for the poetry, bound up as it was in bardic allusions and filled with the magic of those high lakes and mountains. She spoke what she remembered, the light of recollection on her face. "In the sacred time of the May, the way opens for the blessed . . ." Edra's voice spoke in her mind and she stopped.

"A dear friend taught me what little I know of

that. She is dead now but always I see that most beautiful land with her eyes." Luisa thought of the overlook with Marcus in the time when he had loved her body. She knew that if she lived she would return there in the truest of all pilgrimages.

As Lady Travers bade farewell, she whispered, "If there is anything I can do for Philip's daughter, she has but to ask."

Luisa smiled and thanked her. "I will remember the vow as you must, my lady."

The next day was rainy and cold. Henry did not come since he had business to tend but she and Philippa made music and read and helped Dame Elizabeth with the endless tapestry repair. Luisa began to feel restless and nervous, seeing no way to be sure Arban would not find her other than to simply vanish into the London streets. Her efforts to try to find a way of getting a message to Marcus were useless. Her hostess maintained she knew nothing.

Late that afternoon an authoritative hammering came at the door. The servant came to them in the solar. "There is a litter sent for Lady Martin. The bearers have a message." She extended the parchment to Luisa, who took it eagerly.

"Your presence is urgently needed. I send for you in the name of the golden dragon. In his name, fail not."

The bold black script resembled what she had seen of his penmanship and the scrawled *Marcus* looked imperious enough to be his. The golden dragon could only be Glendower. She glanced up at Dame Elizabeth and extended the note.

"The summons is valid. You need not fear for me. This must mean he has changed his mind and decided he needs me, after all." Happiness spiraled up in her. She could not wait to leave.

"But Malcolm has sent no word and they were together. Surely he would have sent one of the men you knew. Is it wise to go?"

"I must." She was in a fever of haste. Glancing down at the yellow gown she wore, Luisa decided there was no time to change. Had not Philippa said to keep the clothes? She took the brown velvet cloak that hung from a peg near the door and placed it around her shoulders. "I'll send a message when I arrive. Don't worry."

She kissed Dame Elizabeth, hugged the excited Philippa, and entered the litter which was borne by several husky men and escorted by a man-at-arms in plain livery. A sense of caution made her ask him, "Who has sent you?"

The stolid face never altered expression. "I was told to tell you if you asked that you are to remember the overlook."

Luisa relaxed. Who but Marcus could know that? "All is well!" She waved back at the Breconts and then was carried away into the rainy streets.

The litter bounced along over what seemed to be an endless course of twists and turns. Luisa told herself at first that she was simply impatient to know what was going on, eager to see Rob and Marcus and the others, anxious to be back in the thick of the plans. She swayed from side to side with the motion, wondering that the course was so rough. Several times she peered out at streets so narrow the close-set houses shut out all light.

The smell of refuse was nearly overwhelming. She saw a few incurious people moving along and trying to shield themselves from the chilly wind which blew gusts of rain about. The cloak she had wrapped herself in was not sufficient to keep her warm. The minor physical discomfort did not matter for soon she would see Marcus.

They came to a sudden stop and the litter was set down with a thump. Luisa started to push the curtain aside but before she could do so it was jerked back and a familiar voice said tauntingly, "Welcome, Mistress Marmoor, or Lenley, whatever name you prefer. Welcome to my house. It is time to meet your former betrothed."

It was Charles Arban. Behind him stood Adam of Wenlock. He was certainly well into his sixties, but his stance was that of a much younger man and his body was trim. His hair was thin and dark, his face well-lined and the cheeks red. Luisa thought of a waiting vulture. Both were sheltered under the jutting roof. They burst into laughter at the expression of horror she was unable to conceal.

Luisa was never more thankful for her gift of mimicry. She was the very image of the great lady as she ignored the hands of the minions who came for her and stepped out into the rain. Calmly she walked up to them and to a dry corner. There she shook out her skirts and gathered the cloak more closely to her neck.

"Where is my husband? What have you to do with Marcus?" She was pleased that her voice did not shake despite the deadly fear that had come upon her.

Arban flashed a grin at his friend. "I am afraid we do not actually know the doubtless estimable Marcus. As to what we have to do with him—well, that's another matter. He is not here. Lady, I fear you have been duped."

"But the message? The dragon and the overlook? How did you know of that? And what do you want of me?"

Sir Adam, looking increasingly like a vulture, stripped her with his eyes. "After fortune brought you and Charles together in the street, we had you followed. We know what the Lollards do; it was the work of only a few minutes to discover where you went and why. Marcus Lenley is not a stranger in the ranks of traitors and we have sources. Anyone knows the dragon is Wales and as far as the overlook . . . we have those in the ranks of the outlaws who are loyal. So here you are."

He opened the door behind him and bowed to her. She gazed past him into a small, barren courtyard. A covered walkway led to a stone house. Trails of smoke rose from it and the few windows were covered with dirty cloth. She heard cries from the street for drink, for free passage through the muck, and the throaty laughter of a woman.

Her lip curled. "What is this place?"

Arban said smoothly, "One of the places in which I maintain a most profitable interest, a drinking place and worse, most pleasantly worse. These are the very stews of London, my dear. No place for a lady. Shall we go in?"

Luisa looked at the bearers who stood watchfully behind and at several other evil lackeys, just emerging to await their master's bidding. No escape. Guile would serve her better.

"Why not? Will you offer wine? The journey was long and bumpy. Is there a fire? I vow I'm freezing."

They bowed elaborately. Each one took an arm and escorted her into the building, through a door off the courtyard, and into a dusty corridor. She felt her flesh crawl at their touch but did not dare pull away. Their men walked behind, ready for any difficulty. Arban opened a panel which led into another section of the house. The room into which they emerged was richly furnished with elaborate hangings, candles in carved holders, padded chairs, and heavy carpets instead of the customary rushes. She sat down unbidden and took the wine but did not drink.

"Why have you taken me? Do you think you can take me from my friends without queries being started, a search instituted?"

He laughed. "We are the most powerful in the land. To what authority shall we answer? Let us say, my dear Luisa, that my dear friend Arban is most helpful regarding certain matters. The king is in full accord with us. As for you, I have a score to settle. I am not easily flouted, as you will learn." His eyes were greedy upon her.

Charles Arban licked his lips. "Aye, there is a score to settle."

Luisa surveyed the two men and understood that they were utterly evil. She knew they intended to kill her, not by poison or a swift dagger, but a slow, drawn-out death administered by those who delighted in such things. The knowledge showed in her face despite all her efforts at self-control. They were swift to see.

"That is what will happen. There is justice, after all." Sir Adam's expression had a kind of gleeful righteousness as he measured out his words for their fullest effect on her.

She felt the fear coming over her in waves. With all the contempt she could muster, she demanded, "How can it be that you have not been trapped in your own vileness?"

Both were unperturbed. Arban said, "Let us explain to you that the true power is not always invested in the wearer of the crown. Officials of the court often have more power than he." He turned to Sir Adam. "Shall we proceed?"

"Certainly. But we must make sure of her strength. Death must be deliciously slow."

Luisa had nothing to lose and ran at the tight-lipped Arban. Angered and terrified, she raked her nails down his face and spat a curse at him before the servant tore her away.

He came close and slapped her on both cheeks before drawing away. Sir Adam grinned, the hunger glittering in his savage eyes. "You're really not much of a lady, are you? Such a bad temper. We'll just let some of your energies wear off." He waved at the servant. "Take her away. Drag her if you have to."

Even with her arms pinned behind her and evil incarnate in front, Luisa could still be defiant. "Any air I smell has to be better than that which you two pollute with your presence! Walking obscenities! No wonder you have to steal your pleasures! What perverted horror of the London streets would come willingly to such as you?"

Arban had not staunched the blood from her scratch and it ran down his parchmentlike skin into the corner of his mouth. Sir Adam watched eagerly. Now Arban said softly. "You will come willingly, longingly, Luisa Marmoor, to our feet and beg for the mercy you pray will come. Defiance and subservience whet our appetites alike. You excited me that first day when you pleaded and then challenged. I knew Sir Adam would find you exciting as well. You might have even lived long enough to bear him a son. It was sheer luck we found you again, and in the middle of conspirators, too! How amusing life can be!"

Sir Adam reached over and pulled her gown away to show her full breasts. His hand cupped her right one and he fingered the nipple. She struggled but it was useless. Her full skirts hampered her so she could not even kick.

"Damn you!" She started on other curses but Sir Adam shook her roughly.

"You need to be prepared, my dear. Really, you are most rude."

At his nod the servant pulled her away and half carried her from the room, a short way down the hall, and thrust her into a chilly cell so quickly she barely had time to balance herself on the shallow steps before the door slammed behind her.

She was once more captive and this time it appeared that there was no way out.

Chapter Thirty
HELL LIGHT

LUISA'S CELL WAS just wide enough for her to take several paces back and forth, stretch out her arms, and reach upward. There was no window but a faint illumination was always present. She had a thin straw pallet and a crude wooden mug was pushed back and forth through a hole in the bottom of the door with the few morsels of food and water she was allowed. She was given no water for washing, no other clothes, and was never permitted out of the prison. The filth was almost as intolerable as the lack of fresh air and sunlight.

Anticipating the plotter's plans was worst of all. They meant it to be. She tried to occupy her mind with songs, stories, poetry, scriptures, languages, and the invention of wild tales. Every minute she kept sane was one more blow to those who waited for her to crumble. Wales, Marmoor, and Marcus were recalled in every detail. She relived every moment, good and bad alike, with Marcus. In the end she did not regret any of it for that was not her way.

"At least I have loved." That thought served to sustain her in this period of waiting. She was always cold but the memory of past summers helped, as did the program of exercise she began so her body would not totally weaken. Although it was difficult to move about in the cramped area the exercise made her feel better. Her tormentors were a long way from driving her mad although despair was her constant companion.

There was no way to tell night from day so she slept and waked as she felt the desire. She roused once to the brilliance of torches and movement. Sir Adam, immaculately dressed and holding a pomander to his nose, stood in the doorway and watched her. She had long since ripped the bottom of her skirt away in the need to move more freely; the rest of the gown was stained and torn. Now she sagged limply on the pallet and gazed dully at him, blinking in the light.

"You grow riper by the day." The vulture look was on his face. "Come, girl, we don't fool so easily. We've watched you daily through peepholes. We can gauge your strength very accurately. The decline has been amusing and we are readying for a fresh pastime."

"I thought so." She kept to her dull pose. It might come in handy. While she lived anything was a possibility. She was buoyed by her very strong desire to live.

The servant took her arm and led her back to the opulent room she had entered on her arrival; it seemed as though nothing had changed except herself. Food and wine were placed at a table. Charles Arban, all in black velvet, and Sir Adam, in opulent rose velvet, bent toward her just as they had done previously.

"Eat. You need not fear poison."

She heard one of them speak the words; it did not matter which. She looked furtively about lest the food be snatched away. Once she would have abstained, given invective and fury, but now she ate as rapidly as possible, not caring that some of the stew fell on her bodice or that the wineglass trembled in her hand. She had never been so hungry in all her life. With every bite and gulp her body was restoring itself; it seemed to her that her blood ran more richly for this meal.

Sir Adam sat down a good distance away. Luisa had grown used to her smell but he clearly had not. "Haven't you wondered about your friends and the fate of their planned rebellion? I mean, in addition to worrying about your own plight, that is?"

Luisa lifted her head and stared at him. "Rebellion?"

"Don't play the fool. That does not amuse us. Are you surprised we know of it? There are very few secrets we do not know. We support it, you see."

"You support Wales? Why?" Her voice came out in a croak of incredulity.

Arban broke in. "We must admire a mind that can be concerned about matters of the realm when it should be more properly reflecting on the various ways of pleasing its captors."

"Why not tell her? It's a goodly joke." Sir Adam was almost petulant.

"As you wish. I hope she is pleased with the quality of our humor."

He resumed. "Your dear husband thinks you have taken up with a young lordling who caught your eye the day of the king's procession. You have since traveled with him to the south country. It was easy to spread this amongst those at the Lollard's house."

"Marcus!" His name escaped her lips briefly

before she shut her mouth, and gazed determinedly ahead.

Arban took up the taunting now. "The rebellion will take place as planned with all the disaffected units of the realm. King Henry will die; he has not proven himself malleable, nor has he acted swiftly enough against these selfsame malcontents. His brothers will fall with him. Kings are extremely replaceable. They change and the same faction remains in power. Have you not found it so in your history lessons? Oldcastle, that fervent Lollard and once the friend of the king, will rise up against him. Some say he has ambitions for the throne himself."

"You will set Mortimer, the heir of Richard, in his place, use Oldcastle's name as a rallying against rebellion, and reduce those who have actually brought it about. Then you'll rule through Mortimer who is probably weak enough for you." Luisa did not try to conceal her horror. Her mind was momentarily distracted from her own fate although she knew quite well they told her these things as a prelude.

"A clever wench it is!" Arban grinned down at her. "We have supplied money, arms, encouragement, rumor, and hope to those elements wishing change in the land. Our people, men and women alike, have wound themselves in among the factions, subtly telling them what they wish to hear yet saying just enough to make them doubt each other when it comes to the matter of rule later."

"What month is it?" She wanted to orient herself in time.

"The last one of your life." Sir Adam came to stand beside her chair. "If you want to measure them out then consider that you have been our guest for nearly a full month. It lacks two days until November. Has the time gone by rapidly for you?"

"And when is the rebellion?"

He cuffed her lightly, his fingers lingering along the curve of her jaw and dropping to her neck. "Why do you care? You'll not be here to witness it. But still, why not? Early January is the date." His eyes moved up and down her body. Arban came to stand beside Sir Adam and they both began to laugh.

Luisa stared at them and through them. Her pretense of dullness had faded with her questions. She understood that they were completely aware of all she felt and thought. This was not a new enterprise for them, but a treasured pastime.

Arban said, "You will wonder at our amusement. A friend of yours has made an amazing defection to the Lollards. He was so outspoken against them before, now so fervently for them. A price has been set on his head. They are minded to think of St. Paul himself. He has been denounced from several pulpits, decried by the king. Later, of course, he will have the names of the Lollards and know where to find them throughout the kingdom. The heresy will be suppressed and England's new ruler will be grateful. Rome may consider the cardinal's hat."

"Not to forget France and her king. It will be a most profitable alliance." Sir Adam poured himself a glass of wine and drank deeply. "Now that you have been acquainted with affairs in the world you are about to quit, I think it is time to reintroduce you to a certain gentleman." He shook his head in a mock reproof. "No, my dear Luisa, you must not think we are gathered to destroy one girl, or several for that matter. We gather, even as do the Lollards and the other dissidents, to plan for the future."

The door swung back just then and a black-cowled figure strode in. It was Father Sebastian. Nothing about him had changed. Fanaticism was stamped more heavily onto his harsh features and his eyes burned with zeal.

"Well met, Mistress. It has been some little time since I have seen you. I see your pride still overwhelms you despite the state into which you have fallen. I am glad to have the opportunity to cure you of the abominable heresy to which you adhere."

Luisa glared at him, at them all, and contempt hung in every syllable of her steady voice. "Foul traitors all, you belong on a dung heap! I wonder, Father Sebastian, that the God you purport to serve does not strike you dead for all the terrible deeds done in his name."

He rounded on her, his face lit with an unholy passion. "Nothing is dishonorable when it roots out heresy. Nothing! I have seen the deplorable state of this land! I used my authority to find evil and deal with it. The king had ordered me to. He was said to be devout, a true and faithful Christian and servant of our Lord. The fires had been ignited; I knew how and when to strike more fully. The king rebuked my honest faith, commanded me to moderation and silence saying we must move slowly so that some might be convinced to come to the true faith. But fire is the cleanser! Only that! God and I have turned from Henry of Lancaster!"

Luisa felt her head ring as his voice rose to a near shriek. There was distaste on the faces of the other two but also a satisfaction. They would use anything to set the realm in profitable turmoil. What was any of this to Luisa Marmoor? She ought to try and think of some way to escape, but her brain would not function; she could only stand and listen to the priest's mad tirade. One blessing was in evidence. Father Sebastian was so entranced by his crusade that he would not have noticed had the Blessed Virgin herself walked in front of him.

"I sought those long in power, of good religious faith, wise in rule. They agreed with me and I will have a free hand with heretics after our battle is won! There are indeed bastions of the church in this land who will declare against the ruler who does not strongly uphold the faith!"

Luisa burst into raucous laughter. They whirled as one man to gape at her. Of all the reactions she might have had, it appeared this one was the least expected. Father Sebastian turned mottled red and brown as he nearly choked on his words. She laughed all the harder, not knowing how long she could keep up the pretense. The door behind him was open. No one expected a weak and emaciated prisoner to dash through it. They had watched her exercise but had no idea she did it continuously or that her slenderness belied her strength. She poised herself to flee.

"Guard! Take her!"

It was too late. Four huge guards came rushing in response to Father Sebastian's angry howl. They held her firmly so that she could not move. Arban and Sir Adam closed around him and began to remonstrate. She heard them as from a far distance.

"Too soon. We have her here for a special purpose."

"You overstep yourself, Father. The woman is ours."

Father Sebastian cried out, "It can be slow. She is a heretic!"

They whispered together for another few minutes and then Arban waved to her captors. Apparently the dispute had been settled for they were smiling. Luisa began to struggle but it was hopeless. The men carried her effortlessly down the dark corridors, through a heavy door, and into another courtyard with high walls. The sounds of the street were faintly heard. It was very cold and flakes of snow drifted down from an overcast sky.

They set her on her feet and stood back, ready to seize her if she should attempt to run. The old men followed, their faces eager. Luisa stared at them and then at what stood in one corner of the yard.

The stake stood tall and black against the wall. The pile of fagots was ready to be ignited by a torch held by a nearby servant. She fulfilled all their hopes then, for she comprehended their intention. She screamed in terror and panic, her body shaking with it.

"Behold your fate, woman! You are one of many!" The powerful voice of Father Sebastian rose over her cries. The others laughed in the reality of their triumph.

Luisa had been afraid before, but she was numbed at this terrifying prospect. This was waking horror, bestiality beyond belief; she could not realize the enormity of what was about to happen to her flesh, her slender body, the mind and heart encompassed within it. She was half-crazed with the prospect and without defenses.

The laughter and comments of her tormentors brought her partially back to her senses. She knelt in the muck of the yard, her hands over her face, sobbing and crying out but her mind still noted that the nearest guard wore his dagger loosely in his belt and that the loose coat Sir Adam wore had a little curved blade on the sash. If only she might get close enough for one grab! Life still surged too strongly through Luisa's veins for her attempt to take her own life, but at least she could try to bring one of these monsters with her on her deathly journey.

Sir Adam called, "Bind her to the stake! Have a care for she is devious!"

Luisa shrieked with all her might as the guard pulled her, almost dislocating her shoulder. She kicked at him and he struck at her. She dodged and grabbed at his dagger which came away easily in her hand. There was a movement behind her and one of the slighter guards rushed to twist her arm, deadening it so that the weapon fell to the ground.

"You shall pay for that. Green wood burns more slowly and we mean to have a care that you don't suffocate." Arban was amused but there was a lash of anger in his voice. "Bind her, you guards, and hurry up about it!"

Luisa was jerked across the yard and toward the stake. She felt utterly defeated; nothing was left for her but this horrible death. Her mind was empty and pride had no meaning before the facts. Her mouth opened and her desperate screams rang out, carrying her last remaining struggle with them. She fought against the hands of the guard and those who came to help him. Now she was a fear-maddened creature, giving vent to the extinction of life, crying to an unhearing heaven and earth.

Her battle brought even more guards, who were still unable to halt the manic screams searing her throat. She saw the blazing torch, the black stake rearing up as she was taken closer to it, and already she felt her skin shrink from the flames.

Chapter Thirty-one
DE PROFUNDIS

THE VOICES AND noise reached Luisa through a mist. There was a great hammering, streams of curses, more hammering and kicking. "Open up! What's going on in there? Open up, I say!" The heavy gate tottered against the kicks. She summoned her strength and screamed with all her might.

The guards set her on her feet but continued to hold her firmly as Arban gestured to them. She swayed and bit savagely down on the hand one of them tried to hold across her mouth. He motioned for the gate to be cracked but the guard who did so was immediately shoved backward by two very large, red-faced men built as though they wrestled daily. Both carried clubs, wore rough clothes, and had a dull, angry look.

Arban snapped, "What is the meaning of this intrusion? How dare you disturb the business of the church?"

One of them laughed loudly. "It's no church you've got down here, friend. Long way from it. Listen, my customers at the tavern are complaining! They can't enjoy the beer or the girls for all that yelling and it has to be real noisy for them to object. What're you going to do about it?"

The other intruder gaped at them as a frown creased his face. "What's that stake for? What's going on here?"

Father Sebastian came forward, black robes flapping in the icy wind, his gaunt body seeming

frail and his eyes blazing with fanaticism. He
held up one hand in reproach. "We are interro-
gating a heretic and the flames are most useful
for this work. I explain this much to you so that
you may understand we work the Lord's will in
this matter. She will be gagged so that your customers are not disturbed. The guilty have much
to fear, you see. Now go in peace and leave us to
His work."

The man looked around uncertainly and
moved closer to the other as he began to fumble
with his club. He backed away a few steps at
Father Sebastian's authoritative stance and manner. The guards grouped together as a loud muttering came from the street. Someone shouted,
"Can't even drink in peace anymore! What's happening?"

Luisa's wits sprang to her aid then as she saw
a possible chance ebbing. The miracle that had
produced these surly knights should not be allowed to go to waste. She had utterly despaired
of her life. Now there was a dim possibility of
survival. Her voice was now that of the water-
front, the very intonation of the London-born
waif who fought for a living against all odds.

"How now! That's the old bastard's story!
Picked me up on the wharf, the old one did,
promised me all kinds of things so I'll come with
him! Sure didn't say there were two more just
like him. Old perverts, ruining my trade, give
me a bad name, it will! Me a heretic? Me that
spends time on my knees in the church praying
for my dying old father! The idea!"

"She lies. Leave us so that this business may

be concluded." Father Sebastian spoke with all
the awesome power of the church behind him,
all the centuries of unquestioning obedience that
it demanded.

"Heretics are burned for all to see. Make examples of them and right to do it, too." Luisa
put her shaking hands on her hips and swayed
blithely back and forth, grinning at the staring
men, hoping they would see an invitation.

One of them said, "The girl is right. That's
exactly what they do. Examples. Have a proper
go. Sure."

Sir Adam came up beside Father Sebastian and
spoke in the tone he must have used with the
king himself. "These are great matters. You must
not interfere."

"So he says!" Luisa gave a screech. "Old per-
vert can't even be a man!"

The first man frowned again as if he were
working something out in his head. "All this is
bad for business. People can't enjoy themselves
while things are going on like this." He beckoned to Luisa. "How about you come with us?
You look like a tasty morsel and my brother and
I'll give you good sport. How's that? Better than
these old ones, eh?"

She shook aside the guards who released her
with questioning glances toward Arban and the
others. The red-faced man hefted his club and
some of those outside the gate chose that moment to bawl another query. Sir Adam made a
barely perceptible gesture. She darted to the side
and then walked all the more slowly to the man,

making sure he saw each curve of her body in the torn dress.

"I'm right glad to see some men for a change!"

He pulled her close and thrust a hand into her bodice while she looked challengingly into his eyes. His hard mouth closed greedily over hers and she almost choked from the rancid taste of bad ale. It was consoling to think that her own smell was not likely to disturb him and she looked the part she was playing.

Father Sebastian cried warningly, "There is no force which can stand against the holy church! She will not be mocked!"

Luisa felt the hand on her breast go still. She did not really think they would go in the face of the populace just yet. The rebellion was not fully formulated, the careful early planning must not go awry for too much was at stake. Lest they waver, she cried, "Churchman, indeed! The things that one wanted to do! Make you blush, they would. I think he used to be a mummer, do a real good job of it, don't he?" She burst into her raucous laughter and pushed her body boldly toward him.

It was sufficient. He and his brother pushed her out the gate, laughing as they went, and into a crowd of some ten or more men and a few women who had heard it all. Luisa knew Arban and the others would quickly find a subtle way to get her back if they all did not leave immediately. A crowd swayed one way could easily be handled in another, and Father Sebastian had a powerful eloquence.

"Let's take her down in that cellar over at Merry Jack's place, what say you, brother?"

Both of them grinned and pawed at her. The people around them began to laugh and make lewd jokes. Someone cried, "Well, maybe now we can drink in peace!"

Luisa said, "Whatever we're going to do ought to be done far away from here. Let's go before those old goats start out after me again." She swung her hips once more and saucily gazed at them. The pretense was not hard for she was just beginning to realize that she was alive and free, not slowly charring and half-dead on a stake. She was sorry to do so, but she bent down, picked up some dirt, and threw it at her lustful companions. Then she ran and ran.

Having stolen some boy's clothes from a laundry line, Luisa roamed unhindered in the next few days, sleeping in corners when dark came, stealing food and running with it, drinking brackish water or catching up the dregs of an ale cup as she begged in the darker inns. She made sure that she went always away from the section of the city where Arban lived although she knew full well he might be anywhere. In the streaming crowds there was a modicum of safety. A boy could go anywhere. During this period, Luisa Marmoor disappeared into the urchin who moved constantly, always aware, ever alert.

Once she skulked by a tavern and, when a drunken fellow slouched out, followed him into the dark, stuck her foot in his path and relieved

him of his belongings, dagger, and cloak. She
was now a thief but she did not care. Danger
made her wary; she was constantly turning and
shifting in her efforts to watch those around her.
Her hand stayed near the dagger, her green eyes
darted craftily, and the person who inadvertently touched her was generally repelled by the
fury with which she whirled in challenge.

Survival was her first concern during these
days, which soon melted into weeks. Food,
drink, a place to rest, the freedom to move about
were all she needed. Life itself. She had no other
thought. She savored the cold, the rain, the increasing grip of winter, the rushing, fighting
people, and her own struggles for the tossed
crust of bread, the warm corner of a stable. The
odd coin came her way by begging, sweeping
out inns, tending horses, giving directions from
one place to another, or by clowning in the en-
tertainments which often swept through various
sections of the city. She never stayed more than
one or two nights in any one place. Drifting and
mingling, melting into the London dregs, she
learned again that she was a survivor. The way
she had used the two men who had saved her
life did not disturb her. The true horror was the
malevolence and torture to which her mind and
body had been subjected. It had been by the
blindest spin of Fortune's wheel that she had not
been slowly destroyed, for in the aftermath she
began to believe they would have taken her from
the stake again and again over days or weeks
before death came.

She burrowed deeper into her cocoon of

safety, refusing to think, allowing herself concern only with the moment at hand. Her disguise was near reality; the dirty face and clothes, the smells and language she had adopted provided security in a world where many fled the searching eyes of the great. As she grew bolder in her role, she earned more. Her tumbling skills grew, she was adept at the quick bawdy saying, which produced food or money if the hearers were amused. Innkeepers fed baggage-and-errand boys heartily now and then. Fastidious Luisa Marmoor, who had had to bathe every day, was no more. In her place was the boy who ran before the winter wind and lived. No more was necessary. This was her way of protecting herself until the scars healed.

One morning she was roused from the straw where she had spent the night in return for tending the horses at an out of the way inn. There was a great commotion in the street outside, with commands to hasten, feet slapping in the mud, and beasts stamping. Her first instinct was flight but her common sense reasserted itself. She was far too ingrained in her part to be suspect now. Her fingers jerked the hood in place and settled the dagger within easy reach.

As she emerged into the cold, gray morning and adjusted the heavy cloak she had taken from the drunken man, she collided with an apprentice who was moving so rapidly he did not have time to stop. Between his curses and the jeers of his friends, she heard a far-distant blast of trumpets.

"What's going on? What's happening?" She

assumed the easiest role to play, that of the lad
from the country, stupid and gullible, awed by
the city, voice just changing.

"Where've you been, boy? Don't you know
what exciting things are going on today?" He
was in too much of a hurry to be angry or pick a
fight, as might normally have been the case.

"I don't know. Around." That much was true,
she reflected. In the depths of the city she had
been frequenting, rumor was constant. She had
heard nothing of rebellion or religion or perse-
cution, only concern with human comforts, gossip of neighbor for neighbor, tales of survival in
a hard winter, and general quarrels. Even
Marcus had been shut in some compartment of
her mind. The present was sufficient.

"I've no time to explain things to a dullard."
He adjusted his cap and took a lordly air. "It's
enough to say that the body of King Richard is to
be reburied this day at Westminster and there's
much to see. I'm not taking the time to explain
who he was or where Westminster is!" He burst
into roars of laughter and dashed away with the
others.

Pageantry often produced largesse. Luisa's
better judgment told her to stay away from pro-
cessions since the last one had been her undoing, but few if any could recognize her as she
was now. She would go for a little while, grab
what was available, and leave. Surely there was
no harm in that. Images of Arban's courtyard
flickered uneasily in her mind and she began to
sweat even in the cold.

The trumpets sounded again, closer this time,

and now she hastened in their direction, telling herself over and over that there was no danger. Chanting came to her ears, at one time low and dire, at another triumphant. When she reached a side street, she darted in front of two large good-wives and was brought up to an impenetrable wall of people. A party of scholars in black gowns and caps were talking among themselves and her sharp eyes caught part of the conversation.

"King Henry is indeed confident. This is a great honor done to Richard."

His fellow was testy. "It is done to show those who persist that Richard lives in exile, that this regime knows him to be dead. This king gains much by this action. Richard's memory is piously respected and now he will lie with England's other kings. Even those who dislike Lancaster will applaud the decency of the idea."

"And cleave more strongly to him because of it. Devious!"

They spoke more softly and Luisa heard nothing but the thoughts whirling in her mind. The rebellion was not far away according to what Arban and Sir Adam had told her. The time was well past that Marcus had been given to report back to the outlaws. The followers of Richard who believed him to be alive and those who wanted his heir, Mortimer, to reign were among those to be included in the rising. Was the plot known? What of the Breconts and Marcus? Would he have believed the tale circulated about her? She had safely shut herself away, concentrating on survival, choosing safety in the best way that had presented itself. In so doing, was everything lost?

Guilt swept over Luisa then, swamping every other emotion. Her life had been saved; she should have tried to warn Marcus and the Lollards someway. She owed a debt. How she could have done so without placing them and herself in mortal danger she knew not. There had been no indication of conspiracy or uprising in anything she had heard. But she should have tried. The tears she had not shed since her captivity flooded her eyes. Her sense of responsibility to something other than herself returned, and with it came the bitterness of loss.

Chapter Thirty-two
ROD OF AFFLICTION

THE CROWD SHIFTED suddenly and Luisa was shoved forward so that she was able to see something of the spectacle. She dug her fingers into her eyes as they ached and burned, but she forced herself to concentrate. Now she was in a fever to know what was happening in the city, and with the planned rebellion and the Lollards.

The cortege came into sight and the people grew silent. The candles and crosses came first, followed by richly robed clergy measured in tread and bearing sacred objects. The bier was draped with banners and hung with black. A troop of men and women rode behind; their faces were somber and their clothes subdued. Another procession of clergy moved along, this time singing the lovely chants for the dead in Christ.

Luisa half expected to see the tall figure of the king, but she could not see into the crush of courtiers and priests and there were no visible trappings of royalty. Her tears came again and rolled unchecked down her face as she stood with the Londoners and watched the cortege wind solemnly along, taking him who had once been the anointed king of the realm to the resting place of kings and to the side of the wife he had so loved. Luisa felt unbearable sadness rise up as she remained there in the winter wind, listening to the low-cadenced psalms, and heard the tramping feet die away. Inadvertently her hand came up in the sign of the cross. She could not have said why she did so. Richard was before his God these many years and Lancaster sat on the stolen throne but Luisa Marmoor, who held with none of them, could still weep.

It was not the urchin of the streets but the proud daughter of nobility who began to walk aimlessly and did so for hours as she pondered courses of action. The Lollards had to be warned. Marcus must be informed. Those were her established goals. She could only pray it was not too late. Life was too dearly won to be tossed aside. Risky as it was, she determined to try to contact the Breconts.

The early winter evening was closing in as she

began to think of retracing her steps to an inn where she was fairly certain of some scraps. Her head was bent against the wind and she did not at first notice the figure watching her from the corner. His head turned as she passed and he began to follow her, his steps slow and sure.

She became aware of him too late to jump aside but she pivoted as he caught her arm. Dagger in hand, teeth set hard in her lip, she lifted it to strike. This time she meant to kill anyone who molested her. Not for this fate had she endured so much. She would not die at the hands of a footpad for the three coins tied in the corner of her cloak.

He held her arm firmly as Luisa clutched the dagger and spat, "Let me go, swine, or you'll lose the use of that arm!"

"Where's Marcus? Tell me that or I'll gut you right here!" The lean face with its ragged beard and deep-set eyes looked very familiar, and the hard voice seemed to have remembered intonation.

"Marcus?"

He said urgently, "We have to find him. There's much to settle. Tell me, Luisa!"

"Ian! Ian! I didn't recognize you! You're so changed!" She lowered the dagger and reached out one hand. "I haven't seen Marcus. I thought you dead. What is happening?"

She realized too late that this was an enemy. He hit her wrist so that the dagger fell to the ground and then twisted both her arms up behind her in one quick motion. His voice was a savage snarl of hatred and fury.

"Tell me where he is or I'll break them. Your choice."

She knew he meant every word. "He came to London with me and the few outlaws agreeable to the course he suggested. I was abandoned, imprisoned, forced to roam the streets for weeks. Adam of Wenlock tried to kill me and I am lucky to be alive. I haven't seen Marcus!"

"You lie." There was uncertainty in the words.

"All right, I lie. How do I convince you not to break my arms? Look at me, Ian, by the wounds of Christ!"

He turned about and she was unresisting while he looked long at her thin face and the ragged clothes. Almost absently he said, "I thought Marcus loved you, that if only we could find you, we'd find him."

Luisa felt a long-checked tide of longing and desire sweep over her. "Why do you seek him with such anger? What has become of you? Ian, you're so changed!" She wanted to demand answers but forced herself to hold back.

He drew her into the partial shelter of a crumbled doorway. The youth was gone from him; he was hardened into a man. "You would lie for him. You love him."

"Gladly. I do and I always will but that does not alter the fact that I speak the truth now." Her eyes locked with his. "We were true friends once, Ian. Think of that and know I do not lie."

His face softened. "Edra liked you so much. I, too. Marcus has played us all false. What can I do but believe you? It was so strange to be standing, thinking of revenge, and then to see an urchin striding along just as you did around our camp. You are distinctive and that's why I took such a chance." He paused and touched her questioning face. "I'll say it once and quickly, then no more. I was away when Edra was killed and the others with her. When I came back Marcus was storming about as though crazed. He sent parties out to look for you and cried out your name in his sleep. He apparently forgot everything else for a while. I determined to avenge my sister but was wounded in a skirmish and laid up for a time. I was with the band later after Marcus and you others came to London to report back within a short time. Weeks and weeks passed with no response either from you people or our sources in the city. Men deserted and who could blame them? They had been forbidden to fight and now were confused and leaderless. What was to be done?"

Luisa felt tenderness well up in her. "So much has come about. I just can't understand the lack of some sort of communication. Marcus would not behave so."

"He has. We are weary of waiting and some of us have come to find out the reason for the delay and to deal with him if we find him. Some people even say he is traitor to our cause and has made a separate peace. We should have begun the battle earlier and not listened to him at all."

Luisa saw again the hawk eyes of Glendower. "Marcus simply obeyed his true prince and tried to follow his conscience as best he could."

Ian gave her a cynical smile. "Princes are all alike. It is our lands, our children, and our livelihoods that suffer. Glendower is from the legends."

She thought of Marmoor and could not gainsay him. "What will you do, Ian? You must believe I have not seen Marcus, and try also to believe in his honorable intentions. Something must have happened to him." She gave Ian a quick, edited account of their journey to London and of all that had come about in the interim. He was unimpressed by what Arban mentioned of the rebellion.

"Plotting clerks and perverted lords! They can't be that powerful. You are lucky you still live, Luisa. Our plans to find Marcus and discover what is going on will continue! If we have no success here, Wales will rise anyway. That much is certain."

She tried again to dissuade him but to no avail. The darkness came closer and the wind bore snowflakes in its blasts. Luisa shuddered and drew her cloak closer. Ian was a soldier now; no trace of the lively lad in the mountains remained.

He said, "We are few and you would be welcome as far as I am concerned; I know your worth. There are those who do not and who spoke out strongly against what they considered to be your corrupting influence on Marcus." He fumbled briefly in his pouch and drew out several coins. "Take these. I don't need them. Find a place and stay hidden until after Wales rises."

She drew back. "No."

"Don't be silly, Luisa. For Edra's sake. And don't worry about Adam of Wenlock. I shall find and kill him with great relish. I honor you for trying and understand something of what you have endured, but he is mine now." His eyes burned with hatred and more—a pleasure in the kill.

Luisa felt a chill not born of the wind. He was right, of course. "I am grateful, Ian. We all do what we must but try to heed my warning. Be prepared for betrayal if you can. Go, and luck be with you."

He lifted a hand in salute and was gone.

Now Luisa was plagued anew. She feared not only for the rebellion, which was near, but for Marcus, whose men sought him in anger. Only some great danger or his own death would have prevented him from fulfilling his duty. The Lollards were all suspect and known. She did not doubt her enemies sought her still. She returned to the inn's stable of the night before and tossed and turned on the straw, struggling in her mind with the difficulties. She was proud of her recent endurance; although of the nobility, she had survived in the London morass. But she could no longer exist for herself alone. Danger or not, she would return to the world of Luisa Marmoor.

In the morning her course was set. A debt for a debt. A life for a life. She mopped at her face with snow and bound her hair more tightly under her hood.

The gray, snowy morning was half-spent before Luisa found the place she sought, a rich and imposing house with grounds running down to the Thames and in close proximity of Westminster. She marched boldly up to the door and hammered on it. Such effrontery was her only hope for success.

"Is the Lady Barthampton here? I have urgent business with her!" Luisa had hesitated long before taking this course, but she knew Lady Barthampton had power and influence. If carefully approached, she might use it for Luisa's own purpose. No one else—least of all the Breconts, who were Lollards, or Ian, who distrusted her— had the power to help. Luisa would dissemble as best she could.

The horrified servant who answered the door stared at Luisa in distaste and tried to slam it, but she thrust one foot inside and gave the woman look for look.

"I warn you, boy, this house is guarded night and day. You'll gain nothing here."

Since Luisa had prowled among the nearby trees and given several shrieks of truly breathtaking volume embellished by both male and female voices, she knew where the guards were. Icily, she said, "Do not let my appearance deceive you. My message is urgent." It was the voice of command which had stirred those at Marmoor to action. "Get on with it, woman! Is she here or not? If so, fetch her. If not, where is she?"

The servant was uncertain. Urchins did not speak so. Luisa had deliberately copied Lady Barthampton's manner. "Who do you come from? I must have a name to give her ladyship."

"So she is here!" Luisa was inordinately thankful for this bit of luck. "Go and tell her I serve Lord Ranald of Connemarth, counselor and friend to the king in the matter of Ireland, and must see her immediately."

"Yes, yes, follow me."

Minutes later Luisa stood in an ornate room hung with rich tapestries and warmed by a roaring fire. A cup of heady wine was in her hand and she dipped into a dish of spiced meats with the other. The woman had rushed away with no further arguments. In spite of the precariousness of her position Luisa grinned. Had the title or the mention of Irish matters secured her entry?

"How now? What's all this? I know of no Ranald of Connemarth and nothing of Ireland, nor do I want to! I'll wager you don't either. I am going to have you searched before you're thrown out by my guards who are just outside. Are you part of a gang of thieves?"

Luisa turned around and looked at Lady Barthampton. She was as full fleshed and hearty as ever, her cheeks red and her dark hair glossy. There was an air of satisfaction about her which was unmistakable.

"Forgive my little deception. I did not know if you would receive me and my need is great." Luisa spoke in her normal voice as she threw back the hood.

"Who are you?" Lady Cecelia put a hand to her large bosom and backed away.

"Luisa Marmoor, whom you rescued. I was taken captive for ransom and wed to an outlaw and much more. Do you not remember the night of the raid?"

"Of course, but word came that you were slain in the mountains. Where have you been and how did you come to this?" She waved a beringed hand at Luisa's garb.

"Am I welcome in your house?" Tell part of the truth, be bold but not overmuch, remember her passion for amusement, forget her predilections and lead her into gossip. It was a dangerous game Luisa must play and one that would require all her skill.

"Thrice over! How can you doubt it?" She came close to Luisa, then drew back with a grimace.

Luisa burst into laughter. She had been in the warm room long enough for the grime of the streets to become apparent even to a less than fastidious nose. "I can barely recall my last bath. I who used to horrify our family priest by bathing daily in summer! He vowed my soul was in danger!"

"You shall bathe as much as you like. I'll have water prepared now. Your hair! It's a veritable nest! And those clothes are a sin! My dear, what an exciting tale you must have to tell!"

She started to roar for the servants but Luisa stopped her. "Forgive the way I must speak to you. It is necessary. Adam of Wenlock has sought my life and continues to do so. Father Sebastian, a certain renegade priest, you may recall, has also surfaced. If you are of them or feel you must contact them, tell me immediately so that I may go. I'll not be imprisoned again!"

"Darling girl, there are factions within factions within factions at the court." She grimaced at the repetition. "Am I not dear friend to Queen Joanna, the king's stepmother and powerful in my own right? I am very glad you chose to come to me. You will find that your trust is not misplaced."

"Thank you." Luisa was so relieved her voice shook.

"Your apartment shall be just across from my own. Your bath water will be carried there immediately." She shook her head. "From the looks of you it'll take some time to become presentable."

Chapter Thirty-three
ALPHA AND OMEGA

CANDLE FLAMES WAVERED on the scented air and cast strange shapes on the delicate tapestries in Lady Cecelia's solar. A fire at one end gave warmth in plenty. Luisa wore a loose gown of pale green velvet with a furred robe of emerald satin over her shoulders. Her chestnut hair gleamed with lights and hung to her waist in a brilliant flow. She sat in a high-backed chair piled with cushions, her bare feet extended to the blaze. A platter of half-eaten meat and sweets stood beside the wine decanter within easy reach. Her hostess sat in the chair opposite and listened to Luisa's story eagerly.

"It is an incredible tale, to be sure. Did you ever think to have such adventures?"

The note of the inquiry struck Luisa as somehow wrong. She was tired with the effort of piecing the tale together. The fine wine was making her slightly dizzy and the sheer heaven of being clean relaxed her body beyond all other sensations. She sat up and said, "This is no romantic dream for a winter's night, Lady Barthampton. It is stark and real."

"Of course, I realize that. You should have told me at the very beginning you were of the nobility. I pride myself on recognizing breeding when I see it. Adam of Wenlock would have been a good marriage for you; old men have their little ways but a wise woman can control them. Tell me more, Luisa."

The greed in her voice shook Luisa, telling her that she must be very cautious. She wanted Lady Cecelia to help her, but she was unsure how to approach the subject. She had given her right name but was not surprised when it was unknown. The struggle to keep Marmoor and the king's edict as well as what followed was described in detail. Her sojourn in the mountains, Marcus and the outlaws, and the general conditions there were somewhat glossed over. She made her concerns personal, the return of Marmoor and her determination to order her own life as the goal. The Lollards were spoken of only in passing.

"Things were done to me by Adam of Wenlock and that horror Arban that would make your soul shudder." Knowing well from Lady Cecelia's face that description was what she wanted, Luisa described the recent horror and the plots that had been revealed to her. Then she added, "I think the Lollards are basically good citizens. They will be led into this foolish rebellion and slaughtered. The government will be taken over by those like Arban. They mean to kill the king and blame others. It will be a bloodbath; old scores will be paid off, new ones discovered. The Welsh will die and they were kinder to me than those of my own country. You have influence, my lady. A few words in the right places and all this can be prevented."

Cecelia leaned forward, her dark eyes diamond bright in the flickering light. One corner of her mouth was turned up in amusement. "Dear girl, you are rather transparent, aren't you?"

Luisa was taken aback. "I don't know what you mean."

"Were you dreadfully in love with the handsome outlaw? Does he haunt your dreams? Did you marry him to save your life or was it more? Some other reason for a marriage? It shines in your face, Luisa!"

Her blood froze. Did Lady Barthampton really know this was why she had come? A woman so privy to secrets and intimate with the court must be aware of plans concerning the Lollards and Wales, and must have some idea of the comings and goings of the leaders, namely Marcus. Surely one so friendly with the royal family would not want it destroyed and replaced with the likes of Arban and Adam of Wenlock? Luisa again vowed to be careful.

"I had hoped none of it would stamp my face permanently. I admit I found him interesting at first for he was the only man I had ever known and he is wonderfully handsome. The marriage was done by a priest and under duress. I have never wanted any bonds of that sort. Freedom, that's what I want! Is that so hard to comprehend?"

"And you come to me for that?" Lady Barthampton rose and paced before the fire, stretching out her jeweled fingers to admire them.

"Of course not. You are powerful and you know it. Who else do I know in London? My enemies are strong. Does it take a logician to figure this out?" Luisa's head was ringing with wine and weariness.

"Luisa, listen to me." Her face was very serious. "You needn't concern yourself with the vagaries of government and rebellions. All this pother is useless. They'll play themselves out and what is left will have more power than the actual ruler." Triumph surged in her voice.

"I see." Luisa thought it must be the wine talking for her words seemed to come out slowly and loudly. "You and heaven only knows who else plot also. You'll use both sides to gain your own ends just as Arban thinks to do. Everyone in a great scramble to get or control the throne!"

"Of a certainty! When the ruler is weak, that is the natural thing to do. As for Arban, he forgets he is only a clerk for all the power he has been given." She smiled at Luisa. "You're very tired, aren't you? The wine is potent. You shall rest and on the morrow we'll take a journey." She bid Luisa goodnight.

Later, Luisa found herself in a maelstrom of horrifying dreams. Seas, fires, mountains, and pools of darkness overwhelmed her as faces sped around her own in dizzying bands. She tried to run and could not, fell and found it impossible to rise. There were parching deserts and high winds before everything faded into a red haze.

"Mistress, can you wake? Lady Barthampton is outside!"

The urgent voice pierced Luisa's head as though a hammer blow. She opened her eyes, which was even more painful. The feeble sunlight of the winter day spread across the covers and the down pillows of her bed and seemed to blaze up at her. A frightened maidservant held out a robe of tawny silk and fur. Luisa brushed her tumbled hair out of her eyes and shuddered as the events of the day before settled into place.

"Close those curtains! I think I have the plague!" She thought her voice was a shout but the girl strained toward her as if unable to hear.

"Saints, Luisa, will you sleep all the day long? It's near noon." Lady Cecelia, resplendent in green satin, strode in, brushing the servant away as though she were a flea. "You had too much of my special French wine, that's all. I've brought some good cheese, fine white bread and breast of fowl for you." She held out a golden goblet. "Drink, this has cured many a head of mine. You're just not used to imbibing."

Luisa pulled the covers up around her nakedness and did as she was bidden. It was easier than complaint. While she drank she reviewed the conversation with Lady Barthampton. In essence she knew nothing more than she had before. Marcus had told her Lady Cecelia had a hand in every plot hatched, doubtless it was a

game with her. All Luisa's instincts told her that
this woman was dangerous. And moreover,
whatever happened in the circles of power, the
Lollards and the Welsh were to be the scape-
goats. Her head started to pound again and she
frowned.

"You're too kind, Lady Cecelia."

"That isn't one of the words generally applied
to me. I have a proposal for you."

Luisa reached for the ornate robe and slipped
into it. Already she was feeling better. A quick
bite of the cheese and fowl from the tray Lady
Cecelia had deposited beside the bed helped
even more.

"I don't understand." Her gaze was limpid.

"You will. I realize you want no husband at
present but that is the way of advancement.
Later, much later, I can make sure you have a rich
and harmless one. Your marriage to that outlaw
will be nullified, I promise you that. Your estate
of Marmoor will be returned in your name and
that of any heirs you wish to designate if there are
none of your body. In your name, Luisa, forever.
Also, you will have an income to run it."

Glory sang through Luisa's mind and heart.
Her eyes filled with tears as she saw the beloved
acres stretching out before her once more. The
fields alive with animals and crops, the villagers
content and prosperous, the castle refurbished
and restored, she the chatelaine of it all and the
Marmoor name once more powerful in the land.
Her own mistress, answerable to no one! She
needed no husband, either. Then she swung to
earth again and met the dark stare.

"At what price?"

"Silly girl, you act as if I were trying to steal your soul instead of help you! You wonder that I want to? I see myself when I was young in you. I am a wealthy and powerful woman; I can afford to indulge my whims. That ought to be enough for you." She turned to the servant and snapped her fingers. "Bring me some of that wine. Hurry about it! And start preparing some clothes for Luisa. Have that other matter seen to at once!"

"The price?" Luisa tried to imagine what it could be.

"Luisa, you're a very clever girl. I would have been hard put to survive under such circumstances as you endured at that estate of yours, in the mountains, and here in London against the many enemies you've made. Be my companion, Luisa, until things settle in the realm. Come to court, be part of it, meet Queen Joanna and have a part in the changing ways. Women can be powerful in their own right. You are fair, and as you circulate in the court you will hear things we need to know. You can pass along information to those who must know it. The king will marry and we shall choose his bride. If he sickens, as is sometimes the case with the best of us, there are others to rule. . . . You take my point, Luisa?"

"I would be a spy. Like Arban." She spoke very softly. "If I did this, I should want more. I want the deaths of those who tortured me. All of them." She could offer that much to Marcus and his Wales, to the Lollards who had sheltered and been kind to her.

Lady Cecelia burst into loud laughter and clapped her hands together. "You're blood-thirsty as well! I'll see what I can do. Those men are no part of our plans for the future, anyway."

"Good." Luisa did not try to keep the pleasure from her voice.

"Now for the rest of it! You shall swear to me that the outlaw is nothing to you, that you wish the marriage ceased, and that all these schemes of rebellion you've been involved in are no longer any part of you. You will forsake them utterly and forever. Do you so swear so?"

Faced with it, Luisa did not know her lips were moving until Cecelia's Barthampton's countenance went from red to white with muffled fury. One hand went back as to strike Luisa and then returned to clasp the side of the bed.

"Did I hear you say what I thought? Does this mean you will reject my offer and return to the streets, where you will likely meet with an unpleasant fate?" Her voice was low and dangerous.

All that was strong and proud in Luisa wanted to repeat the words that had just risen to her lips; Get thee behind me, Satan! But she was human and she loved the home of her fathers, the pride of her name, and her own life. She had not endured so that now she might have another enemy. This was no temptation of scripture, nor a romance, but survival itself.

"Are you trying to put a denial in my mouth, Lady Cecelia? I said I'd accept Satan's own bargain to be free of the life I've had up to now. Right gladly do I accept and my hand on it!" She made her face open and frank, her mouth slightly awry in a gesture of surrender. "And my thanks!"

Lady Cecelia looked hard at her. "Fetch the priest in!" When he came, small and bowing but bearing the stamp of all authority from God, she continued. "This lady here has some vows to make. They will be binding until death, will they not, Father?"

"Assuredly, my lady." He seemed to see nothing odd about the scene nor Luisa's disarray.

"Then I will repeat the words and you after me, Lady Marmoor." For the first time she used Luisa's title. "You do this in full awareness of what you say and all the penalties of hell if you break your sworn oath, not to man but to God?"

Luisa thought again that she had little to lose. Lady Barthampton would deal with Arban and the others. They were already marked and deserving of death. Marcus had abandoned her or lay dead somewhere. She was unable to do anything about him or for him. It was best to be free of that coil. She would somehow get a message to the Breconts and Ian. What more was to be done?

"I do and I accept it freely."

"Excellent." Lady Cecelia repeated again the words she had spoken earlier to Luisa, reiterating the separate vows of repudiation and waiting for Luisa to say each phrase after her in a firm, clear voice so that nothing could possibly be mistaken.

"Your word is given to God, daughter. See that you keep it or your soul will suffer." At her nod he raised his hands in the blessing, the solemn words resounding in the quiet room.

Luisa told herself again that she was swearing to nothing which was not to come about in any event. The word of a Marmoor was held to be inviolate. An oath before God more powerful yet. She must draw the lines of conscience if Lady Cecelia demanded too much but that would not absolve her of this oath. "Not murder, but all else." The phrase whispered in her mind. She was Cecelia Barthampton's now and who was to say Satan had not offered her the world and she had not taken it?

"Dear Luisa. You'll not regret this." Cecelia clasped her cold hand and smiled brilliantly. "Now we'll let you get dressed and go out. You'll need just everything! Jewels, too! You are to be presented at the king's Christmas court. I've just decided! We're going to have such a fascinating time!"

"I am grateful." Luisa tried to brush aside the depression she was beginning to feel. She was still herself, wasn't she?

"Oh, by the way, Luisa, look over at that door. I think you'll be interested in what you see there." Her voice was limpid, smooth, somewhat amused.

Luisa turned in the direction indicated and could not stifle a scream of pure horror. Marcus, hands bound in front of him, face bruised, stood there with a guard. His brown skin was slightly faded but the lean body, arrogant face, and brilliant blue eyes were the same. His mouth twisted sardonically as she winced from the blazing contempt in them.

He stared at her, all his suspicions confirmed.

She was deceitful, a traitor to all he believed in, all they had once shared.

Chapter Thirty-four
CROWNED AS THE LOCUST

MARCUS AND LUISA stared at each other across a limitless chasm. She felt nothing and could only stand and gape. Perhaps this was another nightmare and she would wake in prison or shivering on the London streets.

Lady Cecelia waved one beringed hand and crossed to a table to pour herself a cup of wine. She gave them an amused look and said, "I have brought husband and wife together; have you nothing to say to each other? For shame! I would have sworn that you, Marcus, were able to hear all conversation in this room very clearly. Is it not so?"

"I heard." His voice was low and steady, laced with contempt. "It was of no interest to me. How long will you hold me prisoner, madam? Or have you decided on murder?"

"Speak to this lady, sir!" Cecelia's red flush was mounting.

He surveyed them casually, then turned to glance around the room questioningly. "I see no ladies. Perhaps the servant is one but she isn't here, is she? Ah, no. I see only a plotting, treasonous, perverted bitch and a doxy whom I once bedded. What do you wish me to say?" He cocked his head attentively.

She slapped him with her open hand, which had all the power of a man's blow. He reeled and the guard held him in place. Her rings opened up a cut and blood ran down his cheek. Nothing could alter the utter contempt in those burning eyes.

"What do you think of your lover, now, Luisa?" Cecelia whirled to face her, fingers clenching and loosening spasmodically. "He doesn't exactly speak love words, does he?"

It took all the control Luisa was able to summon, all her willpower to subdue the bitter anger and sudden hatred she felt, in order to hold calm in this situation for which she had so clearly been set up. "What do you expect me to say? Or him, for that matter? Why are you holding him prisoner?"

"He's nothing to you, remember?" Lady Cecelia fairly hissed the words.

"One does not forget one's first lover. I have no wish to see him treated harshly." Luisa shrugged and let her eyes drift casually over Marcus. "I suppose you will turn him over to officials of the king?"

Marcus said, "That course is far from your purpose, is it not?" He spoke calmly. "I expect an accident will soon occur or possibly I'll contract a fever."

"A scapegoat to allay suspicion!" Luisa said coolly. "Who could be more perfect than Marcus Lenley? Both outlaw and Lollard! A fighter against Richard, then Henry, and now the new king. How very useful! Lady Cecelia, I am impressed!"

"Both of you deserve the other," Marcus said. "Have pleasure in the unholy bargains you make. I fail to see why I should be subjected to more of these maunderings. My cell is far more desirable."

Cecelia eyed Luisa narrowly. "Shall I tell you what will happen to him?"

"For God's own sake, enough of this! I'm sick of it! Do what you will. I don't want to know! Are we going out?" Luisa put all the weariness and revulsion she felt into her tone as much as her words. The woman's vanity must surely be such that she would find it inconceivable that Luisa would direct such feelings toward her benefactress. She must be careful not to overdo it. "Haven't I been through sufficient turmoil as it is? What am I supposed to be doing?" It took little effort to make her voice rise toward incipient hysteria.

Lady Cecelia was smiling once more but she was not convinced. "You have sworn an oath, Luisa. You shall be held to that oath."

Marcus gave a bark of laughter. "Oath, indeed! None of you know the meaning of the word. My dear wife there, soon to be widowed, takes and breaks oaths in the same breath!"

Luisa whirled on him and cried, "One forgets oaths sworn on the mountaintop and thinks of survival, of the death of honor and all that it can mean! I do as I must! Take that thought with you as you go to whatever fate is to be meted out!"

She met his impaling glare with her head high and prayed he would understand that she reminded him of the overlook and of Glendower, not in mockery but in simple practicality.

"Oaths of the mountaintop are the only true ones." His tone went from heat to ice. "May both of you remember it in hell!"

The guard struck him and he fell face forward. Lady Cecelia made an imperious gesture, he was carried away, and the door slammed shut behind them. She started to speak but Luisa held up her hand.

"Spare me, I pray you. I have had all of outlaws and rebellions and threats I can endure. Let's go, Cecelia, please." She raised her face to the other woman so she might see that no tears marred its smoothness.

"You are either a most accomplished actress or extremely cold in nature. Heaven help you if it is the first." She probed Luisa's eyes as the minutes drew out. "Heaven help me if it is the latter."

Luisa merely smiled and shook out her skirts. It seemed as though the first round was hers. She had no idea how to help Marcus but she knew she must try. Lady Cecelia must certainly mean to keep him alive until after the rebellion. Then she would produce him for punishment as an overall scapegoat. The other factions would have fallen and she, along with whichever cause she chose to champion, would then be in full power. Luisa knew she must bide her time and wait. She wondered how Marcus came to be prisoner but dared not mention him after all her protestations.

She thought her face might surely crack that afternoon as she exclaimed over fabrics, colors, leather for shoes, jewels, gauzes, and laces. It seemed they went to nearly every shop in London as her worry and exhaustion grew. The merchants were delighted that so powerful a lady and her protegé came in person, and they lost no time in fawning over them, admiring and exclaiming at their differing beauty. Lady Barthampton introduced Luisa boldly and they spoke all the more respectfully.

Luisa said once, "Why are you so free with my name? I have gone to such pains to hide from those such as Arban and his sort! It will all be undone."

Cecelia patted her hand and said silkily, "Then you'll be far less inclined to forget your oath, won't you?"

"There are some things I can never forget."

Seeing no victory in arguing, she gave herself up to mindless cries of pleasure over all the goods and trinkets she was obtaining, often chaffering with the tradesmen and even driving down a price or two. Her voice rose and she exchanged lively remarks with Lady Cecelia, who continued to watch with suspicion. Luisa prayed inwardly that the woman would believe her intoxicated with her good fortune and generally uncaring what happened to her outlaw husband.

"I'd not have thought you cared so much for fripperies," remarked Lady Cecelia as they moved homeward in her coach, a great unwieldy thing not really made for the narrow streets.

Luisa allowed her fingers to linger possessively on a golden bracelet set with rubies. "You've not worn the same gown for days or gone barefoot because there was no leather to repair your shoes or slaved for hours at some menial task for a scrap of food! Those are not enriching experiences. Poverty does not require a noble name. Oh, can't we hurry! I want to try some of these materials! And can't your seamstresses fashion something for me to wear soon? The things you've furnished are nice but they weren't made for me. You do understand, don't you?"

"Of course, greedy child! Enjoy yourself. I take the greatest delight in watching you." The words were both indulgent and a warning.

Luisa played her part well during the next several days. She strained her ears for the servant's gossip and the idle talk of the men-at-arms as well. She listened closely to Cecelia's own words, but there was no mention made of Marcus or his location. His circumstances were not even hinted at. Luisa tried on gowns, arranged her hair, spent hours looking at jewels and laces to match them. Her own taste for the understated was allowed to lapse as she was guided by Cecelia into flaming colors and boldly cut necklines. She made much of her own past lack of material things and spoke of all she wanted to have in the future.

It was agony for Luisa to go on in this manner when she considered what Marcus's situation must be. She thought of the oath she had sworn to Glendower. She would keep the spirit of it but not the letter. The oath to Lady Barthampton and before her priest had been made in reasonably good faith, but to help Marcus she must gladly break it. The lady might not be totally evil but she stood in the way of those who wished to live their lives in peace. Surely the God of Catholic and Lollard alike must understand that. Luisa tried to rationalize her situation as she lay in her warm bed each night, tried to formulate some plan of action.

One morning as they sat late over their morning meal, Cecelia said, "Are you pleased with all that you have now? I think it is time to introduce you to a select few people of the court, but I must be sure you will not rush about speaking of outlaws and rebellions. In other words, my dear, it is time to begin to implement our bargain." She sat back in her chair and adjusted the bodice of her red satin gown. As always, priceless jewels flamed on every finger.

Luisa looked down at her own hands, which were decorated with the emeralds Cecelia had insisted she wear even at this hour. "You have been vastly generous and I am grateful. But, really, I know little of court etiquette or what to say. Suppose I disgraced you?" She added, "I'm frightened I might."

"No one who has been through what you have can be afraid of a court function! But rest yourself in peace on one score. The king and court will spend Christmas at Eltham Palace, outside the city. There is a reason for this but he thinks it is his own idea. Easily led, our sovereign lord!" She laughed conspiratorially. "I have a house close by. What would be more natural than that visitors should come informally and see my protegé, Lady Marmoor? She, of course, is shy and a bit fearful, just up from the remote country. You do see the emerging pattern?"

"Yes, of course. I'll do what I can." Dared she push this? Was it safe to assume that Lady Cecelia would take Marcus outside London with her? He was certainly too valuable to leave behind and risk an escape. "It lacks a good few weeks until Christmas. Might we not go early? I could become familiar with the surroundings, learn something of the ways of the court—the dances and mannerisms, perhaps be tutored in these by someone conversant with them. You naturally haven't the time." She thought she had achieved a good balance of hesitancy and boldness.

Cecelia studied her nails, keeping her face averted. The silence drew out as Luisa struggled to keep her composure. "True enough. The city can be most distracting. When I leave, others will follow suit. Yes. Very well, prepare yourself. We leave in two days' time." She rose abruptly and bawled for the servants in a voice that could be heard the length of the house.

Luisa burst into laughter. It relieved her feelings but caused Cecelia to whirl on her. "That is foremost of the things you will not do, madam. It is most unseemly in a shy maiden."

"Aye. As you say." Luisa folded her hands meekly.

Their eyes met then and both dissolved into laughter. It was one of those moments when Luisa came perilously close to liking this conniving woman and wondered again at the strange forces which shaped people and made them as they were. If Luisa survived this, what might she be like afterward?

As she tossed and turned that night, she could not help but think she had urged the wrong course. What if Marcus were now in more danger? Perhaps he would be left here or taken to a separate prison. He may already have been. If he were dead, she would know, but some things were worse than death. The self-torment went on endlessly.

They left London on a gray and threatening morning when the icy wind seemed to envelop them and pull their breath away in spite of their furs and warm cloaks. The clouds were so low that they appeared a separate ceiling. The few folk abroad huddled down and rushed frantically about their business. There was nothing to indicate the holy season was close.

Luisa felt cold in every inch of her body even though she was clad in tawny and russet, with a matching coif, gloves, and boots of supple leather. Jewels sparkled at her ears and around her neck. She was just as much a prisoner as Marcus and these were the badges of her confinement.

They had a coach filled with luggage, two servants, and extra covers for warmth on the journey. Open wagons rumbled behind them filled with more baggage, plates, household furnishings, and other materials for the stocking of the house near Eltham. Men-at-arms rode close by and more servants came behind them. A small coach, very plain and simple, trundled in the rear and it was heavily guarded. Luisa had got only a glimpse of it as they had entered their own, and she had not dared inquire for Cecelia's eyes gave away the malice she felt. She knew this had to be Marcus's prison and her heart sang. At least they were together.

"He's with us. I know you've been wondering. I'd not leave my useful prisoner behind. He'll be my Epiphany present to the king." Cecelia's gaze did not leave Luisa's face.

When she began this baiting, Luisa had learned the best method was one of direct attack. "Of course I've wondered. It would be inhuman not to; I'm still married to the man!"

"Likely not for long!" She laughed immoderately and, leaning back, appeared to doze.

The trip was not a long one, but the weather grew worse and it slowed them. Cecelia had chosen a very roundabout way of travel and, when Luisa peered out the narrow slit that served as a window, she saw sparsely inhabited open country. Luisa assumed Cecelia's route was chosen to keep her prisoner and destination a secret for now. She shut her eyes in pretended sleep but the face of Marcus as she had last seen him rose up to torment her.

Suddenly there was a great clashing of swords, much shouting and cursing. The coach rocked back and forth while the horses neighed in terror. Someone began to beat on the side door. The servants shrieked and covered their faces. Cecelia lunged for the window but her bulk covered it so Luisa could not see.

"Come out! You have him and we'll tolerate no resistance!"

Luisa recognized the voice. It was Ian.

Chapter Thirty-five
COVENANT

"WHAT DO YOU want? How dare you intercept me this way? You'll hang, I vow it!" Cecelia's courage was never in question as she swung open the coach door just as the bearded man outside jerked it hard. She nearly tumbled out and would have fallen had he not held her firmly.

Luisa looked over her dark head and saw only a few of Cecelia's men-at-arms were being held at bay by several armed men. The small coach was overturned and Marcus was being pulled from it just as Ian caught her eye. He grinned devilishly and looked far more cynical than when she last saw him on a London street.

"You led us to Marcus, Luisa. Did you really think I believed you or that you would not be followed? How prosperous you look! What is the going price for souls these days?" He gave her a dismissing laugh as he turned to Cecelia. "You needn't look for the bulk of your men, madam. We arranged a distraction for them. All we want is your prisoner."

"By God, you can't do this!" Her face was redder than ever and the brown eyes snapped with rage.

"Thank heavens you found me!" Luisa heard Marcus saying some distance away. His whole demeanor was altered; he radiated excitement. "Ian, let's hurry and get away from here. There's so much to tell."

"You misunderstand me, Marcus. You have played us false. Many name you traitor and I aim to settle the score. You went off with Luisa; it appears you quarreled and she's joined with Lady Barthampton here. I don't know what your goal really is and I don't really care." He swung toward Luisa and she saw the savagery in his eyes. His lips flattened against his teeth, giving him a feral appearance. "Sir Adam is mysteriously dead. A robber, perhaps. A very bloodthirsty one. It seems the noble lord was a bit hacked up. Pity."

"Don't be a fool, Ian," Luisa shouted. "This woman plots against us all! I did not know she held Marcus captive . . ."

"Lying little slut!"

"There's too much at stake for us to quarrel among ourselves! Listen to me!"

The cries of Cecelia and Marcus crossed each other and mingled with those of Luisa. Ian leaned over and cut Marcus's bonds with one quick motion. Then he handed him a sword.

"You shall defend yourself, Marcus. Right here and now. When I have satisfaction for my lost illusions and my sister, you shall be taken to our hiding place and there you will be tried as a traitor by those you once led. Amusing irony, is it not?"

Luisa leaned toward him, all her heart in her eyes as her hands reached out to touch his sleeve. "Please, Ian. Let me explain!"

The bitterness in him overflowed. He jerked his arm away and pushed her backward so that she almost fell. "You seem incapable of comprehension, Luisa. Say more and I'll have you gagged. Go where you will and do what you wish. You are nothing to us."

She stared numbly at him and then at Marcus's blank face. A kind of vengeful pleasure shone on Cecelia's.

Ian waved at the men. "Take Lady Barthampton and the members of her entourage into the woods and bind them securely. If they are fortunate someone will find and release them. If not, they deserve their fate. Take the coaches apart and leave the horses for us. The girl can be taken down the road and left. Give us a little while here and return."

Marcus stood as though graven stone. Luisa did likewise. Lady Cecelia protested until one of the men lost his temper and silenced her with a blow on the temple. Then they carried her away, the rest of the servants and her own men-at-arms following in obedience to the drawn swords of the outlaws and Ian's deadly manner.

Ian faced Marcus at the side of the road. One of the outlaws stood close to Luisa, his weapon ready. The clouds seemed tangled in the bare branches of the trees but the snow had slowed. The wind whipped their garments about. A dog howled mournfully in the distance.

Marcus held the sword he had been given point down. His brilliant eyes were hard as he stared at Ian.

"Fight, Marcus, or before God I'll kill you as you stand."

"Then do so. I will not fight you." He stood perfectly still, his whole body exposed, utter sadness on his face.

"To think I once worshiped you!" Ian's voice shook with pain and rage.

"Perhaps you chose the wrong god. We are all but human."

The quiet words struck Luisa's heart to the core. They were unlike the bold Marcus she knew.

"Traitor! Traitor twice over!" Ian lunged at him and the pointed tip of the sword tore at Marcus's sleeve and down to the skin. Blood appeared and ran down his arm. He did not move. "Next time it'll be your heart!"

Ian drew back his sword arm as he spoke and the feral look on his face deepened. Just as he moved to slash at Marcus again, Luisa jumped in front of him. Her cloak, fur underlining, gown, and heavy bodice were pierced by the force of the attack. She felt the blade on her bare skin but there was no pain, only numbing cold. Ian's hand twisted at the last moment and it went no further. The watching outlaw sprang up to grasp her.

Suddenly there was a flash of steel and Ian's sword lay in the ditch nearby. Another motion and the other outlaw was on his knees clutching his bleeding wrist. Ian started to rise from the ground where he had fallen but Luisa snatched up a dagger Cecelia had let fall in her struggles and put it to his neck.

"Don't tempt me. I don't have the compunctions Marcus does." She fairly gritted out the words and he was silent.

Marcus came toward them with the pieces of the rope that had bound him. "Tie and gag him. I'll see to our friend over here. Hurry." He guarded Ian with the sword until she was done. Then she watched until he prodded the other man up. "Wait here."

Luisa stood where he left her, puzzling over the turn fortune had taken. She felt chilled and shaky by turns. When she investigated her torn clothes, she saw that the blood had already dried on her flesh. The point had been deflected; another thrust and it would have gone into her chest.

"Well, madam." There was a step behind her and Marcus appeared, leading two of the horses that had drawn his coach. Incredibly, he was smiling. "All our captors, would-be and otherwise, are bound and in the woods or chasing a false lead or waiting a good distance off. This is a state of affairs I'd not have expected an hour ago."

Luisa smiled hesitantly and then, as reaction hit her, began to laugh. Marcus joined her. He held out one hand, his blue eyes intense.

"I thank you for my life. You risked your own just then. Ian has been driven nearly to madness by all that has happened."

She looked into his face. "Would you have let him kill you?"

He shrugged. ''Mount up and let's go from here as fast as we can.''

''We?'' The word was stuck on her stiff lips. She expected his fury, his demand for explanations, even his scorn.

''Of course.'' In one motion he pulled her to him and gave her a hug that was totally devoid of anything except friendship. ''Come on.''

She scrambled onto the horse as she was bidden and followed after him. In the aftermath of fear and reaction the only thought in her mind was that she was free and in the company of the man she loved. It was a glorious blessing.

They rode into the forest proper, down trails that were no more than footpaths, through clearings, out into the countryside, and back into the shelter of another stretch of woodland. The snow drifted down and the wind pressed at their backs as they moved steadily along. It was nearly dark when Marcus finally led them into a glade and paused in the shelter of a giant oak.

Here the air was still and freezing. Luisa looked around to see the outlines of several huge stones covered with vine skeletons. Directly under the tree itself was a raised and polished one with a glinting surface. Behind it and to the left she saw a dwelling covered with evergreens.

''Where are we, Marcus? What is this place?'' These were the first words she had spoken since they had begun their journey. They had traveled so quickly and were so muffled against the weather that conversation was not feasible. Now her throat felt dry and parched.

His voice was light as he dismounted and assisted her to do the same. "I have been much in this section of the country and used this place of refuge before. That stone is a type of marker, a protector if you will, of this place of refuge. There are legends about it but we need not fear the old demons, Luisa."

The hut had a hearth, a supply of firewood, cloaks and covers, a store of food and ale, even some old clothes, a cache of daggers, and a few swords. Marcus explained that such stores were kept there for people fleeing the anger of the state and were used by various bands in the network of outlaws. "Each who uses it replenishes it as he can. I'll leave some money when we go and what we take can thus be replaced."

"Are there many such places this close to London?" At his nearness Luisa was finding it difficult to breathe although his words were totally impersonal in nature.

"Many." He did not elaborate but knelt to build a fire, carefully nurturing it to give maximum warmth as quickly as possible. When it blazed up, he found a cup and poured out some ale, then handed the cup to her.

"To our lives." She lifted it in a toast.

He regarded her over the rim of his own cup. "To life itself." They drank solemnly. "Make yourself as comfortable as you can. I must see to the horses. And try not to worry. We're as safe here as we can possibly be under the circumstances. Any pursuers will think we are rushing away from London."

The gentleness in him was not what she had expected. "We have to talk, Marcus. I've so much to tell you. I don't want you to think . . ." Her words trailed off as he waved his hand.

"We've both been prisoners, Luisa. I probably more so than you." His blue eyes went darker with contemplation. "Let's be at peace for a little while."

It was a withdrawal and she knew she must accept his feelings. She wanted to explain, inquire, compare experiences, to find out everything and purge herself of all that boiled up within her. "As you say."

He was gone a long time and the early winter dark settled in. The fire gave sufficient warmth for her to remove her outer garments and furs as well as the torn upper part of her gown. She wrapped her shoulders in a dark shawl and let her hair spill free. Then she spread out cloaks and covers so that they would have a place to sleep near the fire. She was careful to prepare two separate places. He must not think she sought to make demands on him. Dark dry bread and cheese and more ale would constitute their first meal in freedom. She thought it better than a feast at Lady Cecelia's board. Then she recalled what Ian told told her of Sir Adam's demise. She smiled as savagely as he had.

"He has gone to his master, Satan. May he rot there in eternal torment." She meant every word. The land was rid of one monster. Pray God others would soon follow him. How many children had he slain? What of them? Weariness began to take its toll now and she drowsed.

She woke to find Marcus sitting beside her, sipping ale and staring moodily into the fire. At her movement he turned and looked at her, his face somber.

"Go back to sleep. I will doze lightly. No outlaws will come here in search of us; they ready themselves for the rebellion and anyone else will think ghosts walk in this part of the forest."

Luisa could wait no longer. All her concerns flooded in as she asked, "I need to know what happened, Marcus. To Rob? The others? The Breconts?"

He sighed heavily and drank before turning back to the fire. When he spoke his voice was low and strained. "I don't really know about the others. I've worried about it. I thought you safe, at least. They may have been taken although I don't think there's any plan to interfere with the Lollards until after the rebellion."

Luisa shifted position and pushed her hair back. The hut was very warm now. She wanted to remove the shawl but was conscious of her nearly bare bosom under it.

Marcus continued in a flat voice. "We went to a meeting of Lollards and others that day. I knew it no place for a woman; you were excluded on my orders. We laid firm plans and then I set off to contact a member of the group that supports Mortimer's claim to the throne as Richard's heir. A united front is so essential. These people feared the Welsh meant to take over the country. I was determined to assure them this was not true. It was to be a most secret meeting and my directions were explicit. There was no reason to doubt them or the motive. When I arrived, however, I was ushered into the presence of Lady

Barthampton, who informed me that certain people found my efforts too successful and desired them to cease. She mentioned something of the plan those she represents have for England and Wales alike. I was angered and drew my sword as might a fool. I was set upon, taken prisoner, and held so. The rest you know."

"You did not think of supporting them and gaining much by so doing?" She asked the question out of sheer perversity, wanting to rouse the old angry Marcus she had once known.

His eyes met hers with a peculiar look as he said, "Not everyone is for sale, Luisa."

"Does that mean you think *I* am?" The defensive words tumbled out before she could stop them.

"You alone are the judge of what you are. You stand before yourself, as we all must."

One part of Luisa's mind recorded the sound of his words as familiar, something heard long ago. Now, out of her own need for vindication, she said slowly, "We once said we were comrades, Marcus. You left me. Are we still?"

"Each of us does what he must. Insofar as I can, insofar as you can, we hold to our bargain." He was the commander, not the man who had once held her in mingled anger and passion.

Knowing she must not, Luisa goaded him. "Friends have an obligation to each other. Had you not left me at the Breconts I might not have fallen into the mire that I did."

Even now he did not flame out or make a sharp retort. He swung around to face her, his features cast into sharp planes by the fire's flickering shapes. She smelled the scent of cold fresh air and saw he had changed into the shabby clothes left in the hut. His blue eyes were intense. "Tell me, Luisa. Tell me and ease your burden."

His remote gentleness made the tears come. Through them and unabashed by them, she spoke of all that had happened.

Marcus took her hand in his. He wanted to comfort her, promise her anything, hold her safe forever. His old habits of withdrawal and reticence held him back. Neither of them was the same; they had endured too much. He told himself sternly that was their bond and that alone.

Chaper Thirty-six
MARCUS AND LUISA

THE FIRE WAS low when she finished. The tale was spread before him in its entirety. He may not have intended for her to tell about her plan to destroy Sir Adam after the massacre, but she was driven to speak of it in detail. His face did not change during the recital.

When she was finally silent he reached over and touched her cheek with one finger, tracing the path of her tears. Then he pulled her slowly to him and held her in a firm embrace. She put both arms around him and clung to him. It was the embrace of friends who had endured much together, devoid of passion but filled with tenderness.

In the warmth of that shelter, Luisa said, "Why did you so nearly hate me, Marcus? After that time at the overlook, I mean?" She felt as though they were back to their earliest days in one sense; in another, more profound way she seemed to speak of two other people from a different place.

He put his hand on the back of her head and caressed it. He, too, might be talking of others. "I told you, I think. You lied to me, not directly but by omission. I thought you wanted adventure before wedding the old man, that you played with loyalty and hearts. Lie and circumstance piled up and I would believe nothing decent of you. Perhaps I *could* not. I have seen too many lies in high places, in my friends, in my own life. I saw how easily people forsake friendship for the winning side, in my youth as well as now. My betrothed went eagerly to the man chosen for her at the time. She wanted nothing of a boy like myself who was so foolish as not to know a courtier must walk carefully. Wise, of course, but I was an idealist in those days."

Luisa raised her eyes to his, catching a look of pain on the carved face before he glanced away. "And now? What do you believe of me now?"

"Now is a different time in a different world. You have endured much but you remain your inviolate self. Is it not so?" He moved slightly away from her and shifted positions. "We've talked long. You must be very tired as I know I am. I'll build up the fire."

Luisa cut across his speech. "I am myself and I live. That is nearly enough. But you are altered." It was true. Much of his anger had vanished. A more sober and responsible air was part of him now and loss shone in his face instead of the old mockery. "I think I know." She stared at him in sudden and very real horror.

Very quietly he said, "Yes. I am a Lollard."

Luisa sat back on her heels and watched him closely. The declaration stunned her, for despite all her rebellious spirit, she had never taken the little she knew of the belief seriously and had thought of its adherents as another kind of fanatic.

"They could burn you at the stake." She thought of her own ordeal and the sweat sprang out on her forehead.

A shadow of the old gay laughter of their early times together rang out. "They'll have to catch me first!"

Luisa grew reflective. "Tell me what it is that transforms life for you, Marcus. Do you not think you may just have come to some sort of terms with yourself and your misfortunes?" She did not want to suggest that he might have seen his battle lost and turned to this dangerous faith in order to fill the gap. If that was so, might she not turn him from it? Yet she easily saw the new compassion and surety in him as well as the melting down of anger. He was purged, as she had been.

"Try to grasp this, Luisa." He was off on a maze of theology, pounding his fist earnestly into one palm, his eyes brilliant with eagerness as he spoke of Wycliffe, Christ, the Pope as man only.

His words faded in Luisa's ears as she listened instead to the faint snap of burning wood from the fire and the slap of tree branches against their refuge. Her shadow and that of Marcus loomed long on the opposite wall. The rest of the world was shut out. This should be the time of their peace.

"All this comes down to the fact that a man can call his soul his own with no need for a go-between," he was saying. "A personal relationship exists between a man and his God. Elaborate ritual and the vast machinery of the church are unnecessary. Men ought to try to imitate Christ, be responsible for their own actions and contrite for wrongdoing. How can this be heresy?"

"This will destroy you if you speak of it. Have you no regard for your own life?" Luisa could not understand his fervor. To her the world of taste, touch, feeling, and all the everyday delights of life was too dear to be sacrificed for a belief such as he was explaining.

His eyes were grave on her fire-flushed face. "This isn't an instant thing. I think it must have grown over the years. What can I do about the past? There is the present and the hope for the future." Conviction rang in his words and might not be gainsaid.

"Does this faith teach you to love Lancaster?

What of your men, the rebellion, all those plans for freedom?" Her tone was hard.

He rose and began to pace about, his tall, lean body imposing in the small area. "Did I not say men must be responsible for what they do? I have not changed in that. I care as much as ever. More, possibly. I just don't serve a boy's first disillusionment any longer." He put his hand up to cover a yawn. "I grow very sleepy. What about you?"

Luisa suddenly wanted to shriek at him. Had he forgotten all the delights they had once shared? This was the perfect opportunity and now he talked of heresy and treated her as though she were one of his soldiers. She moved so that the shawl slipped from her shoulders and her white breasts showed to full advantage. Her hair fell silkily down her back, the fire turning it to bronze cascades. She reached out to touch the pure line of his jaw with one hand. He quivered under her touch.

"You're not really sleepy, Marcus. Do you remember those first days we truly shared together in the Welsh woodland? We drank of each other's bodies as if we could never have enough? Marcus, it has been forever."

Luisa reached up to kiss him, the motion studied and slow, her longing for him reflected on her face. He stood very still for a second, then pushed her gently from him, pulling the shawl together as he did so. He put both hands on her shoulders and held her back so that they stood facing each other for several seconds.

Anger and humiliation flamed in Luisa. If he

had openly scorned her or turned away in anger she would have known how to react, but this placid endurance shown by the hitherto bold Marcus was too much. "Forgive my advances. I had no reason to think I repelled you."

Marcus's brilliant eyes flared with something of the old arrogance. "I have strategy to plan, matters to coordinate, supporters to rally. How do I have time to consider matters of the flesh? I swear, I think all women are Eve at heart." He released her and turned away. She was dismissed.

The blood drummed in Luisa's head as her fists clenched with impotent rage as she cried, "Your own men have named you traitor, remember? They seek to punish you even as the forces of the other side and Lady Barthampton's men do. That ought to concern you more! There's nothing and no one for you to lead, my noble warrior!"

He whirled back to her, his face twisted with fury. One hand went up to strike her while the other jerked her toward him. She was helpless in his grasp, but her green eyes flamed unflinchingly into his. For a long moment they stared at each other, then his mouth came down on her with an inevitability born of need and long-postponed desire. Marcus had known all along he could not resist her. Anger, feigned indifference, concern with battle plans, theology, and violence all vanished when he touched her. She was his nemesis and his fate. He struggled against his own desires, knowing he must always yield to this fair temptress. As he so often thought when confronted by Luisa, Marcus wondered if it were so impossible to uphold his cause and care for her as well. Had he learned nothing over all the years?

Luisa opened to him, instinctively knowing that at first he must be the master because of her goading and his own contradictory feelings toward her. His arms were bands of iron around her and his lips were harsh on hers even as their tongues met and probed. She felt him hard against her. Her breasts were aching and heavy; it was a relief when he put his fingers to one nipple and caressed it. She put her arms around his neck and drew him powerfully to her body as if to envelop him. Marcus moaned something unintelligible and crushed her to him.

They wound together in such hunger that neither was aware of how they came to be naked in the firelight. Marcus still held Luisa captive in his arms; he did not release her mouth from his nor take his hands from her body except to move them down her supple length. Luisa let her touch rove over his flat stomach and hard buttocks and long back. His excitement mounted as did her own. There could be no waiting, no prolonging. Their tide poured into a sea of fulfillment as he entered her and she closed about him with a relief only dreamed of in the long time past.

Luisa rolled over and savored the look of him as he lay with eyes shut in passion's aftermath. His chiseled face was almost stern in repose, and his dark curls clustered over his high brow. She saw the hard muscles of his arms and legs, the slight rise of his powerful chest, and the new lifting of his manhood. The bards sang of the beauty of women; did they not know how glorious a man's body could be or was that left to the Greeks? She giggled at the thought and Marcus opened one eye.

"Are you not exhausted?" He smiled as he said it. The sadness which had covered him as a pall at times was gone and his blue eyes were dark with desire. "Share the amusing thought with me?"

"I was thinking how beautiful you are." It was no more than the truth but she blushed, the color staining her face and dipping down to her chest. "Perhaps I should make an ode to you."

He reached for her in a lazily commanding gesture. "What we do here shall be a hymn to the loveliness and bravery of Luisa Marmoor. Bold in love and bold in battle."

"So I am." In one quick motion she eluded his grasp, twisted so that her hair swirled over her breasts. She stepped over him and lowered herself upon him. "You are my warrior, my prisoner, my lover whom I shall not release no matter how you plead." She moved lower with each word until she had totally absorbed his length. Then she began to move up and down, balancing herself lightly and watching the eagerness on his face as their desires meshed together.

His hips lifted to her rhythm and his hands took hers. "Suppose I plead to remain captive? What then will you do?"

She increased the motion, willing herself to hold back and take this to the last bearable second before allowing the release. "This! This! This!"

"Yes!" He cried out in the joining of their words and then it was no longer the time for speech.

His movements became swifter. They were one in the burning, melting flesh, joined in the most elemental of struggles, fused and taut at the edge of darkness. Their eyes met and locked as the flames of immolation rose. Neither could look away as the shuddering passion rose to an unendurable peak and burst over them.

This time they were too exhausted for anything except rest. Marcus gathered Luisa close to him and she relaxed, her head in the hollow of his shoulder, their hands clasped together. He pulled an old cloak over them, murmured her name once and soon began to breathe evenly, their naked bodies relaxed against each other.

The edges of sleep were beginning to claim her as well. She thought only of this moment, this instant in time when they were close as they had been in the beginning. The strangeness of her feeling puzzled her for a second and then she realized it was pure crystalline happiness; untempered by anything else. Usually she knew such only in retrospect; now it was real and understood. "My cup runs over." She repeated the words softly and was thankful with all her being.

She was awakened by a thrashing at her side and hands pulling at the cloak, which was wrapped snugly around her. Half asleep and wanting to return to the coziness she had been experiencing as she dreamed of Marcus, Luisa slapped at the nearest hand and was rewarded with a muffled curse. She pushed the edges of the cloak back and looked in the direction of the sound.

Marcus was sitting close by the fire, which now gave off only a few faint sparks. Several pieces of wood lay near at hand to be added. He had found her discarded shawl and draped it around him as he rubbed his bare arms.

"What on earth are you doing?" She could not keep the laughter from her voice. "It's cold in here."

"I know it is. You took the cloak and the other piece of coverlet and wouldn't let me have any. No wonder I'm freezing." He grinned at her, one dark brow arching up. "You fight even when you sleep, my dear wife." He rose, tossed the wood on the fire, and reached down to draw her to her feet. "My dear wife." His tone was tender, no longer bantering.

"Marcus." She put both hands on his face and looked deeply into his brilliant eyes. "Love."

His fingers moved over the softness of her skin. He put his mouth on hers and she gave way to his probing tongue so that their mouths were alive together in passion's sweet prelude. Luisa leaned against him, warm and drugged with desire. He put his hands on her breasts, teasing them into blushing peaks as she moved invitingly, urging him on.

They came together standing, he thrusting into her with long, hard strokes and she holding him until the last motion, unwilling to let him go and knowing she had the power to rouse him to even stronger pitches of hunger. He thrust and withdrew, only to thrust again. They played each other's bodies skillfully and with rivalry, delighting in expression and movement. He went more deeply and she arched, moving delicately in a revolving push that threatened to make her slip off balance. The quaking began then, the earth opened up, and all the stars swung together. She and Marcus clung together, awed by the storms they could create.

They sank down beside the now-leaping fire and wrapped themselves in the cloak and shawl. Laziness enveloped them both but his hand was still possessively around her waist, and she caressed his broad shoulder gently.

"Are you cold now?" He nipped at her ear, missed, and settled for a soft kiss on her neck.

She turned to smile at him. "Warm and in no position to jerk the covers away from you."

"I'll have to see you stay that way, won't I?" He tilted her chin to kiss her again and then pushed her back to settle his body on hers.

Luisa's arms rose to embrace him as they moved again in love's rhythm.

Chapter Thirty-seven
TO BECOME A DESOLATION

LUISA TOLD HERSELF sternly that she should have known how it would be, the pain she felt ought to have been expected. She knew the capability Marcus had for isolating feelings and duty, but even now as they rode through the icy back trails she found adjustment difficult. It was only by force she had been able to keep from making demands and urging explanations earlier this morning. Marcus was as he was. Why couldn't she accept that? The pride of the Marmoors was always strong in her; she would never make overtures to a man who truly did not desire her. There was no question of the fact that he did.

The humiliation replayed itself in her mind, rendering her oblivious to the gray weather and freezing wind. She was warm enough in the remnants of the once-fine gown worn from Lady Cecelia's, a heavy-patched cloak, and muffling, caped hood. The future was in abeyance; once again she was caught in a net of strangeness.

Early that morning she had roused first and turned to Marcus in a manner that seemed quite natural to her in view of the laughter and intimacies shared the night before. He was just waking when she reached toward him and the recoil from her, the chill in his blue eyes, was quite unstudied. What followed was far worse. Luisa felt her cheeks burn at the recollection of it and the memory that it had been she who first began their lovemaking the previous night.

Reaching for his clothes and running both hands through his tangled dark hair, Marcus had stared at her as if he barely knew her. He whose body and mind had delighted her anew in passion and understanding! He had said, "Not now, surely! Matters of the flesh have no place in what must be done this day or, for that means, in the future. Cozen me no more!"

Luisa had wanted to spit out her rage at him. He had been as full a participant as she, after all! Teeth gritted, she had answered, "How you do misinterpret a simple motion. I merely meant to wish you good morning. I trust you will forgive that?"

"Hurry and dress. We must go from here. I know a place where our people very often meet. They'll have news if anyone does." He turned his back and walked out. He had spoken no word to her since.

Luisa lifted her head proudly. She would bear herself as though nothing untoward had happened between them. Did his religion prevent the enjoyment of natural feelings? She knew Marcus in many ways and found him a stranger in more. The love and passion they felt in varying degrees for each other, the mutual understanding and tenderness, could not cross their unknown barriers. Still, she was bound together with Marcus and nothing would alter that. Luisa did not count herself fey in any regard but she had felt the anguish of the seer in the Welsh mountains, had known something terrible was about to occur when Marcus left her at the Breconts, and now she knew very well the future, dark and forbidding, was about to unfold around them.

It was midafternoon before they reached any sign of human habitation, an outcropping of small houses finally giving onto a village shuttered against the weather. There was no one about and everything appeared deserted. They rode up to the one inn, strangely called The Broken Bar, and Marcus took the horses around to the stable, which held only a few mules. Luisa followed him without comment, noticing the way he moved warily, always watchful. He placed the animals close to a side door which faced onto a muddy track leading to the woods.

"Wait for me here. If I have not returned for you in a very few minutes, take one of the horses and go from this place as swiftly as you can. I do not have to tell you how to survive." One corner of his mouth went up and he touched her hand briefly. "Will you do as I say?"

Their personal conflicts had no part in this. She was his soldier. "I will, Marcus."

He nodded and was gone before she could say anything else. She stood in the iron cold, staring at the bare-branched trees and listening to a lone bird call. Was the village truly empty or had folk just withdrawn to their homes at this relatively early hour? What if the silent houses were filled with men from whatever faction seeking dissidents? Marcus might be going to his death. She tried to turn her thoughts into a more cheerful vein but it was useless. Thoughts of the Christmas season, now so close, brought renewed knowledge of the rising where many would die.

Luisa walked back and forth, wondering how to tell what a few minutes were. He had been gone an eternity already.

"Luisa!" Marcus was at her side. He had moved so quietly even her alert ears did not hear. "Come quickly."

She dashed after him and they entered the back door of the inn, coming into a little room furnished with several trestle tables and crude benches. Tallow candles illuminated the walls and cast shadows on the row of men who sat with their hoods pulled low. Luisa counted ten and the leader, a burly, balding man who stood to bid them greeting.

"God's greeting to you, madam, and to you, Marcus. You were fortunate to find us here. We leave very soon to meet with others. Welcome to our council. Your name is a legend among us." He beamed impartially at them both.

Marcus spoke urgently. "Does the plan still stand? I have grave news which may alter it for all of us."

The leader said, "If you were other than who you tell me, I'd not speak of this. But you know things only Marcus Lenley could know. We are to move to Eltham during the Christmas revels, there to take the person of the king and royal family. The meeting to which we go is one of all those in London and the immediate territory in order to arrange strategy. After the king is in our hands and our terms made plain, a general call will be issued for a march on London. Messengers have gone forth in the kingdom to tell those who are with us to hold themselves in immediate readiness. The Welsh, the followers of dead Richard, Lollards, all the disaffected. We cannot fail!"

Marcus looked at them somberly and spread his hands. "I must tell you that we are betrayed! My wife will bear witness to what I say."

Luisa stood beside him, her face grave, as he spoke urgently of the plan beyond theirs, of the greater plot that would leave the current faction in power with an even more malleable figurehead than the present king. The group sat petrified, the first shocked rustle stilled. Her own senses were at fever pitch, for not only their lives but those of many others were being decided.

"Madam, is this true? There has been no misinterpretation of facts?" The burly leader's ebullience had faded, the sheen of his ruddy cheeks gone yellow.

"It is true." The words were dry and hard in her mouth.

"What would you have us do?"

"We must wait," Marcus said. "Dissemble. Choose another time. Nothing can be successful now. We are known, as are our plans!"

One of the men rose and tossed back his hood. His wrinkled face blazed with emotion and his white hair shone in the light. One hand lifted his sword high. "We cannot alter what has been set in motion. We are in communication with Oldcastle, who states the time is right. The country will rise. Once we are in power we can set matters to the way they should be. I say we rise!"

"I, also!"

"And I."

"I agree!"

One by one the others rose up, baring their faces and holding their swords before them in agreement. The leader did the same. Marcus and Luisa stood alone.

The leader said, "We are grateful for your warning, Marcus, but we are agreed and there can be no turning back. When we have won we shall be most careful to look for those you have mentioned and, naturally, you yourself can point out some who might otherwise hide themselves." He rubbed his hands together after putting his weapon away and the others sat down. For him it appeared the matter was finished. "Now tell us what words you will send to stir the Welsh, or will you go yourself and explain matters?"

There was no sound in the room; they hardly breathed as all eyes turned to Marcus, who stood, hands looped in his belt, blue eyes almost black as he faced them. Luisa clenched her fingers tightly and could not look away from him.

"I withdraw from this enterprise. I will not encourage disaster, nor will I make a compromise with evil." For one last time he made his plea. "Can you not see? We are all being used. When the rebellion is done, those who are the true perpetrators of evil and unrest and cruelty will remain and be all the more firmly entrenched."

He was cut off by cries of outrage and disbelief. Some of the men started toward him but were waved aside by the leader, who said, "The Welsh know you best. I do not think they will rise in force unless you raise the call. I know it is said some are disaffected and against you, but this is surely not the verdict of the whole. Do not betray us, Marcus. Your name has been one of the rallying cries ever since Glendower retreated from view. We have a real chance to accomplish something now." He was pleading in his turn.

The clear, cold voice of Luisa dropped into the hush. "You will accomplish only more death and imprisonment. The fires of the stake will be lit and all dissenters will die. England and Wales alike will know the oppressor."

The white-haired man cried, "Then we go without you! We have to! The persecutions increase anyway, and Oldcastle must soon be caught by his friend the king. So much for loyalty! Get away, Marcus Lenley, you are none of us!"

"I know that well enough." His voice was bitter. "I thought it my duty to try and save something out of all this. You were the nearest group and could tell those in London. Will you at least mention the matter?"

"Never! We'll not weaken our cause!"

"No! We can conquer."

"He loses his nerve now that he is wed!"

The yell of the others rose around Marcus as he touched his sword hilt and dangerous lights shone in his eyes. Luisa saw the vein throb in his temple. He said nothing as he controlled himself with obvious effort. The leader roared for silence again and again.

Under cover of the noise he said to Marcus, "You will stand apart from both sides? What do you intend to do?"

Luisa spoke for them both. "This is not the way. We support the same cause you do. Why not wait?"

"His wife speaks for him! Is that the way of councils now?" One of the younger men laughed as he shouted the words. "Now we know what has happened to our brave warrior!"

Marcus's sword flashed out. "Perhaps you would care to repeat those remarks?"

He would take no insult for her, only for himself. Luisa's heart overflowed toward him. "Only the foolish will not listen," she cried. "Let us go as we have been bidden."

Marcus turned his back on them deliberately and together they walked to the door, heedless of the clamor behind them and the reasonings of the burly leader.

They mounted their horses without speaking and rode out into the cold darkness. The first trail they took was wide enough to go two abreast; it led deeper into the wood and they were able to make good time. Luisa thought at first they might be pursued but then realized the network these people had would put out the word against them and that was sufficient.

"Marcus, what are we to do now? There's no real safety for us anywhere. What can two people do against all the forces leveled upon us? We can't stop the rebellion or turn the tide."

He turned his head to look at her, his body swaying easily with the motion of his horse. "I still have some friends I can count on. You are another matter. England is unsafe for you and Wales will soon be ablaze. I once did a favor for a high personage at the court of France. For my sake, he and his would shelter you. The bonds between us could be dissolved and you set free to live your life as you choose. What do you say?"

Anger swamped her. "I say no and no! This is my battle as much as yours! This is my country as much as yours! I lost my estate as you did and have risked my life time and again just as you have! Go to France and be a useless ornament in some noble household! I'll have none of it! France helped Wales for her own ends; she would rejoice to see England torn apart. No, here I stay!" She paused to catch her breath while her mount began to shift uneasily and whinny.

"There are battles to be fought. What is to be done with you?"

"What do you mean 'done with me'?" Scorn rang in her voice. "I can fight as well as any man! That has been proven. The country is full of unrest; I'll wait for another opportunity and use it. I'll get Marmoor back, you'll see!"

"You are the most determined wench I've ever known." His teeth flashed in the darkness as he smiled at her. One hand went up. "I know. You're a soldier, not a wench. Forgive me?"

There was the faintest hint of tenderness in his manner and she was quick to respond. "The soldier need not forgive the commander, but Luisa can do so to Marcus. We are comrades, still."

"Aye." He urged his horse ahead so quickly that she was hard-pressed to follow.

After this they concentrated on putting as much distance as possible between themselves and the village. Luisa had assumed they were not too far from London but the very depth of the wood and the lack of human dwellings made her think otherwise. It was beginning to seem to her that they rode forever in the cold, gray world where no sun existed and rain or snow always threatened.

She was surprised when they came upon several houses in the fork of an adjacent road. Horses stamped, a voice was raised in an unintelligible song, and torches flamed over a broken sign which announced to the world that this was The Blue Hart Inn. A crude picture further showed this name to the many who could not read.

Marcus said. "This time we're simply travelers who need lodging. Just a down at heels man-at-arms and his wife. Will you be my wife this night, Luisa? This time I ask. Tomorrow will attend to itself." He shifted himself in the saddle to look at her, the carved face oddly at peace in view of all that had happened. He would take this time with her no matter what. They were two lovers holding time at bay. He knew the time was nearing when all his stored-up defenses must fall before the reality of his caring for Luisa. He would have to yield himself up to her.

Luisa forgot all her resolutions and thought only of her encompassing love for this man. "With all my heart, husband."

Chapter Thirty-eight
RUBICON

Luisa burst into a fit of giggles so intense that she put her hand over her mouth. It would not do to be heard. Marcus tried to keep his face straight but found it impossible. They collapsed on the bed, clutched each other, and roared with muffled laughter until their sides ached. Tears came to their eyes and were dashed away. The tension of the past days vanished for the time being and everything grew even more amusing.

"Did you see the landlord's face when you waved that gold piece and demanded his best for you and your new wife? He'd been ready to throw us out until then and all of a sudden it was 'sir' and 'my lady' and bows and orders to the servants. And he bit down on the gold when he thought we weren't looking." Luisa giggled again at the thought of the once-suspicious host who was now so affable it was cloying. "He thinks we stole it."

Marcus grinned, "I did! Lady Barthampton was careless and I pocketed her purse. You never know when gold will come in handy. Of course people here will think we're lovers running away from your angry old husband. I was careful to look both furtive and triumphant, did you notice?"

"I was too busy being demure. Didn't you notice?"

They laughed together again and stretched out on the rather narrow bed in what the landlord had proudly said was his very best room. "Once used by mighty lords and their noble ladies, it was. The tales these walls could tell!" He had smirked and put a finger to his lips as if to assure them of his discretion.

The room was small and dark, with very few furnishings—a chest and two stools besides the bed, but candles had been brought and braziers kept it warm. There was even a window covered with hides which Luisa had immediately stripped away so as to let the cold fresh air enter. They had further amazed and horrified the landlord by demanding water for washing. He had protested that it was December; no one bathed at such a time of year. Another gold piece had silenced him while also convincing him they were totally mad.

Now a tub of hot water sat cooling in the center of the floor along with the remains of half a roast goose, reasonably fresh brown bread, and some ale. The innkeeper had asked in an incredulous tone if there were anything more. What else could there be? His manner implied nothing.

"I'm first for the bath!" Luisa jumped up and stripped all in one quick motion, tossing her clothes everywhere before Marcus could do more than stir himself from the depths of the bed. She sank down in the water and soaped herself, laughing up at him as she did so.

He came to stand by the wooden tub, his blue eyes shining down into hers. There might never have been barriers between them. Everything retreated except for this particular moment in time. Luisa realized suddenly that she and Marcus had always had this ability to shut out every other distraction for such opportunities as these. Was it their blessing or their curse?

"You're thinking and that's forbidden! There's a penalty!" He was naked now, the light revealing his lean, muscular body and proud manhood. Reaching down, he scooped her to him, suds and all, and began to run his free hand over her smooth breasts. She shuddered with excitement as she struggled to get free.

"The water's getting cold and we'll never make them heat it for us again! Please, Marcus!"

"Fine." He sat down in the tub, holding her all the while. "Close your eyes." When she did not, he splashed water in her face. "I thought you wanted a bath."

Luisa sent a sheet of water toward him and caught him in midsentence so that he gurgled and mumbled before seizing and ducking her. An instant later water was flying in all directions.

Luisa put both hands on his shoulders and prepared to push him under once more as they laughed together. Their eyes met and he crushed her to him in a hard embrace. She clung to him and raised her lips to his. His tongue found hers and probed deeply. The familiar sweet fire began to burn in them both and she hardly noticed when he swung her up and drew her toward the bed.

This coupling was different from all the others. They lay side by side, bodies wrapped so closely that they were indivisible. Now he touched her with slow, exquisite tenderness; she teased him with a delicate brushing motion that stirred them to deeper caresses. Their kisses were a merging of flesh, the union of their separate beings soon joined into one. Luisa pressed herself to him, took and received him as he did her. They two were one flesh and heart in a tender fire of ecstasy.

Marcus looked into her face and spoke her name. "Luisa." It was so close to a declaration of love that tears came to her. He kissed them away while she caressed his brow and cheeks.

"Again. Again." For all the words and declarations she instinctively understood neither must make, Luisa lifted her body to his in passionate longing and avowal.

Much later when they slept, it was with bodies intertwined, their faces so close that their lips nearly touched. Luisa woke once in the darkness and saw Marcus smiling at her. He was half-awake and started to whisper something. She kissed him softly and his eyes closed. Snuggling down once more in the curve of his arm, she dreamed of summer meadows and the mountains of Wales where she had walked with him, secure in his love.

She woke to the sound of his pacing. Bright sunlight poured through the small window, adding warmth to that of the replenished braziers. He was only half-dressed, his lithe, powerful body moving as if it could not bear to be still. The dark brows were met in a scowl and his face, when he lifted it to her, was as remote as a carved mask.

"I have to tell you something." His voice held no inflection.

Luisa sat up, her chestnut hair tumbling around her shoulders and over her breasts. The laughter and sharing of the night were gone. Marcus had retreated from her once again. She reached for the patched coverlet and drew it close for warmth.

"What is it?" She was proud of her restraint.

He said, "I would prefer to send you into France. For the last time, will you go?"

"No." It was flat, unequivocal.

Marcus reached for his loose shirt and held it for a moment. "So be it. Listen to me. The conspirators, one branch of them, plan to kill the king although they said he was only to be made prisoner and have better counselors set around him. Civil war would result and it would destroy England. The land cannot endure another death such as Richard's. I mean to warn him. I have known this since I was made prisoner at Lady Barthampton's. They spoke of their plan in front of me." He pulled the garment over his head and stared at her, his face reflecting no emotion.

The words beat in Luisa's brain so that she thought she had not heard correctly. "You hate Lancaster and have fought against the usurper for years. Richard took all. You have said one king is like another. Are you mad?" Panic struck at her. Perhaps he was truly mad in some strange and unknown way.

"Do you think I come by this decision lightly? More than anything else, this realm needs a firm, strong hand. The king may well have such. Only a determined ruler can ward off domination by those who would manipulate us all. Killing

Henry would not destroy the real despoilers. I have to turn back and think of this country now."

"But, Lancaster!" All her hatred of the regime that had taken Marmoor from her and set her on this course of wandering rose up in her tone of utter loathing. "By all accounts this king is guided by whomever approaches him first. He delegates all to ministers. How can you do this, Marcus?"

He put both hands on his narrow hips and turned to face her. His bronzed face was set, his bearing forceful. "He is new to the role of king. He is still choosing his course. Glendower holds him high. There is no real choice in this matter. Henry is not as his father was, not a usurper."

"No one will believe you! You'll be killed! A known rebel leader, outlaw in the sight of three kings! They'll laugh as they take you to execution, and you'll never get within shouting distance of Bolingbroke's spawn." Luisa put all her power of persuasion into her voice. "What of the cause you have served? Your men? They have called you traitor. Will you be so in truth? Even Glendower fought! Retreat for a time. Gather the forces after this rising and we'll take our chances on who is in power! Please, Marcus!"

Luisa watched the vein jump in his temple and the blood rise to his cheeks as he tried to remain calm. It was utterly strange to her that she should stand here with her lover of the night before, her comrade and beloved, arguing this matter while the sun streamed brilliantly in and they were both young and free. A sense of the preciousness of life overwhelmed her, making her all the more angry at Marcus, who pursued a fool's course to sure death.

"My choice is made and I hold by it. I have forsworn my oaths and have to live with it."

"But that's just the point! You won't live. Don't you know you'll be tortured into telling all you know and thus giving everyone away? You are not just Marcus Lenley. You are a leader of the Welsh!" Luisa felt her face twist with the sheer effort to convince him and avoid tears. "Come away, then. We can go into France, come back at a safer time. You can teach me of your faith. We can be happy. Marcus, if you stay here you will die. Henry hasn't spared Lollards or his friends; he certainly won't hesitate to kill an outlaw."

"Nevertheless." He stood there, inflexible and grim, a believer in an honor that went beyond the dictates of man.

Luisa watched him and a great pride welled up within her. Their lives had been joined on the London road and, as far as she was concerned, that union would last until they lay dead. She knew life was possible without Marcus; if she must go on alone, her time with him was still well worth all it had cost. Her throat threatened to close up. When she opened her mouth to try once again to dissuade him, no words would come.

"There's some gold, not a lot, which you must take. Go to one of the coastal cities if you won't leave the country. Go to ground and when this passes, as it must, petition whoever rules for Marmoor. But be careful when you do so." He watched her face as he spoke and saw the rebellion there. "I do what I must, Luisa. I may succeed. It may come to nothing and the king may be as weak as many say. But it is the only hope."

"You're trying to kill yourself! Are you so eager to die?"

"I can do nothing else and there it rests. No more." He went to the tiny window and stood looking out at the sunlit land.

Luisa knew there was nothing more to say. This was the end for them and it was unbearable. He set up his death and would preside at his own sacrifice. She was thankful for her practical nature. Life was the important thing.

"How do we proceed to warn the king? Have you a plan?"

Marcus whirled around to stare in amazement. He was no more surprised than she. Luisa would have sworn she was about to speak the words of renunciation and separation. But now that she had spoken, she knew her words were inevitable. She had come to her choice just as Marcus had.

She said slowly, "We may not change the course of the kingdom, but we shall have acted as best we could according to the truth as we believed it. Not as ciphers. Not in overweening hatred. Not as puppets to be manipulated. We act as a free man and woman." This was the truth for Luisa, it shone in her face.

Marcus cupped her chin in one hand. His eyes were the color of the mountain lakes and the sky above them. Luisa was reminded of the eagle that had soared from the overlook in Wales on a faraway day, and she thought its proud, invincible beauty stood before her now.

"We? You were so much against it, Luisa. Don't say such things for the sake of the feelings that are between us. This transcends all else. I cannot let you risk your life. All the arguments you gave were true, of course."

God give her wisdom! It was partly for love of him and partly because this was a choice for action rather than flight, but the deeper reason she herself did not yet know. She smiled confidently. "Better the known enemy. One king is like another, I am sure, but this one is at least thought to have some right to the Crown. He is young and possibly easy to lead when one has achieved his favor. I will dare much for my estate, you much for the Welsh. So we'll approach this as a problem to be solved and not as some blessed sacrifice. On that basis, I join your enterprise, Marcus."

Unpredictably, he began to laugh. After a shocked moment, Luisa joined in.

"You do think this is a mad enterprise, don't you?" He reached for the purse of gold and began to check it. "If I could think of some way to prevent you from coming, I would. Your about-face is too quick, the danger too great." His eyes blazed into hers and there was no mistaking the dedication there. "Even if we were well and truly wed, with children about us and all estates restored, I would still do what I could to restore some form of justice to this realm. It is the very toleration of evil which makes it possible. What good is accomplished if the figurehead is brought down and the old advisors who seek only their gain remain? Many have done so, you know. During Richard's reign and earlier. The ruler is a symbol."

Luisa said, "I think it may be possible to warn Lancaster, but I should like to live in the process. I'd hate to think your only goal in this was expiation and suicide." Let him be angry. It had to be said.

His voice was dry. "Well, I'd not decided to burst in the first gate crying news of a plot. I've done a bit of mimicry in my time, as have you, my dear. This will take a bit of planning. Some of the conspirators were going to be dressed as mummers to go about the great hall and entertain. I thought one more would make no difference."

"And now we are two." She went to stand beside him.

"Why, Luisa?" He put both hands on her shoulders and looked directly into her eyes.

In the end it was only the truth which would suffice. "Our lives are woven together, Marcus. I go because I care about myself, you, and our land."

He drew her into his embrace and he looked deeply into her eyes.

"Thank you, Luisa." He held her all the more closely. Her allegiance meant more to him than he could ever say. He wanted to try to tell her but his mouth went dry and he did not want her to see the shimmer of tears in his eyes.

Luisa would not let herself think too far into the future in this shared moment. The consequences of success might be as unfortunate as failure, but that was not to be considered just now. She stood with the man she loved and they were allied. What came after would not truly matter, for this was the time above all others, a time of decision and action, going beyond chivalric ideals to the ultimate responsibility of the individual before his God.

Chapter Thirty-nine
BATTLE PLANS

MARCUS AND LUISA made their way slowly in the direction of Eltham Palace. They knew that conspirators and rebels alike would be watching for them so careful plans were necessary. He did not try again to dissuade her from accompanying him, nor did she speak negatively about their mission. They worked together now, one in mind and heart, true soldiers in the common cause.

With the gold they bought several changes of clothing, a harp in good condition, a stout staff wreathed with strange carvings, some glittering and gauzy materials, and face paint along with two well-honed daggers. Marcus concealed his sword in one of the packs; he could not bear to part with it, dangerous though it was to keep. They would sell the horses for what they could get. No mummer ever had such transportation and it was not safe to ride them much longer.

They paused for one final night at a very scruffy inn and had the unbelievable luck of obtaining a tiny room with no one else in it due to the weather, which had remained fine for the holy season allowing folk to travel rapidly. There was no fire and very little comfort for they dared not spend their few remaining pieces of gold, but cuddled together on the hard bed they managed their own shining warmth.

Marcus held her closely in his arms while the dark glory of her hair tumbled over them both. "Mummers can go anywhere. There's no problem there. I don't think we'll be recognized in our disguises. Many of the rebels will be recruited from the south of England, and Lady Barthampton's people won't be that quick to suspect those they think of as being their own. The king will have guards, of course, but who can know if even they are suspect or not? There was an attempt on his life soon after the crowning, remember?"

Luisa recalled something about poisoning and the relief it had brought to the remoteness of Marmoor. A king concerned for his very life would have little time for the people of her estate and village. Quite an error that thought had been!

"Once we're in the palace and established, we ought to have a good chance to gain the ear of the king. Impromptu entertainment will be everywhere." Marcus stretched out his long legs, bumped the nearest wall, and bent his head to look at her. "Are you listening to me?"

"Of course." She curled closer to him.

"I don't think you are. Prove it. What did I just say?"

"You were recounting strategy. Strategical positions." Luisa slipped one hand under the folds of his shirt and the cloak which covered them. She caressed the warm flesh and felt him move with pleasure. Her other hand moved downward under the bulk of his clothes. "What strategy shall we discuss now?"

He breathed her name into the stillness as they looked at each other. Both knew this might be one of the last opportunities they would have to come together in passion. Once embarked on their endeavor, every second must be accounted for lest they lose track of the roles they played and forget to be aware of the danger in their absorption with each other. The sense of last things touched them and they clung together tightly.

They made love with a tender hunger which welded them into one being. His hands imbued Luisa with a fire that fed upon itself and could not be assuaged. She covered his naked body with kisses, but it was not enough. It would never be enough. He caressed her breasts, soft inner places, stroked and touched but always held back as desire mounted higher.

"I want you now, Marcus!" She lay on her side as he explored her rosy nipple with his tongue. Her fingers held his manhood as she arched toward him in her urgency. "Now!"

"Ah, Luisa!" Marcus could say no more for his fierceness matched hers. He half sat up, she leaned to meet him, and then they were moving together as the flames roared up and the world dropped away in the mutual passion and love that was their gift to each other.

They slept for a short time and returned to their enjoyment, rousing and stirring themselves to a mutuality of the flesh that melted into exhaustion and tenderness. Hands, lips, eyes, mouths, all their bodies worshiped in the act of caring. In the end they lay fused, arms wrapped about each other and limbs tangled closely. Their breaths mingled. Luisa's last conscious thought before the delicious languor of sleep took her was that she had never before known what the words *one flesh* meant. She had to come to the very edge of death and loss to know it. She intended to fight until the last breath to preserve the precious thing she shared with Marcus. He would not admit it but she, as she had told him, understood they were bound together by some fate not to be sundered in this life. If they lived and yet went their separate ways, that fact would still be true.

The wonder of their passion was with them in the very early light when they woke to make slow and gentle love for one more time. Afterward, they nestled cosily close, unwilling to break the spell laid upon them by emotion. Marcus played with a tendril of her hair, winding it first around one ear and then both nipples. She kissed his fingers and blew out her breath noticing how it hung in the chill of the room.

"Marcus, what shall we do to attract the king's attention to us?" She hated to put reality in front of them again, but it was already past the hour upon which they had planned to be on their way. "Think of all those competing for it, the royal nod or glance! We want to speak to him, explain, and make sure we have time to do it before the others, real mummers and otherwise, surround him.

"I don't know about you but I'm an indifferent juggler and tumbler." He sat up, pulled his shirt over his shoulders, ran his fingers through his tousled dark hair, and regarded her seriously. "We've talked about this act and that, but timing and skill are so important, you know. There are many tales of Richard's punishments to those who failed to amuse him. One can hardly expect more of Bolingbroke's son."

Luisa settled the cloak over her body, then shook her hair out of her face. "You don't really care for any of them and still you risk your life. Men are strange and I suppose I am, too, because I follow you."

Marcus lifted her hand to his lips. "And I am honored that you do, lady mine."

The idea hit her as though a hammer blow. Odd it had not come to either of them earlier! "Marcus, I know! There was admiration between the king and Glendower for all those summers of fighting in Wales. He was born close to the border, wasn't he? And hasn't Wales been claimed by England for many years? The citizen surely has a right to approach the ruler!"

"What are you saying, Luisa?" He pulled her to him, his gaze searching her face.

She was so excited she did not even feel the cold air on her bare skin. "Audacity can at least win us a hearing! We can be the Welsh! My voice

carries well and yours will also. Remember John,
the seer, and the respect accorded him! We'll
have to work all this out, of course, but the
words of the Welsh poet, Dafydd ap Gwilym?
Marcus, let his words resound in an English hall
for the ears of the king of England!"

"You are too bold." His voice was flat, almost
bored, but he could not hide the dawning excitement in his eyes.

She said, "We'll have to be. Our danger is
tripled before we even reach the king. One lifted
finger and he can send us into prison or worse,
as you well understand. Boldness from the out-
set may take the day! You're enough of a soldier
to see that."

"Against all odds." He rose and began to
dress. "If only you'd stay clear! Listen, let me go
and do this. You take shelter in the forest; you
have that ability to look like a peasant if you
must. It'll stand you in good stead—I'll come to
you as soon as possible or if everything fails you
at least will live."

"No. Marcus, I ceased to implore you and
have taken up your struggle as my own. My
decision is made and you know it. If we don't
work together now that we are so close, what
can happen to us when everyone is ranged
against us? Together, Marcus, until the end,
whatever that is." She rose and faced him, regal
in spite of the ragged cloak and tumbled hair.
"The Marmoors have always fought for their beliefs and their daughter is no different."

Marcus smiled. "You speak as though this
were a noble tale of knights and a quest. Those

times never existed except in the romances. This is real."

Luisa was undaunted. "So it is and all the more reason to do it properly. I am a free woman and I do what I must."

He held out his hand. "I am rebuked. Comrades?"

She put both hands over his. "As always. Equal comrades."

Once more the smile touched his carved mouth. "So be it."

Later that afternoon Marcus and Luisa went on foot through the rolling fields and woodland to the royal palace of Eltham, which had been a favorite of English kings for years. The court had streamed after the new king in this first Christmas of his reign; the gaiety and pleasure were expected to be unrestrained. They stared at the troops of the great who went by, the ladies in velvet and furs, veils streaming, the men lordly in bright mantles and rich cloaks, the clergy opulent in furred gowns. It seemed all the kingdom wished to be present for the Christmas festivities, which were to last many days as was customary.

Luisa had felt Marcus withdraw to his own privacy after they left the inn. She guessed he had come too close to fully admitting his feelings to her; not even as close as they had been and all they had shared could allow him to come nearer. He was no longer angered by their passion but it made him uncomfortable and reticent in the aftermath. When they were safely in the wood and their disguises well in place, she had started to kiss him only to experience his rapid recoil. The touch of pain she experienced was not completely wiped away by her understanding. Since that time he had spoken only in monosyllables.

The day was still brilliant but the sun was dropping into the west by the time they reached the castle's drawbridge. They joined the ranks of people waiting to cross. Luisa wore boy's clothes in varying shades of brown and Marcus was bent over, well wrapped in a heavy cloak. Both carried packs from which bits of food and clothing appeared. She guided him as he bent over his stout staff. Their look was that of the very poor, come hoping for Christmas largesse. When she glanced cautiously around at the others, she saw that some might have been performers or gleemen for they were light on their feet, exchanged lively remarks, and indulged in much laughter. She observed that some of the poorer ones had the look of petitioners, even as they did. Others might have come from the surrounding villages to work in the palace by day and night. Many were undistinguished; Luisa hoped she and Marcus blended in.

As they stepped onto the bridge, several guards surrounded them and seven others. Luisa saw this procedure was followed with all who entered by this bridge. Scrutinies were severe and questions sharp. This was one of the common entrances. The nobility would enter elsewhere. She wondered if they were being checked and doubted it.

"Why do you come here, boy? What purpose do you have?" The words were harsh but perfunctory. Whatever they had been warned against, it was not a slender boy and a bent man.

"We're mummers, sir. We've come to participate in the revels. I take the parts of maidens and lads; my friend has many an amusing tale. He's a little hard of hearing but his voice is good." Luisa did not have to try very hard in order to allow fear to creep into her voice as she rattled on. "All are welcome at the holy season, surely? We heard they were and we're in sore need. Hungry. Not many clothes. Can we go in, please?"

The guard's eyes narrowed. "What is in those packs?" He jabbed at Marcus who cowered away.

"All our belongings, sir, and a few crusts," Luisa patted Marcus's arm and murmured soothingly under her breath. "He's been beaten, you see."

Some of the people around them began to grumble and one of the other guards motioned for the next party to come forward. "Let them go! This rabble is cold and hungry. At least let them pass." He turned to Luisa and added, "Get on with you! You'll have to sleep wherever you can find a place and the pickings of the kitchen will feed such as you and more. Now move!"

Luisa gabbled her thanks while Marcus tottered along using his staff. The impatient ones behind them nearly knocked him off balance as they surged ahead and earned a cuff from the guard who had first addressed Luisa.

Thus did they gain entrance to the park buildings and outbuildings of Eltham Palace. The entire area was huge with sprawling gardens, trees, and winding ornate paths that would be blazing with flowers in the spring. The palace, Marcus told her, was as most of its kind and filled with special chambers for the great lords, inner ones for the king and his family, extras for court officials and keepers of the household, treasure rooms, chapels, and great halls for pageantry.

Marcus drew her aside in the crush of people and whispered, "I've been here once or twice but I don't remember that much about the place. We both need to familiarize ourselves with it. I don't think anything will happen until Christmas is done. No conspirator will dare risk the curses which might be placed upon anyone breaking the holy time. But after!"

Luisa said, "We'll separate then and meet in several hours to compare what we've seen." Excitement shook her as she thought once more of their daring scheme, which surely had at least a chance of success.

Marcus said nothing for an instant as they stood together in the evening chill which was now far more pronounced. The scene about them was one of endless activity. Guards marched and drilled, their eyes watchful. Several ladies walked with their escorts, laughing and chattering. A group of maskers practiced the entertainment they meant to give, possibly that night. A fair maiden cowered convincingly as a giant bent over her. Several jugglers kept a fantastic array of objects in the air and sang at the same time. Several hooded friars clustered together, the hum of their Latin rising above the general hubbub.

"God keep us both." His voice was soft in her ear.

Luisa spoke the words which were her credo. "We have to help ourselves first."

She looked at Marcus as she spoke and saw his blue eyes alight with the laughter they had often shared. A smile illuminated her face in answer. The battle had begun.

Chapter Forty
CHRISTMAS COURT

THE BLESSED SEASON of Christmas was kept with full ceremony at Eltham Palace. The holy day was filled with rejoicings, many Masses, and exhortations to the faithful while choirs sang and prayers resounded. Food and drink were given unstintingly to the gathered people who praised the king and his largesse loudly. Even the weather was strangely mild after the previous numbing cold, and it was said that even this honored God's anointed.

Marcus and Luisa wandered about as much as they were allowed without calling suspicion to themselves. They could not fail to notice the plethora of guards everywhere and the strict watch kept on the people. At night they slept in

one corner of the huge stables with many others
and ate of the communal food. Marcus maintained the pretense of deafness and of having a
twisted back. Luisa was his young helper. They
never allowed the roles to deviate for an instant.

They had been at Eltham for two days and
Christmas itself was over, though the celebration of the high festival would continue for a
while longer, when Marcus approached Luisa as
she stood watching some tumblers at work in
the vast courtyard.

He spoke urgently. "Time has run out. I saw
two of the conspirators from London, wearing
the habit of the Benedictines. I remember them
from Lady Cecelia's house. I don't think anyone
could recognize me in this garb but it's a signal
that something is about to happen. The Lollards
and others were scheduled to rise very soon after Christmas Day. It must be tonight that we
make our move."

Luisa was horrified. "But we've not been permitted within the banqueting hall. No one has
except the nobility and the entertainers. How
will we know what to do or how to make ourselves known in the festivities? We really need to
watch for one night at the very least."

Marcus glanced up at her white face. "You're
afraid. I am, too."

She looked at him oddly. The old, arrogant
outlaw would never have admitted so much. "I
wish I were as brave, Marcus." Her hand went
out to him and he took it unashamedly.

"I've been wandering a great deal and I just
happened to hear that the next few nights will be

given over to all those who have come to honor the king and the season. They are to be permitted in the hall and watched carefully. It'll be our chance."

"So it will." She would not show herself less brave than he. They were, as she had so often said, soldiers in a common cause. "We'd better go and practice."

They went on to search for a secluded corner somewhere on the spacious grounds to prepare for the most important event of their recent lives and one that would spell life or death for both.

Feasting and celebration began that afternoon in the great hall of the palace. A special area at the back was kept for the people to gape at the doings of the mighty. Guards were stationed at various intervals there. Candles by the hundreds obliterated all shadows. Braziers burned high and fires were blazing in several tall fireplaces. The long tables were covered with ornate cloths and a huge feast was spread on them. Luisa saw all manner of ales and heady wines, apples, pears, pastries, sweets of all sorts, loaves of white bread, fish, fowl, pigeons, mutton, boar, venison, and other elaborate concoctions beyond her experience.

"That's enough to feed my village for a month." An old man just behind Luisa grumbled into his beard. "Sinful, it is."

She and Marcus were engaged in pushing their way up to the front where they could see more. Some of the people gave way, crossing themselves as they noticed his bent form and apparently twisted neck. Others shoved back, lessening their efforts as they saw the sharp eyes of the guards. Luisa saw one beckon to the old man, who turned away and was quickly removed in the same instant. None protested; it was obvious this celebration was well regulated.

Above and below the salt, all ate heartily of the various courses. The Lord of Misrule capered wildly about, issuing commands in a high, eager voice. The minstrels played in their gallery, now a lively air, a tune of the season, ballads, and love songs. The courtiers wore fantastic creations of silk, satin, and fur in all the brilliant shades of a rainbow. The gowns of the women showed nearly bared bosoms crusted with rich jewels and opulent laces. The ransom of a kingdom sparkled in this one hall. This was a place where Luisa and Marcus, by virtue of blood and birth, might sit in honor but it might also turn out to be the place of their doom.

Luisa's eyes moved over the extravagance of color and light to the figure who sat on the dais, his brothers and their ladies slightly lower. On this occasion, Henry wore cloth of gold with white and red velvet. A simple golden circlet was on his head and a cross hung around his neck. The brown eyes were heavy-lidded and watchful. As she watched, he lifted one long hand and gestured in the direction of the people. Immediately a gorgeously dressed official stood up.

"You in back there! Mind your manners and you may come closer to watch the revels! Silence now and be orderly. His Grace is concerned that all shall see the wonders."

Someone roared, "God save His Grace!"

Others took up the cry and in the resulting commotion Marcus and Luisa were able to edge near to the end of one of the tables, which needed only to be shoved aside in order to give them access to the cleared space directly in front of the nobility. This would be a blessing when the time came. The guards had moved with the surging people but now they seemed unsure of how much enforcing was to be done.

The Lord of Misrule waved a gaudy arm and several mummers tumbled in. They wore bright cloaks and gaudy masks. Amid cries and shouts, roaring songs, wooden swords clashing, much posturing and gallantry, they formed a circle into which a lion strode. He turned this way and that so it might be seen, the royal coat of arms of England on his broad chest. The mummers gave instant and loud homage while the assembly cried approval.

"Soon, Luisa." Marcus looked at her and his blue eyes blazed with their own warmth. "I'll give the signal."

"I'll be ready." Fear caused knives in her stomach and sweat on her upper lip but she spoke the truth. Everything but the moment was receding. She thought of the many battles she had waged for Marmoor. This was but another. Losing was not a consideration.

There was a sudden blare of trumpets and a new company entered the hall. Some members were dressed as demons in black and red, others wore white and had streaming golden hair. Masked kings and emperors moved behind them. Knights clad in unrelieved black and bearing jeweled swords surrounded the regal ones. Then men in Eastern garments, their hair oiled and sporting fierce black beards, appeared. A battle in mime took place while the minstrels played martial airs. The demons and the men of the East were speedily vanquished, a great cross was upheld, and everyone bent at the knee.

Now the Lord of Misrule bade a fat knight rise and sing a ditty in which he, the Lord, would lead him. The knight began but flushed an angry red when he realized he was singing of a fair maid who sought a capable lover but wept because all she found were fat knights who were useless abed. The whole assembly, nobility and poor alike, roared with laughter. Even the king applauded. The knight raised his arms and bowed this way and another, grinning with pleasure. Another round of applause began.

It was still going on when Marcus touched Luisa and nodded his head. Their communion was instant and total; she felt very near tears. In this moment before they entered into the supreme gamble, she and Marcus stood as one in love and faith. Once it would have been a time to cherish but now there was no more time. She nodded in return and it was as though they lay clasped in love.

Luisa loosened the enveloping cloak she wore and shook free of the brown mantle. She wore tight red breeches and a full shirt of the same shade. Her hair was plaited under a bright yellow hood and sparkling bangles on both wrists caught the light and stirred the air as she moved.

Placing her hands in front of her, she vaulted up and over the table in one swift movement. Landing on her feet, she did another tumble which brought her up to the Lord of Misrule's feet. She bent her knee in a caricature of obeisance, spread her arms wide, and brought them together under her chin as she implored him in a loud, whining voice.

"A boon, great lord! A boon of the mighty lord!"

The bright figure turned to her, the black eyes under the red and white mask viewed her with some sourness as the little mouth pursed.

She lowered her head as if in awe and cried, "One little boon, my great lord. You alone are supreme here. Your greatness is sung in all the courts represented this night. Of your kindness!"

The Lord of Misrule was by tradition ruler of the court at this time. Like much of their planning, this part was a gamble but the language she used and the very appearance she made would make it seem as if this were part of the entertainment.

Those seated at the tables nearest her began to chant, "Grant it! Grant it! Of your courtesy, lord, grant it!" The cry was taken up until the hall rang with it.

The Lord of Misrule said, "Done. Boy, what is this boon?" He swung his string of bells over her shoulder. "Rise and speak. You have my permission."

"I am with a teller of tales who has a surpassing one to relate. The spirit is upon him this night from viewing this great assemblage and our most noble lord. He beseeches time to speak. His voice is a mighty one." She pitched her voice at its most compelling and dropped it on the last syllables so they had to lean forward to hear.

"Let him come forth." The decree of the Lord of Misrule was echoed in the other throats as well.

Exultation rose in Luisa and she suddenly wanted to dance in delight. The first part of their struggle was won. And it had been so easy! She waved to Marcus who pulled his hood down and stumbled toward her. The lord and the company began to laugh, thinking it part of the entertainment. Someone called out a jest, which was answered by another. Marcus came closer and held out their harp, which he had taken from the folds of his cloak. Luisa came to stand beside him as if to support him. She looked around the hall and saw that every eye was on them, even that of the king, who leaned forward, his face grave.

Marcus swept the cloak from his shoulders and threw back his hood. He stood revealed in bright blue and yellow, colors donned to catch the attention. His dark curls rioted over his head and his piercing blue eyes fixed themselves on the king. Luisa's mind went in an odd flash of fancy to the old tales of her youth, of Ulysses and his return from Troy when he confronted the suitors who had wronged him and was changed by Athena's grace from a beggar to the king of Ithaca. She had worried that he might be recognized before giving the performance and carried away to prison but he had said wryly, "No difficulty there. These proud nobles can't imagine one of their own being a lowly minstrel. It may dawn on them later but with the first surprise we'll be safe."

The hall quieted at the rich timbre of his voice. "I speak in honor of this company and for the lord king. The boy and I are from Wales and it is of that land I am moved to speak."

One noble called out, "Arrogant minstrel! That land is in foul rebellion. Take care how you speak to your betters."

"Aye, sing of England and her triumphs."

"No, a jolly tale instead."

Others chimed in with demands but the Lord of Misrule stretched out his hand and there was silence. He was capricious as only such a one could be at this time of year. He said, "I command the minstrel, the storyteller, to sing of his land of Wales. Silence to all the others!" He was currently the law and they obeyed.

Marcus was not a real bard nor was his voice trained, but the lovely cadenced words in Welsh and English wove their own tracery of magic over the hall. He spoke the Welsh most of the time and Luisa the English, but often their voices mingled in the refrain of the mosaic they had put together and memorized, repeating it over and over in the long days of preparation and later here at Eltham.

Now in memory and dream they walked in the greenwood in May when the wind was soft and sweet and the days ran together in a white haze. Young lovers met in the first passion while summer abounded in the mountain sheltered valleys. When the black ice came and men huddled in halls against the wrathful storms, they remembered green May and were restored. Love came again and walked among them until all knew what it meant to long for the presence of the beloved, to weep and be returned to life again, to experience the glory of living in things small and large.

Their voices drifted together and paused. Into the utter stillness, Marcus spoke the words of the poet, Dafydd ap Gwilym. He spoke of the eagle in flight, of its proud freedom, of its shadow on the crags. The eagle fell, pierced by the careless arrow, and lay in death while the mate screamed her agony to the unrelenting skies. Freedom was the breath all men and all things needed for life. Without it everything sickened.

Luisa translated the powerful, singing words—which really needed no explanation—and thought of Owen Glendower's gray eyes. She said to herself and to his mighty spirit, "This is for you, true Prince of Wales, at the court of England."

She touched the harp in a waterfall of sound as love and sorrow blended. Now it was her voice alone, lifting in the endless tale of Taliesin, who was beginning and end, mountain and eagle, black magic and white. She gave her delight in the tale full play; reality faded and she stood again in the Welsh mountains with her outlaw and found new meaning in living each day. Then she let the final notes drop into a stillness, which was the highest compliment it was possible to give.

Applause poured over them as hands and goblets hit the tables and coins fell at their feet. The Lord of Misrule started forward to clap them on the shoulders but was stopped by a movement from the dais. The quiet voice resounded into the complete silence.

"Minstrels, who have greatly pleased us this night. Will you accept this ring from one who knows the land of which you sing?"

King Henry was tugging a large ring from his finger and did not notice at first that Marcus assumed a proud stance, head thrown back and hands on his hips, while Luisa swept her own hood aside and let her loosened hair tumble over her shoulders in a chestnut stream. When he raised his head to look at them there was no surprise on his face. He paused with the ring in one hand and waited. The guards at the walls stepped closer while some of the people began to whisper.

Marcus said, "Nay, Your Grace. I will not accept this gift at your hands. Instead I choose to give you one."

Henry plainly thought this was all part of the entertainment for he spoke indulgently. "Ah, what diversion this is! And what do you give me, minstrel?"

Luisa lifted up her voice in words she had never thought to speak in this life. "The gift is your life, Henry of Lancaster! Be warned for there are those in your very court who seek it! You are offered your life this night!"

Chapter Forty-one
GRIEF OF THE WORLD

The great hall exploded in outrage and shock, but Henry's upheld hand stopped all sound. The faint smile had not left his mouth but his gaze was hard and his face held no expression.

"I trust you will explain yourselves?" His tone was almost conversational.

Marcus said, "There is a plot, several in fact, against you. You and your family will be taken and held captive, eventually killed. They and others will march on London before Epiphany, there to storm the city and take over its rule. There are plots within plots and things are not what they seem. Be warned now for some come as mummers, others as friends, and in force."

"Treason!" "Seize him!" "Surround the king at once!" The simultaneous cries began as Henry raised his hand again in one swift gesture. Instantly guards surged forward, some to Marcus and Luisa, others to stand between the royal party and any who would approach, and still others to prevent anyone from entering or leaving the hall. Some of the nobility started to protest but looked at the drawn swords of the guards and sank back down.

The quiet voice had not altered, nor had the king moved. "Who are you, Welshman? Who is this woman? Why do you warn me? Perhaps you seek to trick me when the real danger is from another source?"

"I am Marcus Lenley and this is my wife, Luisa

Marmoor. I have fought with Owen Glendower and led battles on the border for the cause of Welsh freedom. I have been named outlaw."

The guards pressed closer at his words. A dull red flush built up on the king's face. Luisa waited for the outburst that would surely send them to their deaths.

She cried, "They who plot are within your own government and call themselves your friends. They would rule by exploiting those who bear grievances against you for religious or state reasons. The Lollards and other dissidents are not your true enemies; they are used as shields by the real plotters who desire your death!"

Angry cries rose up and continued even as Henry said, "I will be answered on this. Why do you come to warn me when you fought against my father's rule and mine as well, Marcus Lenley? The woman is your wife and must follow you. That excuses her. But you? A noble of my realm?"

"You have not yet conquered Wales, your grace!" Pride rang in Marcus's voice.

Luisa burned with anger that a man should be accountable for his deeds while a woman was considered a mere appendage. "I, too, fought against Lancaster! You took my family estate and sought to order my life so that I was forced to flee for my very sanity! Neither of us has reason to love your house, lord king, yet we risk our lives to warn you this night."

Exasperation was plain in Henry's voice. "Why? Can either of you answer so simple a question?"

"You may be a strong ruler one day. The land

must unite or all is destroyed." Marcus spoke with all the certainty at his command. "What else is there? The ruler changes, the evil behind the throne does not."

Henry looked at them expressionlessly, then turned to a noble standing close at hand. "Take these people, guard them securely, and find out all the details of this. See to it immediately."

They were pushed toward the nearest door by the guards, who were none too gentle. The other mummers and onlookers were treated in the same fashion. Clerks and scribes moved among the guests with papers in hand, evidently making sure there were no imposters among them. The king was conferring with a group of men and flanked by his guards. The general atmosphere was one of bedlam. They were given no chance to speak to each other but were hustled rapidly along.

Marcus and Luisa were taken to a large quiet room of the palace which was richly ornamented and hung with tapestries depicting the many phases of a hunt. Shelves of books were carefully arranged, great windows gave onto the park and were of glass painted with pictures of birds and mythical monsters. The nobleman, Sir William Rays, who had been informed of his duty by the king, joined them and offered wine in golden goblets before telling the guards to stand far back.

He spoke in a conversational tone which did not hide the iron behind it. "I fought in the Welsh wars. I have respect for the Welsh people but I cannot subscribe to treason for whatever motive. You can be tried for that. I am not aware if change of heart is a mitigating influence. You may speak freely to me for I stand in the king's place here." He was grizzled and white haired, but the determination of a much younger man rang in his voice.

Marcus said, "If he is simply aware of the danger and takes steps to guard his person and London, I think the main power of those who seek his life will be averted. Will he act on what I have said?"

Sir William answered, "You have played the double game. How can you be believed? Your name and opinions are certainly familiar to this court; you are called traitor in three reigns, Marcus Lenley. Suddenly you declare for Lancaster?"

"Not for Lancaster. For England and Wales."

Luisa said, "It is a matter of conscience and personal responsibility."

Sir William folded his hands and put them under his chin as he viewed them reflectively. "You will naturally give all details of these plots, name the plotters, and vow allegiance to King Henry. You have likewise been associated with the Lollards and that is heresy. You will be eager to wipe them out, I know."

Luisa and Marcus stared at each other. So it had come to this. Traitors of noble blood were beheaded; heretics were burned at the stake. Would Marcus be such a total fool as to declare his faith now? He must not! Hurriedly, she demanded, "You have not said if the king will be watchful in his own household."

Marcus ignored her as he said, "The king has been warned. I give no more details. The greatest danger is in his so-called friends."

Sir William shrugged. "I expected no more from you. The matter rests in other hands now. I'll tell you this much. The king has had spies among the Lollards and other groups for some time. We, too, had heard of a plot involving mummers and investigations have been arranged. His man, Arban, is most efficient in—"

"Arban is one of the plotters!" Luisa fairly spat out the words.

"You are overwrought, madam." Sir William beckoned to the guards. "Take them away."

From between the encircling guards who started to take them out in different directions, Marcus and Luisa exchanged agonized looks. They both knew they might never see each other again. His head went up and the brilliant eyes blazed into hers as they had done on the London road so long ago.

"No regrets, lady mine?"

Luisa regretted many things about their relationship and the political aspects of it, but never would she regret her love for this passionate, contradictory man. She lifted her chin and smiled at him, the smile of her ancestors in the old stone church at Marmoor. "No regrets, lord husband!"

Marcus spoke as if they were alone, his voice warm and intimate. "You have been my joy, lady wife." He knew, as she did, that he spoke the utter truth.

Then she was pulled roughly away. Her final sight of him emblazoned in her mind the tenderness on his carved face. She would carry it with her in what remained of her life, be it long or short at Lancaster's whim.

In the long stretches of time that followed, Luisa was reminded of her ordeal as the prisoner of Arban and Sir Adam. She was now, as then, kept in ignorance of day and night, never allowed out of her room, and seldom allowed to speak. Her questions, no matter how trivial, were not acknowledged much less answered. She was beginning to realize that there was no mental torture so acute as not knowing the fate of a crucial issue. She lacked no luxury for the room in which she was confined was richly appointed with tapestries, comfortable chairs, an excellent bed, and books and various musical instruments. But the door was kept locked and there were no windows. She had many gowns and most of them fit. Hair ornaments and dressings as well as a mirror were furnished. Her meals were composed of the finest foods and wines. Nothing was demanded of her; no one asked questions or seemed interested in her at all. She had no idea of the passing of time and could not measure it by the way her meals were served since even that varied. Her only visitor was a priest, who exhorted her regularly at times and left her alone at others. Often it seemed to her his attention was perfunctory but she knew better. Women died at the stake as well as men. It might have been days or weeks since she last saw Marcus; he could be dead now. Such thoughts nearly drove her mad.

"Do you pray, daughter?" Father Otho advanced toward her on soundless feet as the door was relocked behind him. "Now, no questions. We discuss religious matters only. Have you meditated on the principles of Aquinas as I asked? Have you reflected on the vast learning of the church and its power as placed against the puny railings of a few hedge preachers who haven't the mind to grasp the wonder of the faith?"

Luisa had read some of the books; she had little choice for they were all religious in nature, some abstruse in content. She demanded, "You wish to prove me heretic! Convict me out of my own mouth!"

Father Otho, rotund and cheerful, was truly horrified. "Lady, you wrong me. You have been in ill company, exposed to heresy. The mother church is ever compassionate."

Luisa laughed shortly. "For souls, I suppose. She seems to care little for the bodies of people. I am no Lollard!" She dared not add the truth, that she simply did not care about doctrine, that the real world of flesh and blood, the blessed world of earth, was enough.

"Ah, the soul is the most important thing. I will leave you in the hope your bitterness will cease. It stands between you and reconciliation with God. A woman should be meek and pliable; you suffer from the abomination of pride."

"How about the mercy of man to man? Does my husband live? What have you done with him? What has happened and why am I held so closely?" Luisa felt control leaving her as the priest turned to go to the door.

"Pray for the mercy of God, my lady." He went out and the door slammed behind him.

Luisa put cold hands to her face and tried not
to weep. Her wits must be alert for whatever
might happen. They could not keep her this way
forever, could they? She sat down and schooled
herself to remember Marmoor and the Welsh
mountains, her times with Marcus and their
closeness at the end. If she ever attained freedom, she meant to ride and run and dance in the
sheer ecstasy of movement. More than anything
except reunion and safety with Marcus, she
wanted to be out in the winter world. Now, as in
Arban's prison, she began to exercise briskly,
practicing the tumbling motions and strengthen-
ing movements that had helped her then.

Tired from her efforts, she slept well and came
awake to find a woman she had never seen before
bending over her. "Get up and dress. Hurry!"

"What is it? What's happening? Damn you,
tell me!" Luisa shoved her hair back and eyed
the servant angrily.

"You have five minutes or the guards will take
you as you are. I'll say no more, lady." She went
out rapidly.

Luisa jumped to her feet and tossed on a warm
shift and a gown of red wool with furred sleeves
and skirt. The neckline was low and showed her
bosom to full advantage. She fastened a shawl of
priceless lace over her shoulders and picked up
a cloak of white velvet banded in fur of the same
shade. Her hair was swept back from her brow.
She pinched her cheeks fiercely to give them
color. The mirror showed her to be both calm
and fair in spite of her gnawing fear. She was
thankful once more that the clothes she had been

given were those of a noblewoman. She would
need all the help she could get this day. She
murmured the talisman. "I am Luisa Marmoor
still." So she was but she was the wife of Marcus
as well and dead or alive he would glory in her
beauty and courage.

When the woman entered again Luisa said
coldly, "I am ready."

She was taken quickly out into a bare corridor,
down some icy steps, and put into a litter with
black leather coverings fastened over the one
tiny window. She had time to see that guards
ranged around it and that it was a dark evening
or morning. Then she was jolted away.

During the course of the journey Luisa reflected that she approached an ending. As she
reviewed the crowded events of the past few
months, she knew there was very little she
would change. Last January all this had not even
been considered, Marmoor had been fairly safe,
and Dame Matilda was still living. She had not
understood herself very well then, and Marcus
had not been a part of her life. So much had
happened in such a short time and she now
wondered about the future.

After what seemed an eternity, the litter was
put down and she was escorted out by a silent
guard. This time she did not bother with questions but simply followed him down a damp
incline, up a flight of stairs, and into a spacious
warm room where a fire blazed. Some books
were placed out on a table and a chessboard lay
beside it. As she glanced around, she heard the
bolts on the door as they shot home. One prison

was exchanged for another. The sounds and cries of London could not be mistaken. Perhaps this was one of the minor palaces. But what was wanted of her? She wondered again at the lack of demands. She was a helpless mouse being played with by a cat. Disgust made her lips curl.

In search of diversion she crossed to the table and picked up one of the books. It was beautifully designed and illuminated in rose and gold. Birds and beasts flew and pranced down the pages. Luisa sighed thinking it was probably a dreary text on the soul but the beauty might well distract her. She turned one page and recoiled as though she had reached into a nest of vipers. Men and women with overlarge sex organs, huge lips, and fatuous expressions moved in the most bizarre positions, all graphically illustrated by a master hand. The Latin text was graphic and explicit. Another section dealt with the jaded sexual appetite, grossly illustrated in brilliant colors.

Luisa clutched the book in both hands, afraid to investigate the others and yet drawn to plumb the full list of horrors. Why were such books left for the attention of a political prisoner? What sort of captivity was this? Angrily she opened another. It purported to be an account of the demons in hell, some of whom wore faces where their organs should have been and outsized organs on their heads. The descriptions of these were lurid. She looked for a moment and put it down. The religious books of her earlier prison seemed all the more desirable now.

There was a grating noise at one end of the room and one of the tapestries moved aside. A man appeared from the passageway and stepped into the room. It was Charles Arban.

Chapter Forty-two
CHOOSE YOU THIS DAY

LUISA STOOD very still. It seemed to her that the world slowed as he approached her. Instinct told her not to show fear for he appeared to be in a very excited state.

"Well, Mistress Marmoor, you had not thought we'd meet again. May I wish you well?" The small cruel eyes bored into hers. He was the very color of his gray robe except for the flush on his hollow cheeks.

"What do you want with me?" She took an objective pride in the fact that her voice was rock steady.

His thin lips creased in a smile that showed his yellowed teeth. "Have you found the books interesting? They were specially prepared and the results are truly unique, don't you think?"

Luisa was done with dissembling. "You have a diseased mind fit only for a charnel house. Why have you had me brought here?"

"My dear Luisa, how can you think that I, a mere clerk, had anything to do with the disposal of a state prisoner? You are here at the direct order of King Henry."

"Where is *here?*" She emphasized the last word.

"Westminster Palace, of course. Yes, your presence was ordered by the king but, good servant that I am, I anticipated your arrival and arranged for you to come early." His laughter was filled with venom.

Arban came close to her. She could smell sweat overlaid with a heavy musky scent. The wrinkles in his face seemed carved there with a knife. Luisa backed away slightly and he followed. This time she stood her ground.

"You've been to a great deal of trouble."

"I thought you'd be full of questions. Don't you want to know what has been happening?"

"You would tell me the truth?" She made her question purposely light.

"Probably not, but it would be a pity to die not having made the attempt."

"What do you mean?"

"I mean, Luisa Marmoor, that you shall not live to leave this room. I have a debt to pay. Sir Adam was my dearest friend and he was foully murdered by those connected with you." He gritted his teeth savagely and glared at her.

"He but went to his master, the devil, as I hope you do soon." She saw nothing to lose by provoking him.

"I'll admit to a bit of a shock when I learned that the mummers were taken and Henry alerted, but my family lives long."

Luisa heard his words but some part of her brain could not fully take them in. It was as if she watched another drama being played out at a far distance. The plot at Eltham had failed. What of the one at London?

"I don't suppose you'll tell me about Marcus. How are you planning to kill me? You said I am a state prisoner. Will the king not wonder at my fate?" Her voice sounded high and strained to her.

Arban laughed as she recalled him doing on that day she had pleaded with him for Marmoor. "Marcus Lenley has remained in prison even as you. It took little effort to ascertain he is a Lollard and he will die at the stake. The dissidents—Lollards, followers of Richard, and that ilk—marched on London and were taken. Oldcastle was said to be ready to take over but he was warned in time and fled. That rebellion is broken and the king triumphant. That was day before yesterday, Luisa Marmoor, and in several more days our group will act to remove him and blame it on secret Lollards here in the palace. He is confident, our Harry, little knowing that his days and those of his house are numbered. He called me clerk and spymaster. After we are in power I shall be a lord and wield great power."

Luisa heard him but most of all she heard his voice saying Marcus still lived. It didn't surprise her. She thought she would have known if he lay dead.

Arban watched her narrowly for a reaction. "You don't seem very interested. Perhaps you think to prepare your soul for death? It's really too bad the good Father Sebastian couldn't be here. He hates you almost as much as I do. But the heretics needed his attention. You understand. As to what the king will say, he'll not be in any position to be concerned about anything for he will be dead. If questions come up before that time, it will be said that you killed yourself with a dagger. Simple, isn't it? And so neat."

Reality burst upon her as she saw him grinning at her. This was no play or dream, but a horrible truth. She thought of attacking him for she was as tall as he and certainly her body was in better condition, but her skirts would hamper her and she was unarmed. He was giving vent to that cackling laughter again.

"So we come to the end of our battle, Luisa Marmoor. Do you think it would have ended differently had you approached me in another fashion that day last summer? We discussed that while you were my guest, remember. Was it fate which drew us all together? Adam's shade shall rejoice when I dispatch you. You are a strong-willed, forceful woman and would have given him many sons. I despise the type!"

Luisa knew he meant to torture her with unanswerable questions. She said, "I behaved as the person I was born and became. Being Luisa Marmoor, I could have done no less." And because she now had nothing to lose, she added, "I have loved Marcus with my whole heart and I have ever had the well-being of this land at heart. Can you say even one tenth of that, foul traitor?" Generations of Marmoors sang in her proud voice as well as that fierceness which had caused the Lion-heart to honor it on a Saracen field.

Arban's skin went a strange mottled shade and, before Luisa could move, he had come close to her and thrown a very thin cord over her neck and was now pulling on both ends as hard as he could. Blood drummed in her ears and the room whirled as she began to strangle.

The stench of fetid breath reached her fading senses as Arban crooned, "Die, bitch, die! You shall pay for all you have caused. Die!"

Luisa reeled back against the table as she tried in vain to reach up to the cord. Arban's head seemed twice as large now and the malevolent eyes were bright with delight. He was enjoying himself immensely. One flailing hand caught on something from the table and she brought it forward. It was the small, heavy chessboard. With the last vestiges of her fading strength, she brought it down on the side of Arban's skull. She heard a crack and a gasp, then the pull on the cord ceased and he fell at her feet.

Luisa jerked the cord away and took several deep breaths in the brief respite. Now he was trying to rise, the next move would bring him upright, and if he called the guards he had probably brought with him, her life was truly at an end. He had tried to kill her several times over. She picked up the chessboard again and, aiming precisely, slammed it into his temple. This time the bone cracked and blood poured out. He fell back on the floor and his eyes rolled back as his breath ceased.

He was her enemy and that of England. She could feel no shred of pity but the bare fact of having taken a life made her weak and faint. It is war, she told herself sternly, and stepped over his body to go to the table where a small flagon of wine was set. This would strengthen her and help her to decide what to do next. She did not see a cup and raised the flagon to her lips as she tried to still her shaking hands.

And then, Luisa Marmoor sank down in one of the chairs at the table and wept. Wept for life restored and in sorrow that her enemy had had to be slain by her hand, wept in gladness that some reprieve was given her and in despair that her struggle seemed to never end.

There was a rattle of bolts at the door just then and at the same time the tapestry over the passageway by which Arban had entered was thrown aside. Guards rushed in from both entrances and one caught Luisa by the arms as she rose to face them.

Their leader, a slight man in black, surveyed her and the body with a cold detachment. "Take her to the arranged place. Immediately."

"Where are you taking me? What is this all about?" Her voice was strong again as she prepared to face this new adversary. "This man tried to take my life. Can you not see the marks on my throat?"

"You are not to speak and no information is to be given to you. Do you fully understand that, madam, or must you be restrained?"

Luisa spread her hands in resignation. This time it must be to the stake. Where else could it be? "I demand religious comfort. I am unshriven! I demand a priest! It cannot be done this way!" Her cry went higher and higher for all that she tried to control it. Any moment of life, however short, was preferable to that death.

The leader stared, momentarily dumbfounded. "Madam, you shall have that. I promise. Your death is not yet. Now come."

Shocked into silence, Luisa subsided and went meekly with them. In the aftermath of what she had endured, she assumed this lethargy and weariness was natural. She knew only that she could endure little more.

They went out into a passage lit by torches and well guarded. The air here was cold and fresh in spite of being inside. She inhaled hungrily, wondering what sort of prison they escorted her to now. She soon lost count of the turnings they took and the flights of stairs they climbed and descended. When they paused before a door which was guarded by four men with drawn swords who inspected her own guards with careful eyes, she longed to ask one last question but there was no time.

"This is the woman. Admit her and double the watch." The leader surveyed her and said, "Madam, the prisoner is obdurate. Do your duty and pray for him. Also for yourself."

The door was held open and she passed through. The strangeness of his comment and the odd way she was being handled held her bemused for an instant before she took in the comfort of the spacious room with its hangings, featherbed, books, and table set with food. At least she was fortunate in her prisons! The thought struck her as mordantly funny and she laughed aloud.

"God's greeting, my lady." A figure moved out of the shadows cast by the candles and into the full light of them.

"Marcus!" Luisa could only stare at him as he approached. Speech froze on her tongue and she could say nothing.

He wore blue velvet which nearly matched his eyes and his shoes were of softest leather. His bronzed skin was smooth and supple. Dark curls tumbled over his high forehead and his mouth was calm. She saw the marks of strain around his eyes and a deepening of the tiny lines around his mouth.

"Is all well with you?" It was a courteous question, one a stranger might ask.

She cried, "I've been worried to death! What has happened? What does all this mean? How are you? They said you were obdurate. How so?"

He said, "I was brought here yesterday from Eltham. No hand has been laid upon me but the questioners have not spared their efforts. They want to know about Wales, Glendower, Oldcastle, the Lollards, everything. Naturally I could only explain my part and my decision. They account me traitor and they know I am a Lollard. I could not hide it. It is the fire, Luisa."

"And they brought me to change your mind." The deep, hammering fear began inside her.

"You cannot." His gaze was grave on her face. "I shall not try. That is your decision to make." She knew that only a short time ago she would have begged and pleaded with him to alter it, but now matters were different. She could not presume to dictate to Marcus about his responsibility and his God. Each person must settle that as he or she saw fit. "Marcus, has it been worth the price?"

His brows lifted in the familiar gesture. "Who can say, Luisa? The outcome of all struggles is in the hands of God and there it must lie in safety. We have done what we must. I am content except for you. We must make sure you go free."

"And leave you to die? No! Oh, Marcus, I have much to tell you."

"Come and sit. The wine is good." He waited until she was seated and a goblet in her hand. "Now . . ."

She told him what had transpired in a voice that did not shake. "I killed Arban and I cannot pray for his soul. I loathed him and those who follow such evil. If that damns me, then well enough!"

He laughed. "You are fierce, lady wife."

"Surely they cannot prove you traitor, Marcus!" She explained all that Arban had told her.

"They seek Lollards out. I cannot disavow the faith that restored me and it would do little good if I did. Those determined for my death are those who seek to bring Lancaster down. We are caught in circumstances, Luisa." His face was grave as he watched her.

Just then the guard opened the door to admit Father Otho. His eyes were filled with compassion, but that did not intrude in his voice as he said, "Husband and wife should cleave to each other in times of trouble. Your bodies may suffer but your immortal souls will go to God. Madam, have you spoken with him about this heresy? The mother church's arms are ever open to her penitent children."

Luisa said, "The things of earth should concern you, Father. The king goes in peril of his life now more than ever. There will be an attempt by his friends, who will blame it on the Lollards while the old evil goes on. Warn him again. It is our gift, freely offered."

Father Otho's face reddened. "Traitors and heretics will do anything to save themselves, it seems. Beware, woman, lest you suffer his fate."

Then madness came over Luisa and she cried, "I will share anything with him for I do love Marcus Lenley beyond all else, even your cruel God!"

"Out of your mouth, you stand condemned." He turned and went out while Marcus looked at Luisa in amazement.

Chapter Forty-three
DEO GRATIAS

"I THANK GOD for this final mercy, that we have been given some time together before they come for us." Luisa put her head in the hollow of Marcus's shoulder and savored the feel of his arms around her.

He raised himself on one elbow and said, "I love you, Luisa. I have not said the words before for I am chary of such things, but you have known, have you not?"

She smiled. "Not always. You have a way that makes one think otherwise."

"You are not the obedient wife whose virtues are sung in the ballads and related in the chronicles. Yet I would have no other."

"And I no other husband."

He kissed her long and deeply and it was as if they stood again looking down on the valleys of Wales in the shimmering sunlight with the eagle soaring over them.

Father Otho had been gone for several hours. Luisa knew her outburst had doomed her, but she could not regret it at this moment. Common sense told her they would kill her anyway and who knew what was to happen in the meantime? These moments with Marcus must be savored. She remembered his words just after the priest left.

"You are a brave woman, Luisa. How I fought against loving you! I am blessed by your love." He had held her to him. "You have fought so hard to survive."

If they continued in this vein she would weep bitterly and that must not be. "Hold me, Marcus. Hold me closely."

Since that time they had made passionate and tender love several times. Each time lifted them to the very highest of places and was all the sweeter because of the horror that lurked so close. Then they lay together and spoke after the manner of lovers, recalling this memory and that, laughing here and growing grave there.

"When did you first begin to feel something for me? Besides anger, I mean." Luisa stretched against him, enjoying the feel of his powerful body on hers.

"When I saw you fighting so boldly with my men there in Wales. When I saw you with the pilgrims. When first I tasted your kiss. Perhaps I have always loved Luisa Marmoor. My feelings have been held in check for a long time. Anger was the easiest thing to feel, you see. You freed me from that."

"I fought against caring for you, too." She put her mouth against his chest and felt his fingers sifting through her hair.

"What children we might have had to grow up in a united land! A boy might have been the king's advisor, but the girl would have had to do without your temper. Her husband would find it trying."

Luisa sniffed. "She'd have chosen him properly or perhaps not even wed at all. I certainly never intended to, until I met a Welsh outlaw who took my body and then my heart."

He kissed her passionately and said, "You were so bold and proud there before my men, demanding your rights and your life. I was determined to wed you and have you for my own. That was a perfect opportunity although I didn't want you to know my feelings for you, or maybe I did not understand them myself. I suppose I was afraid." He cupped her face in both hands, drinking in the loveliness of it while her eyes searched his to see the unveiled love there. "My lady of love and war, who has been my joy, my pain, and my delight."

For the last time they were joined in sweet

fusion, a passion and a union so complete that Luisa thought the fields of heaven could offer nothing to match it. She caressed his mouth with her fingers and tried to smile at him. It had begun with a curtsy on the London road and it must end in the flames. God alone was their judge and He who had made them would surely understand.

Later they rose in mutual consent and dressed, knowing it could not be much longer until the reprisals were made after Father Otho gave his report. Luisa was wearing the red gown which Marcus admired extravagantly and her hair was loose around her shoulders. He was elegant in the blue velvet. They held hands, drank the wine, and once more recalled the past.

He said, "We have loved many times in past days. What if you are with child? Our bold son or lively daughter?" He cocked an eyebrow at her expression. "Well, it is possible, you know."

She sat forward. "I had not thought."

"And why not? It is a natural thing. They dare not take your life under such circumstances. The child is a soul and they risk damnation."

"But I'm not pregnant."

"How do you know? How will they know? Will you do it for my sake? Who knows what shifts fortune will take?"

She bent her head, mortally ashamed of the thankfulness which surged over her. Death was too fearsome and awful to contemplate even when they were to suffer it very soon. Luisa, the practical, the life lover, still could not see how one could deliberately court death for an ideal.

She was spared an answer for a small door in the opposite wall opened and a guard glanced around, then stood aside for another to enter. This man was tall and roughly dressed, a dagger at his belt and a hood pulled low. Her first thought was of an assassin. Marcus believed the same for he looked about for some sort of weapon.

The man gestured and the guard vanished behind the closing door. Then he swept the hood back and stood looking at them. He was somber and new lines were cut in his face, but his brown eyes were curiously alight.

"Your Grace!" Marcus and Luisa knelt as one.

"Rise." The king gave the command harshly. "There are things you must know. The rebellion of the Lollards and others in the city was put down some days ago. There was fighting and some confusion, and many are in prison. My spies have apprehended those here at court who sought to work behind them for their own gain. A man of my bedchamber accounted my friend, a friend of my lady stepmother, my own chief clerk whom I raised high, even Canterbury may be involved. And there are others. It was your warning that made us know what we had suspected was true. I am grateful, grateful to a Welsh outlaw who has tried for years to destroy this throne and to a lady who is a fighter in her own right."

Marcus asked, "What will happen to the conspirators?"

"Lady Barthampton and several of her friends will spend the remainder of their days in a very

strict nunnery. The false priests, including one
Father Sebastian, who abused my trust most
grievously, will be imprisoned in a far castle in
the North. There they can pray incessantly for it
is all they will be allowed to do. Arban is dead
and none will mourn him." He shrugged. "Oldcastle was not taken. He escaped to rally rebellion again. Treason and religious dissent have
mixed with discontent and sincere belief. Many
consider that Lancaster usurped the throne."
The dark eyes pierced them both. "You are a
Lollard, Marcus Lenley, and I doubt not your
wife is close to it. I have sworn to uproot that evil
doctrine. Oldcastle was my friend but I am England's king and when caught he shall burn."

Luisa heard the implacable note in his voice
and knew he came to explain only because he
owed them a debt. He would not have the slightest compunction about burning them. How she
loathed fanaticism! She said, "We have held the
king to be the authority, that the rule must be
centered in him. We warned you because of that.
We do not advocate dissent."

The long nostrils flared. "I have sworn a great
oath against heresy."

It was Marcus who said quietly, "Your Grace
must do as conscience dictates, even as do we."

Marcus now spoke to the powerful king of
England as though he were a boy to be schooled.
Luisa's heart lifted with pride as she listened to
her husband's words.

"I have seen what war can do, just as you
have. It has seemed to me that each man ought
to be able to live out his life in a reasonable

amount of security, to have a quiet fireside and be free of petty upheavals and the quarrels of the lordlings. Whatever Lancaster has done, you alone offer a strong hand, a rallying point, and a demonstrated sense of conscience. Glendower understood that in you. Much of this unrest has been because you were new to the throne and the ways of power."

Henry stared at him in no little wonder and said, "God's will cannot be challenged."

"But you are not His interpreter." Luisa was bold in her turn.

"There speaks the Lollard for all to hear. The king is God's anointed, the distributor of His will."

She retorted, "There speaks your honest English citizen and Welsh as well."

Henry flushed and started to reply, but Marcus intervened. "What of the Lollards who rose? You surely will not burn them all?"

The heavy lids rose and his gaze was once more sharp. "I have already given orders that no man shall fear unjust punishment; all shall be reviewed and tried by the laws of the realm. There are to be no wide-scale reprisals and some pardons will be issued. But examples must be made."

"Your Grace is merciful."

Henry looked at Marcus for signs of sarcasm and saw none. He turned to Luisa. "Madam, you and your husband will be relieved to know that each case involving the outlaws is to be judged on its merits. No hasty action will be taken."

She spoke for them both. "We thank you, Your Grace."

"And now we come to your particular situation." He hesitated and the silence drew long as the candles burned lower and the light flickered over their faces. "All this might be a misunderstanding. Perhaps you had the welfare of the realm in mind and worked for it as best you saw fit. Perhaps you joined the Lollards to observe and nothing more. Is that it?" He half smiled and waited.

Luisa and Marcus looked at each other. Was he offering life at the expense of truth? Temptation pulled at them. What was honor beside a cruel death? Life was the important thing. A life with Marcus in freedom. Acknowledge error and retreat from the court, survive as best they could. She gazed into the brilliant eyes of her husband and let the ancient Marmoors give their answer.

"No, my lord, it is not true. We stood for what we had to and continue to do so. There is no misunderstanding." Now both their lives were doubly thrown away. The beating of her heart hammered in her ears, but she smiled bravely at Marcus whose admiration shone out for her.

Henry hooked both thumbs in his belt and surveyed them without expression. "You have strange ethics and you hold to a pestilent doctrine which must be wiped from this land eventually, but I would trust you at my side and behind my back. I will tell you a thing which has been rumored but none knows for certain."

They had expected exhortations, shouts of

rage, the summoning of the guards. This mild discourse was surprising.

"I invade France within at least the next year or eighteen months and must leave the realm secure. By virtue of the way Lancaster obtained this throne, I do not think my house shall reign long. God will be with me as I seek to unite England and France in one great bond. To this end, I may safely use every available means at my disposal since the cause is just." He was erect and his eyes blazed with zeal as he seemed to see a sight beyond them.

Luisa's heart twisted. Another fanatic after all! They had helped to save his throne, discounting the usurpation and Lancaster's history of blood for the sake of the realm. Was all this worthless?

King Henry said, "I offer you pardon, Marcus Lenley, if you will fight with me in France. I offer it to your lady freely as well. What do you say?"

They were taken in shock. From death to life in as many words. Marcus caught Luisa's hand and managed to say, "The Lollards, too?"

"I am God's instrument." The words were flat and uncompromising.

Luisa asked, "Beyond conquest, do you not envision an England united in a cause that will make all these petty battles as naught? Holy crusade, a uniting war, and a means by which men come together in a common cause—they are likely the same but we would have you know where we stand."

"How could I not know?" He smiled suddenly and his face was illuminated. "I know a great deal about the both of you. I have studied your records. I did not think you would have accepted my offer of a misunderstanding. You had life then but not my trust. I believed you from the beginning, but I have learned to be cautious. The guards heard what Arban said to Luisa but could not enter quickly enough to help her. I know also about a fiery young Lollard and outlaw called Rob who sits in another part of this palace and kicks at his guards as they come near. He talks about Marcus, his lord, and Luisa, the fairest in the land. Do I not know of you? Believe me, this battle is for God, who has set me on this throne. All who serve under my banner—zealots, cynics, idealists, Welsh, outlaws, even Lollards—shall be simply Englishmen in a common cause. My ranks are open to all so long as they do not flaunt their beliefs. Do you understand?" He crossed to the table and drank quickly of the wine there, the dark eyes never leaving their faces. "Will you serve me?"

"With all my heart."

Marcus knelt before Henry Plantagenet, fifth of the name, placed his hands on those of his lord, and swore the ancient feudal oath of loyalty. "I do become your liege man of life and limb and earthly persuasion." He rose the servant of Lancaster.

Henry said, "You, too, Luisa."

It was unheard of that a woman should swear allegiance in her own right, but she did so and felt the feudal kiss on her lips. She, too, was now the vassal of Lancaster. Privately she thought Henry was equally in love with God and war, but that would now work to England's benefit since the ancient dream of conquering France was to be revived.

He was saying, "The rebellion and all this about the nobility has caused a great furor. Your names have figured rather prominently. I have a small holding in the washes near Walsingham. You shall go there, live in peace, and tend the land. When the standards are lifted for battle, I shall summon you."

"Marmoor, lord king," Luisa said. "What of it?"

Jerked from dreams of crusade to the disposition of a castle, Henry burst into laughter, then sobered to say, "Ah, yes, that started all your adventures, did it not? Marmoor and the Lenley estates shall be held in fief to the Crown, to be returned to your firstborn son or daughter. I did say daughter, my lady." He grinned openly. "I need the revenues for France."

Marcus clasped Luisa's hand while Henry called to the guard, who came forward to hold out a pouch of gold and some old clothes for them so that they might make their way out of the city in disguise. Horses were to be left for them at an inn along the way.

"I must go. I've been here far too long as it is. God keep you for you are the very lifeblood of this land."

They knelt before him. "God save you, Your Grace."

He raised them up. "Go in peace for now. Until France!" Then he was gone into the shadows.

The one guard bowed deferentially. "Will you

deign to come with me now, Lord and Lady Lenley?''

Marcus and Luisa started at the tone and at the mention of their names. They smiled at each other and melted into a passionate kiss that held all the promise of life given back and a future of freedom.

AUTHOR'S NOTE

In October, 1415, Henry V and his followers overcame the might of France to win the battle of Agincourt and a place unequaled in England's history. It was less than two years after the failure of the rebellion to unseat him from the throne.

A Message To Our Readers...

As a person who reads books, you have access to countless possibilities for information and delight.

The world at your fingertips.

Millions of kids don't.

They don't because they can't read. Or won't. They've never found out how much fun reading can be. Many young people never open a book outside of school, much less finish one.

Think of what they're missing—all the books you loved as a child, all those you've enjoyed and learned from as an adult.

That's why there's RIF. For twenty years, Reading is Fundamental (RIF) has been helping community organizations help kids discover the fun of reading.

RIF's nationwide program of local projects makes it possible for young people to choose books that become theirs to keep. And, RIF activities motivate kids, so that they *want* to read.

To find out how RIF can help in your community or even in your own home, write to:

RIF
Dept. BK-2
Box 23444
Washington, D.C.
20026

Founded in 1966, RIF is a national nonprofit organization with local projects run by volunteers in every state of the union.

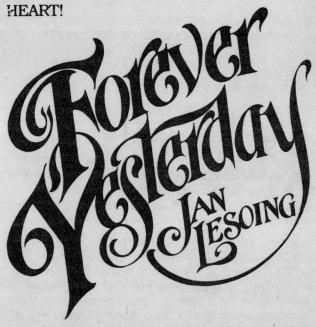

A HISTORICAL ROMANCE
TO CAPTURE YOUR HEART!

KAT MARTIN
MAGNIFICENT
PASSAGE

Mandy Ashton is fleeing her stifling existence at
Fort Laramie and is heading toward Califor-
nia. Travis Langley, a white man raised by the
Cheyenne, is hired to escort her, although he
mistakenly believes she is the rebellious daughter
of the governor. This dangerous deception becomes
even more perilous when the two discover they've
become captives of a passion as untamed as the
wilderness of the American West! Will they be able
to overcome their contest of wills and let true love
reign?

ISBN: 0-517-00620-0   Price: $3.95